LLANTATHAN

Chris W.

Christine Went

LLANTATHAN

Published by Ambercroft Books, York

A CIP catalogue record for this book is available from the British Library.

ISBN 978-1-7390814-0-9

Book layout by Clare Brayshaw

Cover design by Kate Went

Prepared and printed by:

York Publishing Services Ltd
64 Hallfield Road
Layerthorpe
York YO31 7ZQ

Tel: 01904 431213

Website: www.yps-publishing.co.uk

THE TIME BEFORE

Now is the dramatic moment of fate...
When you hear a step upon the stair which is walking
Into your life,
And you know not whether
For good or ill.

Arthur Conan Doyle

Lake Lucerne, with its backdrop of harsh peaks, had no more charm than wallpaper for Matthew Howells. Less: wallpaper could be changed. A steamer edging to the pier, flags fluttering, made a pretty scene, but the Welshman, leaning on the balustrade of his terrace, gazed out unseeing, his thoughts wholly occupied with another place: with the village at the centre of his estate in Wales. Llantathan.

Llantathan has a rich historical heritage yet no information boards tell the tale of its Roman origins or of the long-vanished priory and the thriving town which grew up around it. There are no amenities to attract tourists: just a pub whose catering is reluctant and basic. No bus service; no facilities. A Godforsaken, dead-and-alive place, some called it. And that, as Howells knew, was closer to the truth of Llantathan than anyone could possibly believe.

He went there once a year on estate business. Routine usually, but this time there were concerns: complaints about the new rector and the need for extensive work on the church. That dealt with, there would be the only social event: the annual party at the Hall to commemorate the first Matthew Howells who had purchased the estate in 1755 and saved it from ruin. A big occasion, this very long-standing tradition. Drinking the lord's health, they called it. Plenty of drink, certainly, and always the one special toast courtesy of the guest of honour.

A sudden, sharp memory, wholly unwanted, thrust itself to the forefront of his mind: that long-ago special guest from one of the tenanted farms. Josh, they'd called him. Dark hair, dark eyes. A good looking lad who behaved with a dignity far beyond his 15 years. With, Howells thought, resignation. There had been nothing dignified, nothing resigned about last year's guest. They hadn't managed to get enough alcohol into him before he realised what he'd got himself into. There'd been no trouble with Josh, he recalled, only a look from those brilliant eyes: a little reproachful, infinitely sad. So long ago but, if he lived forever, he would never forget that boy.

Words: something remembered from his scripture-steeped childhood, followed the memory. *Your hands are defiled with blood, and your fingers with iniquity...* It was the sort of thing Imogen Vine might have said. Perhaps she had, along with all the other insults she'd hurled at him over the years. His aunt was clever with the words she chose to voice her hatred.

* * *

Imogen Vine. 82. Born with the century, bedevilled by arthritis; mind like a scalpel and a guilt-ridden soul. But, Angela Morton knew, a heart as generous as anyone could wish for, however she tried to conceal it.

When Angela came to Allington there had been only Imogen. Servants, yes, but the family... All gone. Unless you counted that devil at Llantathan Hall. Miss Vine did not count him.

He called her aunt and she refused to acknowledge the connection. How could she? Who would believe that her carefree, loving little sister could have given birth to such a son? There was nothing of Penelope, of the Vines, in Matthew Howells. It would have broken Pen's heart to see her baby turning out just like his father. He'd been a devil too.

From her window Miss Vine could just see the tower of St. Michael's. That was a comfort now. The old rector's death hadn't changed anything in the village, but change might come with the new one. John Holmes was of a very different ilk. A good man. If only, she thought... if only John Holmes stays... And that persistent self-accusation: If only I'd done something when I was able...

After dinner, when Angela brought her knitting to the sitting room, Imogen Vine shared her troubled thoughts and Angela, in her confidence for years, counted stitches, nodding. 'You didn't know then,' she said patiently.

'I should have made it my business to know,' Miss Vine snapped. 'And I should have listened to Uncle Arthur instead writing him off as an old fool.'

Arthur Vine, Angela thought. She'd heard about him soon after she arrived at Allington. Batty, he'd been, according to Doreen, the other housemaid. Convinced that Miss Penelope had been murdered by her own husband. And Doreen had heard stories... things old Arthur claimed Howells got up to at the Hall with the rector's connivance... well... Enough to make your liver curl. 'They're gentlemen,' she'd said. 'They'd never do stuff like that.' 'Stuff like what,' Angela had asked, and been told primly that it wasn't fit to be spoken of. Well, she'd soon figured out what Doreen meant but, over the years, she'd come to suspect quite independently of Miss Vine, that what James Howells, and then his son, really got up to was infinitely worse.

Miss Vine cut across her thoughts. 'I shall tell John Holmes,' she announced.

Angela's fingers stopped in mid stitch. 'Wait,' she advised. 'If you tell him now, he won't believe you. He's seen nothing yet.' She finished her row. 'People always believe their own experiences before the word of others. It won't be long.'

'Too long,' Miss Vine grumbled. 'And what if he leaves?'

'He won't.'

'He'll need help.'

'Then he'll get it.'

The needles clicked on. Angela consulted her pattern and changed the colour of her yarn. 'Matthew's back at the Hall,' she said, her tone conversational. 'And Anne-Marie Pritchard is going to marry Paul Williams.'

Miss Vine made a small, disgusted sound. 'Anne-Marie Pritchard should be at university enjoying herself. When is that abomination going to take place?'

'Next spring, I believe.'

Silence overtook them and Miss Vine seemed to doze until the clock's mechanism whirred. At the first note of the chime, Angela laid aside her work and rose to turn on the television set for the news.

'I shall have Vine Villa put in order,' Miss Vine stated abruptly. Get me some estimates tomorrow. That builder in Newport, and the one who fixed the roof after the gales.'

Angela reflected that her employer's sudden decision made sense. John Holmes would need help. When it came there must be somewhere safe. Apart from the rectory, only Vine Villa, built on the last scrap of Vine land within the ramparts, was free from Howells' influence. Except for a period when it had been occupied by Allington's estate manager, it had been empty since Arthur Vine died.

Just before the bell was recast, that was, Angela thought. 1952. I came to Allington that summer. Penelope had died ten years before. The bell was to be her memorial.

* * *

The last notes of the Evensong recessional faded as John Holmes took his place in the porch. Kind words to his parishioners as they straggled out brought the usual non-responses. Eyes slid away from his. Only the Allington people lingered a little to chat. He'd known from the start that his appointment had raised objections in the parish, but surely by now...

John knew a sudden longing for tea and a bright fire: comfort after the cheerless service; and this despite the evening sunshine. September was turning into Indian summer. He paused to thank his organist, Mrs Lewis, and went back to the vestry. The verger, Elwyn Pryce, moved silently along the pews checking for fallen prayer books and lost property.

The vestry calendar, its pages curling in the musty air, reminded John of one last task. He called his verger in. 'We should be fixing a date for Harvest Festival,' he said. 'And you'll want the hall for the supper.'

Pryce stared blankly. 'No,' he replied.

'You mean that you don't need the hall?'

'We don't have a supper. Never have had,' Pryce elaborated, clipping his words. Nor a festival neither, see.'

John gazed at him, perplexed.

'There's no harvest festival in the prayer book,' Pryce went on. 'Rector Blayney said it wasn't right.'

'It's true that the custom only dates from the last century but that doesn't mean it's wrong. Look, why don't we have a meeting – quite informal – at the rectory next week and make some plans?'

'There'll be no meeting and there'll be no festival. We don't want it.'

It took a lot to rouse John to any level of temper, but the insolence in the verger's tone did it. 'Tell me, Mr. Pryce, just who you think you are to stop me holding a meeting if I choose?'

Pryce's pale eyes turned full on the rector and he smiled. 'You hold your meeting, and see who comes. Maybe you like talking to yourself.'

Really angry now, John demanded to know just who would prevent people from coming to a meeting to plan a church service. 'You?'

'We'll do as we've always done. You just let it alone. You don't want to get across Sir Matthew.'

With that, Pryce turned and walked back through the body of the church to wait pointedly by the door, keys in hand. John, choking on a goodnight, hurried away. Visions of tea had become an urgent, unaccustomed need for a good, strong drink.

Elwyn Price watched him walk along the Rector's Path through the churchyard to the little gate in the west wall. Only when he saw the side door of the rectory close on its incumbent did his impassive expression relax to a hard smile of satisfaction.

'That's settled the bastard,' he murmured. Whistling softly, he locked the church door and secured the porch grille. Then, aware that the minister was watching from an upper window he lounged against the wall, smoking. Let him, he thought. He wouldn't watch for long.

Withered flowers on a new, raw mound nearby prompted a memory: the coppery smell of blood spreading over the grass in Tudor's clearing. Pryce let his mind track back to the previous month, the same hard smile distorting his mouth. Well organised, it had been. And clever. Important, that: the world was changing fast, but Tudor and Reece had done a first class job throughout.

He dropped his cigarette butt onto the path, ground it out with his heel and, sauntering towards the lych gate, he resumed his whistling. His tune, if tune it was, reached John's ears as he stood at his bedroom window: slow cadences in a minor key, compelling and repulsive, dying away as the verger's bulky outline was lost in the gathering dusk.

Apart from services and last month's funeral, the parish made few demands upon his time professionally, and none at all socially. John was lonely, depressed, and, though he tried to dismiss it, increasingly prey to a feeling of deep unease. He fought it, but there were times when it threatened to overwhelm him. Like the day, soon after his talk with Pryce, when the archaeologist from Newport visited to discuss the possibility of excavation in the church before the restoration started.

They'd been talking in the churchyard when the hot lunchtime stillness of the village was disrupted by a coachload of students, their laughter echoing along the empty High Street. He'd watched one of them, a small, dark haired woman, catching up with another at the lych gate. How vivid and vital she'd seemed! For an instant he coveted her and knew a pang of regret when she passed out of sight with her friend. Friend. He'd almost forgotten what it was like to have friends. When the church was restored, when the people were more used to him... perhaps then things would be different.

Much later, he would confess to Adam, Marina and Stephanie that his disquiet went far deeper than he wanted to acknowledge. 'I refused to see it,' he told them. 'Llantathan was nothing like my previous parish. I'd been well and truly spoilt there and I blamed my disappointment on that. I was trying to go too fast, I thought, and if there was a problem it arose from my way of dealing with people. So I had to persist. One doesn't change parishes on a whim. It's done because the minister concerned believes that it is God's will. And God doesn't make mistakes.'

Marina's gaze was long and thoughtful. 'No, I don't think he does,' she said.

* * *

It had been a long morning, hot and tedious, and Adam Pembury was relieved to be out and away. Even the prospect of lunch with a clergyman was preferable to the interminable nit-picking he'd just listened to. Discussing budget allocations was necessary, but did they have to make such a meal of it?

Driving south through the town to pick up the A48, he reflected that a year ago such meetings would have been unimaginable. Well, things had changed and he wasn't complaining, but he was a practical archaeologist, not an administrator. Still, if that was the price to be paid for a real job, so be it.

For years he'd gone to work in worn jeans and ancient sweater, spent eight hours digging and, tired and often filthy, went back to whatever accommodation passed for home. The pay, for 40 hours' bloody hard work, was a joke. Job security was a sick joke. A ridiculous state of affairs. He was an experienced professional with a good degree, but at almost 30 he'd been little better off than when he left university.

Rumours that Thatcher planned to introduce a scheme which could mean the end of local authority funded archaeology sounded dire. But there was nothing else he could or wanted to do, so he went on digging and looking at the pitifully few ads in the Wednesday *Guardian*. It was possible that a proper job would come up, eventually. If one did, it was vaguely possible that he might get it.

He'd been working in Haverfordwest when it happened: a real job with a real contract paying, for archaeology, real money. At the beginning of 1982 Adam Pembury became senior supervisor with the Hafren College Archaeology Unit. He bought some new clothes, added to his excavation kit, and rented a bedsit in Newport. Sometimes he returned to it of an evening with relatively clean hands. After six months a general review gave him a salary increase and, co-incidentally, he was made Field Officer and placed on a higher pay scale. Feeling cautiously prosperous, he bought a better car.

Girls drifted into his life as they'd always done and, usually, conveniently drifted out again. To the ones who didn't, Adam explained that serious relationships and archaeology didn't mix. The pay was poor and there was no security, no stability. All this was true. But what he didn't say, because he didn't know, was that he was never in love with any of them. If he had been, he would have found a way round every difficulty.

But Adam was not to encounter love: real love with all its gut-heaving misery and its damn-fool persistence, until he also encountered Llantathan. The two came together not once but twice. The first time was a foretaste which might have been forgotten eventually, but the second would be a reiteration and a confirmation. Signed, sealed and delivered. He was well and truly fucked up and he knew it.

That day in September, when summer was enjoying a last flaunting of almost tropical proportions, he'd gone to Llantathan to get an idea of the extent of the job should excavation become possible. The prospect of digging on such a scale intrigued him, and growing ambition already visualised prestigious publication. It could be a very significant project for him if it materialised.

The rector, John Holmes, turned out to be a lot younger than Adam expected and a decent sort who would co-operate fully should there be an excavation. 'Though at present it's only in the archdeacon's mind,' he warned. 'Nothing's been decided yet about the amount of restoration work.'

As they went round the church, inside and out, he gave Adam all the information he could while Adam made notes. He was more reticent about the village, though, and what little he imparted was cautious. 'It is rather insular,' he mused. He paused under a spreading yew near the gate and fumbled in his pockets for cigarettes. 'The main families are very old-established and they don't like change.'

Adam accepted a cigarette and offered his lighter. Then, for a few minutes the quietness of the churchyard was broken by the low rumbling of an engine: a coach negotiating the tight turn into the nearby car park. Both men watched as it disgorged a party of students whose shouts and laughter seemed oddly out of place here.

Adam listened politely to the rector's speculations about finance, then he only half listened. A girl had detached herself from the little crowd and was heading through the churchyard gate. A mass of darkish hair framed her face and fell in long strands to her slim waist.

Seeing them, she smiled and spoke a soft, conventional greeting then, called by a friend, she turned back and was gone. Adam thought her the loveliest woman he had ever encountered. And, as men have done for ages past and will continue to do until the end of time, he fell in love with a beautiful face.

A year later Llantathan would bring her into his orbit again, and he would do all he could to keep her out of his life and, failing, he would resign himself to the novel experience of unrequited love. He never asked himself why he knew that it was a hopeless case. He just knew. He had no conscious memory of the person who had joined her at the churchyard gate, no recollection of what passed between them. But often over the following year, in dreams he forgot on waking, his mind replayed all he had seen and heard that day. And he had seen and heard more than he knew.

* * *

It hadn't taken long for Stephanie Turner to realise that her marriage to Howard Hargreaves was a mistake. It took a lot longer to be free of it, but late in 1980 the divorce came through. About the same time Stephanie, who had long wanted to go back to university to do a higher degree, discovered that her old department was offering a two year M.A. course. Part taught, part thesis, it looked ideal, if she could fund it. That matter was still unresolved when her widowed mother arrived from Scarborough, unannounced and bent on finding out exactly where things stood.

People always said that Alice Turner, as aggressively Yorkshire as they come, was not a woman to be trifled with: hard-headed; intimidating; bent on getting her own way. She might be diminutive, but she was afraid of no-one, and she was fiercely protective of her own.

'You can give me another cup of tea, Stephanie,' she ordered, 'and tell me how you and Howard are sorting things out.'

Satisfied that Stephanie had come out of the divorce with the house and that Howard had agreed an equitable division of funds, she relaxed a little. 'Well,' she conceded, 'it's better than I expected. I never liked him, you know.' Stephanie did know: she'd been told often enough.

Used to her mother, she'd expected all this; didn't really mind it, but sharing the university idea was something else. Alice could understand why her daughter had wanted shut of her marriage, but she would never grasp why anyone, once out of it, would want to go back into education. Despite having left school at 14 with nothing more than a head for figures and an abundance of practical common sense, Alice had had a successful working life, and she was proud of the fact. Once wed to Stephen Turner, she'd taken over the office side of his family's small joinery and shopfitting firm. With his craftsmanship and her growing business acumen, they'd made a very successful team. Turner & Co. of Eldersfield, known throughout the West Riding, had prospered.

Alice respected education but too much of it was, in her view, pretentious. It was Stephen who'd encouraged his daughter to go to university after she left the grammar school. Though forced to acquiesce Alice hadn't approved. Nor did she approve now.

'What for?' she demanded. 'You've been once.'

Patiently Stephanie explained. 'But I can't apply until I'm sure I can pay for it,' she finished. 'I wouldn't be able to carry on working and what I have in the bank isn't enough for the fees and for me to live on. I'd have to sell the house.'

'Nay, you mustn't do that,' Alice said, observing Stephanie through narrowed, calculating eyes. She was a bonny lass even if she did have some crackpot ideas. Alice blamed Stephen for that. But... if she could go back to university, get out more, she might meet someone... So: 'Tell me how much you need, love. There's a tidy bit coming to you when I'm gone but you might as well have some of it now. Not,' she added darkly, 'that I think you've a cat in hell's chance of getting in, at your age. You'll be 34 by the time you get there, *if* you get there, and 36 when you leave. You won't find it easy to get a job. It'd happen make sense if you wanted to do summat sensible like teaching, but history! What can you do with that?'

* * *

Marina Graham, lecturer in English medieval history, was not fanciful. Already, depressing thought, turned 30, and regarding herself as plain and practical, she'd long since abandoned attempts to look otherwise. Fanciful or not, though, she had known exactly what her departmental head, Gordon Murdoch, meant when, at the second staff meeting of last year's autumn term, he called Becky Scott, Alison Prentiss and Stephanie Hargreaves the Three Graces.

There'd been appreciative laughter from the 20-odd people around the table. Dr. Bell, who taught ancient history and was, therefore, classically minded, agreed that while fresher Becky and third year Alison undoubtedly represented the mirth and elegance of Euphrosyne and Aglaia, post-grad Stephanie, at 34, could not be called youthful. 'Maybe not,' Richard Maynard (Renaissance Studies) had put in, 'but Thalia represented beauty as well as youth and Stephanie's certainly beautiful.' And he'd added, very softly, to Ian Forrester (Medieval Europe) on his right, that he wouldn't mind seeing the three of them posed like Canova's famous statue. Forrester, catching a filthy look from Helen Cotton (Early Modern Political), suppressed a snigger and Professor Murdoch called the meeting back to order.

'Gordon's right, though,' Helen said to Marina later as they made their way down from the conference room to the car park. 'There's Becky with that unusual combination of blue eyes and red hair; sort of witchy: all tunic tops, coloured tights and pixie boots, and fun. She seems to trail laughter wherever she goes. Flirty little devil too... Then Alison... Elegance could be her middle name...'

Alison, tall and fair, had that underlying bone structure which would ensure the durability of her classical good looks. But what her companion thought of Stephanie, Marina never knew. As they reached the car park Helen was side-tracked by a student with a late essay. Marina sketched a goodbye and drove home, relieved not to have to comment on any of the Three Graces. Becky, uncomplicated and essentially harmless, would never trouble her, but Alison... Marina gave silent thanks for the umpteenth time that she didn't have to teach her.

In the kitchen she considered coffee and, instead, reached into the fridge for the bottle of supermarket Italian wine, thinking that Richard, too, had been right: Stephanie was beautiful. There was nothing cool or serene about her, and nothing flirty either. As slender as Alison, though not as tall, her face was neither classical nor in any way fey. Just very lovely, though Marina, pouring a second glass of wine, would have been hard put to say why. If Becky was the witch and Alison the ice maiden, Stephanie was the gypsy, always slightly dishevelled, her long brown hair invariably escaping from clips or braids, huge skirts swirling under the ridiculous, obviously home-made cloak she wore which, she insisted, laughing, kept her warm waiting for buses.

Marina had been drawn to Stephanie from the moment they met during registration for the new M.A. course. The list suggested a mixed bunch. A dozen continuing students were easily dealt with as were the retired teacher, the former dancer and the ex-police officer. Those three should do well, Marina thought. Years since their first degrees but they had real enthusiasm and discipline. And then came Stephanie with her silly cloak and her messy hair. Stephanie who, when invited to say a little about herself and her interests, spoke with fluency and depth of understanding about medieval church politics. When Marina lifted her head from her note-taking, to look into eyes warmed by Stephanie's smile, she, not at all fanciful, realised that unless she was very careful indeed, she could find herself in difficulties.

Now, a year on, she knew she hadn't been careful enough. Attracted by Stephanie's lively mind, by her obvious enthusiasm and her willingness to argue her point in the face of disagreement, Marina had, for a time, enjoyed some rare socialising. In itself harmless but potentially dangerous, because it wasn't only Stephanie's mind that beguiled her, and that hadn't gone unnoticed. She'd done what she could by way of mitigation and it might just have been enough but for what had landed on her desk that morning.

Heavy-hearted, she looked again at the scribbled telephone message passed on by the department's secretary. Professor Murdoch was ill. Would she take over his field trip? The very short notice was a difficulty she could overcome with some intensive reading. The fact that Stephanie would be on that field trip was another matter.

MARINA – AND ME
1981 – 1983

Lovely as a garden sprung with flowers
Where lilies shake and leaves spread with the moon,
Oh come love, aching love, and laugh
Before me like the ghost who soon
And transparent floats in silent eye awakened dreams
Oh nothing is that is, nothing seems that seems.

Sue Lenier

I

When a woman you hardly know makes a point of singling you out to give you friendly advice it invariably means three things: it isn't friendly or advice. It's a warning. It didn't take much thought to arrive at that conclusion. What did mystify me was why.

It was almost the end of my first term: a term during which, since her seminar on medieval queenship, I'd had some lively discussions with Marina Graham. Another, about Eleanor of Aquitaine, began in the common room one afternoon and continued at the Fox where Ted behind the bar obliged with toasted sandwiches and chips. We were still debating when Marina said that she had to go. 'But we'll conclude this tomorrow lunchtime, Stephanie, if you're not doing anything else.' I wasn't, and we did, and though we disagreed completely about Eleanor, we enjoyed it enormously. But, after Marina left, there was an odd, unpleasant consequence.

I stayed on, checking a list of references I needed from the library. Nearby, a group of third years were making final arrangements for the department's Christmas party. One of them, Alison Prentiss, detached herself from the group and came across. 'Mind if I join you, Stephanie?' she asked. 'They're trying to decide whether to order Old Peculier and since I really don't care I'm rather superfluous at the moment.' She took the chair just vacated by Marina and I thought that the contrast could not have been more striking. Marina, small, dark-haired and neat in jeans and jersey, and Alison, tall, elegant, and looking out of place in her silk blouse and tailored jacket, her fine blonde hair twisted in a smooth coil at the nape of her neck.

Since I hardly knew Alison, I had no idea what to say to her but it was soon apparent that she hadn't come to listen. What she said, in her cool, carefully modulated voice, was something and nothing: an ideal technique for the politician I knew she meant to be. It was nothing if you didn't understand or chose not to; something if you were sharp enough to realise what she meant. I opted for the former, made some anodyne response and left for the library, but she knew I'd understood.

In the library, trying to note the references, I was distracted by what Alison had, and had not said about Marina: that she was a lesbian, that I should discourage her from being friendly, that there could be unpleasant consequences. It was a clever, and a very horrid little speech about which I could do nothing but which made me feel somehow smirched.

Over the Christmas holiday Alison's words returned again and again to annoy and upset me. Marina's sexuality

– something I'd assumed without ever really thinking about it – just wasn't an issue and I wondered why Alison thought it should be. Was she a moral crusader who saw Marina as a danger to other women? Maybe, but she couldn't really think that I, in my thirties, needed to be warned, particularly by someone barely out of her teens. No, but it was certainly a warning off. And what sort of unpleasant consequences could she mean? I didn't know enough about her to work all this out, nor could I think of anyone who might enlighten me. One thing, I did know though: however beautiful she was, Alison Prentiss was a nasty piece of work: a woman to avoid.

* * *

As it happened Alison, with Finals that year, was hardly in evidence during the spring term. Nor was Marina. I can't say that she was avoiding me, but she certainly wasn't putting herself in my way. A couple of times when I did run into her and suggested a drink at the Fox, the regret of her refusal sounded real. I knew her workload was heavy this term, but there was something... something else. So I let her be and got on with my own work, disappointed that the friendship I thought we'd begun to build had stalled. But the less I saw of her, the more I wanted to see. As the weeks passed, the idea of Marina took hold of my mind, and grew.

* * *

The first day of the summer term fell in late April, when an unusual cold snap covered the city in snow and caused chaos. I managed to get a bus as far as the town centre and walked the rest of the way, arriving in the department chilled and wet.

'Stephanie!' Marina, just coming out of the library, greeted me with a smile. Not an everyday smile, but one of pure pleasure transforming her face to a beauty I'd never imagined. She took a step towards me, stopped, and the smile died. Behind me, footsteps. Turning, I saw Alison Prentiss cross the hall from the ladies' cloakroom to the stairs.

'Go and get warm,' Marina said. 'I'll bring you some coffee.'

In the common room I pulled a chair closer to the gas fire, exchanging a few words with Marina about the weather before she disappeared to her top floor domain. Solitary, comfortable and distinctly bemused I sat, hands cupped round the heavy green salt-glazed mug I recognised as Marina's own. I'd never seen Marina smile like that, ever. But then Alison had come out of the cloakroom, and in an instant the smile was gone. It made me wonder.

Alison didn't appear again but around 11 Professor Murdoch came in, his woolly bobble hat dotted with snowflakes. He collected some stuff from his pigeonhole, told me to go home and left in a flurry of Burberry and multi-coloured Dr. Who scarves. I stayed, yawning over *The Just War in the Middle Ages*. All very well for Gordon to talk about going home. The snow was easing but the buses wouldn't be running properly yet. Soon I made more coffee and took some up to Marina.

'Gordon was in,' I said.

'I know. I saw his car.' Her window overlooked the car park. She finished the sentence she was writing and looked up. 'Are you going home?'

'Not yet, I replied. 'It's quiet. I can get on with some work. If you're not too busy we could go to the Fox at lunchtime.'

A pause, then: 'I can't Stephanie. I'm sorry.' I gazed down at her dark head for long moments before retreating. Work I did not. I couldn't: I'd seen her face. She'd been crying.

* * *

The cold weather died suddenly. Across the campus the flowering cherries scattered their petals in great confetti drifts and exam fever swept the department. A good thing I had no exams that year for my concentration was shot to pieces. The memory of that day haunted my mind: Marina's smile and, later, her tear-wet eyes. I couldn't begin to imagine what was wrong. Work? Family troubles? If I'd known her a little better than I did there were things I might have done or said but, as it was, I could do nothing.

It was probably as well because although I skirted around the idea, the one thing I'd really wanted to do was put my arms around her and hold her, and that, since Kara, was a can of worms I'd been very careful to avoid. I met Kara – wild-haired, exotic, fascinating Kara – about a year before Howard and I finally split up, and had an affair with her. It had been a joyful time, remembered without regret: a time of exploration of mind, body and emotions. But, though it had ended when and how it should have, that ending had hurt, and I didn't want to be hurt again. Even so, I spent much of the summer term wanting to see Marina, telling myself to keep out of her way and then doing the exact opposite.

II

During the long vacation a week spent with my mother in her claustrophobic retirement bungalow in Scarborough brought me face to face with the reality I'd avoided confronting throughout the previous term. On edge one day and tired of my mother's endless nattering, I offered to go and pick up some more milk, leaving her amid the afternoon tea things for the brisk wind of the seafront. Fifteen minutes later, I leant on the wall near the North Bay beach huts staring out at the grey sea. I was soaking from a sudden downpour and in emotional upheaval, hating my mother's probing questions, hating myself for my inability to tell her to mind her own business. Yes, I'd made friends. No, there wasn't anyone in particular.

A veering gust of wind blew salt-laden rain hard into my face: a slap from the elements for lying to myself. It wasn't true, was it? For most of that year I'd had Marina on my mind. Yes, and there was more that I wasn't prepared to admit. Cold and wet, I turned and walked back past the Corner Café where ice cream sundaes had been a childhood holiday treat. Life had seemed so straightforward then. Now, no. I had the M.A. but after that, what? I saw myself drifting around in some empty future. I didn't regret my divorce and I certainly didn't wish Howard back, but I did wish for someone and if that someone was small, dark-haired, slim and green-eyed, with the loveliest of smiles, that was probably just a case of propinquity. Wasn't it?

Escaping at last from my mother's warnings, advice and misplaced sympathy, I managed to get a seat on the overcrowded train down from Edinburgh. I felt hot, sticky, and the fretful wailing of a toddler outraged my aching head. All around me people were talking, eating, drinking. Every sound, every movement fretted me and the smell of chocolate, grease and beer turned my stomach. Would I be sick first, or start to cry? It would be a close-run thing. I stared unseeing out of the dusty window, listening to the steady beat of the wheels over the track and to the thoughts

I could no longer deny. I was in love with Marina. In all probability this had been growing for months. I couldn't stop it; didn't want to stop it. I wanted her.

Between York and Church Fenton I made a rush for the lavatory and threw up. I did cry then, my face damp with stale water, my feet in a litter of wet, crumpled paper towels and cigarette ends. A long time after, I remarked to John that if hell existed it would surely be managed by British Rail.

At home, insomnia-plagued and able to settle to nothing, I brooded on a situation which, I believed, had no sort of resolution that I wanted. So, on the second Saturday in September when I set off to Gloucester to join one of the department's field courses, I was in a hellish frame of mind. The course – *The Parish Church as Historical Document* – meshed with my research. It was to be led by Professor Murdoch who, if his lecturing style was less than enthralling, was sound enough on all things ecclesiastical. I'd been looking forward to an interesting week. Now, though, I was in no mood for it.

III

I was the last to arrive at the hostel, a converted Edwardian villa on a quiet, leafy avenue off the London Road. In the cool, semi-basement, the office door stood ajar and inside I found not Professor Murdoch, but Marina. She looked up, her expression strange. Relieved? Afraid? Defeated? All of those, perhaps, but gone too quickly for me to be sure.

Gordon was ill, she explained, ticking my name off the list and handing me a key. 'The rooms are shared,' she went on, 'but I thought you'd prefer some privacy so I got you a single staff room. If you'll hang on five minutes, I'll take you up.'

Two flights of once-elegant stairs lit by tall panels of stained glass gave way to a set of narrower, steeper steps. Passing floors humming with the muffled sounds of students settling in we reached a little landing at the top of the house. 'You're here,' Marina said. 'I'm opposite. Bathroom... pantry... Coffee, tea, biscuits, and milk in the fridge. Let me know if you need anything.'

The small, square attic room was pleasant: plain, clean, and warm with the light of the late afternoon sun. A thick red wool carpet and pretty bedcover added homely comfort to the simple furnishings. The dormer window overlooked a garden: high hedges enclosing a rough lawn flanked by narrow rose beds. At the far end a vigorous pear tree shading a weathered wooden seat had scattered its windfalls in the grass around. Everything looked slightly neglected, slightly overgrown, rather charming. Beyond the hedge, beyond the nearest houses, between distant rooflines, I caught a glimpse of the cathedral tower, pale against a cloudless sky.

Dragged away by the faint echo of the dinner gong, I pulled a comb through my hair and washed my hands at the basin in the corner. Marina's door opened and closed but she didn't knock or wait. Did I expect her to? Securing this privacy for me was kind, but probably meaningless. What might mean something was that, despite her obvious tiredness, she seemed rather more her old self. The last week's vast misery acquired boundaries. Well, I was ever a clutcher at straws.

After dinner there was a restrained rush upstairs followed a little later by an enthusiastic exodus: the first pub crawl of the week. I couldn't be bothered to go out. I unpacked, had a quick bath and read until around 10 when Marina knocked, offering tea. Her goodnight was soft, with the trace of a smile.

Four days. Eighteen churches. Five architectural styles. A thousand years of history. Sketches. Notes. Photographs. Guide books. Marina, compensating for hurried preparation, was trying to include as much as possible. The days were Indian summer hot, the pace exhausting. After dinner most people revived and went in search of liquid suppers, but I worked: it was the only way to keep track of everything before it was blotted out by the next day's avalanche of information.

I wrote and worked up 'reminder' sketches. Marina, I knew, made notes and checked her material for the next day. All this rushing from place to place, church to church, scribbling frantically to catch the gist of the mini-lectures... snatched lunches, dehydrating coach rides, aching feet... I felt what it was doing to me, could see what it was doing to her, and on the Wednesday evening I made us both stop. Acting on impulse for the first time in months, I crossed the landing to her door, knocked, and said, 'Come for a drink.'

Caught off guard she nodded and we went down to the quiet, warm street. Dusk was turning to dark. Windows were lit and somewhere a baby cried. On the London Road we found a little, old-fashioned pub off the tourist trail. It had a small, empty back room with an uneven, faded mosaic floor, and there we sat in a corner with our drinks, avoiding eachother's eyes.

When women are tired, they're vulnerable. Marina was very tired. Uneasy, too: nothing like she was when we were picking the Plantagenets to bits. I began to doubt the wisdom of this. What good could it do when she was obviously bothered and I... Yes, I was in love with her, but wasn't this just reinforcing the misery?

She said, 'I can't stay long. I haven't finished my notes for tomorrow.'

'You work too hard,' I told her.

She sighed, scraped her hair back, picked up her glass again. 'I got very little notice of this trip. Gordon sent a rough outline and a list of churches. He doesn't need notes. I do. This isn't my field.'

'Seems good to me.' I reached for her empty glass. 'Another?'

'My turn.' She stood up and I watched her walk to the bar: dark hair, longer than usual, shadowing the thin, intelligent face. I closed my eyes to shut her out. When I opened them again, she was regarding me with concern. 'Are you all right?'

'Just thinking.' Then, suddenly, I reached a decision. I said quietly, 'Marina, I need to talk to you.'

Her eyes met mine, alarm flaring.

'Listen, I don't know what's happened since last year to make you bothered about me, but if you're worried because I know you're gay, you've no need to be. I've known for ages.

Leaning back, eyes closed, she sighed. 'I suppose Alison told you.'

'Nothing directly, and nothing I hadn't already assumed.'

'Alison never does say anything directly,' she replied angrily. 'I shouldn't say this but I will. That woman is vile. She spins poison into words and when you try to grasp what she means, it falls apart like cobwebs. Only it niggles and you suspect that there's a smidge of truth in it, so that you half believe.... What did she say?'

I recounted it as accurately as I could and she nodded. 'But what she meant by it all I can't imagine.'

'Oh, I think I know what she was getting at,' Marina said, her voice hard. 'Look, Stephanie, there's an unpleasant back story to all this and, given the right circumstances, there really could be dire consequences.'

'But Alison's gone now,' I objected. 'Surely...'

Marina shook her head. 'I wish! She's coming back to do a Ph.D. She got her First and with Daddy's money behind her, Gordon wasn't going to say no, though I think we'd all be glad if she took it elsewhere.'

Daddy's money? Ah! Godfrey Prentiss, the millionaire industrialist. No wonder Alison swanned around in silk blouses and condescending arrogance. 'So what's the back story, Marina?'

'I need something stronger than cider for this,' she said, making a move to get up. I forestalled her, brought two double whiskies and offered my cigarettes. She took one, lighting it with an unsteady hand.

'Alison Prentiss,' she began, 'is a manipulator. If she does go into politics and gets any sort of power, God help this country because she won't. She'll use anyone and anything to get what she wants, just as she's tried to do in the department. Oh, don't get me wrong: there's nothing shady about her degree. She came by that through her own efforts and I would never deny her intelligence or her work rate. Technically, she's never put a foot wrong.'

She paused. Sipped her whisky.

'So?' I prompted.

'So... You know Alison's reputation in the department? The iceberg? In three years she's never shown the slightest interest in men.'

'Or women,' I replied. 'Not to my knowledge.'

'No... but in her first year she claimed to be interested in me. She wasn't, I'm sure, but what she really wanted I don't know. A cats-paw, perhaps. I told her flatly where I stood and she didn't like it. I thought that was that, but then she found out about the departmental politics and the hints started about the trouble she could cause me. She would do it, too, if she saw an opportunity... if, say, she thought I was getting too close to someone else in the department...'

'Some sort of blackmail?' I suggested.

'Something like that,' Marina said. 'But what I don't understand is why on earth she spoke to you as she did.'

I was curious about the departmental politics but there were things to clear up first. 'What has Alison been saying about me?' I wanted to know. 'I take it that she has said something?'

'Something and nothing,' she replied, with a glimmer of humour. 'A hint that you were trouble; a vague suggestion that you wouldn't give me the time of day if you know what I am. That sort of thing.'

I nodded. 'Divide and rule. It all makes sense now,' I said grimly, 'including why she spoke to me.'

Marina looked up sharply. 'There's only one reason why...'

I nodded. 'That I'm not as rock-solid hetero as one might suppose. Didn't you guess? Alison must have.'

'I wondered, sometimes, but I didn't really imagine...'

That was interesting: clearly, she'd tried.

I had a lot of questions but the barman called time and we walked back to the hostel chatting peaceably about nothing much. The air was cleared, the barrier down, and I hoped that now, at the very least, Marina and I could be friends.

Thursday evening, and my concentration was nil. I pushed the books aside, opened the window wider to lean on the ledge and look down at the garden and the pear tree, indistinct and fading into the dusk. Perhaps I should have gone out with the others to the Fleece instead of sitting here forcing my mind towards architecture as a reflection of wealth and status, and away from Marina. I'd been trying to do that all day but Marina the historian merged, separated and merged again with the Marina of the previous evening... with the Marina of my imagination. All day she'd been within sight and sound. All day I'd watched her and it wasn't enough. I wanted to see her again.

This time it was easy. In the same little pub we talked as we used to talk: about the state of academic history; about campus politics and the iniquities of the University Grants Committee. And, now, about ourselves: how she had always known about her preference for women; about my failed marriage, and Kara who had added such an unexpected dimension to my life. 'She refused to stick labels on herself and I don't think I can either,' I said, and, in response to her question: 'No, my mother doesn't know. God knows what she would say if she did.'

'At least it's only your mother you have to worry about,' she replied. 'I've got to keep it completely quiet.'

'Must you? I know you said that Alison would cause trouble if she could, but can she really? After all, you're not the only one. GaySoc's flourishing, judging by all the posters in the union building, and I know of a number of staff members in various departments: two in Archaeology, Dora Gainsford in Earth Sciences, and that woman in Fine Art... as out and extrovert as it's possible to be, and nobody bothers.'

She snorted. 'Vanessa Lambton. Nobody bothers, true, but her image overshadows her work. I'd hate to be talked about as she is. It's not just that though. Stephanie, keep what I'm going to tell you to yourself. This isn't precisely confidential but it isn't common knowledge either, and we'd rather it doesn't become so. It's what gives substance to Alison's insinuations. All this Grants Committee business and the need for campus-wide cuts. Arabic Studies is going, Drama may close too, and we're under threat.'

I frowned, wondering where this was going. 'They're small departments,' I said. 'History isn't.'

'No, but we're not getting the numbers or the quality of students we need. Increasingly we're second or third choice and too many of the ones we do get come through Clearing. Why? Simple. Gordon and Dr. Bell. Bell's fossilised, and Gordon's second rate. You must know that. Ours was one of the best history departments in the country but between them they've blocked the introduction of new courses and new blood lecturers and dragged our reputation right down. Bell's retiring next year so he doesn't matter but Gordon...

'I don't see what...' I interrupted impatiently. She cut me off.

'Listen. About three years ago we had a hell of a scandal. A lecturer had an affair with a third year. Yes, I know. It happens. But he also gave her information about the Finals papers. Well, Gordon knew, and he didn't act. Claimed he'd seen nothing untoward.

'It was hushed up as far as it could be. The lecturer left and the girl's degree was rescinded. Gordon got away with a reprimand but with Senate looking for ways to satisfy the Grants Committee he can't afford another scandal. Senate also wants to bring History back up to scratch and that means getting rid of Gordon. Difficult, because he has tenure, but if they had an excuse, they could pressure him to resign. I don't want to be the excuse. I'd be glad to see someone younger in charge of a restructured department, but if Gordon went because of me, sure as hell I'd have to go too. End of my career.'

If what she said was true, she was right to be cautious. Right, perhaps, to be worried by Alison's poison, though I didn't think there was enough mileage in the mere fact of Marina's sexuality. There had to be more, but she wasn't telling, and I couldn't ask, so to change the subject I made some remark about longer hair suiting her better.

She made a face. 'I'm having it cut next week.'

'Oh, don't! It's softer... prettier...'

Another grimace. 'I was never pretty.'

'No. Beautiful.'

She raised her eyes to mine in a sharp, questioning gaze, wondering, perhaps, if I was mocking or mad.

'No, I mean it, Marina. Especially when you smile.'

Her expression was half amused, half disbelieving. Then she shrugged slightly and lit a cigarette, and we talked trivia until we left.

'God, it's warm!' Marina exclaimed. 'If it doesn't change, tomorrow will be hell. I may have to cut some of the churches.'

We reached the hostel, steps flagging, stopping simultaneously where the drive gave way to the darkness of the garden. 'It'll be baking up there in the attics,' she remarked. 'I'd sleep outside if I could.'

Any second she would tell me that she had to go and write notes, and would there be another evening? The barrier was down. It was staying down. Madness it might be but I had to be myself, and the devil fly away with Alison Prentiss.

'Pity we can't, but we could just sit out there for a while,' I said. 'Unless you have to go in.'

'Not yet.'

In the deep shadow of the pear tree I swept windfalls from the bench and we sat down. Quiet. Close. Through the branches the moon was the merest sliver of light in the indigo, star-hung sky.

'Stephanie, were you serious... what you said about my hair?'

'Yes, every word.'

Silence, then: 'Your hair is amazing. Will it get any longer?'

'No, it's at its limit. It hasn't been cut in years.'

She lifted a strand twisting it gently round her fingers; letting it slide loose. I had to be myself. 'Marina...' As my hand closed over hers, she made a soft sound. The tips of my fingers touched her face and our mouths met in the gentlest of kisses.

Then, agonised: 'Oh God, Stephanie, don't... I can't... I'm so sorry... *I can't*...' And she was gone like a ghost flitting across the grass.

Nothing is that is....

I looked up again at the black mosaic of the leaves, still in the heavy night warmth, and let the madness of hope have its way. Her words might have been a denial, but not that kiss.

* * *

Friday was the hell Marina predicted. Tracing the influence of the Cotswold woollen industry in the architecture of churches, we visited Northleach, Fairford and Cirencester. No-one took notes now: we bought the guide books to read later, and had to be chivvied out of cool interiors back into the wilting, sweat-heavy air of the coach.

On into south Wales, and Llantathan for lunch. Still and hot and silent, the village looked as if it might crumble to dust under the power of the sun. Wanting time to think I made for the leafy shelter of the churchyard where, in the shade of a big tree by the path, two men, one in a dog collar and the other holding an official-looking clipboard, were conducting a discussion. I smiled, said hello, and turned back when I heard Marina's voice calling from the lych gate.

Dear God, if only I could have held her then! Voices along the road reached us, threaded with Becky's high, bubbling laugh. In the churchyard the two men continued their quiet conversation. 'Come on,' I said. 'Let's get out of the sun.'

At the village's only pub we heard chatter from the garden: Becky and her courtiers, but there was no-one inside. I ordered cheese sandwiches – the only ones on offer – and we retreated to a corner with glasses of shandy.

Marina was agitated. 'Last night. It shouldn't have happened but running away like that was silly.' She pushed her hair, damp with sweat, back from her face. 'Stephanie, what have we done?'

'Nothing much, yet.'

'No! There can't *be* a yet.' She shook her head in fierce impatience.

'We need to talk, Marina.'

'Yes, but not now. My room this evening. About nine.' She finished her drink and from somewhere she dragged up a kind of resolution. 'I'm sorry, Stephanie. It shouldn't have happened. But... I'm not as sorry as I should be.' A shadow of her entrancing smile, and I gave it back.

'I can't be sorry at all,' I said.

The smile grew then the light died from her eyes. She said softly, sadly. 'It can't go on, Stephanie. It can't.'

I couldn't work that evening. I did the crossword in a paper I'd bought in Cirencester, and read about the car crash which had killed Princess Grace earlier that week: such a mundane end to a fairytale life. Then, impatient, I paced, smoking, waiting. Footsteps hammered on the stairs below, muffled by doors and floors and ceilings and carpets. Sporadic laughter and shouts drifted up from the street and faded. Still I waited. Went to the window and stared out at the dark shape of the pear tree. Remembering... *leaves spread with the moon...* but the moon was dying. A distant clock struck the first note of the hour. I picked up my cigarettes and lighter and went to her.

She was closing books, tidying her papers, her eyes bright with unshed tears. I put my arms round her. 'Marina... It's all right...'

I remember kisses before she pulled away, shaking her head.

'It isn't all right! It isn't right at all! Oh, Stephanie, *please* understand. It's no use!' She retreated, leaning against the window frame.

'Marina, I *don't* understand.' I sat down and lit a cigarette. 'So why don't you tell me?'

She kicked her toe into the pile of the carpet, raking furrows in its dark blue smoothness; pushed her hands into her pockets. When she spoke her voice was cool. 'Stephanie, last night should not have happened. I told you how it is with Gordon and the department.'

I flared. 'Do you really imagine I'd go around telling people that I'm in love with you?'

'Are you?'

'Yes. Oh God, *yes* Marina! Did you think this was just a game? There, so now you know. But no-one else does or ever would. Could you honestly see me announcing that we're having an affair? Which we're not.'

'And won't be. I told you,' she snapped. 'Oh for heaven's sake, use your brain, Stephanie. Look what happened when all we did was talk history: we got Alison Prentiss stirring things. I tried to protect us then by backing off but I can't swear that it worked entirely. Even if we're nothing more than friends she could kick off and then we'll both be in the shit.'

I shrugged. 'So we keep it very quiet and right out of the department. It's not impossible.'

'True,' she conceded, 'but I'm not prepared to chance my job, your M.A., our careers and our reputations. I don't want this, Stephanie.'

'You did last night. And just now.' The cold in my voice matched hers.

'What I might want, and what I can have are not compatible. I was wrong to let the situation develop and I won't let it happen again. The risk would be bad enough without Alison Prentiss. With her it's completely unacceptable. I'm sorry, Stephanie. But facts are facts. You're a student and I'm a member of staff. I have responsibilities to you, to the department and to myself.

'I know you mean it when you say you would be discreet, but how long do you think it would be before someone worked it out? Alison would be onto it before the cat could lick her ear. And that would be that. No, no, and *no*, Stephanie. I do *not* want this.'

I crossed the room and put my hands on her shoulders. Slowly, gently, my hands slid to her face. She didn't move. I kissed her. Not gently. Caught the quickly damped response.

'Marina,' I said, 'you're a liar.' I turned, picked up my cigarettes and walked out.

It was almost ten months before we spoke to each other again.

IV

Seething anger, through which I could barely grasp the possibility that Marina loved me, gave way to ice, and ice got me through the autumn term. But when that passed I was left with hopelessness and a sort of confused guilt. I couldn't deny her integrity but surely, I thought, if she did care about me, there were ways round this. Was she right? Was I? Whatever the case, my reaction in Gloucester must have hurt her, and that bothered me a lot but, avoiding eachother as we did, and with Alison Prentiss an ever-present threat, I couldn't see a solution. And, as another Easter vacation loomed, I realised that time was running out. I had one more term, one round of exams and the submission of my thesis, and that was that.

I did, however, realise something else: that the day I walked out of the department for the last time, Marina's case fell flat. All very well but how likely was it that she had any feelings at all for me now other than dislike? And if there was a road back it wouldn't be easy. Anything I did would have to be gradual and, of course, completely secret. It wasn't in my nature to be cautious, subtle, slow. Ideas came with difficulty and nothing seemed feasible until someone mentioned Marina's birthday the following Friday. If I could do nothing else, I could send her a card. Something that might make the first vital dent in her defences.

A developing and printing place in town made a card for me from a photo I'd taken that week in Gloucester: the pear tree, caught at dusk, and the bench strewn with windfalls, its muted colours and outlines softened by fading light. Beautifully, painfully evocative. Inside I wrote:

'Marina

"Lovely as a garden sprung with flowers
Where lilies shake and leaves spread with the moon,
Oh come love, aching love, and laugh
Before me like the ghost who soon
And transparent floats in silent eye awakened dreams
Oh nothing is that is, nothing seems that seems."

Stephanie.'

Not trusting the post office or the university's internal mail, I got hold of Marina's address and put the card through her letterbox early on the morning of her birthday. Then, for the first time ever, I cut lectures and went home to spend the weekend worrying. Finding a 'leave me alone' letter in my pigeonhole would be dreadful. Silence would be worse. Her response, when it came, was wholly unexpected.

'Stephanie

"Why must you follow me
When I come to the threshold of this holy place?
My resolution falters and it seems death to enter
When, turning back, I look upon your face.
I could renounce you when I lay alone;
I ran from you as from a hungry light
Into the gentle, the infinite, the healing
Clemency of the night.
I crave an eloquence that is not words
I seek fulfilment in the kiss of stone –

But you, you come with your mouth and your dark hair
And at your feet a leaf that the wind has blown."

Marina.'

That, written in her small, precise script, was inside the card I found on my mat the following Saturday morning. The picture on the front was a reproduction of an old sepia print of Gloucester Cathedral. It was all the answer I needed.

How strange those last weeks were! I worked with an absorbed intensity: revision, and hours at the typewriter working on my thesis. But there was another intensity just as absorbing: that of a love affair growing in silence. No word spoken. No looks exchanged. No kisses, caresses. No physical contact of any kind. Only the interchange of cards, and the endless search for words written by others to say what I could not.

Madness? Probably. We were making love in the only way available to us, and it was a dangerous game. When the cards had no further function, what then? This was a fragile fantasy whose foundations were small and weak: a paper edifice which could collapse to nothing at a breath of reality. What would we do when we could face each other openly? When we could speak and touch? Would words fail us when we had to find our own?

Towards the end of June the results notice went up and I knew I had my M.A. After the elation came a deflated emptiness. All was finished. Term had another week to run but already people were making plans to leave. There was an end-of-year party but I didn't go. My sense of belonging had evaporated and I was afraid, as if the last two years had come to nothing.

If I'd been sure of Marina, I don't suppose I would have felt so disconsolate. But there had been no card from her for several days and I began to imagine horrors. In another week we would be free from all ethical restraints. I'd longed for that. So, the cards suggested, had she. Now, perhaps she'd had second thoughts.

Monday. Nothing.

So... In a mood of brittle resolution I caught a bus to the deserted department, cleared my locker of the year's accumulated rubbish and said goodbye to the secretary. At the main campus library I returned two overdue books and paid a large fine. Then, afterthought, I went back to History to check the notice board and my pigeonhole. Futile, and I knew it. She never sent cards that way.

Stripped of its timetables and options lists and flyers, the notice board displayed nothing but the results paper, already yellowing, an envelope addressed to one of the second years, and a request for a lift to Birmingham. My pigeonhole yielded only a reminder for the books I'd just returned. All at once the emptiness, the quiet and the finality overwhelmed me. I went into the library and shut the door on a bout of stifled weeping.

My mind registered footsteps, voices and the slam of the main door: the secretary and her assistant going to lunch. In the cloakroom I splashed cold water on my face, repinned my hair. A last coffee, a last cigarette in the common room, then I would go.

I did, but I didn't do it alone, for there was Marina, travel bag on the floor at her side. In her hands a pen and a card...

* * *

Time meant nothing that day. We moved from coffee in the common room to wine and a salad in my kitchen, from wine to whisky, from the kitchen to the sitting room, and we talked. Enough to fill every corner of our long silence. The paper fantasy had blown away after all. Our words were our own.

She'd been at a conference. 'I thought you knew. I wasn't going to see you until the official end of term,' she told me. 'But I couldn't manage to hang on for four more days.'

'It's been a long time,' I said. 'Ten months...'

'Longer than that, Stephanie. Your first term... that seminar... those times in the Fox. Then there was Alison and her lies but even when that was sorted out there was still nothing I could do except hope you'd understand. Until the first card I thought you wouldn't. Oh God, it's been hell!'

For long minutes we gazed at each other from the corners of the big sofa. 'What now, Marina?' I asked. Her eyes, clear and lovely, held her answer. Every answer for me. I touched her face. Gently. Kissed her. Gently. Oh, it was all so gentle. The kisses, the caresses, the murmurings. So very gentle in the gentle, fading evening light. A deception. Tenderness a garment cloaking passion.

She lay against me, fragile as old lace; warm as I had not known warmth before. Close... Closer... The softness of her breasts against my own. Marina... *aching love*... unfolding flowerlike beneath my hands. Opening to the warmth. Blossoming at my touch. And then, the glorious flowering over, closing, drooping, falling; curled petal-like in my arms to sleep in garden serenity. A distillation of every summer night there in my bed.

In waking I thought I slept, dreaming of Marina in my arms, and found no dream but truth. I lay, eyes closed, willing myself to believe what I felt. To touch. Open my eyes to find that I still touched. No dream. Or, yes, eye awakened dreams. *Nothing is that is...* I thought no more, emptied my mind and warmed myself against the reality of the moment.

JOHN, MARINA – AND ME

1983

Just when we are safest, there's a sunset touch,
A fancy from a flower-bell, someone's death,
A chorus-ending from Euripides –
And that's enough for fifty hopes and fears
As old and new at once as nature's self,
To rap and knock and enter in our soul.

Robert Browning

I

We were together until Wednesday afternoon in a time out of time, detached from the world, from the past and from the future, our absorption in each other total, our mutual happiness unclouded. Such times cannot last. No-one can exist in complete isolation for long. The mechanics of life have to be maintained. The phone rings, the postman calls, the food runs out. So the interfaces are blurred. Interaction with the world begins again simply because it must. We revelled in our solitary hours but when Wednesday came and Marina had to go back to the department for a staff meeting, we moved without regret into normality, and enjoyed that too. I saw bright days ahead, unaware that a shadow was growing, that Fate was spinning threads with a view to a dark fabric…

A phone call from my mother in the afternoon reminded me that I needed to make plans for the future. When was the degree ceremony, she wanted to know because, having paid for this educational extravaganza, she would like to see the result, thank you very much. Oh Lord! I thought and, grabbing pencil and paper, scribbled messily while she talked. Cap, gown and hood to be hired from Ede and Ravenscroft. Form to fill in for guest ticket and whatnot. Sort out the spare room. And beyond all that, what? Start looking for a job because the allowance from my mother would stop at the end of August. Thinking furiously, I tidied up, threw a heap of washing into the machine and went to Marina's for supper.

In the kitchen, where the detritus of cooking suggested spaghetti bolognaise, a bottle of Frascati stood open on the cluttered table. I found somewhere to sit and she told me to pour the wine while she stirred the sauce.

'Steph, have you had any thoughts about jobs yet?'

'No, but it's a priority.' I told her about my mother's phone call.

She ran hot water into the sink and started clearing up. 'Well, I can't do anything about your mother but I've some news which might solve your job problem. Let's get this sorted out and I'll tell you everything while we eat. It's about ready.'

So, containing my impatience I washed up while she set the table and served the meal. Then, with glasses refilled, she began.

'Last year, I was told, unofficially, that the post of Senior Lecturer in Medieval History at the Hafren College of Higher Education would fall vacant some time in the next 12 months. Hafren's in Newport, South Wales, and they have a Department of Archaeological and Historical

Studies. It was suggested that, as and when, if I chose to apply, I would be appointed. No, don't ask, Stephanie: there's a lot of chicanery in the groves of academe.

'Today I heard that the post is now vacant, but that isn't all. My contact also told me of another position they're having difficulty filling.'

'She looked at me over her glass and smiled. 'Want to know more?'

'As long as it isn't teaching.'

'No, it's not. The college has a very active archaeology unit and they need what they call a Field Historian: someone to undertake all the historical background work for the excavations. A lot of it will be documentary research but there would be some site work and you'd have to liaise with the archaeologists. They're also talking about setting up a local history archive and resource. Still interested so far?'

'Yes, though I don't know much about archaeology. I did a basic subsidiary course for my degree but that was years ago.'

'I don't think that would matter. You're an excellent researcher and you write to a very high standard. That's important because you would have to contribute to reports and bring out a series of local history publications.'

'It sounds good.' It sounded ideal but I was being cautious. 'What about the post you're being offered. Do you want it? Isn't it a step down? Wouldn't it be primarily Welsh history? And surely they'd want a Welsh speaker?'

She rested her fork on her plate and leaned back. 'I'd like to accept for several reasons. On the personal level I'd probably be happier there because the current head's an old associate and I wouldn't have to pretend to be anything I'm not. Professionally the prospects are much better than staying put: a lot of scope for advancement because the college is slated to become a polytechnic within the next five years. First of a new breed of polys intended to encompass both extremes of the practical and the academic and to allow students to move in either direction as their abilities develop. Hafren was chosen because it's already doing this with remarkable results. Yes, there would be a Welsh slant, of course, but that doesn't bother me. And no, Welsh isn't a requirement, though it might be useful to start learning it later.

'So you'll go for it?'

'It's not as simple as that.' She looked up at me, eyes luminous with love. 'I can't possibly go without you, so would you go with me?'

'I'd go to... to Baluchistan with you if you wanted me to. Do you think it matters to me where I am as long as you're there too?'

She squeezed my hand, let go and stood up to clear our plates. 'Where's Baluchistan?' she asked.

'I've no idea. But you know, Marina, I might not get the job.'

'Oh, I'm sure you will.' She dropped the plates into hot water. 'The question is whether you'll want it. They've been trying to get someone for months.'

I frowned. 'What's the snag? With jobs so scarce I should have thought...'

'It's not a snag precisely,' she said thoughtfully. 'Come on. Let's take the rest of the wine into the sitting room.'

Settled with refilled glasses and cigarettes, she went on. 'Right. This autumn the archaeology unit will be excavating in the parish church at Llantathan.'

'I remember Llantathan,' I interrupted. 'It was where...'

She cut me short. 'I know. Don't remind me. Look, the church needs extensive renovation. Lifting the floor will allow the archaeologists to investigate what was there before. Priory remains, probably; traces of a Celtic monastery, maybe.'

'So what's the problem?'

'The community. There's serious opposition to the excavation. It'll go ahead but the strength of feeling's such that anyone involved could have a pretty rough time.'

'Surely that's more of a worry for the archaeologists?' I suggested.

She shook her head. 'You'd be doing the historical recording of the fabric, so for the duration of the excavation you'd be there at least part of every week.'

'Hmm. I see... But can these people really do anything?'

She shrugged. 'I wouldn't have thought so, but it must be serious because the rector of Llantathan said that anyone involved in the dig has to be fully informed of the situation, and no-one must be compelled to take part.'

'Sounds rather melodramatic.'

'It does, but if you want the job you have to talk to the rector first. Hafren won't see you unless you do.'

I lapsed into thought. What was the worst I was likely to encounter? Weirdos with placards picketing the lych gate? Verbal abuse? Eggs and tomatoes? But that could be dealt with and it wasn't forever. Llantathan was only one project and I couldn't afford to let this go because of short term local difficulties. I needed a job. Marina wanted to take up the post she'd been offered. I wanted to be with Marina.

'You'd better accept that post,' I said abruptly. 'Even if I don't get this Field Historian thing, I can find some sort of work in Newport.

'I'll phone tomorrow,' she promised. 'There will be formalities of course but...'

'Hang on a minute,' I said. 'I assume that these jobs start in the autumn. Shouldn't you give at least a term's notice?'

'Ah well...' She reached for the cigarette packet. 'Do you remember what I said last year about Grants Committee cuts? That staff meeting today... Applications are well down this year. The department will open in October with about twenty per cent fewer students. Courses are being rationalised and those of us who don't have tenure can leave on a salary in lieu of notice basis. Three have accepted and I'll do so tomorrow. Oh, and by the way, my post at Hafren starts in September but you would have to be available from the 1st of August.'

'Well I am available. Oh, I see! No, it's not long, is it?'

'Not if I have to put my house up for sale and find somewhere else. You too. Which brings us to something you didn't mention. Stephanie...' She looked up quickly. 'I don't want to take anything for granted but if you could consider the possibility of us living together...'

I gazed with love at the bent head. Her face was hidden by the heavy fall of soft, dark curls. She'd let her hair grow, I thought inconsequentially. And it did suit her.

'I never imagined anything else,' I told her quietly.

* * *

Marina made all the Hafren arrangements, including a meeting with the rector, John Holmes. More than a meeting. He'd given, and she'd accepted, an invitation for us to stay at the rectory the following weekend. I was doubtful about that, unsure that she and I, love spilling from us, could maintain the necessary circumspection. 'We can cope for a couple of days,' she assured me cheerfully. It makes sense,

Steph. Means we can go on to Hafren for our appointments from Llantathan. Anyway, isn't the Church all about love?'

'Not our kind,' I replied tartly.

She sighed. 'I know. Some so-called Christians are amazingly lacking in love when it comes to homosexuality, aren't they?'

'Let's hope John Holmes isn't one of them,' I said. 'Or that he's some old fogey of a saint who's never heard of lesbians.'

Marina said that he'd sounded neither old nor fogeyish. 'I don't know what a saint sounds like,' she added.

Saint or not he would expect us for tea at the rectory the following Friday when he would have a lot to tell us. Then she frowned. 'You know, Steph, this is odder than I was led to believe.'

She went on frowning and shook her head. 'I don't know. I was told that he's worried but... Oh damn it! I can't convey it. He sounded besieged.'

On the strength of the job interview and the fact that my house was up for sale I beguiled my bank manager into letting me have an overdraft. And then, because I was a sentimental idiot in triumphal mood, I persuaded Marina to leave for Llantathan a day early so that we could spend a night in the hostel in Gloucester.

I wanted to go back to where Marina and I began; to do what, professionally, I could never countenance. I intended to rewrite history. And, in a way, I did. Looking out on the garden at dusk, on the pear tree and the bench, I let all I'd felt last year: all the love and the longing and the pain, wash over me. And then, turning into her arms from the past to the present, the night we kissed under the branches and the dark summer sky melted into the night we made love in a small room sweet with the air drifting from the garden. Thus, it seemed, all the silent months of misery were quietly edited from my life; and though my mind accepted that those months had existed, my feelings knew only a moment from the pear tree to her bed.

On Friday morning we went shopping: film for my camera, sandals for Marina, and flowers for the church. The flowers sparked a conversation about our religious backgrounds as, later, we went on to Llantathan.

'C. of E.,' I said. 'Christened, confirmed but rather lapsed.'

'How nice and straightforward. Do I turn off at the next junction?'

I consulted the map. 'No. Next but one. Go on: I take it you're not so straightforward.'

'Hardly.' She laughed. 'I'm Jewish. You must have realised.'

'I did. You had a mezuzah on your door frame in the department. 'But Graham's Scots, surely?'

'That's right. My father was a Scottish Presbyterian. Interesting mixture, isn't it?'

'Were you a confused child?'

'Not at all. My mother wasn't orthodox and my dad wasn't strict. I grew up with bits of both worlds. They encouraged that and let me decide for myself what I wanted to be.'

'Which is?'

She took one hand off the steering wheel to scrape back her hair. We were crawling along now behind a lorry whose driver appeared to have all the time in the world. 'Both and nothing,' she replied evasively. How far is it to the turning? Is it worth trying to overtake?'

'No, I don't think so,' I said, estimating the distance. 'But Marina, when I asked you, you immediately said you were Jewish.'

Tapping her fingernails on the steering wheel, frowning, she agreed. 'In Jewish culture I take my identity from my mother, but I can't accept that any one religious system has a monopoly of truth. I believe... Oh, I believe there is a God: a power for good, and I believe in a power for evil too. I believe there's an afterlife of some sort. And telepathy, ghosts and even, so help me, fairies. But whether I believe because I believe or because I want to believe...'

The turn-off for Llantathan appeared and she said no more on the subject. Nor did I pursue it. The remnants of her frown suggested that this was something important to her but, for the moment at least, too deeply personal to share.

A largely lapsed Anglican and a both-and-nothing Jewish Presbyterian. Not, perhaps, ideal guest material given our host's calling! We'd agreed in advance that should we be invited we would, out of courtesy, attend Sunday service. We did, and not merely from politeness. But I'm running ahead. Let me go back to the point where Marina drove along Llantathan's main street. Because this is where things first started to go wrong.

It's a pretty enough village, tidy and very silent, which was, centuries ago, an important market town. Picture a dusty B-road running north from the A48 and cutting through the south side of a rectilinear bank-and-ditch system: the ramparts of the former medieval settlement. Inside the bank the road passes between small fields where telltale irregularities betray the remains of structures under the soil.

Today Llantathan is hardly more than a cluster of cottages around a tiny green just north of the junction between the High Street and the B-road. The High Street runs east-west through the village, piercing the banks to meander through fields and woodlands to other hamlets. Along it you will find a few more cottages and the tiny primary school on the north side, with the Cross Guns Inn and the post office-cum-general store to the south. Beyond these, a small car park backs onto a pig farm, some allotments and four small industrial units. The church of St Michael and All Angels, the late Georgian rectory, and the church hall opposite are the last buildings at the western extreme of the High Street. Apart from some other scattered houses and farms, and Llantathan Hall, there is little else. The church, the pub and the Hall have medieval origins but most of the other buildings were probably put up in the 18th century with stone robbed from the town walls, parts of which still survive. There is no secondary school, no significant industry, no new housing development and almost no through traffic.

As we approached the T-junction and Marina prepared to turn left, I looked about, struck by the orderliness of the place: at well-tended gardens bright with roses, at neatly clipped hedges and sparkling windows uniformly hung with net curtains. Nothing stirred: no children played on the close-mown lawns; no dog or cat lazed in the sun. It was deserted. A film set of a village.

We turned into the High Street past the post office on the corner and Marina started to accelerate. Then she swore, stamped on the brake, and the car stalled.

'What the hell...?' Pale, scared, she darted a glance at me then, with some effort, she restarted the car and we crawled as far as the lay-by in front of the church.

'Give me a minute, Steph,' she said. She switched off the engine and sat there shaking, arms resting on the steering wheel, eyes closed.

'What happened?'

'I don't know. What did you see?'

I shook my head. 'Nothing. What was it? A cat?'

She seemed to struggle with herself as if she could find no suitable words. With a few deep breaths the shaking eased, but still she said nothing. Then she wiped her palms on her jeans and reached for the ignition. 'Let's go. No, Steph, I'm all right. We're nearly there. I must have let my concentration go. I thought I saw something but it was only a shadow. You know how it is.'

Yes. Perhaps she imagined some small animal darting across the road. The reality was probably a bit of litter blowing in the gutter or the shadow of a tree stirring in the breeze. I looked back along the High Street. It was as still and empty as before. The wide road which had once, long ago, accommodated markets and fairs, shimmered with heat haze. There was no hint of a breeze. Litter? No. And no shadows on a road running east to west. Only an airless summer's afternoon and sunshine, and parched gardens ablaze with roses.

II

The rector's welcome was warm without being fussy, and my first impression of John Holmes was favourable: a kindly man; a good man. I've never revised that view except to upgrade it. In my opinion he's a saint.

He gave us a generous tea at a long, battered table in the kitchen, filling the teapot from a big old kettle hissing comfortably on the aged Aga. While cups were passed and plates handed, I took stock. A bachelor, certainly, this reverend, in his later 30s, and just about everything medium or average: height, build, brown hair, blue eyes. Regular features and a lightish, pleasant voice.

What wasn't average was his aura of unobtrusive warmth. He had a way of being at ease so that it was impossible to be anything but easy with him. In his job that must have been quite a gift. One couldn't ignore the implications of the dog collar but they didn't obscure the man. And the great charm of the man was his unselfconsciousness. He had no idea of his own worth. That unknowing made a good man great.

Meals with strangers can be awkward but this one wasn't because John remained a stranger for no longer than it took to pour the tea. Conversation never lapsed, continuing as we cleared the table and helped with the washing up. John looked bright and happy; Marina's face was unusually pink and her eyes sparkled. It was impossible to imagine that the man who laughed so freely as they exchanged Cambridge anecdotes was desperately worried. Or that only an hour ago she'd been white and shaking. That incident was forgotten. It was to be months before it was talked of again.

The rectory was a rambling place, the top storey empty and echoing. 'Ridiculous,' John said, 'but it goes with the job. The archdeacon talks about a new, sensible house, but...'

He put down our bags and opened a door. 'You're both in the one room. I hope you don't mind...' I caught Marina's glance: too solemn to be real '... but as you've seen, most of the house is never used. Now... the bathroom's opposite. There's a bath and a shower and the water's always hot. Make yourselves at home. Come down when you're ready and I'll show you the church. Then we'll have a drink. Anything you need, give me a shout.'

Marina closed the door and hugged me. 'This isn't bad at all,' she said. There was a bubble of laughter in her voice.

I kissed her. 'It'll do,' I allowed. The walls are pretty thick.'

'He isn't.' She was suddenly serious.

'No. But do you think he'd mind?'

She lifted her bag onto the bed by the window. 'Perhaps not, but there are ways and ways of finding out. He's a really nice man and I wouldn't want to offend him. Let's err on the safe side, Steph.'

We took turns to shower and change, and it was while she was watching me battle with my hair that Marina asked, apparently casually, whether I thought she looked very Jewish.

I turned, surprised. 'It never occurred to me to think about it. Why?'

She shrugged. 'It never occurred to me either.'

'Well don't start now,' I replied. 'It doesn't matter whether you do or don't. Marina, is this to do with Alison? Something she's said to you?'

She shook her head. 'No. It was just a random thought. Come on. Let's go and look at this church. And see what sort of a drink John meant.'

* * *

St. Michael's is pleasing if, now, relatively unremarkable. The first stone building known on the site had been put up in the 12th century and remodelled on gothic lines in the 14th. As John said, it must have been like a miniature cathedral then. 'This was a rich town, by all accounts,' he added.

'Yes,' Marina agreed. 'There's plenty of evidence for that.' She settled herself into the corner of a pew to tell us something of the rise and fall of Llantathan: a pocket history she'd put together last year for the field course.

'There was a Roman camp here, and a fort later,' she said. 'But the site was abandoned in the second century AD, probably due to the growth of Caerleon and the rise of Caerwent. There's been no archaeology, not even the antiquarian sort, so it's hard to be sure, but after the Romans, there's no known evidence of occupation until the sixth century when St. Tathan or one of his disciples supposedly founded a monastery here, thus giving the place its name. It's only tradition, though, and not unique hereabouts. Caerwent has a similar one.

'From 1066 it's all much clearer. The Normans soon reached Gwent and William FitzOsbern, Earl of Hereford, built castles at Chepstow and Monmouth. Since he was dead by 1071, you can see that the county was at least partly overrun within five years of the invasion.

'From the late 11th century Llantathan is increasingly referred to as a town or township, and a significant piece of evidence – a charter of 1120 – establishes a community of Augustinian canons here. The charter refers to a church described as ruinous but of great age and dedicated to St. Michael, and it reiterates the tradition of a foundation by St. Tathan.'

'How odd!' John exclaimed. 'I should have thought that it received its present dedication much later. In fact I'm a little surprised that such a dedication should have been given at all. Churches dedicated to St. Michael are frequently sited on hills or sometimes on what the pagans believed were entrances to the underworld. Magical places.'

Marina smiled. 'The explanation may be much more prosaic. The cult of St. Michael was very popular in the 8th century and you find many such dedications throughout Wales and the Marches from that time. Of course Llantathan may overlie a lost prehistoric ritual site. Echoes of that in folk memory might account for the adoption of St. Michael but, equally, it may have been just a fashion.

'So. After 1120 the documentary evidence is very straightforward. The canons put up a monastic range and a hospital, and the rebuilt church served the town too. The guest house was extended twice and the fact that there were three inns fits with what we know of the town's growing prosperity.

'Llantathan's market charter dates from the 12th century and two fairs were granted less than a hundred years later. Around that time the walls went up and a small stone castle was built. The motte – the castle mound – is still there, near the south eastern angle of the ramparts. In places you can see where the medieval builders bonded their walls onto remnants of the Roman defences, but the area enclosed was much greater than that of the fort.

'The Great Revolt following the death of Henry I in 1135 caused widespread hardship and there was more devastation throughout Gwent early in the 15th century with Owain Glyn Dŵr's uprising and Henry IV's reprisals. Still, the town and the priory were rich enough to sit it out and recover, and decline only came after the Dissolution. All the Welsh monasteries were gone by 1539 but the priory church here, albeit reduced, survived because of its parochial role.

'The end of the priory needn't have meant the end of the town, but it did. Many of Llantathan's tenants owed rent to the priory which took half the revenues from the fairs and markets. After the Dissolution most of the priory holdings went to a Sir Richard Thomas who held the manor of Llantathan, and he received what had been ecclesiastical revenues too.'

'Most? Who got the rest?' I wanted to know.

'The Devigne family. They held the adjacent manor of Allington along with some land within the parish, and tenements in the town itself. John, your rectory is built on a former Devigne tenement.'

He smiled and nodded. 'That I did know,' he said. 'There is still a member of the family at Allington, though the name is just Vine now. What happened next, Marina.'

'The inevitable,' she said, 'Sir Richard was greedy. He raised market and fair fees so traders put their prices up and custom declined. With fewer people coming two of the inns closed and that, more or less, was that. There's no mention of fairs after 1575. The market became just a little local affair, staggering on until the beginning of the 18th century. Sir Richard's grandson sold the estate, and it was sold again twice more, being acquired, finally, by a Matthew Howells in 1755.'

She paused again.

'Is that it?' I asked. John said nothing.

'It might as well be it,' she replied. 'Because from that point, although Llantathan didn't decline further, it never recovered. During his first year in Llantathan Matthew Howells repaired the church and what was left of the town walls but he didn't do much else in the village beyond demolishing superfluous houses and rebuilding the inn. For himself he added a wing to the manor house and introduced new farming methods. He seems to have been a very wealthy man so it's a bit surprising that he didn't do more. His son and heir improved some cottages and established a plantation behind the Hall, and that, so far as I can tell, is that. He was made a baronet but I don't know why. Probably lent some money to the Prince Regent.

'A Howells still owns most of Llantathan and he seems to be as unenterprising as his forebears. In 200 years the village hasn't really changed. Beyond the odd house built on Devigne lands, there's been no development of any kind, though that may be down to the fact that almost every building is listed and a big area is scheduled as an ancient monument. Historically and archaeologically it's a treasure, and I'm surprised that no work's been done on it before now.'

She stood up and stretched. 'Well... There you have it. There's every justification for excavation. Uncovering the Augustinian priory would be enough but the opportunity to look for confirmation of St. Tathan's putative foundation is too good to miss. And then there's all the Roman stuff.'

John nodded. 'That's what the archdeacon thinks.'

'And you?' Marina's look was quizzical.

'Oh, of course. If only it wasn't causing so much trouble...' He said more, but I didn't hear. I'd remembered the flowers and thought they might serve to lighten John's mood a little: during the latter part of Marina's monologue he'd seemed less at ease.

'How thoughtful of you!' he exclaimed. He unlocked the vestry door and rummaged for scissors. 'I'll get some water,' he offered, leaving us with the heavy sprays of chrysanthemums and carnations. A thought niggled and Marina put it into words, idly, as if it meant nothing.

'There are no flowers at all in the church.'

We snipped stems and arranged, admiring the rich colours against the stone above the altar and the dark oak of the chancel screen. On some impulse John lit the great altar candles. The soft, flickering light gave the blooms a jewel-like quality and the church, cold despite the season, felt warmer. An illusion, but a comforting one.

Marina touched my arm and nodded towards John. He was standing before the altar, head bowed, hands folded before him. In silence we withdrew to the back of the church and sat in one of the short side pews by the font. She took my hand and we waited.

My eyes traced the interlacings carved in the stone panels of the font and I wondered whether they were as genuine as they looked. Marina might know. But Marina was, for once, not with me. Her face, eyes closed, was a mask of concentration. And pale... I thought she was praying too, and I was strangely unsurprised.

I watched her. In the dim light and against the whiteness of her skin her hair was very dark; the tilt of her head emphasised features which, until then, had seemed to me to carry no particular racial stamp. But now I thought of Rachel, of Rebecca, of Sarah. In that moment anyone might have guessed her ancestry. I, who saw only beauty, couldn't care less; yet in another time, another place, it would have signed her death warrant. My grip on her hand tightened. Marina... *lovely as a garden sprung with flowers*... but the garden was the Garden of Eden and the flowers the roses of Sharon.

Why? Why should it matter? Why should she question her appearance now? I gave myself a mental shaking. Told myself that I – we – were silly. That our talk about beliefs that afternoon had sparked a sudden odd insecurity and I had merely empathised her disquiet. The holocaust was decades ago and no-one persecuted Jews now. Not here. Not in Britain. It was nothing, nothing... silliness.

* * *

Amid the comfortable clutter of John's study we found that a drink meant what we hoped it did. When we were all settled with generous measures of whisky John beamed. 'I can't tell you what a welcome change this is for me,' he remarked. 'I'm a social drinker only so I've been almost teetotal since I came here.'

We made sympathetic noises. 'The natives must be very hostile,' Marina said, and John's smile faded.

'I'm afraid that's truer than you know.'

'The excavation?' I prompted.

'Yes, that...'

But not just that, I thought, though I let it pass. 'Why don't they want it?'

He shook his head slowly. 'They call it sacrilege, but that isn't the real reason, I'm sure.'

Marina said quietly, 'Start from the beginning, John. From when it was decided that restoration was necessary. When was that?'

He smiled ruefully. 'Oh, it's been necessary for years. The archdeacon talked about the dilapidation when I arrived and a survey was carried out. They found every kind of rot. And woodworm, fungus, plaster fatigue and even rust. The only sound part of the church is the tower which was restored when a new bell was donated earlier this century.

'An appeal was launched and I must say that the people were very generous. All that stopped of course once they realised what would be involved. I knew it would be something major when the archaeology people sent someone out to talk to me about excavation. That would have been last September. But it wasn't until I had the archdeacon's letter with the schedule of repairs that I understood just how much work was needed.

'He wrote that in view of the historical importance of Llantathan and because deep excavation was necessary to investigate the damp problem, he had agreed to allow the Hafren Unit access to discover what they could of the Augustinian foundations and to attempt to verify the tradition of a Celtic church. He added that the archaeologists would remove all bones and funerary material for study, and these would be reburied in accordance with the wishes of any surviving descendants. And that's what started the trouble.

'Of course I understood that people here wouldn't like the idea of disturbing the dead but I never anticipated any serious objections. After all, the last burials inside the church were over a century ago and only the Vine family was affected. Ironically the sole remaining representative of that family didn't object at all. So you can imagine my surprise when first the Vestry then the whole village protested.'

He paused to refill our glasses.

'A meeting was called,' he went on. 'I spoke. The diocesan architect spoke. He told them that if the work wasn't done the church would have to be closed because it was rapidly becoming both a danger and a health hazard. He said that naturally their feelings were understood: exhumations were not undertaken lightly; but he stressed that the archaeologists would carry out the task with consideration and efficiency.

'It was useless. One of the churchwardens claimed that the problems had been exaggerated. Someone else appealed to the village's sense of decency. Incidentally, there was a lot of play on the average man's superstition: his fear of death, the unknown and the wrath of God. And in all this there was constant stress on the fact that Sir Matthew wouldn't like it so it wasn't to be done.'

Howells... I said nothing.

Marina's expression was impassive: she was in analytical mode. 'They, and Sir Matthew, are going to be disappointed, she remarked to no-one in particular.

'Oh yes,' John agreed. 'The diocese had no choice but to overrule all the objections. The necessary Faculty to allow excavation to take place has been obtained along with the Home Office licence to exhume, so it will go ahead as planned, with restoration work following. The village, however, says it won't.'

John stood up and switched on the lamp. I hadn't realised how dark it had grown. Then he closed the curtains too and, excusing himself, went to lock up. Marina looked at me, lifting her eyebrows.

'People can be very funny when it comes to the dead.'

She made a face. 'They have a reason, but it isn't superstition.'

When John returned he replenished our glasses again and put a match to the fire. 'These old houses can be chilly even in summer,' he explained. He settled himself in his big, worn leather armchair again, and took up his story.

'Letting the people air their views was a courtesy and it was explained at the meeting that they have no legal rights over the fabric of the church or any burials. It made no difference. The restoration fund has stagnated and, barring a handful of people from outside the village proper, no-one attends services. I have no choir, no organist, no sexton. Not even a cleaner.'

'A boycott... And I suppose no-one's talking to you either,' Marina said shrewdly.

He admitted it and sighed. 'But they never were friendly.'

'What about funerals?' I wanted to know. 'Weddings? Christenings?'

He shook his head. 'Fortunately none of my parishioners has died since this began. We haven't had a birth either though Mrs. Griffiths' baby is due any time. Let's hope it's all settled before the christening becomes an issue. The church will have to be closed for the duration anyway. We'll be holding services in the hall over the road – if anyone comes.'

'That's crazy!' Marina exclaimed. 'Surely not every single person in Llantathan feels so strongly. There must be some...'

'The actual village, that's the households within the bank, is solidly against,' he said. 'In the wider parish feelings are more diffuse, but many of those families are estate tenants who won't go against Howells. In fact, only the Allington people are still coming to church. That's Miss Vine, her companion Miss Morton, and three or four of her tenants and their families. Imogen Vine is the one with the ancestors buried in the church and she has no qualms about disturbing them. A wonderful old lady, but not much help, I'm afraid. Twenty years ago, maybe. I gather she's been at loggerheads with the village for decades, but she's pretty infirm now.

'So you see,' John finished, 'that unless the situation is resolved before the Hafren people arrive, anyone working on the church could be in for a most unpleasant time. The village is adamant that it will stop the excavation and believe me, they're a dogged bunch. To say that it might be dangerous is, I think, no exaggeration.'

'I still don't see that they can *do* anything,' I insisted. 'Not without breaking the law. If they do that, they're in deep trouble.'

'You'd think so,' John replied and, leaving us to puzzle over that remark, he went off to the kitchen to check the

Aga. Marina followed. I yawned, looked at the clock. Was it really half past one? No wonder I felt tired and washed out. And uneasy. Nothing John had said had convinced me not to attend the interview on Monday afternoon but I did wonder if he'd told us everything.

'No, not by any means.' Marina sat up in bed, hugging her knees. 'This furore over the excavation isn't the half of it. John's not just troubled – he's scared. And he doesn't strike me as the type to scare easily.'

I turned onto my side. 'Yes, he's scared,' I agreed. I'd seen him check and recheck the locks and bolts on the front door before we came up to bed. 'And I'm not entirely happy. Nor are you.' I paused. Then: 'Why, Marina?'

She ignored my question and put one of her own. 'Do you still want the job, Steph? Considering what you could be taking on?'

Earlier I would have given her an unqualified yes. John had failed to persuade me that real trouble was likely. But now all my feelings were negative. I didn't say that, though. 'The background noise is a nuisance,' I told her, 'But, yes, I still want the job.'

'You mean you're still going to apply for the job.' She stared very hard at me, and I had the oddest feeling that she'd put me to some kind of test and was satisfied with the result.

On Sunday morning the service was thinly attended. I surprised myself mightily by going up for communion: something I hadn't done in years. Marina surprised me too, kneeling beside me for a blessing. When we left after lunch on the Monday, John was cheerful and my unease had lifted. Llantathan seemed harmless then, its associated problems diminished to realistic proportions. It was easy enough to blame my temporary antipathy towards the job on whisky and a late night.

III

We travelled to our appointments on a day of butterflies and ripening cornfields, of sun glinting on the silver-grey water of the Usk, and the promise of the night. All that weekend Marina and I had kept custody of hands and eyes, careful not to betray ourselves with loving words. Our nights had been passed in separate beds but that night we would be in some anonymous, uncaring Newport hotel.

My memory traced the lines of Marina's body and a languid, crimson wanting engulfed me: a tidal wave in slow motion. As if she knew, she pulled off the A48 into a narrow lane where hawthorn luxuriated and the verges were thick with unmown, seeding grass. Cutting the engine, she unfastened her seatbelt and leaned back, eyes closed, her breasts rising and falling with each deep, dragged-in breath.

'I want you,' she said softly. 'Dear God, how I want you!'

I stretched my hand to undo my seat belt but she put up an arm as if to defend herself. 'No. No. Don't, Steph, or we'll never get to Newport on time.' And then, in contradiction, she turned and kissed me. One kiss, no more. But it was enough to shake the essence of my being. The key of my need turned and the tension of my wanting tightened. And again and again, before that day was over.

When I left the interview room Marina pounced. 'Did you get it?' Her voice was sharp, anxious.

'I don't know.' I took her arm and pulled her along to the staircase. 'Alan Foster suggested getting some coffee. I need it. I feel wrecked.'

We found a drinks machine in the deserted refectory and fed coins into it. 'So what happened?' Marina demanded. 'When will you know?'

'I've to see Foster again at four,' I told her. I took the plastic cup of hot, frothy sludge from the machine and sat down at the nearest table. 'But I don't think I'll get it.'

Marina sat down too, rummaging for cigarettes. 'Why not?'

'Because two of them didn't want me.'

'Two of them? How many were there?'

'Four. Foster, who runs the archaeology unit. Fred Denton, the departmental head, a Dr. Taylor, and Adam Pembury. Foster and Denton were OK but Taylor was very sniffy and as for Pembury...'

'Oh, don't worry about Taylor. He's very keen on having staff with clear research agendas but he's a realist too. They have to make an appointment and he knows that the longer they leave it the less likely they are to get anyone good. You did make a big thing about your own research, I hope?'

'As much as I could, but he didn't seem impressed, and Pembury looked bored.'

'I don't know this Pembury guy.' She pushed her cup away. 'That stuff's vile. Who is he?'

'The unit's Field Officer. He's the one I'd have to liaise with at Llantathan. No, I don't know him either, but I got the oddest impression that he knows me, and that he did not want me at all. To be fair, it could have been because of the potential problems because he made it clear that he favoured a male historian.'

'I suppose he might have a point there.' She made a face.

'Only if he has an all-male excavation team, and he doesn't. I did ask. But he wanted to know what archaeological experience I had and if I understood the processes involved. All I could say was that I was applying for a job as a historian, not an archaeologist. I was competent in my own field and respected the validity of other disciplines. Which I don't suppose helped at all, though Taylor was amused. I don't think he likes Pembury. Can't say I did, either.'

'Oh well... Thank goodness I don't have to go through all that rigmarole.' She pulled out more coins. 'I wonder if the tea's as bad as the coffee...'

It was, but we drank it anyway, watching the clock and talking sporadically until four when, to my surprise, Alan Foster offered a three year renewable contract, a tiny office, a file full of paperwork 'to put you in the picture before you start' and a salary which was larger than I'd ever earned in my life.

'Told you so,' Marina grinned smugly. 'Let's find a phone and tell John.'

And my mother, I thought. Worlds apart we might be but if she hadn't funded my M.A. I wouldn't have this job, I wouldn't be here with Marina, and the night, and a life together, ahead.

* * *

Half an hour before our dinner booking, we went down to the hotel bar and sat in a padded alcove with white wine spritzers. It was Monday quiet: just a small knot of middle-aged men in business suits, and half a dozen women celebrating a birthday.

'Well?' Marina said. The question mark was emphatic.
'Well what?'

'Any particular thoughts?'

'Yes,' I replied. 'They can wait. But one definite statement can't.'

'What's that?' She smiled at me over the rim of her glass and I felt the crimson tide building again. That smile. More than lovely now. I took a deep breath, raised my eyes to hers. She knew that look and all it signified, and her face burned as she reached for a cigarette, hand shaking as she held the lighter. I closed my hand over hers to steady it, let my fingers trace a light track across her wrist. 'Stephanie...' she whispered. 'Oh Stephanie...'

I said softly, 'Marina, I will never again endure a weekend like this last one. Not for the sake of anyone's scruples. I will not share a room with you if I cannot share your bed.'

She nodded weak agreement and opened her eyes. And smiled. And the key turned once more.

It was well for us that the hotel's interior designer had suffered from an alcove fixation. The partitions in the dining room were high and deeply upholstered in red velvet. Our faces were hidden, our movements masked, our voices absorbed. Throughout the meal, of which I recall nothing, we made love with words, with looks, with gestures. We stripped each other naked with our eyes and when, at last, the table between us became an unbearable barrier, when we could no longer restrain the urge to touch, we left. Left coffee cooling, cigarettes half smoked, brandy hardly tasted.

I remember the storm of her love breaking over me, her tear-wet face; the sob in her voice when, on the brink of the long, helpless, ecstatic fall into peace, she cried out, inarticulate in her passion. Claimed by the demands of the night, she was lost... lost with me... out of time and place. A little death.

IV

We were packing Marina's books when John phoned on the Friday to say that all objections had been withdrawn. According to the verger, Sir Matthew had decided, and that was that. No reason given. 'But,' said Marina, 'John thinks it's because it got into the local paper. He says that Howells is coming back, and he sounds agitated.'

I looked at her blankly. 'I didn't know Howells had been away.'

'Since last year, apparently.'

'Then how...?'

'No, I don't know either.' She sighed. 'All I know is that John's still bothered. He thinks you shouldn't have taken the job and he wants us to go down again as soon as we can so that he can tell us what he didn't tell us last time. And, though I didn't quite grasp what he was on about, something about a house we might like.'

I was doubtful. 'There's so much to do....'

'What about Wednesday? We'd have to be back by the Sunday evening because your mother's coming on Monday... John says that if we want, we can store things at the rectory so we could take a carload with us.' Then: 'I told you we hadn't heard the full story. Remember?' She bit at a fingernail. 'I wish we could make sense of this. You'd expect him to be OK now that the protest's over.'

'Maybe it's Howells. It would be understandable considering all the trouble the guy's caused.'

'Yes, but...' She looked horribly worried and I hated that. She passed me a stack of paperbacks and I fitted them into the box.

'I know Llantathan's a funny place, and this Howells sounds like a real control freak, but there must be hundreds of little, old-fashioned villages resisting change and newcomers. That's all it is, Marina.'

Her gaze was steady but her tone was uncertain. 'I don't know, Stephanie. There's something...'

There was something about her, for sure – a stillness, an intensity – something, and it made me nervous.

'What else could it be?'

'I don't know.'

'Well, then...'

She remained thoughtful throughout the rest of the evening and eventually I became infected with her mood. I think now that if only I'd thought to mention the odd incident on the High Street, she might have told me what it was. But I didn't remember. And though it must have been in her thoughts, Marina said nothing.

By the following day, though, her mood had changed again. We started packing up what we planned to take down to Llantathan and before we left, I had an offer on my house which was better than I expected. When we set off for south Wales again, the car crammed with boxes and bags – and two bottles of Glenmorangie for John – we were both buoyant, travelling in happy anticipation.

After tea John helped us to unload the car and carry everything up to an empty bedroom. The dusty sash window overlooked the west and south sides of the church and from it Marina noticed someone in the churchyard. 'Who's that,' she asked, and John peered over her shoulder.

'Elwyn Pryce,' he said shortly, and turned away.

As we watched, the man flicked a cigarette end onto the path then, hands in pockets, wandered idly along the path, disappearing from sight round the east end of the church. I had an impression of a bulky, late middle-aged individual whose bearing smacked of arrogance and whose general appearance suggested the farm.

'Yes, pigs,' John confirmed as we went for more boxes. 'He's my verger. It's not unusual to see him hanging around in the churchyard.'

The phone rang as we brought the last bags upstairs. John went down to answer it and we followed slowly, Marina commenting on the dreary emptiness of the house. 'I'm sure he'd feel more cheerful if his home could be sorted out. And it could be lovely.'

She was right. There was a fundamental elegance about the house which no amount of neglect had destroyed. 'One day, maybe,' I said.

In the study John had just put the phone down. 'It was Miss Vine at Allington,' he said. 'Asking me to bring you for tea on Friday. I visit her most weeks for what she calls a good gossip. I'm not entirely sure what's in her mind, but she's heard about you and thinks she may be able to help with finding you somewhere to live. She owns several properties around the parish and I think I know which it might be.'

We were very curious. 'Vine Villa,' he said. 'Not far from here on School Lane. It's been empty a while but it isn't neglected and lately there's been a lot of work done on it. If it is that house, I think you'll like it. But for now...'

And then John, hesitant and uncertain about our reaction, began to tell us about Llantathan. Really tell us. 'You have to know what I believe even if you dismiss it as nonsense,' he said. 'Very likely you'll think I'm losing my mind; for all I know, that may be true.'

He went on to describe the hostility of the village and Llantathan's rejection of everything normally associated with parish life, and his growing bewilderment and dejection. 'Christmas was terrible,' he told us sadly. 'I tried, of course, but it was quite useless. Some, like poor Anne-Marie, seemed sympathetic but I couldn't persuade them to do anything. I opened the church on Christmas Day for communion, and Miss Vine and Miss Morton came. No-one else. And next Christmas won't be any better.'

'Why did you say "poor" Anne-Marie?' Marina asked. Perhaps she was trying to change John's mood, to distract him. If so, she failed. He looked at us with horror in his eyes and I knew that here, at last, was the core of his fear.

'I buried Anne-Marie early in the New Year.' He gazed from Marina to me and back again. Then he dropped his head. 'She was only 18. That made it particularly bad coming after the Mason boy last summer.' He looked up again and now his expression held defiance. 'You can doubt my sanity if you wish,' he said, 'but I believe...' He stopped, took a deep breath, went on: 'I shall always believe that they killed her.'

Time froze. Even now, with so much gone between, I can still remember this moment in diamond detail. John, his words hanging between us, leaning forward, head down again, fingers pulling distractedly at a loose thread in his sleeve: crinkly grey wool, well washed. Marina unmoving, her face impassive, her eyes fixed unblinkingly on John. The snapping of the fire, loud in the silence and the blue drifting swirls of smoke from forgotten cigarettes. And then the chime of the church clock telling the quarter hour across the still night air.

A cold shock possessed me. I remember it all, I think, because I knew with absolute certainty that John spoke true. There was no logic to it, no reason why I should accept his statement so completely when I knew nothing of the circumstances. I did accept it though: I knew John and I knew that he believed what he said. My scalp tingled and I felt sick.

Marina's voice was gentle, calm. 'What happened, John?'

'What happened? Or what appeared to happen?' he countered.

...*Nothing is that is*...

'Just tell it your way,' she suggested. 'But go back to... What did you say the boy was called? Mason?'

John was puzzled. 'There's no connection,' he began.

Marina put her head on one side: her quizzical look. 'You did make a connection though, didn't you? Subconscious maybe, but...'

'I mentioned it because since I came to Llantathan I've only had to conduct two funerals. Both were teenagers. Just a very sad coincidence, Marina.'

'Probably,' she replied with a touch of briskness, 'but tell us about it all the same. When did the Mason boy die?'

'Last August. About the 9th or 10th, I think. Marina, I really can't see why you think this is relevant. Andrew Mason's death was the result of a farm accident. Nothing mysterious.'

Marina sighed. 'I'm a historian, John. Experience has taught me never to discount any information because I can't see its immediate relevance. I dare say it is a coincidence as you say, but I can't make any judgment if I don't know. Do you see?'

He nodded. 'Yes. I'm sorry. Well, there isn't much to tell. Andrew was helping on Bert Tudor's farm in his school holidays. Tudor had felled a tree in his far copse and they were cutting it up. Andrew took a turn with the chain saw and lost control of it. The poor boy was horribly mutilated and died before help arrived.'

We said nothing. John helped himself to more whisky.

'The inquest returned a verdict of accidental death. Derek Mason – the father – testified that Andrew had had proper training and was certainly strong enough to handle such equipment. Bert Tudor's son said that he'd seen the saw kick a little just before Andrew lost control but the firm that does maintenance on farm equipment hereabouts checked the saw and reported nothing amiss. And there was the medical evidence which I'll not repeat if you don't mind, Marina.'

Had the coroner apportioned blame, Marina wanted to know. 'Did he, for instance, suggest that Tudor had been irresponsible in allowing Andrew to use the saw? Or that he wasn't properly equipped?'

'No. And he wasn't exactly a child. He was 16, tall and well-built, and all set to go into farming with his father. The post-mortem did show alcohol in Andrew's blood so there was some suggestion that he might not have been in complete control that morning, but witnesses said they saw nothing to be concerned about.'

'Hmm. OK. The funeral. Here?'

'He's buried in the churchyard, not far from the porch where most of the recent graves are. There was quite a turn-out and a lot of flowers. Sir Matthew paid for everything. The Masons weren't well off.'

'Were they popular in the village?' I asked.

'Not particularly. They were incomers, you see. There isn't much mixing between the old families and the tenants. The Masons came about five years ago. I didn't know them well. They weren't churchgoers though Mrs. Mason did a lot for the fundraising. The poor woman was in a dreadful state as you can imagine. Andrew was her only child.'

'And now?'

'I don't know. The Masons left. The new tenants at Ty Gwyn are from East Anglia. I've visited a couple of times. They seem nice enough.'

'Who owns Ty Gwyn?' Marina wanted to know.

'Howells. It's one of about two dozen properties leased to outsiders.'

Marina stretched and reached for her glass. 'OK, John. Let's move on. Between August and New Year no-one dies.'

'I didn't say that, Madam Historian' he pointed out, smiling. 'I said that I only conducted two funerals. Jim Johnson at Bodnant Farm died in December but he was a Methodist and his funeral was in Newport. And before you ask, Marina, he was 93 and died in hospital of an assortment of degenerative complaints.'

Another slightly teasing smile disappeared with his next words. 'And then,' he said heavily, 'there was Anne-Marie.'

Anne-Marie Pritchard and Paul Williams were to be married in March. The date was set, the church booked, the banns about to be called. 'This was before all the trouble brewed up,' John explained. 'If the timing had been a little different, that poor girl might still be alive.'

As was his custom he'd interviewed the couple, noting their wishes as to music, hymns, flowers, and so on. All very routine but when John began his usual talk about the duties and responsibilities of marriage the young man cut him short. 'She knows what's expected of her and what to expect,' he said curtly. 'And I know my responsibilities. Isn't that right, Anne-Marie?'

The girl nodded but John had seen the misery behind her smile. 'Well,' he'd said, showing them to the door, 'If there's anything you wish to discuss, just call round. You may change your mind... about music and so on.' This last for Anne-Marie. An excuse, just in case.

'You see,' he explained to us, 'I believed that she was having second thoughts. He was happy enough but she... no. I thought that if only I could get her to talk, the wedding could be prevented.'

'Presumably she did talk.' Marina lit yet another cigarette: the only sign of her tension.

'Oh yes, she talked.'

On the pretext of requesting a particular piece of music Anne-Marie visited the rectory about a week later. A little probing provoked a torrent of words and tears, but it wasn't as John surmised. This was an arranged affair between Evan Pritchard and Paul Williams' father Owain.

'I don't want to marry him, Mr. Holmes,' she'd wept. 'I can't stand him, but Dad said I have to, or else. I said I wouldn't and...'

The methods of compulsion had been dreadfully harsh. Medieval, John said. Incredible, yet there had been no disbelieving the girl.

At first John had tried to persuade her to call in the police, but she'd refused. It would be pointless, she said, and it would only make things worse for her.

'I didn't understand this at all,' John told us, 'Nor why her mother didn't intervene. Anne-Marie wouldn't explain. She just kept saying that Neil Griffiths was family.'

Marina raised questioning eyebrows and John said, 'Griffiths is our local constable. She meant, I think, she could expect no support from him.'

Eventually John persuaded the girl to let him take steps to stop the wedding. If she kept quiet and went on as usual for a few days, he would make the necessary arrangements, and get her to a place of safety. 'She began to look a little happier,' John continued, 'but before she left she told me to watch out for myself. "When they find out," she said, "When Mr. Pryce hears of it, there'll be the devil to pay."'

'And then?' Marina prompted.

'The following afternoon her father came to arrange her funeral. He told me she had a weak heart caused by rheumatic fever as a child. Her doctor said the same.'

'But you don't believe it.' Marina said. A statement, not a question.

He shook his head. 'Someone knew she'd been here, and for far longer than it would take to make a simple alteration to the wedding service. What they did to her I can't bear to think, but I do believe they killed her.'

'They?'

'Pritchard or Williams. Or both.'

'But surely the doctor... the post-mortem...' I groped for sense, for escape.

'There was no post-mortem. The doctor who issued the death certificate told me that he'd treated Anne-Marie for a heart complaint since childhood and that he'd prescribed for her several times in recent weeks. He said, after the funeral, that she would keep rushing around, overdoing things and getting into a state about the wedding. Because he'd seen her so regularly there didn't have to be a post-mortem, you see. Heart failure.'

'It may be true. But the doctor is Richard Reece who is cousin to Williams' father and to Pritchard's wife. Yes, I will have a little more. Thank you, Marina.'

V

We'd been going to ask about Matthew Howells and his imminent return: whether it might signify more problems for the excavation and for John, but we never got round to it then, and later we all had far more urgent concerns to deal with. During breakfast next morning John was summoned to the church by Elwyn Pryce to witness the latest evidence of decay.

'It's the plaster,' he told us when he returned. 'Most of what was on the north wall of the chancel has fallen off. Pryce reckons more will come down, and I'd say he's right.'

He sat down, his pleasant features marred by worry and dust. 'The church will have to be closed,' he went on. 'I'll need to let people know what's happened and that we'll be holding services in the church hall... get on to the archdeacon... and... something else...' He sounded tentative now. 'Given that the church is in a dangerous state I really shouldn't ask, but I noticed something odd about the stonework. You'll probably think I'm being fanciful but if you could take a look at it...'

'You're right,' Marina said, peering again at the stone exposed by the fallen plaster. 'Isn't he, Steph?'

'Yes,' I agreed. 'It's a wall painting.'

'You'll have to do something about it, John,' Marina told him. 'It might deteriorate very quickly now that it's exposed.'

'What do you suggest?'

Getting hold of an expert, Marina thought. Getting out, I insisted, as more plaster slid from the south wall filling the air with noise and dust.

While I wrote notices to put up round the village Marina phoned the college and spoke to Alan Foster. Who, cursing, she said, promised to come out and look at it after lunch. 'And Steph, he wants you to be on hand.'

'Oh Lord!' I exclaimed. 'What am I supposed to do?'

'I don't know but you are the team historian.'

Alan, hair all over the place and glasses sliding down his nose, arrived with a box of bright yellow hard hats.

Looking and feeling faintly ridiculous we all trooped across to the church and as John unlocked the door, Elwyn Pryce sidled round the corner, seeming inclined to attach himself to the gathering. Marina and Alan went inside, but I hung back a bit: I wanted to hear how John dealt with the verger.

'No, I'm afraid you can't come in,' I heard him say. 'It's dangerous and you're not properly equipped.' And then, more firmly: 'Out of the question, Mr. Pryce. The building is closed until further notice and I must ask you to surrender your keys to me now.'

I was dying to hear Pryce's response to that but Alan called me over to look at the wall. 'How's your Latin?' he wanted to know.

I made a face but followed his pointing finger and squinted at the faint, patchy lettering painted on a ribbon banner. John came up behind me. 'It looks,' he said softly, 'as if half the first word is obscured.'

I could see it then: '...*minus... Dominus vobiscum... et cum spiritu tuo!*' I pronounced triumphantly. My Latin wasn't great, but this I could translate. '*The Lord be with you, and with thy spirit.* Yes, John?'

'That's right. Now, what have we got? And what's to be done about it?'

Alan looked rather grave. 'I'm no expert on this kind of thing,' he began, 'but it may belong to the period when the church was in its heyday. Let's say early 16th century at the very latest. It appears to be pretty extensive but it's hard to tell until all the plaster's off, and it may not the only one. What do we do?' He shook his head. 'Hope that the rest of the plaster stays put for the time being. We'll need an expert out to assess this. Meanwhile I'll get some people in on Monday morning. It'll have to be cleaned, recorded and so on.'

'Preserved?' John asked, hopefully. 'Restored?'

'Preserved, certainly. It'll cost...'

'I'll speak to the archdeacon. I'll have to anyway, about all this mess.'

'Good. Well, for now...' Alan turned and surveyed the chaos. 'Lock the church, play the danger up and don't say anything about the painting. I'll get back and try to organise things for Monday. Mr. Holmes, I know you're a busy man but do you think you could have the church emptied by Monday. All movable items?'

'Of course,' John assured him. 'That must be done anyway.'

While they were discussing details: availability of keys, facilities for the workers and so on, Marina and I drifted towards the door and into the fresh air. She took her hard hat off and shook out her hair. I glanced around. No sign of Pryce, but when Marina asked what John had said to him, I shushed her. 'Later,' I said.

Soon John and Alan came out too. John closed and locked the heavy oak door and the grille. 'I'll leave the hats,' Alan said as we made our way back to the rectory. 'They'll be needed on Monday. Make sure that whoever clears the church uses them too.'

'That'll be us, I imagine,' Marina smiled.

'It'd be as well,' Alan remarked. 'The fewer people in there the better.'

He drove away, his car loud in the afternoon quiet. Marina put the kettle on and John disappeared into the study to phone the archdeacon and arrange for the removal of the pews, the font and the other large fittings. I sat on the kitchen table swinging my feet. 'So?' Marina said.

'So?' I echoed. 'It's going to be pretty lively round here next week one way or another. I hope he's going to be OK.'

'Why should he not be?' She reached for the big blue tea caddy.

'I think he's taken Pryce's keys away.'

'Aah. Pryce won't like that. He does seem to regard the church as his personal property. You can't look out of a window without seeing him roaming around in that horrible, greasy cap. Yes. I suppose things could be made uncomfortable for John.'

She brought the teapot to the table and pushed me off. 'It can't be helped,' she said. 'We can't do anything more.'

Nor could we. And to be fair, John did seem more cheerful. Far less worried. He'd spoken to the archdeacon who thought the financial side could be dealt with. 'I'll enjoy having people about,' John said. 'They were going to put site huts in the garden, but I've got more space than I need here so they might as well use some of it.' And, yes, he had got the verger's keys. 'I'll have to hold an emergency Vestry meeting to suspend normal procedures and get the churchwardens' keys too. And if I have my way, Pryce at least will never get them back.'

I had my doubts about that. It might be OK as long as the church was out of commission, but there would have to be a verger and churchwardens, and didn't the parishioners have votes? I didn't say anything, though. John was so happy. I wasn't going to cast clouds.

VI

On Friday morning we dealt with the last of the small items from the church and a van took the pews and whatnot away to temporary storage. John had a diocesan meeting in Newport. 'The wall painting and so on,' he told us as he left. 'And apparently there's been a huge, anonymous donation. But I'll be back in time for us to go over to Allington.'

'Oh yes,' Marina said. Sleeves rolled up, she was polishing the altar cross and candlesticks. 'Tea with Miss Vine.'

Sensing her disquiet, I pointed out that we weren't obliged to accept Miss Vine's offer.

'I think we may have to,' she sighed. 'Sorting even a rental property might take more time than we've got.' She reached for the Brasso again, and a clean cloth. 'Vine Villa! It sounds like an Edwardian monstrosity.'

'John thinks we'll like it,' I consoled. 'But you're right. I think we will have to take it. We needn't stay there for long, though.'

'No...'

She sighed again. 'Let's have some coffee, Steph love. Maybe I'll be able to get my head together...'

She tried to smile but didn't quite manage it. 'All this rushing backwards and forwards between Yorkshire and Llantathan. Changing jobs. Moving house and not knowing where we're going to be or when. Doing a million things and feeling I've achieved nothing. It's all a shambles.'

Then sensible, capable Marina put her head on my shoulder and cried like an overtired child. I held her, made the right kind of noises, sympathised and offered practical suggestions, like putting me on the insurance so that I could share the driving, and wondered if there was more to this than I knew.

* * *

John was back in time for a late lunch, burdened with padlocks, hasps, chains and whatnot. 'I'll make a start this afternoon,' he said.

Marina, brighter now, was amused. 'The excuse being that the church is now a dangerous place.'

He grinned. 'Exactly.' Then he told us something of the morning's meeting. 'The main thing is that we won't have to worry about funds. That donation I mentioned really is huge. The diocesan surveyor thinks it should more than cover all the restoration work and the archaeological investigation.'

'And you've no idea where it came from? Could it have been Miss Vine?' I asked. Marina ran hot water into the sink and I began to clear the table.

No. It came through a legal firm in London. That's all anyone knows.' Then: 'Talking of Miss Vine, please don't expect a sweet little old lady. She can be perfectly outrageous at times.'

'But you like her.' Marina squeezed Fairy liquid into the bowl.

'I do. And I only hope I've as much life in me when I'm in my eighties.'

'Tell us about her,' I invited. I pulled a tea towel from the big overhead drying rack while John, reaching past Marina, filled the kettle.

'I hardly know where to begin. As you know, she's the only person in the parish who owns land apart from Matthew Howells and the Church. Howells has tried several times to buy her out but she says that her family has held its property here since the Conquest and no upstart baronet is going to get it.'

'Good for her.' Marina grinned. 'Go on, John. The line's going to die with Miss Vine, I take it.'

'Yes and no. The name will die, certainly, but Howells is Miss Vine's nephew. Her half-sister was his mother.' He took another tea towel and started drying cutlery. 'I know she detests the man but I don't know why. Something going way back.

'Her companion, Angela Morton, has been trying to persuade her to finalise her will. Apart from the Allington estate there's another in Lincolnshire, a house in Mayfair and some other London properties. She's an extremely wealthy woman and if she dies intestate, Howells will get everything. She doesn't want that, obviously, but all Angela gets is a promise that she'll do it when the time is right.

'There's not much leeway for prevarication when you're in your eighties.' Marina commented.

'Quite. Yet except for the arthritis she's pretty fit. Her mind's perfectly sound and there's nothing wrong with her sense of humour. She was at Oxford – Somerville – and I believe she finished at the Sorbonne. And if the names she's dropped occasionally are anything to go by she was on the fringes of the Bloomsbury set. She seems to have had a very interesting life...'

On the way to Allington John told us more about Miss Vine, and Angela, her companion, who came from the Midlands as a girl. 'A nice woman,' John said. 'How she manages that house with minimal help I can't imagine.'

Angela Morton met us at the door. Plump, cheerful, 50ish, she was, with her curly brown hair and pretty summer frock, definitely not one's idea of an ancient retainer, and Allington was no grim and dusty den. It might be full of museum pieces but it was a real home: comfortable and bright. It took me some time and several visits to appreciate its size. Llantathan Hall was a dolls' house by comparison. No wonder Howells wanted to buy her out. It never occurred to me then to consider just how much buying Miss Vine out would cost.

Miss Morton, chattering, led us upstairs to a small sitting room overlooking a rose alley. Everywhere we saw evidence of life lived now: the day's papers, a stack of cassette tapes, a colour TV, the latest Robert Barnard mystery. Whatever Imogen Vine was, she wasn't Miss Havisham.

She was tiny, bent and white-haired, but her fragile appearance was deceptive. Her hand was distorted by arthritis, but it grasped mine firmly. I smiled down at her, liking what I saw: eyes speaking reams for the power of her mind and for a love of life in spite of physical failings.

In a clear, high voice she welcomed us all, inviting Marina and me to sit down. John she despatched to the kitchen 'to help Angela with the tea things'.

'So you're the historians. John has been singing your praises loud and long.' She paused. Her expression, gravely formal, didn't change, but I saw mischief in her eyes. 'I had a very passionate affair with a historian once. Didn't last. Silly girl went back to her husband.'

I tried not to let my eyes widen. Tried not to let the jaw drop. Then Marina burst into peals of delighted laughter. Miss Vine was chuckling too. 'You knew!' Marina choked. 'You said that deliberately because you knew!'

'Of course I knew, child,' she said. 'I can put two and two together even if John Holmes can't.'

I remembered that John had said something about the Bloomsbury set. Yes, well...

'Are you happy?' She was nothing if not direct.

'Very,' my lover told her with serene confidence, answering for both of us.

'Good. Be happy. Be discreet – I can tell that you are – but don't ever be ashamed.'

She said no more on the subject. Not then or ever. I've always regretted that: I would love to have known whether

her historian lover was real or an invention to provoke a reaction by which to judge us.

Miss Vine didn't play about with polite conversation. She proceeded at once to the matter of Vine Villa and offered her extremely reasonable terms. 'I shall be happy to rent it to you on a casual basis and then if you wish we can make more formal arrangements. You may find that you would prefer not to live in Llantathan when you know it better.'

I wasn't sure that I wanted to live in Llantathan at all but we had to do something. I looked at Marina and I could tell that she wasn't sure either. 'May we think about it?' she asked. 'And decide when we've seen it?'

'Naturally. Ah! Good!' Miss Vine turned stiffly as the door opened: John and Miss Morton bringing tea. 'Angela, the keys please.'

Miss Morton crossed the room to a small walnut bureau and returned with a bulky brown manila envelope. She put it into Miss Vine's hand and went back to the laden tea trolley to fuss with the cups and saucers.

Miss Vine beckoned. Mine were the hands into which she pressed the keys. She looked up at me and smiled, nodding. Then she took Marina's hand and held it. Again she nodded but her eyes, fixed on Marina's face, seemed to hold questions.

We didn't stay long after tea. Miss Vine was tiring and we, with the keys of this possible house in our possession, were keen to be off to view it.

'School Lane, you said?' Marina asked. 'I thought the school was on the High Street.'

'Such as it is.' John frowned and eased up on the accelerator as we neared the village. 'It isn't a state school. All the Llantathan children attend a private co-operative set-up in the village. The incomers' children go to Llanfair junior and comprehensive.'

'How very odd,' Marina remarked. 'I wouldn't have thought this place could produce enough teachers for such a scheme.'

'One, qualified,' John told her. 'And that seems to satisfy the Education Authority. Of course they are quite within their rights to organise their children's schooling as they wish as long as it's of a suitable standard, and one assumes that it is. In any case, at 13, all the children go on elsewhere.'

'One hardly ever sees children out and about in the village,' I remarked. The village had no play area and I wondered what these kids did. I would have asked John but by now we were back at the rectory and in a rush to change from what Marina called our party clothes and get off to look at the house.

VII

The lane, named for an 18th century dame school, is a gentle hill running from the High Street opposite the rectory. Bordered by field hedges, it follows a semi-circular route passing Llantathan Hall close to where it re-joins the High Street east of the village green. On the left, at its highest point, a substantial, ivy-clad wall is interrupted by tall stone gateposts. One bears an incised announcement that this is Vine Villa. We had to take that on trust though, because from the lane no such villa was visible. Beyond the wall, trees, shrubs and undergrowth battled in riotous green confusion. 'Good God!' breathed Marina. 'Where is it?' Then: 'Oh, I see! It's all camouflaged with ivy and whatnot.'

The curving gravel drive led us round a stand of beech trees and there, suddenly, was Vine Villa. No monstrosity this, but one of the loveliest houses I'd ever seen. Its basis was a fairly large 18th century cottage, whose rough-dressed, limewashed stone walls stood under a slate roof broken by three pointed dormers. Flanked by casement windows, the deep open porch framed a solid central door painted a rich, dark green. To the original building had been added a wing of about the same size extending back to make a reverse L shape. This was the part of the structure we'd glimpsed through the trees: unpainted stone giving a home not only to ivy but to honeysuckle, clematis and wistaria.

'I think it's worth investigating further.' Marina sounded very off-hand but I knew what she was thinking. Nothing could have kept us from going in.

The key turned easily and silently as did the hinges when the front door swung open. We stepped without a word into a stone-flagged hallway. And without a word we walked from room to room of the house we knew was ours.

Sitting room, dining room, kitchen and store made up the ground floor accommodation of the older part with a passageway leading into the newer wing. There, one room suggested a study and the other, giving onto a conservatory, could be a breakfast room. The central staircase, with its half landing and stained glass window, brought us to three bedrooms and a bathroom in the old house. In the extension a much larger fourth bedroom adjoined another bathroom.

It was lovely. No. It was more than that: as far as any house can be, it was perfect. Someone had taken care that the extension should match the original, and there had been no short cuts. Everywhere we saw evidence of quality in materials and workmanship.

All the features one associates with country cottages were present at Vine Villa: oak floors and beams, wainscotted hall, inglenook fireplaces, lattice windows set in thick walls. Yet there was nothing rustic about the amenities. Marina, opening a cupboard, disclosed the electricity meter with a very modern fuse board and circuit breaker.

The plumbing looked good too. In both bathrooms the fittings were plain but new and included, in the larger one, a spacious, separate shower cubicle. The kitchen had a new electric cooker as well as an Aga, and a stainless steel double drainer sink, also new, with cupboards below. We saw in- and outlet pipes for an automatic washer and though there were no fitted units, we discovered a walk-in larder. Two enormous glass-fronted cupboards had been built into the alcoves on either side of the cooking range, and the floor was quarry-tiled.

When Marina unlocked the kitchen door we found ourselves in a big lean-to porch housing another sink and the central heating boiler, and from there we progressed to the gardens. Every corner was overgrown but it was easy to see the plan: kitchen plot with fruit trees; shrubbery, lawns, flowerbeds. To top it off there was a greenhouse, the panes intact, a modest potting shed, a good garage and a tiny, octagonal summerhouse overlooking a square, lily-choked pond. Beyond the rough-hedged boundaries the fields stretched away, empty, quiet.

When I say that Marina and I viewed the house in silence, I mean it. Neither of us said a word until we were back where we started, at the green front door. Then, and only then, did she speak. 'Oh, Steph, it's a marvellous house.' She wandered inside again, and upstairs. 'I love it. I really do. But let's just rent it short-term until we see how things go.'

We went over the house again trying to decide on what pieces of furniture would fit where and wondering how quickly we could arrange the move.

'It's just packing and some notifying,' I said. 'There's a lot but I'm sure we can do it as long as we can book a removal firm at short notice.'

'Let's go back to John's,' she suggested. 'First thing is to let Miss Vine know what we want to do, then make some lists.'

In the main bedroom she opened the window and leaned out. 'You can see the church and the rectory from here,' she said. 'And there...' She pointed in the opposite direction. 'Isn't that Allington?'

Neither of us saw any significance in that, but later it occurred to me that if one joined the three points – Allington, Vine Villa and the rectory – the triangle so formed encompassed the village.

JOHN, ADAM, MARINA – AND ME

1983 – 1984

Some circumstantial evidence is very strong
as when you find a trout in the milk

H. D. Thoreau

I

After a wild, late drive back to Yorkshire on the Sunday, we fell, exhausted, into bed at Marina's house. On Monday my mother arrived for my ceremony on Tuesday, and helped me finish my packing before she went home on Wednesday. By then Marina had boxed up the last of her small stuff, arranged for the Salvation Army to collect furniture we didn't want, and got hold of a firm able to move us at short notice. Late on Thursday we fell, exhausted, into bed at Vine Villa. That we achieved the move at all in that time was a near miracle. That we did it without a single problem suggests divine Providence. No doubt John put in a good word for us.

Over the next few days he did more than that. He ferried our boxes and bags from the rectory, cooked for us, cleaned windows, moved furniture, plumbed in the washing machine, fired up the Aga, cut the grass and ordered a delivery of coal and logs. And, inevitably, he found us out.

A week on, and we were nearly straight. The kitchen was fully functional and we were sorting out the sitting room. When John arrived Marina was perched on the stepladder hanging curtains and I was about to carry the last box upstairs.

'Steph, pass me that other curtain, would you?'

I went to help her. Over my shoulder I said to John, 'Would you mind carrying that box up for me please? Everything in it belongs upstairs. In the big bedroom.'

Marina didn't take the curtain I held up. 'That's done it,' she said as she climbed down. Her gaze was rueful yet mildly amused. 'Put the kettle on, Steph. John's going to need a nice cup of tea.'

I stared at her. What was she on about? Then it dawned. 'Oh no!'

'Oh yes! Steph, up there is a double bed which has obviously been occupied by two people, in a room clearly intended to be used by two people. In a house with three other bedrooms. He's not stupid.'

Nor was he, but I doubt he'd have said a word if Marina hadn't decided to clear the air immediately. How she began it I don't know but when I brought in the tea tray John was saying something about having known, really, from the start. And he was looking embarrassed and worried. I handed him a mug and sat down in silence, more than content to leave this to Marina.

She said, 'I'm glad you know, John, and I hope it's not going to make a difference.'

'It shouldn't,' he said. 'Oh dear! This is very confusing.' He sipped his tea and went on: 'You see, I've never had to confront this so directly before. I know what the Church teaches about homosexuality of course...' He lit a cigarette.

'Never mind about the Church,' Marina told him. 'What do *you* feel, John? Do you like us less?'

'No, of course not.' He was sure of that. 'But that makes it more confusing. You are my very dear friends who have brought me nothing but good. Yet all I've ever been taught is that what you are, what you do is sinful... wrong.'

Marina put her mug down and sat back. 'May I tell you about us, John? I won't upset you with personal details but if you know something of what we are, how it came about, it may help.'

He nodded and Marina spoke again, giving a quick, vivid sketch of the way our relationship had developed. Then: 'John, I love Stephanie. More than I can say. And she loves me. So now we live together, caring for each other because love is all about caring, as you know.'

'I don't think any reasonable person would condemn you for that,' John said. 'It isn't the fact that you love each other.'

Marina's smile was wry and sad. 'No. It's the fact that we demonstrate that love, isn't it? You weren't troubled by our obvious closeness, were you, John? By the fact of our sharing a house? It only became a problem when you went upstairs just now and saw that we also share a bed. I'm not going to deny it. Of course Steph and I make love. That makes us both very happy and we're hurting no-one. Your Church, would brand us as sinful, and much of society as sick. Are we, John?'

John's distress at her words was evident. 'Sick? Of course I don't believe that. Sinful? Yes, that is the view of the Church which I am supposed to uphold. But...' He shook his head. 'You're right in so many ways. You may be completely right. I don't know.'

Marina had more to say before she drifted back to her

curtain hanging but I took the tea things to the kitchen to wash up. When I returned John had gone and Marina was clearing up the crumpled newspapers from the boxes.

'Let's get this out of the way,' she said. 'Then we're finished.'

'Where's John?'

'Gone shopping. Caldicot. He's coming back for tea. And...' she stuffed the last of the paper into a black bin sack, '...he says that if we've nothing urgent to do tomorrow, why don't we go and see how the church is coming along.'

'Good idea,' I said. 'I ought to anyway. I need to find out what I have to do on Monday.'

Then Marina suggested inviting the Hafren people for drinks one evening. 'A sort of housewarming.'

I thought of Adam Pembury, now in charge of the small team carefully stripping plaster from the church walls. If he was still nursing his obvious antipathy that could be awkward. But Marina was keen so I agreed. 'If John will come along too it'll be OK.'

'Oh, he will, she told me. She grinned. 'I asked.'

So you think he'll cope with knowing about us?'

'Steph, he knew already, really. Yes, he'll cope. He'll work it out by his own feelings and his own concept of God, not by what the Church or even the bible says. And if he ends up not being able to square us with his own religious stance, he'll still take us for what we are and leave the judging to a higher authority.'

'I love John,' I said.

'So do I. And I wish him a better parish than this.'

'Yes, but I don't think he would leave Llantathan now.'

I followed her outside with the boxes and we pushed them into the shed. Inside, washing our hands, I remarked that the women weren't as frosty as the men.

'But the women won't do anything the men don't want. Look at the case of Anne-Marie. Whether or not she was murdered, there's little doubt that she was being forced to marry a man she hated. That can happen in other cultures, but I can't imagine any western girl nowadays, except in some of those weird cults you hear about, allowing such domination. Did her mother just sat back and let it happen? Damn it all, Steph! Why didn't Anne-Marie, with or without her mother's help, just walk away from it?'

'She tried, in the end,' I pointed out. 'And she died. Murdered? Who knows? Perhaps she really did have a bad heart. Maybe she got into a row with her father and her heart packed up. You're right, though: it does look as if the women do what they're told.'

'Yes... but...'

'What?'

She leaned against the fridge, twisting a strand of hair round her finger. 'I'm not sure. Something I've noticed, but I don't know if it means anything. Look, Anne-Marie's grave always has fresh flowers. A couple of times I've seen them being arranged by some of the women who go to Sunday morning service.'

'What's so unusual about that?'

'Nothing. But if you look at the graves in that area, you'll see that the only one tended is Anne-Marie's. Except for hers they're all male Pritchard burials. They don't bother with flowers for their menfolk. Makes you wonder, doesn't it?'

It might have, if I hadn't had other things to think about. The housewarming party was postponed, thankfully, because John was tied up with diocesan matters but, remembering Adam Pembury's hostility, I was jittering more than I cared to admit about starting the new job.

II

The wall paintings – there were three – had complicated everything. When I could do nothing practical, I got on with the revision of a 1930s publication about the fairs and feasts of Monmouthshire, working in one of the empty bedrooms in the rectory where John had set up a table and chair for me. When I could work in the church I was mostly confined to the tower.

Separated from the nave, the tower's thick walls and massive door mercifully shut out most of the plaster dust and the headache-making noise of hammers on chisels. The ground floor had probably been a meeting room. Now it was full of junk. Above it the ringing chamber was, by contrast, orderly and almost empty. Eight faded blue and gold sallies, their tail ropes looped up, hung in the dust motes glistening in and out of the thin shafts of light from the narrow leaded windows. On the walls grimed wooden boards, gold lettering dulled by time, recorded details of the bellringers and their achievements. Hafren's finds supervisor, Joyce Sanderson, suggested a careful wipe over with a soft damp cloth. 'Try an edge bit first,' she advised, 'but if you get paint coming off stop at once.' It worked well enough to let me read and transcribe them all. Photography was another matter, but that wasn't my concern.

The last recorded peal was in 1939 rung by a team of six like all the teams listed on the boards. I wondered why, when St. Michael's had a ring of eight but, knowing nothing then of change ringing, I didn't think to query it. According to John the bells were in working order so it seemed a pity that ringing had been allowed to lapse. The influence of John's predecessor again, no doubt. Or Howells. No. Not Howells. Not if he was Miss Vine's nephew. His father, probably. Something to ask John about.

The blue carpet on the floor of the chamber was good but in need of cleaning. I noted circular mats below six of the ringing stations: a simple device to prevent localised wear. But, again, why only six?

Apart from a set of handbells, two dusty books about ringing methods and a few ancient copies of *The Ringing World*, there were some dog-eared pre-war account books. These, detailing fees and fines, should be archived if John agreed.

In a corner steep, wooden steps led to the bell loft. I didn't like the ringing chamber, and I was in no hurry to visit the bells. The superstition that bells have personalities and power had inspired several of the horror stories I'd read in my teens – stories which I now recalled with uncomfortable clarity. I would have to go up there because the dratted things had names, dates and inscriptions, but when I did, I would try to ensure that I wasn't alone. Finished with the ringing chamber I escaped downstairs and started investigating.

Underlying the tower room's all-pervasive smell of damp was another smell. Mice. Hardly surprising given what looked like decades' worth of abandoned rubbish: torn hymn books, rotting, mouldy hassocks and piles of ancient copies of *The Church Times*. A massive, immovable oak cupboard half obscured more wall boards. Lists of previous incumbents, probably. And under the rotting, filthy carpet there were, as I expected, grave slabs. Nothing could be done until the room was cleared so, since it was 4.30 and the team was packing up, I went to consult John.

'Yes, of course the tower room must be cleared,' he agreed. 'I've been wanting it sorted out since I came but Pryce just prevaricates. Is there anything worth keeping?'

'I shouldn't think so,' I told him, 'But I'd be glad if you'd have a look yourself.'

He nodded. 'Let's see... Monday morning... Stephanie, you shouldn't have to be doing this.'

'Well, who else can? You wouldn't trust anyone in the village to deal with it, would you? If Marina can help it won't take more than a day and I can make up my work time.'

That agreed, I was about to set off for home when I remembered my curiosity about the bellringing. 'By the way, John,' I said, 'How old is this Howells person?'

He started. 'What on earth put him into your head, Stephanie?'

I explained about the end of the bellringing.

'He'll be 41,' John told me. 'According to Miss Vine his mother – her sister – died couple of months after he was born, in the summer of 1942. But I don't think there's necessarily any mystery about the lapse of bellringing. War broke out in 1939 and church bells couldn't be rung for the duration except in the event of invasion. And Dunkirk and Alamein of course. I suppose that since it wasn't allowed, it simply died. By the way, Howells came back to the Hall today...'

This bellringing thing niggled as I walked home. Hadn't church bells been rung to celebrate the end of the war in 1945? Surely the ringers of Llantathan had done that. Or had they all still been in the Forces? Probably: my own father hadn't been demobbed until late 1946. Likely John was right. Only... only... something didn't make quite sense. I tried to make connections but nothing would come, and once in the house I forgot about it. With the prospect of a warm weekend spent with Marina, it was easy to forget, though I did remember to tell her about Howells' return.

III

'Well, well!' Marina said softly. 'I wonder if we'll manage to get a sight of him. I'd like to see this medieval character for myself. How did John seem when he told you?'

'Uneasy. Probably bothered in case Howells starts kicking up a fuss again.' I spooned fresh fruit salad into dishes and poured cream.

'Hmm... Anne-Marie... Didn't she say there'd be the devil to pay when Howells found out?'

'No. She said when Pryce found out. Still, how reliable is that? A scared girl...'

'She paid.'

Suddenly I didn't want to eat any more. 'I thought you weren't sure about that?'

She didn't reply for some minutes. Then, hesitantly, she said, 'It's as if my mind's working on two levels. On the critical level I'm dealing with John's story as a professional historian. Only what the evidence will allow, and taking account of bias in the sources. Oh, *you* know, Steph! You're a historian. You know that any one event may have half a dozen different interpretations. So, looking at what John told us on that basis, I can say that his is the least likely of several interpretations.

'But... The other level's quite different, and entirely emotional. Perhaps it's intuition, though I've never really believed in it.'

'I think intuition's only awareness based on information assimilated subliminally,' I told her. 'But whatever it is, what is it telling you?'

She didn't reply. She was troubled and trying not to be. I brought the coffee, waiting for the answer I expected.

'It says that John's right,' she said finally. 'It says that there's something more wrong about this place than we could ever imagine. And it says all this with far more conviction than anything my logic says and with such force that it's like being hit over the head with a brick.'

* * *

We saw nothing of Matthew Howells nor did we hear anything about him. No portentous messages were relayed from him to John and if he stirred from Llantathan Hall we were unaware of it. He was less trouble, in fact, than when he was away.

Sunday morning had a surprisingly large turnout. Every member of every family seemed to be there, but it was a restless congregation and the singing was off-key. Afterwards. Marina and I watched Mrs. Pritchard, Mrs. Lewis and two of the younger women, cross the road from the hall to the churchyard. Sure enough, when we passed through later with John, Anne-Marie's grave was bright with fresh carnations. Nearby, on the Mason boy's unkempt plot a mass-produced flower vase lay overturned and broken. The Masons, I supposed, had moved too far away to tend the grave. Or perhaps they could see no point. What was the purpose of grave-tending and flowers? Part of the grieving process? The only way left of demonstrating love? An expiation of guilt? Or propitiation of the dead? And did the dead care? I would have given much to know what motive those women had for their weekly floral offerings.

IV

On Monday morning Marina and I found John waiting for us at the church with cardboard boxes and black bin sacks. As the team arrived, he paused to extract a promise of assistance with the cupboard later. I heard Adam

Pembury's laconic assent as I unlocked the tower room door and soon that interminable clunk of hammers on chisels began again.

'Dreadful,' John agreed, looking round. 'Unless it's obviously useful, it can all go, including this disgusting carpet.'

The big cupboard was locked and John could find no key for it. By the time he'd borrowed tools from the team and forced the doors we were half imagining some amazing secret inside but of course it was just more rubbish: mostly paper, ancient curtains and stained altar cloths.

John, with an afternoon appointment, left us to it. We filled endless bins sacks and, at the end of the day, all we kept were some pretty baptism certificates, a box of light bulbs, a little sanctuary lamp, a vast pair of blue velvet curtains, grubby but sound, which Marina thought belonged to the stage in the church hall, and a box.

This last resembled an oversized cash box with side handles. It was heavy: black japanned steel; strong, and locked. When I lifted it down from the top shelf of the cupboard something moved inside as if the contents fitted neatly but not exactly. There was nothing we could do about it until John returned so we started clearing up.

Marina carried a sack to our temporary dump just inside the main door and came skipping back again, looking at once exasperated and mischievous. 'Pryce is lurking again,' she announced. 'By the gate. Look, Steph, we've got to get the good stuff over to John, including that box which may or may not be important, and dispose of the rubbish without giving Pryce a chance to paw over it. Adam Pembury says that their skip's almost full so we can put the junk in it just before it's replaced in the morning. For tonight it can all stay in here and we'll take the good stuff over to the rectory now.'

We contrived to do it so that Pryce, staring over the wall, could see nothing. He hung around for a while but by the time John arrived home he'd given up and gone away. Which left us behind closed curtains with the box on the desk in John's study.

This time John did have a key which fit though the lock needed WD40 before it moved. 'I hope you're not going to be disappointed,' Marina said, amused by John's suppressed excitement. 'I doubt it'll be bags of gold sovereigns.'

'No,' he replied. 'But I don't think I'll be disappointed for all that. I've an idea of what's inside... if only I can get this key to... Ah!'

The lock clicked and John lifted the lid.

Books.

I recognised them instantly for what they were. Parish registers. Baptisms, marriages and burials, and banns books.

Marina said, 'I thought parish registers were supposed to be lodged in archives.'

John nodded. He started to say something but stopped, listening. Then: 'Get them out of sight!' and a moment later the doorbell rang. We scrambled the lot, box and all, under the desk and pushed a stack of books in front while John went to the door.

Elwyn Pryce.

We heard his voice but not his words and then John saying, with reluctance, 'Come in, Pryce. I'm rather busy at the moment but I can give you a few minutes.'

The verger followed John inside. He paused in the study doorway, pale lizard eyes sliding contemptuously from Marina to me, to the drawn curtains, and back again.

'Now, what is it, Pryce?' John asked.

'Thought I'd better let you know, Rector. Sir Matthew is having some work done tomorrow to one of his family memorials.'

'Oh yes. That leaning headstone.

'Looks dangerous,' Pryce went on. 'Don't want it falling over, see. All these strangers messing about round the church.'

'Yes, it would be wise to have the stone made safe. I'll make a note...' John scribbled something on a piece of paper, 'and let the archaeology team know.'

Pryce nodded. He stood there a moment longer. Just long enough to add to the awkward atmosphere. Then he said, 'I'll be off now, Rector. Good evening to you.' He nodded to John, then to Marina and me. 'Dr. Graham. Mrs. Hargreaves.'

I wondered how he knew our names.

'What a creep!' Marina shuddered, when he'd gone.

'A very well dressed creep though,' I pointed out. 'Exceptionally smart for a weekday.'

'Yes,' John said. 'Unusual.'

But we weren't about to start speculating on Pryce's sartorial habits when there were more interesting pursuits to hand. John retrieved the registers and began to explain the procedure governing the keeping of parish records.

'A basic copy goes to the bishop every year,' he said. 'There. You can see in the margin of this one a note to the effect that that was done in 1881. Registers used to be put away safely when full but now they go to the diocesan record office and the parish keeps photocopies. The registers must, by law, be available to any member of the public: copies just save wear and tear on the originals. What on earth these were doing in that cupboard I can't imagine. I knew they were missing but no-one seemed to have any idea what had become of them.'

'They were put away long ago judging by the amount of dust on that box,' I commented.

'I wonder why.' Marina put her elbows on the desk and rested her chin on her hands. 'A whole century's worth. You do have the ones before and after, I suppose.'

'Oh yes,' he confirmed. 'I have copies of all the registers prior to the 19th century. And the current books. But how very strange. A century's worth. Rather more, and the first ones have a few years back into the 1700s. Perhaps my mad predecessor put them away during the war and just forgot about them. I suppose he may have believed that if there was bombing or even invasion the church would have been safer than the house.'

'John, when you enquired about the missing records, whom did you ask?' Marina wanted to know.

'Pryce and the churchwardens. No, Marina, I don't think they knew where the books were. They could only have been boys when these were put away.'

She seemed to accept that and, really, I thought it unlikely that Pryce and his cronies could have had anything to do with it if, as we supposed, the records had been hidden during the war. 'But they were known to be missing and Pryce might be very anxious to know if and when they turned up,' I said, thinking aloud.

John and Marina stared at me.

'Sorry,' I said, and added quickly, 'I only meant that Pryce is a snooper and likes to know what's going on.'

'No you didn't,' Marina contradicted. She gazed down at the registers. 'John,' she said, 'there's something very odd, rather nasty about Llantathan. I can't begin to know what it is, but I want to find out. I don't like people who try to force girls into unwanted marriages. I don't like that creeping toad of a verger and I don't like what all this is doing to you.'

'But my dear girl, what on earth can you do about it?' John asked, bemused and troubled.

'I don't know. It depends on what's going on.'

'It could be dangerous to meddle.'

'Very likely. But listen to me, John. As rector of Llantathan don't you bear a responsibility for the spiritual welfare of your parish? Aren't you duty bound to confront evil where you find it?'

'Yes, I am. But you, Marina, do not have that responsibility.'

She put her head on one side. 'Not even natural responsibility? John, I can't stand by. I just can't. Because of other Anne-Maries. And because I love my friend John Holmes. But most of all because evil makes me bloody angry and I cannot close my eyes to it and say that it's nothing to do with me.'

There was no cant about Marina, no theatricality, and her simple sincerity brought tears to John's tired eyes. He bowed his head slightly. 'I stand rebuked,' he said quietly.

* * *

The immediate upshot of all this was that we took the registers home with us and the following day, in college, Marina made three photocopies. One set went to be bound for parish use, another was deposited in the college strong room and the third came back to Vine Villa. By prior arrangement the originals were entrusted to a clergyman acquaintance of John's in Newport for personal delivery to the record office, and the record office was notified.

'I shall, of course, announce that the long-lost registers are found and now safely deposited,' John told us.

Marina made a face. 'Do you have to?' she complained. 'The less Pryce knows, the better, surely.'

'I can't, legally, conceal those records,' John said but, as he pointed out, with the originals safely out of reach, no-one was likely to interfere with the parish copies. 'That is what you're concerned about, isn't it?' he asked.

'That and keeping one step ahead of Pryce,' she said. 'It seems important. Perhaps it's only paranoia. I can't imagine why Pryce should be interested in the registers and to be fair we've no evidence to show that he is. After all, the records weren't truly lost, were they? Annual copies had been made. But...'

But... Feelings. Always feelings. And none of them good. Sometimes I thought we were like children creating spooks from our imaginations. John had had a difficult time. He was, perhaps, overwrought. Marina and I, sympathetic, had latched onto the hostile atmosphere of a particularly insular community and inflated it beyond all reasonable proportion.

How I wanted to believe that! I did believe it, sometimes. If I could have gone from Llantathan then, back to the familiar, crowded world of university, I would have believed it completely. That being impossible, I rationalised. Often, conveniently, I forgot what I didn't want to know, and toned down what I couldn't forget.

When, in the following months, we all sought answers, the basis of my seeking was a need to discover the reasonable explanation for everything. My intuition told me the same things as Marina's, but I wanted none of it.

V

The day Marina copied the registers she and I had a discussion about rationalisation. Early evening, and we'd started clearing the undergrowth behind the house. Marina wanted to make a scented garden with an old lilac as the focal point.

'Well of course, Steph,' she replied when I mentioned it. She stopped to lean on her rake. 'It's an ancient human trait, surely, and essential, because life would be pretty bad if we didn't. We learn to do it as kids and we go on until we barely know we're doing it. In the end we almost believe our rationalising.'

'Almost?'

'When you were small, Steph, were you afraid of bumps in the night?'

I laughed. 'Yes, of course.'

'Were you scared of the dark?'

I admitted that too.

'Did you think that graveyards were creepy?'

'Doesn't every child? But we're not children now.'

'No, but I often think that children have far more sense than adults.'

'What do you mean?'

'They *know* that noises and darkness and graveyards are things to be scared of. OK, so the funny noise outside the bedroom door turns out to be the cat. Darkness is only the absence of light: nothing changes because it's dark. Graveyards are full of dead people, yes, but your gran's one of them and she would never hurt you.

'But... One time that noise might be a burglar. One time the darkness might conceal a mad axeman. One time the graveyard might be harbouring someone who isn't dead and you get raped or worse. And that's only the ordinary level. What about the monster under the bed? The ghost in the wardrobe? Both of them waiting to get you so that you can't even go and switch the light on.'

She resumed her raking while I thought about it. I said, 'Marina, that's all true as far as it goes. But there's a world of difference between a mad axeman and the ghost in the wardrobe. The axeman could be real, but the ghost's just a typical childhood fear.'

She stopped again. 'Which were you scared of when you were little? A mad axeman?'

I shook my head. 'Never heard of one then. But I was terrified of ghosts. The possibility of ghosts.'

'And now? If you had to walk through a churchyard at midnight which would spring to mind: the axeman or the ghost? No, no need to answer. I can tell by your face.'

I nodded ruefully and she went on: 'Steph, what would you say if I told you I'd just seen a face at our kitchen window?'

I jumped. 'Don't, Marina!' I said, and turned reluctantly to look at the house.

'"Don't, Marina", meaning don't try to scare me for the hell of it?'

'Yes, I suppose so.'

'There you are. Instant rationalisation.'

I laughed uncertainly, but the sudden upsurge of fear had gone.

'And how quickly you seize on the idea that I was merely giving you a practical example. It bears out what I've been saying. As a matter of fact, I *did* see a face, but it was only John. Come on. Let's go and see what he wants.'

Unsettled again, I followed her indoors.

We found John sitting, head in hands, by the kitchen table. When he looked up his white, drawn face shocked me. 'I had a phone call from Angela Morton,' he said dully.

'Miss Vine?'

He shook his head. 'No... No... There's been a dreadful accident...' He shivered. I crouched beside him, an arm round his shoulders. Marina went quickly, silently for the brandy.

He sipped and seemed better. 'It's the Bennett boy,' he told us at last. 'Brian. His father farms Nantoer. Brian doesn't... didn't... like farming... He...' John stopped, close to breaking down.

'In your own time, John,' Marina said gently.

'Brian had a holiday job,' he managed. At Powell's motor business. Robert Powell. One of those little units behind the post office. He does car parts... special restoration work. Chrome stripping...'

I knew what was coming but that didn't make it less horrible.

'Brian fell into the stripping tank. They use sodium hydroxide... caustic...'

Marina was in a strange mood for the rest of the evening, a mood which persisted until the following weekend. She was working on the lecture notes for her Wales and the Normans course, but I didn't think it was that. Two evenings of almost total, abstracted silence worried me and though she assured me that she was only thinking, her face had a tired, dragged-down look.

On Friday when I left St. Michael's after work she was loitering amongst the graves at the east end of the church. I watched her pass Anne-Marie's headstone, move on to another row and pause briefly, crouching to read the inscription on the grey polished marble of Andrew Mason's memorial. And again, three times more. Straightening, she saw me and beckoned.

'Have you got your notebook?' she asked. 'Write down the details: name, date and age. And hurry before Pryce comes sliming back.'

Perplexed, I scribbled as quickly as I could. 'Any more you're interested in?'

'The one with the kerbs... and that black marble cross...'

At home she pulled a beef casserole out of the oven and we ate in more of that horrid silence. Afterwards she took my notebook and went to the phone while I, really disturbed now, washed up.

The phone call was short: soon I heard the soft click of the sitting room door. I dried the last dishes, boiled the kettle, and hesitated. Did I leave her alone or go in with coffee and hope for the best?

The muffled strains of Ravel's *Pavane for a Dead Infanta* from the stereo decided it. If she was listening to music her mood must have changed. Marina never listened to music when she felt down. This had to be a good sign. I made the coffee and went in to join her.

She'd lit the fire despite the warmth of the evening, and was sitting by it looking shivery and preoccupied. I put a mug beside her and sat down opposite, waiting until the end of the track. This was one of her favourite pieces: I wasn't going to interrupt.

As *Pavane* reached its final section: that gentle, bubbling repeat of the main theme, Marina lifted her head and smiled. A wan, rather sad smile, but better than nothing.

The music died. Picking up her coffee mug she walked to the window and back. 'Point one,' she announced, 'Howells is in Llantathan.'

I nodded cautiously.

'Point two: during the second week in August a teenage boy dies horribly.'

'Marina...'

'Point three,' she went on, ignoring me, 'that boy belongs to an incomer family.'

I stared blankly at her, shaking my head. She sat down, then bounced up again, exasperated. 'Think, Steph! Doesn't it sound vaguely familiar?'

'Andrew Mason?'

'Right. Same age. Same background. Same time of year.'

'Are you sure?'

'I'm sure.' Her voice was hard.

I took a deep breath and hoped that I wouldn't get a tirade on rationalisation. 'OK, but Andrew had an accident with a chain saw and this boy fell into a vat of caustic soda. These things do happen. It has to be coincidence.'

'And is this coincidence?' She pushed my notebook into my hands. Go on. Read it. Aloud.'

I looked at the scrawl and read: 'Paul Amies. 9th of August 1981. Aged 16...' I trailed off into silence under her gaze.

'And the others?'

'Darren Whitehead, 10th of August, 1980 aged 15; Gary Dean, 11th of August, 1979 aged 17.'

'I'll grant you that two may be coincidence,' she said. 'But five?'

'Oh, come on, Marina!' I protested. 'We don't know how they died. Or where. For all we know this Paul Amies might have died in a car crash.'

'He didn't, though,' she replied. 'I phoned Angela Morton because I thought she might remember. Paul Amies – yes, another incomer – died in a fire at the pig farm. An accident with fuel for Pryce's vintage tractor. The kid was burned to death. To be brutal, burned to cinders. Howells arrived in Llantathan a few days before, and left less than a week later. Given the size of Llantathan don't you think that three particularly horrific accidents in three consecutive years – same week of the same month – is a bit much? The other two? One was apparently drowned in Wentworth reservoir. Not much left by the time the body was recovered. The other fell under a train. And, according to Angela, wherever Howells spends the rest of the year, he is always in Llantathan from the first week in August until about the 12th. A little strange then, isn't it, that these accidents just chance to occur when Howells is around?'

'Curious, yes. The odds against must be pretty huge. But it's by no means statistically impossible.'

She flung me a look of disgust.

'OK. OK. Marina, if it isn't coincidence, what is it?'

'I don't know.'

'You do know!' I persisted. 'You think it's murder, don't you?'

She turned away and wouldn't reply. I stood and crossed the room. 'Well, there's one way to find out if it is coincidence,' I said. I went out to the hall and dialled John's number.

VI

The next evening: the Saturday, John came for dinner bringing with him the current burial register. No, he said, he hadn't looked through it. Why did I want to see it?

As tactfully as I could I explained Marina's discovery of the earlier accidents and my wish to see if there were any more. John took it calmly, handing the register to me without a word and, after dinner, I took it into the study. For minutes I sat there just looking at the black cover with its stamped gold lettering. Then I opened my notepad and began. And line after line filled with my small handwriting.

It was full dark when I slipped quietly through the sitting room door, glad to see that Marina had lit the fire.

She and John were talking about early Church history but my appearance killed the conversation and they both looked up at me.

Marina, in control, betrayed nothing by her expression but her glance flicked to the paper I held with the register. John saw the paper too, and his eyes suffused with pain.

I sat down, grateful for warmth and the glass of wine Marina poured. John gave me a cigarette. 'How many?' he demanded, his voice harsh as sandpaper.

'As many as there are years in the register. Andrew Mason, 1982; Paul Amies, 1981; Darren Whitehead, 1980; Gary Dean, 1979; Peter Sherwood, 1978; John Collinson, 1977; Richard Finlay, 1976...'

John held up his hand and I stopped. There was, indeed, no need to go on. I said, 'All mid-teens and buried in the second or third week in August. There is no year without a similar entry.'

'Statistically impossible?' Marina asked. I may have imagined sarcasm in her tone.

'Statistically nothing's impossible,' I replied. 'But realistically, it has to be impossible.'

'What now?'

'I'll go through the old records. See if I can discover when it started. Then I suppose we could try to discover causes of death, but...'

'Why?' John interrupted. 'Why is all this happening?'

'I don't know,' Marina said. 'But I'm going to find out, John. And if I can help it, Brian Bennett will be the last.'

* * *

'Come to bed, Steph.' Marina, nightgowned and yawning, leant against the frame of the study door. 'It's very late.'

'I know.' I glanced up, marking my place with a finger.

'Can I get you anything? Tea?'

When she returned with two mugs I'd finished. 'There,' I said. I gathered up the papers and locked them in the desk drawer. 'I think that settles it. The same pattern right through the 19th century and back into the last decade of the 18th. I'll need the previous registers to continue.'

'Do you need to?' Marina observed me over the rim of her mug. 'Surely that's enough to prove that it's not random.'

'More than enough, but I want to know when it began.'

'What if it's been going on forever?'

'If that's the case I can only go back as far as the records go but I still want all the information there is. There'll be patterns within the overall pattern. Why do you think it might always have gone on?'

She screwed up her face. 'Just an idea. You know, Steph, a lot of rural communities still keep some form of pagan custom. Well-dressing. Maypole dancing.' She frowned and seemed to grope for things half-remembered.

'Are you thinking of Lammas?' I suggested. 'That's at the start of August. It was Lughnasadh and it may have been the forerunner of our harvest festivals. But whether it involved human sacrifice, if that's what you mean...'

'I'm not sure what I mean, but something that's been going on from time immemorial.'

'An old custom could have survived, perhaps, but we'll need a lot more data. If Llantathan is a focus for underground pagan beliefs there'll be other clues.'

'Such as?'

'Well, a spate of births every January might indicate that the villagers keep Beltane. If they are into killing people, they're not going to balk at fertility rites, are they?'

Marina rose and carried the empty mugs out to the kitchen. I listened to the sequence of small sounds as she rinsed them, locked the back door, dropped something in the pedal bin. I was very tired yet my mind would not let go of the ideas which kept floating in and out, refusing to be pinned down. It was like trying to hold together a burst feather pillow. Without the data I could do nothing, and I wanted to do everything. Abstract feelings unsettled me but data I understood.

'Tomorrow,' Marina told me, her voice soft in the bedroom's dark silence. 'Tomorrow and tomorrow and tomorrow... There's time, Stephanie.'

She drew me into the circle of her arms and, with gratitude, I rested my head against her shoulder. Breathing in the scent of her skin brought, as it always had, always would, the near-subliminal memory of leaves silhouetted black on black, of ripe, scattered pears and a garden, its rose-bordered limits lost in night, enclosing us in the dark, billowing folds of madness loosed by the meeting of our mouths.

Slim fingers brushed against my hair, my face, her touch reaching into my mind, caressing away all thoughts of Llantathan. Names and dates faded from consciousness and my senses knew nothing but Marina. I turned in her embrace, aching, wanting this to be the only reality, this time the only time.

And time floated. Breezes stirred the heavy air drifting the scents of the garden around us. Her body, lily pale, ghost pale, enfolded me, drew me to its illusive passivity, and separate existence ceased.

* * *

On Monday morning, before I started work, I called in on John to ask if I could borrow the earlier burial registers. He nodded, weariness evident in his eyes. 'Now?'

'After work, please. I've been through the copies of the ones we found and it's the same so I need to carry on and see if I can discover when it started. Marina thinks it may have been going on for centuries. Pagan remnants.'

He thought about that. 'Do you agree with her?'

I shook my head. 'I can see why she got the idea but... I don't know. Maybe if I find a start date...' I glanced at the kitchen clock. Time to go. 'Look, John, I'll work on it and keep you in touch. Please try not to worry. You know we'll do all we can.'

He smiled. 'I know. And I'm more grateful than I can say. But I do wonder what you – we – *can* do.'

'We'll know better how to deal with it when we find out what it is,' I replied.

'Do you believe that?'

'I'm not believing anything yet,' I told him firmly. 'But if there is something nasty going on, we will stop it.'

On that note of determined – lying – confidence I removed myself to the church and did what I was paid to do, and at lunchtime I sat outside to eat my sandwiches, and chatted to Adam Pembury.

So far, I'd had little to do with Adam. He wasn't hostile now but still moody and usually taciturn. When he did talk, however, he was intelligent and entertaining. Adam, not at all didactic, taught me a lot over those weeks and months. But his sunnier moods were unpredictable and I, knowing that he hadn't wanted me for the job, remained cautious.

That day he was talkative because, I thought, he wanted information and didn't like to approach John. So I sat with him on the shady side of the church, eating my sandwiches and trying to answer his questions without saying a thing. Questions about what had happened to Brian Bennett; about the strain John was under; about Matthew Howells' invisible command of Llantathan and, finally, about Llantathan itself. Which, Adam admitted, he found weird.

I parried everything with obvious non-answers and his dissatisfaction was patent, goading him into telling instead of asking. 'I came back here last Monday night,' he began. 'I wanted to see... Oh hell!' As he spoke the church clock chimed the half hour and he rose to call everyone back to work. Before I disappeared into the cool of the tower he turned, his expression indecisive, wondering.

I said, 'Adam...' but he cut me off before I could go on. As if he knew I couldn't think of a thing I could reasonably say. 'I'll see you later, Stephanie,' he murmured.

On my knees, transcribing worn ledger stone inscriptions, I considered Adam's questions. It was easy enough to work out that he knew something. And that he was well aware that I knew things too. Very much did I want to know what Adam had done in Llantathan last Monday: what he'd seen or heard. If Adam could be trusted, and I thought he could, he might be an asset.

Additional brain power would be useful; maybe physical strength too: I'd seen Anne-Marie's father, and Paul Williams. Big men, both, with enormous hands and thickset bodies. And Elwyn Pryce, older than Pritchard, and slower, yet on Tuesday I'd watched him support, single-handed, the massive Howells headstone and hold it tirelessly while the stonemason's men aligned the new supporting blocks at its base.

Adam wasn't in that league: his tall wiriness was in direct contrast to the broad solidity which characterised

Llantathan's male population. But he was light on his feet. He looked capable of speed and I knew that, as an archaeologist, he had to be fit. Which was something, as I said to Marina over dinner.

She was amused. 'You talk about him like someone hiring a horse.'

'It has to be considered,' I returned defensively. 'If these people really have killed one of their own, they're not going to think twice about seeing us off if we get in their way.'

'They don't think twice about seeing these kids off year after year either,' she said grimly. 'Yes, I take your point, Steph. Two women and a peace-loving clergyman make pretty feeble opposition. Even one more has to be an advantage. I vote for Adam provided John agrees. Shall I phone him, or will you?'

'You,' I said, pushing back my chair. 'I want to work on the registers.'

I was twenty years back into the 18th century records when Marina came into the study. 'That was quick,' I remarked. 'Wasn't he in?'

'Yes, he was.' She reached over for a cigarette and lit it. 'But he said no.'

'Why? Doesn't he think Adam's OK?'

She perched on the edge of the desk. 'It's not that. John reckons Adam's safe enough.'

Falling silent, she started fiddling with my lighter, flicking it on and off. So what's the problem?' I asked.

'He's having one of his fits of conscience: says it's bad enough that we're involved without dragging anyone else in.'

'Do you think we can talk him round?'

'We'll have to, Steph, because Adam's just dragged himself in, I think. He's in the sitting room.'

'You're kidding! I never saw him come up the drive.'

'He didn't. Came across the back garden.'

'How very odd.' I stood up.

'I wonder...' Marina mused. 'Well, go and talk to the nice man. I'll put the kettle on.'

The nice man was standing awkwardly by the fireplace in a dust-streaked teeshirt and jeans torn across one knee. Fragments of leaves clung to his not-quite-blond hair and his nose was scratched.

'A hawthorn hedge,' he explained.

'But, why? Look, sit down, Adam. No, you're not that mucky. Sit down and tell me.'

He sank onto the sofa with obvious relief. 'Because I didn't want anyone to see me here. They watch us you know.'

'Us?'

'The team. The rector. You and Dr. Graham.'

'They watch us?' I repeated and wondered whether I was hearing right or he was loopy. It must have shown on my face for he grinned and said, 'No, I'm not mad and I'm sorry if I scared you. But it's true and if you care to look outside, you'll see for yourself.'

So I looked, and after a moment I saw the man mostly concealed by the big rhododendron at the bend of the drive. As casually as I could I closed the window and moved the plants around on the ledge. And thought of Elwyn Pryce, and remembered that John always had a tendency to close his curtains.

I turned back. 'I think it's Gareth Lewis,' I said. 'His mother's the church organist.'

'Last Monday night it was that guy who's been painting the garden gates round the green.'

'Mal Bowen. Son of the people who run the market garden. And Pryce watches John. Who watches you?'

'Usually it's Pryce,' he said. 'He spends so much time around the church anyway, and we don't leave it during the day unless someone goes to the shop. But on Monday night it was that big red-haired sod who I think works in the pub. Until I shook him off.' He grinned at some memory. Speed versus bulk. I grinned too.

'Paul Williams,' I told him. 'His father's the landlord. Paul's a farmer, supposedly. Still, that's by the way. What did you do?'

'Dived through a hedge and ran like hell,' he said. 'He wasn't doing a very good job. It was just dark and the silly bugger stopped to light a cigarette. As soon as he struck the match I went for the hedge.'

I had to laugh and was glad that I could: there wasn't much else to laugh about.

Marina brought coffee then and for a moment I thought that Adam was going to clam up. Drink his coffee politely and go away without saying more. But Marina, handing him a mug, said, 'Don't worry about me, Adam. I know what Stephanie knows. Whatever you say to her can be said to me.'

He regarded her steadily for a few seconds before transferring his gaze to me. I nodded and he relaxed again, and drank his coffee in silence while I told Marina what had transpired so far.

'We should have realised,' she said finally. 'John can't stir without falling over Pryce. If they're so interested in him, they're bound to want to know about us. Well, we can deal with it. Thanks for telling us, Adam.'

'That's not all though, is it?' I said shrewdly.

He didn't answer immediately and I guessed that he still wasn't entirely sure of being taken seriously. Then: 'This place – Llantathan – isn't right. Something's going on but I can't figure it. Can you?'

'We're working on it,' I said. 'If you know anything at all, however crazy it seems, please tell us. It may fit with what we know and help us to make some sense of it all.'

'It makes no sense to me.' A leaf dropped onto the sofa cushion as he pushed his fingers through his hair. His face, hardened by tension, seemed thinner, narrower. I had never thought Adam soft or weak in any way and now he appeared stronger than I'd imagined. More than ever did I want him with us.

'Oh, what the hell...' He leaned forward, resting his forearms on his knees. 'Brian... the kid who died last week... I talked to him a couple of times when he came to look at the excavation. He wanted to dig. I'm not keen on volunteers but after all the fuss over the excavation it was a change to have someone taking an interest. So we sorted out that he'd come at the end of the month for a week before school started, and I said I'd drop a couple of archaeology books in at Powell's place. Basic stuff to give him an idea of site work.

'Right. So Monday night. You wouldn't expect much to be going on in a little village, but it's school holidays and there aren't even bored kids hanging round on the green. It's totally dead. And I'd picked things up from the rector. He's never *said* anything but you can tell he's bothered. So I thought I'd come back and see what it's like at night. Walk round for a bit then have a drink at the Cross Guns.

'It didn't go like that. The Williams guy latched on to me as soon as I'd parked the car, so I went for a wander round the ramparts and got rid of him as soon as I could.

When I'd stopped running, I was in a sort of plantation up at Llantathan Hall and I got stuck because people were coming and going round the house and the grounds. It looked like a party: people on the terrace with drinks, and I could hear music.'

'Did you see anyone you recognised?' Marina asked in the pause he made.

'Pryce. The bloke at the post office. One or two others I've seen around. No women.

'After a bit everyone went inside and I was just going to sneak away when I saw car headlights coming up the drive. Two people got out. One was a man I didn't recognise but I've seen the car in the village: that red E-type Jag.'

I nodded. 'Richard Reece. The local G.P.'

'Sounds like a gathering of the clan,' Marina put in. 'Who was the other man?'

'Boy,' Adam amended. 'It was Brian Bennett.'

Marina and I exchanged glances but neither of us spoke and Adam finished his story.

'I waited a goodish while then made a long detour, keeping off the roads. That's how I spotted... what did you call him? Bowen? I nearly ran into him after I cut through your back garden. He didn't see me though and I don't think anyone else did.

'It was well after closing time so I went home. It seemed odd to see Brian going into the Hall but what bothered me most then was the guy lurking round your garden. You needed to know about that, but I wouldn't have mentioned Brian if it hadn't been for what happened next day.'

He stopped, in a bit of a state now. I offered whisky and he accepted a glass gratefully. Marina too, and I poured one for myself.

How did I feel then? Imagine being a child and making a Plasticene model of a monster. In your child's world the monster lives and breathes and moves and snarls but although it has life in your mind, you know that your own hand moves it and your own voice speaks for it. What, then, if one day your model monster, of its own volition, begins to move its hands and then its feet, growing and coming to a life of its own over which you have no control? I was beginning to feel something like that now. When Adam spoke again, I had no idea what he was going to say. Yet when he said it, it seemed as if I'd known all along.

'Tuesday?' Marina prompted gently.

'Yes. Tuesday. Teabreak. I had those books for Brian so I went over to Powell's, cutting down the footpath between the pig farm and the back of the High Street. I don't think anyone saw me.

'Powell's unit was shut: looked as if it hadn't been open at all that day. I started back and I was just passing that little thicket behind the pub when I heard an engine so I stopped and a van pulled up at the side of Powell's place.

'I nearly went back then. I don't know why I didn't. Instead I edged behind a tree and watched. I think the driver was Powell but there was another man with him. Don't know who. They unloaded some old-fashioned car bumpers and radiator grilles, and stacked them by the workshop door. I thought that was it and I was just wondering whether to go and ask about Brian when they lifted something else out of the back of the van.'

He stopped and finished his whisky. He looked from Marina to me and his eyes were very dark. 'Look, I saw what I saw. What they took into the workshop wasn't car parts. It was wrapped in a dust sheet and from a distance you might have thought they were carrying a roll of carpet. I wasn't at that much of a distance, and it wasn't a carpet.

'Then I heard clattering and machinery whine: the stripping tank hoist, I suppose. They took the other stuff inside, locked up and drove off, and I went back to work. 'I didn't realise what I must have seen until next day when John came to warn me about a funeral and ask us to suspend work during the burial. Then he said who it was who'd died, and how. He looked pretty sick and I didn't feel too good either. Worse when I started putting it all together. I had to tell someone. Not John, though: he was in a state.'

'So you talked to me,' I said.

'I would have anyway: about them watching you, but when you didn't answer all my questions so neatly, I was sure you knew something. So...'

Now it was all out he looked better. I could sense the relief. 'Does it fit with anything you know?' he asked.

Marina bit her lip. 'It adds to what we know. It certainly contradicts nothing. And I think it clarifies one point. May I ask a question?'

'Sure.'

'If it was Brian being carried into the workshop, would you say he was still alive?'

Adam thought, picturing the scene. 'You mean how did the roll of dust sheet look? Not...well... floppy. But not rigid. Lumpy and uneven. That's how I know it wasn't carpet. I can't be sure. Dead, I'd say, but I couldn't swear to it. At least not conscious, thank God.'

'So it may have been the disposal of a corpse rather than the actual killing, Marina reflected. 'Acid would destroy evidence of the real cause of death. Just as you can cover a multitude of sins with a chain saw.'

She filled our glasses again and, concisely, told Adam everything we knew. 'We have ideas, Adam, but only ideas. At the moment Steph's going through the parish registers trying to find out when these deaths began.'

'I'm back to 1774,' I put in. 'Whatever it is, it goes back a long time.'

Then Marina advanced her Celtic ritual idea and I wasn't surprised when Adam shook his head. He didn't like it either. 'Leave it with me,' he said.' 'I'll see what I can come up with.'

'And I'll hit the records again,' I said. 'Then we might be further forward.'

'And I, I suppose, will tackle a more immediate problem,' Marina said wryly. 'John. He's not going to like any of this.'

Nor did he, but being a reasonable man he accepted Adam's involvement with, perhaps, more relief than he cared to admit. Anyway, he had no choice: Adam had opted in of his own accord and though he made no statements of intention, it was clear that he wasn't going to opt out again.

The rest of it was another matter. Unable to soften it, Marina told John the bald facts and did her best to ease his distress. She came home pretty distressed herself, collapsing into her chair. Adam had gone back to Newport and it was very late. 'I can only be glad that John has his faith,' she said. It never occurred to us that that faith might be under growing pressure. 'Come on. Let's go to bed. Sufficient unto the day, as John would say.'

'Mmm. But one thing more. I've found the first burial.

She sat up. 'You're sure? Not just a break?'

'No. 'I've checked. It's 1756. 12th of August. Josiah Abelson.'

She stared. 'Josiah Abelson?' she echoed. 'A Jew?'

'Well, it does sound like a Jewish surname.'

'Yes,' she said softly. 'Yes, it does, doesn't it?'

Bewilderment and fear warred in her expression. I caught her to me and she buried her drained face in my shoulder.

And that's when the nightmares began.

At the inquest Powell claimed that Brian had been working alone that day, manning the office. He wasn't supposed to do chrome stripping unsupervised. No-one brought evidence to refute Powell's statement and a verdict of misadventure was returned. Adam could have cast doubts on it but he had no proof of what had been in the dust sheet and in any case, as Marina said, Powell would have denied everything.

VII

We'd arranged to meet with Adam and John at the rectory on Friday evening. To that end I put in hours on the records searching for sequences which might confirm Marina's pagan idea. I didn't find any. There was no trace of an annual peak in spring baptisms so the idea that Llantathan was keeping Beltane looked shaky. 'Unless they were killing the babies,' Marina suggested.

'I don't think so,' I said, 'because Beltane's about fertility, and there are no abnormally high levels of infant mortality.' And to be honest, I didn't expect to find any, even if there was any validity in Marina's theory. There had always been ways of getting rid of unwanted pregnancies. Risky ways though, so I looked at female deaths just in case, but no pattern showed.

Another did, but it took me some time to spot the curious groups occurring every forty to fifty years. Because, at first, I'd been chasing teenage male deaths in August, I hadn't looked at other months, but once I started considering whole years, I began to notice oddities, and the second pattern, linked to the Howells name, emerged.

Since I hadn't been bothering much about names, I must have passed over a score or more of the Howells family without anything registering. But now I noticed that when James Howells was buried in May, 1874, his funeral was preceded by a flurry of interments during the previous week: three males and three females, all under 16. For Llantathan six burials in one week was unusual. Not inexplicable when diseases like scarlet fever, typhus, diphtheria and cholera were rife, but that small concentration didn't suggest even a minor epidemic, so I went back to the 1750s, looking year by year for something similar. I found the same grouping of burials associated with Matthew Howells in 1782, with Samuel in 1832, James in 1874, George in 1921, and another James in 1966: intervals of 52, 42, 47 and 45 years. Whenever I found the burial of an adult male Howells, I also found that six children had preceded him to the grave.

* * *

On Friday Marina and I joined John for a meal after work. Poor John! From any standpoint the situation was dreadful but from his, infinitely more so, and he was out of his depth. Nothing, he said, had prepared him for anything like this. Plenty of social problems, yes, and he'd had to deal with the occasional outbreak of supernatural dabbling: silly people terrifying themselves with Ouija boards; church and churchyard vandalism with satanic overtones; bored kids playing with witchcraft.

'Usually it just fizzles out,' he told us. 'Very occasionally you get a highly suggestive person who becomes too frightened or guilty and needs help.'

He pushed his plate away and leaned back. 'Sooner or later every clergyman encounters tragic death: suicide,

accident, even murder. All the ills of society. But this...
this is something else. This is wilful evil.' John was angry
now and I was glad. It seemed far healthier than the
miserable depression of the previous week. As long as
that anger could be channelled in the right direction. Just
now he was turning some of it on himself, for his imagined
inadequacies, and on his Church for diminishing itself to
the level of the social services.

Marina interrupted gently. 'John, you seem to be
linking Llantathan with the supernatural. Do you believe
that what happens here has a supernatural basis?'

He regarded her steadily for long moments. 'I do,' he
said firmly. 'All evil has a supernatural basis but, in this
case, I believe that the evil has been generated, and is being
perpetrated, deliberately.

'Listen. Evil prompts people to the commission of
evil acts, taking advantage of human frailty. We want
to be good, always, but we can't be. That's human and
understandable, but sometimes people deliberately
engage with evil for their own ends. Unlike most of us
they recognise the power behind the manifestations and
court that power to harness it for the satisfaction of their
desires.'

'Deals with the devil?' Marina suggested.

'Yes,' John agreed. 'Exactly that.'

'What do you think?' I asked as Marina and I washed
up.

'Well you could say that John's view is predictable
given what he is.' She stacked another plate in the drainer.
'Not having any fixed faith myself I find it difficult to
reduce this to a formula. I'd like to be able to say that
these killings are the work of a madman. It's harder to say
that they're the work of a village which has been mad for

over two hundred years. These murders are systematic. Can madness ever be that precise? No, I don't think it's large-scale, long-term insanity. It's ritualised which means that the perpetrators believe their rituals gain or prevent something. Since they keep doing it, presumably they get the result they want.'

'You're still thinking along pagan religious lines?'

'Maybe. The fact that this only started in 1756 doesn't preclude the possibility that pagan beliefs had declined and this was a revival.'

'So religious motives, therefore supernatural,' I said.

'Not necessarily. Come on, Steph, dry something. I'm running out of space. No, religion needn't involve the supernatural at all.'

'I should have thought it would have to.' I picked up the teapot. 'And John certainly believes it must.'

She sighed. 'Look, I've decided that I'm going to be a... a teapot worshipper. She dried her hands, took the teapot from me and set it, big, brown and squat, on the table. 'Right. That is my god. I am its high priestess. I worship it and bow down before it. I perform rituals with dried leaves and boiling water in its honour. I devote my whole life to its service. On forms I fill in my religion as teapotianity. It is my religion: I follow it as faithfully as John follows his. But it isn't supernatural. I invented it. It's a product of my own mind.'

I laughed. 'Actually, Bertrand Russell invented it.'

'No. That was the Celestial Teapot, orbiting like a planet. It was about the burden of proof. Stop distracting me.'

'OK. Sorry. But wouldn't you, at the end of a lifetime of devotion, expect to be united with the teapot in some other dimension? Wouldn't you, after a while, evolve the idea that the teapot you see before you is merely the representation of the true teapot somewhere else? That would be to bring in the supernatural.'

'No. Because it's still my own invention. There is no true teapot outside my imagination.'

'How can you be sure?' I persisted. 'What if you'd received a divine revelation?'

'I'd probably think that I had,' she said. 'But it would still only be me because the god Teapot doesn't exist.'

'By your argument then, every religion is suspect. They're all products of the imagination. Therefore there is no God and no supernatural. Do you believe that? You can't, on the basis of what you said about believing in fairies and whatnot.'

She leaned against the fridge and, gloomily, surveyed the teapot. 'I don't know,' she said. 'Can anyone ever know? You can start from the teapot and push the argument any way you want. You could even argue that belief in something causes it to exist. Or the opposite. Every time a child says he doesn't believe in fairies, one drops dead. At the very least you could say that once you've imagined something, you've called it into existence, even if that existence is only in your mind. I simply don't know. I wish I did. But as far as Llantathan goes, does it matter?' She picked up the teapot and restored it to its accustomed place on the shelf. 'Beyond the fact that it might help us to discover what, if any, religious belief is governing events, does that belief have any bearing on us?'

'It might,' I told her. 'It depends on whether the force behind it is human or not. Human activity can be countered but what if it is supernatural? Really supernatural? What do we do then?'

Adam's arrival put an end to our private speculations. He came with a sheaf of jottings about every form of pre-

Christian belief known in Britain, plus those neo-pagan cults which had sprung up in the wake of the women's movement. Nothing matched our data.

'Even if this was a distorted version, I think you'd be able to see the original,' he said. 'It's possible but unlikely that they've got hold of something exotic: South American or Afro-Caribbean. Or they've invented something.'

'I'd have thought it would be very difficult to introduce a religion – old, new, exotic or invented,' I mused. 'Especially in the 18th century.'

'Oh come on!' Marina exclaimed. 'That was the great age of Methodism. You can't say that didn't catch on.'

'It wasn't a new religion,' I pointed out. 'It was Anglicanism redefined. And you can probably say that all the modern cults and sects are just Protestant variants offering different flavours, like breakfast cereals. Look at Frosties. Cornflakes with a bit of sugar. Make one small change and you've got a whole new product. Even some of the eastern imports attempt a blend with Christianity. Everything which isn't Christian-based has been imported or revived, and springs from a foundation either in the history of other cultures or in our own. And not one has made any significant impact. Not even the great religions like Buddhism and Islam. I think that given human nature you have to be offering something incredibly attractive to convert people. Or you have to make them too afraid to refuse. Preferably both. You'd have to play on need, greed and fear to impose it. Especially if you want your followers to do difficult things. Nasty things. People just don't like demanding religions. Isn't that so, John?'

He agreed ruefully. 'For the average person, and that means most of us, I'm afraid it is. There are exceptions where faith is very strong, but in general you're right, as

I well know, but there is one religion which takes root anywhere at any time and governs by greed and fear,' he said. 'It enacts evil rituals and hides behind the ordinary, and it's well documented.'

We looked expectantly at him. 'Satanism,' he said heavily. 'Not the games people play, but the real thing. It reverses all we accept as true. For the Satanist, that which we believe to be evil is, in fact, good. It's a completely different way of looking at things which I, at least, cannot comprehend.'

I frowned. 'It's a fairly recent phenomenon, surely? Aleister Crowley and... Anton LaVey?'

'Some of it, yes,' John agreed. 'But don't forget the Hellfire Clubs. There may have been more to them than drunken blasphemy. And the one at West Wycombe was in its heyday when Matthew Howells arrived in Llantathan.'

I still wasn't convinced, but I left it alone as the discussion turned to the spies and what, if anything could be done. 'Keep your doors locked from now on,' Adam said to us, 'Do you have spare keys for eachother's houses? Yes? Good...' I sat, half listening to the rest of the suggestions, and looking at the names and dates abstracted from the registers. That list, that long list of murdered boys... English surnames mostly. A few Scottish and Irish. The first one – the only one – apparently Jewish. Nothing obviously Welsh. All, I supposed, the offspring of the Howells family's incoming tenant farmers.

Not so with the deaths preceding the Howells burials. Every village surname was represented there. Davies, Reece, Bowen, Williams, Lewis and Pritchard in 1782. For 1832 I read Pryce, Evans, Jones, Powell, Griffiths, Tudor. In 1874 and 1966 the first group of names repeated itself and in 1921 the second. Their own children. A high price.

What, I wondered, could they imagine to be worth that? Did the Howells family pay likewise? It must. Nothing was for free.

* * *

I remember that autumn as a busy, happy time. Marina was teaching; the wall paintings had been temporarily conserved, and the excavation proper began. With Brian Bennett's funeral behind him and so much going on in and around the church and the rectory John was much more cheerful. Optimistic even, and when our postponed housewarming party sparked off more social interaction between ourselves and the archaeologists, he decorated the little terrace room and brought some of his furniture out of store so that he, too, could host supper parties.

We were still watched and there was no change in the atmosphere but, involved in our own little community, we could ignore it. It may have been that, coupled with a visit, in November, to the Public Records Office at Kew which caused me to wonder whether we'd all overreacted. That wondering caused the first serious row with Marina. It was very serious indeed and though we got past it, I know that things were never quite the same again.

Three nights without Marina in a hotel on the Cromwell Road where no-one spoke understandable English and the tea was like mud was not enjoyable, but working at the P.R.O. was absorbing and useful, and London... Crowds. Noise. Colour and movement. Smells of exotic food and diesel. People. Strangers, abrupt, sometimes, but normal. It was inevitable, I think, that I returned to Llantathan with the suspicion that we'd all let our imaginations get wildly out of hand.

It was mid-afternoon when I paid off the taxi at the rectory so that I could say hello to John, Adam and the team. Filling time, really, until Marina came home from college.

No, John said, nothing untoward had happened while I was away. Marina had been down for supper and Adam had a cold. That was all. How had my research gone? And so on. A nice chat over a cup of tea.

And that's how, more or less, the row with Marina started. But from recounting my experiences at the P.R.O. and describing the seedy, sinister atmosphere of the hotel, I went on to explain how London had made me feel about Llantathan.

'So what you're saying is that you can't, after all, believe that there's anything bad going on here?' Her voice was calm but I saw anger flash in her eyes.

'You yourself once said that an event can have many different interpretations.'

She didn't answer that. Instead she bounced up from the hearth rug and out of the room, returning to slam some papers down in front of me. The list of August burials. 'And you yourself said that this was realistically impossible. Do you really not believe those?'

'Yes, but what have we got to corroborate our interpretation of them?'

She danced with rage. 'What have we got, Stephanie? We've got Anne-Marie. We've got Adam's eye-witness account. He saw it, remember? He saw Brian Bennett going into Llantathan Hall and he saw his body being carried into the workshop. What more do you want?'

I pushed back my hair and lit a cigarette. This was not what I'd intended: Marina blazing at me; backing me into a corner. I said, 'As far as Anne-Marie is concerned, I'm not disputing anything John said about the forced marriage. We know she died, but we have no evidence whatsoever that she was murdered.'

Marina sat down, her face hard. 'Go on,' she invited, and I didn't much like her tone.

'Yes, Adam saw Brian going into Llantathan Hall on the night of the 8th of August and several if not all the senior male representatives of the village families were present. And, probably, Matthew Howells. I also accept that Adam saw something heavy being taken into the workshop on the day that Brian is supposed to have died there. But Adam did not see Brian's body; he saw something in a dust sheet. It's all circumstantial, Marina, and though it's very suggestive, it is capable of ordinary interpretation.'

'OK, Stephanie. I know that at university you had a reputation for critical sense. I once heard it said of you that you didn't merely examine the evidence: you subjected it to all the savagery of the Inquisition. I know that you're better than I am when it comes to quantifying data. But this isn't just another bit of historical research. This is feelings... fears...'

Some of the anger had gone out of her now. 'Everything you just said is true,' she went on. 'I know that. But it's only a part. We might be fantasising: winding each other up, but I'll stake my life on it that we're not.' She picked up the list of August burials again. 'One teenage male in the second or third week of every August since 1756. You can dispute Anne-Marie's cause of death. You can question what was in the dust sheet but you can't deny this!'

'Of course not. Marina love, just because I argued for the rational side, don't think I'm discounting anything else. I don't know. The odds have to be on a simple explanation but I do accept that there might be something very strange behind all this. It might be satanic but I do wonder if it's child abuse dressed up as Satanism and not supernatural at all. I'll do every damn thing I can to find out what is going on. But if it does turn out to be bad, I don't see what we can do to stop it.'

'Whatever it takes,' she replied.

'Yes, but what? Love, whatever is behind these deaths, it's been going on for over 200 years. Others before us must have made connections. If so, we have to assume either that they tried to stop it and failed, or they got out.'

'Probably, but I'm not going to get out. Nor am I going to fail.'

I walked to the window, to the fireplace, to the window again and back, wishing I could find the right words. Wishing I'd never said a word in the first place. Knowing that whatever I said now wouldn't make it better. But I said it anyway.

'Marina, I'm going to go on being critical with the evidence. I cannot, with integrity, do otherwise. But I can't deny the feelings either. I hate it all. I don't want to believe it and I admit that I'm trying my damnedest not to. I hope that there is a very ordinary explanation though I can't imagine what it could be. Gut reaction tells me that there isn't an ordinary explanation, but if there isn't, and Howells really is carrying out ritual murders, then I don't see what we can do to stop it. I just don't think it's possible.'

Her eyes had gone very cold again. 'So what do you want to do? If you want out, Stephanie, then bloody well say so and go. But I won't.'

'I'm not going anywhere,' I replied. 'Not to the front door without you. If you stay, I stay. I just wish we didn't have to. Oh God, Marina, I'm scared. I've been trying not to be, trying to... yes, trying to rationalise. And after London I know that if I went away from here I could do it.'

'You think I'm not scared? Eyes closed, arms crossed over her waist, her hands gripped her elbows. 'But I'm more scared of letting it go on. No. It's more than that. I *can't* let it go on. I'm not responsible for whatever happened here before we came, before we knew. But now that I do know, I have responsibility. If I say, so what? and let it continue, I'm condoning it. I become an accessory. As bad as Howells. I wouldn't stand by and watch a child drown.' She opened her eyes and looked at me. 'Would you?'

'No, of course not.'

'Well, this is no different.'

'But what if, in the process of saving the child, you drown too?'

'Then I drown.'

VIII

By Christmas our disagreements were... dealt with. I still handled the data as critically as ever but I'd slipped back into speaking and acting as if I, too, believed as firmly as Marina. In Llantathan it was difficult to do otherwise, and Christmas did nothing to encourage a rational view. What the village did I've no idea. Nothing, as far as we could see. No tinselled trees sparkled in cottage windows. No cotton wool 'snow' was stuck to the post office windows. No excited kids showed off new toys on Christmas morning. Not so much as a new football.

We put up a tree and decorations and invited my mother who, refusing to come to 'the back of beyond', went to Bournemouth instead. We sent cards, gave presents, threw a party, and it was good. On New Year's Eve we felt we could all look forward with optimism. 'This time next year it will be different,' John said, his eyes bright. If any of us had reservations we kept them to ourselves. But John was right. It was different.

My real worry during those months was Marina. The nightmares of the previous August had gone on, but intermittently. After Christmas they were more frequent and she began to look tired and frail. Yet steadfastly she refused to tell me what she saw in those dreams. I think, after the row, she didn't quite trust me to believe her. 'They'll go, Steph,' she promised. 'They'll stop soon. I know they will.'

Preoccupied with other concerns, I let myself believe her. My mother's letter, enclosed with a cheque in a birthday card came as an unsettling surprise: she wasn't much of a letter writer, and it was weeks to my birthday. I read the letter and thought it uncertain, evasive, as if she wanted to tell me something and couldn't quite bring herself to do it. Not like her at all. The only thing I could be sure of was that something was up and that I needed to go and see her.

'Yes, of course you must,' Marina agreed, and at lunchtime I went in search of Alan Foster who, as I expected, told me to settle it with Adam.

I left a note on Adam's desk and went back to my office to grapple with *The Norman Settlement of Southern Monmouthshire* or whatever we decided to call it in the end. No writing yet, just pulling information together from the various sources, and I was trying to merge three lists when Adam came in with coffee. 'How's it going?' he asked.

I sat back, took one of the mugs and nodded. 'OK. How did the fieldwalking round Carrow go?'

He made a face. 'Leaving aside some of the worst students I've dealt with yet... one belt buckle, snake variety,

20th century and a lot of pot, medieval. Talking of things medieval, no problem about time off to go and see your mother, but I wondered if I could help. You know I'm in York next week for that medieval archaeology conference? I'm driving up on Wednesday morning so I'd be happy to take you with me and you could go on to Scarborough from there. Anyway, think about it and let me know.'

'It would save a lot of hassle with trains from down here,' I told Marina on the way home. 'I'm only planning to stay a couple of nights so I'll come back with Adam on the Friday evening.'

'Take the car,' she said. 'I can manage without it for a couple of days. Longer, if necessary.'

'Seems daft when Adam's going north anyway. No. I'll go with him.'

* * *

Travelling with Adam was entertaining, relaxing: chatting about common interests, current affairs; nothing demanding and nothing at all about Llantathan. We broke the journey at Trowell services and it seemed no time then before we were on the Tadcaster road.

In York we ran into slower traffic on Blossom Street but Adam had made good time in spite of fog and snow flurries, and it was just on half past two when he pulled into the station forecourt. Lifting my little suitcase from the boot he said that he would meet me in the café there on Friday. 'About four, but don't worry if I'm a bit late.'

I thanked him, said that I'd enjoyed the journey, and meant it. 'I hope things are OK with your mother,' he said, then he gave me a brief hug and was gone.

I envied Adam his conference. I wished I could have gone too, or even just stayed in York, a place I'd always loved. I looked across the busy road to the pale stone city wall and the grassy rampart which, in a few weeks, would be thick with daffodils. And, around me, I heard the voice of Yorkshire. Home. I'd missed it.

But, needs must. I had a train to catch. I bought a period return to Scarborough, discovered that the next train left in 10 minutes, and crossed the bridge to platform 5. I would, I thought with resignation, arrive in good time for tea.

* * *

'It'll be summat and nowt, Stephanie,' Mum said after tea. I'd done the washing up while she explained that she'd been having dizzy spells. 'You know me, love: can't be doing with doctors and hospitals, but I can't be doing with the room going round either.'

I couldn't get her to tell me how long this had been going on but, since she'd shown no signs of falling over at my M.A. ceremony, I assumed that whatever it was, it was recent. Knowing that for all her matter-of-factness she would be worried, I took my lead from her, and didn't probe, didn't show much concern. I said, 'You haven't become a secret gin drinker have you, Mum? That would do it.'

She laughed, made a face. 'Gin? Common stuff. I can't think why you like it, Stephanie. No, love. That's not it. I don't know what it is but like I say, it'll be summat and nowt. We'll see what the hospital says next week. I just thought I'd better let you know.'

And that was that. She said no more and I was left to draw my own conclusions, if any. But, thereafter, disguised as chat, as tidying, as 'clearing out all this junk', I could see that Mum was preparing for the possibility of bad news.

If she had any dizzy spells while I was there, I wasn't aware of them. She seemed much as she'd always been: wanting to know that my job was going well; wanting to know how I was getting on sharing a house with my friend – 'What's her name? Marie?' – wanting to know what 'this Adam' was like.

With more patience than I usually possessed I steered her questions away from Marina and showed her a photo of the archaeology team, pointing Adam out and letting her think what she would.

On Thursday, sorting through some boxes of photographs, she came across a big envelope containing my wedding pictures. 'I meant to tell you, Stephanie,' she said, 'Howard got married last December. It was in the Evening Post...' She went off into gossip and reminiscences about Eldersfield and Eldersfield families and that was OK with me. As long as I didn't have to discuss my ex or the man Mum had probably marked down as my next.

I'd known far worse visits to my mother. This one drifted along quite genially. I did some shopping for her, agreed to take a few things back with me: things she wanted me to have, and left on Friday afternoon in a better frame of mind than I'd expected to be. If she had some sort of health problem maybe it was, as she said, summat and nowt.

'Summat and nowt' could not be said to describe the 'few' things she'd insisted I took with me. When Adam found me in the station café with my little suitcase augmented by three large carrier bags and an old-fashioned and very awkward dress box, he said, laconically, 'Shopping, Steph?'

I shook my head and explained. 'I don't know what the half of it is, but the box contains, apparently, my great-great-grandmother's wedding dress.'

'Did you find out what's wrong with your mother?'

'To be honest, Adam, I haven't a clue. She's got some sort of health issue. She *says* she has dizzy spells but I'm not sure I believe her, and she certainly didn't have any when I was there. She's behaving as though it's nothing except...' I gestured at my additional baggage... 'She's sorting things out; putting things in order. I don't know. She's got a hospital appointment on Tuesday. No, she doesn't want me there. Frankly, I wouldn't put it past her to tell me there's nothing wrong when there is.'

'Do you think there is?' Adam asked gently. And when, not looking at him, I nodded, he put his hand over mine briefly. 'If you need time off... if I can help...'

Underlying worry surfaced suddenly, and I was on the edge of tears. He saw, and said, 'I think you need something a bit stronger than British Rail coffee, Stephanie. Come on. Let's go.'

Adam's car was parked at Marygate so we lugged my stuff over there, locked it in the boot and walked back through Bootham Bar, cutting down Grape Lane and Finkle Street, to the Roman Bath pub. Adam sat me in a corner, bought me a double whisky, gave me a cigarette and made a suggestion.

He could see, he said that I was far more worried than I wanted to show. 'Your mother, of course, but Llantathan as well. If you want to go back tonight, we will, but it might be better to go tomorrow, or even Sunday. Downtime, Stephanie. I think you need it.'

Downtime. Away from Llantathan. Away from the worries, the doubts, the fear. Oh yes... But at home there was Marina. As if he read my mind he said, 'Never mind what you think you ought to do. What would you *like* to do? Would you like to stay here, be a tourist for a day or so; give your mind a holiday?'

I nodded. 'Adam, I'm so tired...'

That decided it. 'I noticed a little B & B place off Bootham with a vacancies sign,' he said. 'Didn't look too expensive. We could get a couple of rooms, then find a phone box so you can let Marina know.'

There was no reply from home so I called John. 'Yes, she's here,' he said. 'Cooking. Shall I...?'

'No, don't distract her, John. Just tell her that I won't be back until Sunday, and give her my love.'

'Sunday?' I heard questions in John's voice.

'Sunday,' I repeated. 'Tell Marina I'll explain then.'

At this point Adam asked to speak to John. I handed the phone to him and stepped out of the box, wondering what Marina would say when I got home.

What did Adam and I do, that cold Friday evening in York? I know we had dinner somewhere off Castle Street. Adam told me about the conference: 'I think you would have enjoyed it, and said that his paper had been well received.

'Next year, we could both go. I dare say Hafren would be willing to cover the fees.'

Oh yes! I thought. How I would love to go to conferences! Tackle history and ransack documentary sources for academic reasons, not this insane Llantathan thing.

My face must have mirrored my thoughts for Adam said, 'It would be good for you to research seriously for... normal... purposes. What you do for work is fine, but a lot of it doesn't need much depth. If you had something you could really get your teeth into, you could give a paper.'

I blinked. Wondered if I, or he, had had too much to drink. Give a paper at an international medieval archaeology conference? 'I'm not an archaeologist,' I objected.

'Nor were about a third of the delegates this year,' he riposted. 'Think about it, Stephanie. For now, what shall we do tomorrow?'

'It's all rather busman's holiday, isn't it?' I remarked. 'Archaeology and history. I used to come here and mooch, mostly. Visit whatever sites were being excavated. Coppergate, Bedern, the Lendal interval tower. Did you ever see the Coppergate dig, Adam?'

He said that he had, adding that the new Viking Centre would be opening in a couple of months. 'We might get to see it next year if we're here for the conference. For tomorrow, mooching's a good idea,' he agreed. 'See where we get.'

On Saturday afternoon, in no hurry, we walked the walls, descending here and there to warm up with coffee, or for a closer look at some building which attracted our attention. It was, probably, the easiest, most relaxing day I'd known since I became snarled up with Llantathan. Marina and I had had times away the previous autumn but, good though they were, I don't think she and I ever really escaped as I did then. Thinking of her, alone at Vine Villa, I should have felt guilty, and I did not.

We reached the viewing point at the northern angle and stopped to look across to the Minster. It was too cold to tempt many people onto the walls and here we were alone. Adam lit two cigarettes, passed one to me, and we smoked in companionable silence until snow – first the odd flake, then a flurry – emphasised the cold and I knew that the wall walk would have to be closed.

That evening we found a little Italian place to eat. Somewhere between the pasta and the pudding, and into a third glass of Frascati, I smiled at Adam and thanked him for suggesting this 'holiday'.

'You needed it,' he said.

'And you?'

'Not as much. I don't live so close to it all, as you do. I wonder how you stand it.'

'I'm used to it now,' I replied. 'And there's John, and when you and the team were there most of the time it was OK. It's not the place, more all this digging into the records, trying to piece together what's going on and what on earth we can do about it. I think, sometimes, that we're all slightly mad.'

'No... not that... But you might be better not living in Llantathan. I don't suppose...'

I shook my head. 'We *like* Vine Villa, Adam, and how could we move and leave John? Even if we could, Marina wouldn't go and if she stays, so do I. It's just that here everything's normal. Sane. It was the same when I went to London last year. Away from Llantathan I can believe that we've got it wrong; that whatever's going on and, yes, something is, it's not what we think. Do you understand?'

He did. 'But I'm pretty sure it is what we think, and for the time being we're stuck with it, but it won't be forever, Stephanie. Nothing ever is.'

Then, something in his expression, his eyes, held me. I don't want to go back, I thought, and wondered at myself. When had I ever not wanted to be with Marina? What on earth was I doing here, in York, playing tourist, having dinner with Adam Pembury? I don't want to go back, I thought. And I went on thinking it: through coffee; on the way to the guest house past the floodlit Minster and the bright shop windows of Petergate; past Exhibition Square where, in summer, fountains criss-crossed their jets of water below the weathered statue of William Etty; along Bootham, past the house where W. H. Auden was born.

'No rush in the morning, Stephanie,' Adam said as we neared the B & B. We've got all day and we can go down by a different route if you like.'

At the door of my room he said goodnight, told me to sleep well and then he kissed my cheek. I ought to have wondered about that, I suppose, but it seemed so natural.

We were off by 10 next morning. Adam thought we would head for Stafford then pick up the A49 south of Shrewsbury. Slower, but more scenic, he said, and we could maybe stop in Ludlow.

We didn't. It started to snow soon after Stafford: sleety snow that didn't settle, and it went on all the way back, making our arrival in Llantathan even more depressing than it would have been. Vine Villa was in darkness and I supposed that Marina had decamped to the rectory. Adam helped me get my luggage inside and stayed long enough to have coffee and cake before he went home to Newport.

'I'll be inside tomorrow, Steph,' he said, 'writing up the fieldwalking report. There's the team meeting with Alan on Wednesday to decide how we're going to go about organising more work in Llantathan. You'll be needed for that. Friday, weather permitting, we're over at Mellyn setting up for a bit of a look at the back of Mellyn House. Might be something for you there if it turns out to be medieval but we'll see. Well, I'd better get back...'

He stood up with obvious reluctance and I went with him to the door. 'It was a good weekend,' I said. 'Thank you.'

'My pleasure. Stephanie, when things get too much, remember what I said. We're stuck with all this crap here for now, but it isn't forever.'

I nodded, gave him a hug and, when I closed the door, felt the warmth of knowing that, in Adam, I had more than a colleague, more than a co-conspirator. Now I had a friend.

IX

Marina came back around 10. She told me that she'd had a good time with John and had been with him to Tintern, but she was tired now. She seemed a bit edgy, a bit distracted, and her face had a shuttered look that I didn't like.

Next day we drove in to college as usual, she to a full day of lectures and tutorials, I to my little office to engage with the Normans in Monmouth. I didn't see her at lunchtime, nor did I see Adam until mid-afternoon when he brought me tea and a Kit-Kat. By that time I'd realised that Marina hadn't said a word about my time away, not even an enquiry about my mother. Nor did she on the way home. The storm broke over dinner.

* * *

On Wednesday, after the team meeting, Adam walked with me back to my office, asking about my mother on the way.

'Tests, tests and more tests, she says,' I told him.

'If you need to go back to Scarborough...'

'I may, but it's obvious that she doesn't want me there just now. Perhaps when she has some definite results. Assuming she tells me.'

As I unlocked my office door he said, 'Work from the rectory tomorrow, Steph. I'll be over at 11 to see John about the next phase of work and you need to be there, then we could all have lunch.'

As it happened, things didn't work out quite like that. By the time Adam arrived John had gone out to see a sick parishioner so, instead, we went for a walk on the ramparts.

'What's up with Marina?' he asked. 'She seemed a bit fraught when I saw her this morning.'

I pushed my hands deeper into my pockets. It was cold: misty, and more snow overnight had made a frozen crust along the top of the bank. 'We had one hell of a row on Monday evening,' I told him. 'My fault. I said that I'd been wondering if we ought to take the evidence we have – all those teenage deaths and the other pattern – to the police. She went through the roof. Said Llantathan would have been ready for that for years and if I was seriously thinking of doing it, I'd better understand that she would deny everything.'

'I can see her point,' he conceded. 'John tried to drop hints to that bishop of his, and the bishop didn't want to know. I rather suspect that we're on our own in this.'

As we rounded the south-eastern corner of the bank, near the motte, the church clock struck the hour. 'We'd better go' I said, 'and see if John's home yet.'

The footpath back to the church took us between the doctor's surgery and the first of the little industrial units. Powell's was open but a sign outside announced that the chrome stripping service was no longer available.

'Served its purpose,' Adam commented.

'Where were you when you saw...?'

He knew what I meant. 'About here.'

I looked back. Yes, Powell's unit was perfectly visible from the thicket. As we paused Powell himself, enveloped in a donkey jacket, appeared in the shop doorway and stood, arms folded.

'Bastard,' Adam said softly as we turned away. And to me, 'Don't worry, Stephanie love. It'll be all right.'

I looked up at him. Stephanie *love*?

We were nearly at the church when he said, 'Why don't we all get together and talk through what we think we can and can't do? Would that help, do you think?'

'It might,' I replied cautiously. 'The problem is that if I argue for the rational: and I must, Adam, whatever I *feel*, Marina gets angry.'

'I'll have a word with John after we've dealt with work matters.'

We ended up having a working lunch with John in the rectory kitchen. According to the diocesan surveyor the foundations of the nave's south wall needed additional attention and there was still a significant damp issue in that area. The surveyor thought that whatever was causing it had to be outside. Much of the churchyard on the south side would, therefore, have to be cleared.

Comparing diaries, we agreed a potential start date. Adam produced a provisional schedule of work and John provided a list of his commitments, offering accommodation for the team much as before. Then both went off to the church to discuss with the foreman how the overlap of work would be handled and I went up to the empty bedroom I used on my Llantathan work days: one with a view over the south side of the churchyard. Across the fields beyond the cottages and the village green, I could see the chimneys of Vine Villa. Could I also see Allington? Yes, just. I lit the portable gas heater John had provided and settled down to write about the establishment of the Augustinians at Llantathan in 1120. Absorbed, I hardly noticed the time until John brought me a mid-afternoon coffee. 'Adam tells me that you and Marina have had differences,' he said.

I admitted it, and told him what I'd told Adam. 'She's right, you know, Stephanie,' he said.

'But John, even if she is, I must be allowed to express my thoughts without being attacked! She forced me onto the defensive before I'd had a chance to explain. That's unreasonable.'

'Yes, but she's very scared, Stephanie. And exhausted. These nightmares she has... Oh, I know, and I know that you're exhausted too, having to deal with them. It was good that you had a rest from it all, but it frightened Marina. She accepted that you had to see your mother but she found it very hard to understand why you stayed in York with Adam. No... no... *I* know why: Adam explained, and I agree with him. You needed that break. If it made you look at the situation here from the outside, that's natural, but it just added to her fears.'

'Adam thinks we should have a time together when we can all be absolutely honest about what we think... feel... Should we, John?'

He smiled. 'Not unless you want to be forced onto the defensive by all of us.'

'I wouldn't mind you, or Adam, but Marina made it... personal... tied it to our relationship. That was what hurt so much.'

'I see. Well, perhaps if I set up a little chat on the basis that personal issues are not admissible?'

'You can try. But John, isn't that a bit pointed? The only personal issues are Marina's and mine.'

His gaze was quizzical and after he went back downstairs, I wondered if it had anything to do with Adam.

Adam.

Now there was an enigma! If anyone had asked me to sum up Adam Pembury, I would have described him as self-contained, self-sufficient. Laconic. Moody. A man I hadn't liked on first acquaintance; a man who'd seemed not to like me. A man who had involved himself in the matter of Llantathan of his own volition and, I realised, without explanation. A man who, with rare understanding, had given me a much needed respite from my worries and tiredness; who had gone from scarcely veiled hostility to friendship. Last July I'd been Mrs. Hargreaves. This morning I was Stephanie love.

The 'little chat' was organised far faster than I anticipated. Adam came in just after five, as I was tidying up my papers, to tell me to stay put: John had phoned Marina and she would be here by six. 'We'll have something to eat and clear things up,' he said. 'At least that's the plan. It could turn sticky.'

'It's sticky already.'

'Maybe, but as well as giving all of us a chance to air our views, John's going to get Marina to talk about these nightmares of hers. You know she stayed here while we were away, and he had to deal with it twice.'

I hadn't known. I doubted that she would tell us anything, and said so.

'She may find herself in a corner about it,' Adam told me. 'John's line is going to be that if people have to cope with her terrible dreams the least she can do is say what they are.'

'It might work, but I've tried and got nowhere. I think there's something behind it that she doesn't want to talk about.'

He looked a question and I hesitated, wondering how to explain. At last I said, 'I think it goes right back to when we first came to visit John, the weekend before our interviews with Hafren. There was that condition that I couldn't be seen for the job unless I talked to John first.'

'I remember.'

As best I could, I told him about Marina's sudden concern that she looked Jewish. 'She didn't make a big thing of it, claimed it was just an odd thought. We'd been talking about religion on the way here and I wondered if that had sparked it. I think there must be some sort of connection because the nightmares started not long after I discovered that the first murder victim had a Jewish-sounding name. But what's in the nightmares I don't know, and she won't say.'

'Surely you of all people...'

'No. She won't talk about any of this. She's quite a reserved person and last July we weren't long into our relationship so maybe then she thought I wouldn't take her seriously. Not knowing what's behind this makes it hard for me to judge. And now I think she won't tell me anything because she doesn't trust me.'

He was startled. 'Why on earth wouldn't she? Just because you suggested a way forward that she disagrees with? Surely not?'

'It was a terrible row, Adam. And it wasn't the first.'

I told him what had happened following my London trip the previous November. 'After that I should have known better than to say a word,' I concluded bitterly.

'Maybe, but even if you're wrong you've a right to say what you think. It sounds like massive over-reaction, and not really like her.'

'It's not, normally. John said this afternoon that she's very scared. Well, yes, so am I when I let myself think about it.'

We heard Marina's car pull into the drive; heard John go outside, and the muffled sound of his voice and then hers, in the hall, cut off by the closing of the study door. I crossed to the window, turned, walked back. And again. 'I am not looking forward to this, Adam,' I said, aware, now, that I felt sick. 'If Marina loses her temper...'

'I suspect,' he replied, 'that John's got her in his study now to make sure she doesn't. But, if she does lose it, walk out and leave it to John and me.'

He hoisted himself away from the edge of the table and suggested drinks. And in an echo of our conversation earlier, he said, 'Don't worry, Stephanie love. It'll be all right.'

Stephanie love...

For God's sake, I thought, *don't* call me that in Marina's hearing. Neither he nor John knew what she'd flung at me during that dreadful argument. 'What the hell did you think you were doing, going to York with Adam, and then staying there with him?' she'd demanded.

I'd shouted back that he was a friend – no more. And then, 'He *may* be just a friend to you, Stephanie, but you're a damn sight more than that to him!'

Choked, suddenly, with incipient tears, I followed him downstairs. In the kitchen, where various cooking pots simmered in and on the Aga, Adam brought an opened bottle of Talisker from the pantry, poured a generous measure and handed it to me. 'Go on,' he ordered. 'You'll feel better.'

I sipped and, while Adam found cutlery and condiments and set the table, I sat and willed my nerves to steadiness, wondering how on earth things had come to this: that I should feel so scared that I didn't want to see Marina. Marina... all my world... So what had gone wrong? The tears caught up with me a minute or two later. I put my head on my arms and sobbed. And then...

'Stephanie...' Marina's voice, Marina's arms round me. 'Oh love, I'm so sorry!' Pushing my hair back, she dabbed my face with a tissue, gave me another and I blew my nose. She pulled me close, kissed me and said, disjointed, 'Oh Stephanie...love...' and kissed me again. Then, 'We'll talk later, yes?'

Opening the door to the hall, she called to John and Adam. I stood up, found wine glasses and brought the Sauvignon from the fridge, quietly consigning the remains of my Talisker to the sink.

John took charge of his cooking, Adam dealt with the wine, and we all sat down to eat. For now, at least, everything seemed OK. Later, things might be, as Adam had put it, sticky, because I didn't think that Marina would, without considerable pressure, be willing to tell us about her nightmares.

John handed dishes, topped up glasses and drew Marina into a conversation about a film version of Orwell's *1984* which, he'd heard, would star Richard Burton. Across the table Adam looked up from his plate, nodded slightly, and smiled. *Stephanie love*, I thought. Had Marina been right?

We took coffee through to the study where John produced brandy and Adam offered cigarettes. Then, with a good fire, drawn curtains and locked doors, I began the discussion, saying that if someone showed me a list of annual deaths over more than 200 years, I would consider it something to be investigated.

'And if you did investigate, what would you find?' John asked.

'Apparent accidents,' I replied. 'But I would think that there were too many to be coincidental.'

'So you would go and talk to Bert Tudor about Andrew Mason and the chain saw?' Marina asked. 'Robert Powell about how Brian Bennett came to fall into the chrome stripping tank? You'd ask Elwyn Pryce how Paul Amies managed to set himself alight with petrol and burn himself to a cinder?'

'Yes, and I imagine that I would get exactly what Tudor, Powell and Pryce said at the inquests.'

'And?'

'And, I suppose, that would be that,' I admitted. 'Because however suspicious it looked, I wouldn't be able to find a single person who would say that it was other than a string of unfortunate accidents. And someone would be sure to point out that, sadly, farm accidents are very common, and teenage boys ditched by their girlfriends do sometimes jump under trains or into reservoirs.' But what if it was suggested that, come next August, around the 8th, a watch was kept on Llantathan?'

'You know the answer to that, Steph,' Adam said. 'On such flimsy evidence no-one would deploy the manpower needed to watch Llantathan. Someone at police HQ would talk to Neil Griffiths. Neil Griffiths would laugh and say it was a load of bollocks: English archaeology nutters causing trouble. We would look stupid, or worse, and Howells and the village would be alerted to the fact that we know something's going on. At best, they'd take steps to force us out. At worst, curtains. If we're not dead in some convenient accident, we're hamstrung, and come next August another kid dies.

'You had to raise the possibility that it might be a way forward, but Marina's right. It won't work and it would just leave us all completely exposed. You see?'

Before I could reply, Marina said, 'I shouldn't have reacted as I did, and I'm sorry, Steph. But I stick to my belief that we can't go down that route. I don't know what's going on in Llantathan, let alone how to stop it, but I will never agree to any plan which involves the police or any other authority. Whatever the solution is, it lies with us.'

'You think we were all, somehow, brought here for this, don't you, Marina?' John prompted.

'I do. John. You left a nice, normal parish in north Wales to come here. Why? Because you felt called by God. And you stayed. Why? Because you believe that God doesn't make mistakes. Adam, you would have been working in Llantathan regardless, but you go home each evening. You didn't have to take a closer look. You didn't have to come to our house that evening and tell us what you know. You didn't have to involve yourself. Stephanie, you needed a job after university, but you knew that Llantathan was a problem. You didn't have to apply to Hafren, and when you heard what John had to say, you could have walked away. My post at Hafren has nothing to do with Llantathan and I didn't have to live here, but I'd met John. I too heard what he had to say and when we were offered Vine Villa, I couldn't refuse. I do believe we were all brought together for a purpose and I've no doubt that each of you could add to what I've just said. Each of you has your own reasons for being here. And so do I.'

She took a deep breath, picked up her glass, put it down again, asked for a cigarette and needed me to light it for her. 'I'm sorry to be so... so feeble. It isn't easy to talk about this. It's going to sound insane.'

John reached across and took her hand. 'More insane than what I told you about Anne-Marie?'

Her expression was rueful. 'Yes John,' she replied. 'Much more.'

'But does it make sense?' John asked.

'It didn't, but it does now.' She looked up at me. 'Stephanie, do you remember what happened on the High Street when we first arrived in Llantathan last year?'

A moment of blankness, and then I saw it clearly: the deserted street, hot and still and empty. 'I'd forgotten until now but, yes, I remember.'

She nodded. 'It was very quiet. No-one around. I'd just turned left by the post office and then I was surrounded by people.' She paused, looked at us, and went on. 'I saw them and they looked as real as you three now. I couldn't imagine how we came to be driving into a crowd but I knew we were going to hit someone. I slammed the brakes on, we skidded a bit and stopped, and all these people were looking at me. Not just at me sitting in the car, but at the me inside: my mind: what I am. My soul, if you like. Then the crowd parted. I started the car and drove through.'

She reached for her glass, and then another cigarette. 'I thought I must have been hallucinating and I was scared. Nothing like that had ever happened before. And if you're thinking of LSD flashbacks, forget it. That was never my scene. Well, I tried to dismiss it as stress but I wasn't stressed. I was happier than I'd ever been before. Still, had it just been a non-existent crowd I might put it down to delayed reaction. Only there were the voices.'

She looked at us; we looked at eachother and back at her.

'Voices?' John asked, uncertainty evident in his tone.

'Voices,' she insisted with more than a trace of defiance. 'Voices all around me. It only lasted a few seconds but it was terrifying.'

'What were these voices saying?' Adam wanted to know.

Marina leaned forward, sat up, pushed back her hair, agitated. 'I'm not sure. You know what it's like when football crowds sing? How it's never quite in unison? You get the overall shape of a word but the edges are blurred.

It could have been "who". It might have been "you". But I thought it was "Jew". I don't know. Whatever the word was, though, it had an interrogative inflexion. They were asking a question.'

None of us spoke. I don't suppose any of us knew what to say. We just waited for her to go on. A log in the grate settled, sparks flying and dying. I heard the wind gusting against the window; the scrape of Adam's lighter; the soft sounds of John refilling glasses.

Marina said, 'I thought I was losing my mind. There was I, a rational being, seeing people who weren't there who were speaking one indistinct word which, out of all the possibilities, I believed to be that one. I promise you that until then I'd never bothered about what I was because, in so many ways, I wasn't. I've never felt either chosen or persecuted. I may take my identity from my mother but my father was a Scottish Presbyterian. Crazy, isn't it? But, God, it scared me. It made no sense at all, then, so I decided that it had to be some weird mental freak: faulty connections in my brain paths.'

'But you knew, really,' I said. It wasn't a question.

'Yes. Underneath I knew it was something to do with Llantathan. As long as nothing else happened I could ignore it but of course things did happen. Then Steph found the start date of the deaths and the first one was Josiah Abelson. A Jewish surname, and that freaked me. Why? I don't know. It may have no significance but I feel that it does. And then the dreams started. It was the same thing: the crowd, the voices and the word I couldn't quite make out. And always it was a question which became more and more insistent. Then, quite suddenly, those dreams stopped.'

'Any idea why?' Adam asked

'Oh yes,' she told him, and her expression spoke of resignation and determination.

'I answered the question, you see. I said yes to them. I had to because I had no option. And once I'd agreed to what they wanted, those dreams stopped.'

She'd lost me. Perhaps John and Adam too. 'What did you agree to, Marina?' I asked. 'What did they want you to do?'

'I don't think you're going to believe this, Steph.' She smiled, but it was very wry.

'Try me. Just now I'm wondering if there's anything I can't believe.'

She chose her words carefully. 'I've come to accept that the crowd I saw that first day, and then in the dreams, was made up of all those murdered people. They were asking me to... involve myself in the matter. No, I still can't make up my mind what the word was. I don't really care now. What was behind it was far more important. What else could I do? I had to say yes.'

Did we believe her then? John did. Adam, maybe. To this day I don't know if I did. Later, yes. Probably. All I know is that she believed it and if it wasn't what she thought, it might as well have been.

Adam said, 'Marina, you told us that the dreams – *those* dreams – have stopped. But you're still having nightmares, aren't you?'

'I'm having nightmares,' she agreed. 'Funnily enough, not so dissimilar to the others. A crowd again, and voices, but these are hostile. The first ones were scary, but hostile they were not.'

'So not the same crowd?'

She shook her head. 'The real problem with these is that they're not dreams at all. I'm not asleep. While it's all going on, Steph, I can see you, the room, everything. But I'm cut off from reality. I know you're there but I can't reach you. And all the while the voices are telling me what will happen to me if I don't go away. Terrible things. Sick things. That I'm going to die.'

She was struggling now: looking distressed. 'They're worse every time. I didn't tell you, Steph, but I've even been to the well-woman clinic. I had a complete overhaul to make sure that there's no physical cause, and I paid for a CT scan because I'd begun to wonder if I had a brain tumour or something. I've made a follow-up appointment for May, just in case something was missed but they say there's nothing wrong with me. Nothing... So...'

Her voice trailed off and we all sat in silence until, finally, Adam got up and made noises about coffee. We were all, I think, in something akin to shock: Marina because she had, finally, unburdened herself, and the rest of us because what she'd said was a million miles from what we might have expected.

With the coffee came a flat statement from Adam: 'We need to get you out of Llantathan.'

I knew what Marina's response to that would be. She shook head vigorously. 'No, Adam. I have to be here.'

He turned to me. 'Stephanie?'

'If Marina stays, I stay,' I stated. 'But I think Marina's right. I don't pretend to understand why, but I think we have to be here. All of us.'

Adam looked uncomfortable: torn, I thought, between a natural wish to get us away from danger and a strong suspicion that I was right.

At this point John, who had been unusually quiet, added his voice to mine. 'If Marina's committed herself by agreeing to the demands of those voices, then she has no option but to stay. And, naturally, Stephanie will not leave Marina, but I don't think she would anyway. I'm also committed and would not leave if I could.'

'But I'm not here,' Adam said slowly. 'Not in the same way.'

'You could be,' John offered. 'If you choose to be. This rectory has more rooms than I can ever use.'

He didn't push it beyond that, and we wound the evening up shortly after. Marina and I drove home through falling snow and Adam stayed overnight with John.

We were unsurprised when, a week later, Adam moved into the rectory. Marina nodded when she heard. 'It's right,' she murmured. And then, 'Stephanie, do you remember that day we first saw Vine Villa and we could see the rectory and Allington upstairs windows? Do you know that Allington and Vine Villa are visible from the rectory?'

'Yes,' I replied. 'And I expect you can see the rectory and our house from Allington. Interesting, isn't it?'

'It's right,' she repeated. 'All three Vine properties occupied by good people.'

'Enclosing the village,'

'You noticed that too? It is right isn't it, Stephanie?'

I thought that it was, but I also thought that we would not have been the only ones to realise.

* * *

The following month was very full for all of us, so I was relieved when my mother confirmed that her dizzy spells had been, as she said, 'summat and nowt'. Nothing to worry about. Marina, anxious for good results for her students' first year exams the following term, was ferociously busy, as was I with my section of the Llantathan report. The renovation of St. Michael's was progressing and Adam and the team were preparing for the start of the churchyard dig. Outside of work there were weekend suppers at Vine Villa or the rectory, occasional evenings out and, several times, Sunday tea at Allington. Miss Vine had heard about Adam and wished to meet him.

Coerced by John, he went with us reluctantly at first, wondering what on earth he could possibly have to say to two elderly ladies. But Angela, not as elderly as he imagined, and completely unthreatening, merely fed him quantities of tea, sandwiches and cake, while Miss Vine engaged him in a mind-bogglingly erudite discussion about the collapse of Roman rule in Britain. On the sidelines, Marina and I watched as Adam, at first disconcerted, engaged with Miss Vine's argument, emerging triumphant only because his reading was more up to date than hers.

'Come again, Mr. Pembury,' she said. 'And we'll see what we can make of Constantius.'

'She likes you,' John told him as he drove us home.

'Oh good...' he replied, sounding gloomy, and turning to glare at Marina, convulsed with suppressed laughter in the back of the car.

Nevertheless, although Adam claimed that he only went for the ginger cake, he never refused Miss Vine's invitations nor did he go empty-handed, always managing to find some book or magazine article to interest her.

X

It was, I suppose, inevitable that the churchyard excavation would provoke more trouble with the village. Once again, the protests had flooded in. Once again John was without a congregation and, with the sense of hostility worse than we'd ever known, Adam was very worried. 'We go ahead,' he told us over supper one evening. 'The Clerk of Works says they've got to get to the bottom of why that south wall is so damp. If they don't, all the work they've done so far will be wasted. And given what we've discovered so far, he's pleased to let us see if we can find more of the early building. It isn't even as if these bloody-minded villagers have to do any fundraising for it since that second donation.'

'Miss Vine?' I smiled. 'She wasn't the donor last time, but since you've been sweet-talking her...'

He laughed. 'Don't know. No-one knows. But this time there will be trouble. They're not going to back down again.'

'No, I don't think they will,' John agreed, but for now at least, he refused to worry. Instead, he asked if I'd been able to do anything more with the parish registers.

'I think I've done everything I can with them,' I told him, 'And with every other bit of documentation I can find. Apart from a few gaps I've got a complete chronological and demographic rundown on the village. Shall I go over it now?'

I brought my folder of notes from the study and began. 'In 1755 land in Llantathan parish, church property apart, was apportioned as follows. The Devigne family had the Allington estate, the plot now occupied by Vine Villa, and several parcels of land to the north-west, close to the parish boundary. Miss Vine still owns these properties. The rest: the Llantathan estate comprising Llantathan Hall and its demesne lands, all the village properties, and all remaining land within the parish boundary, was sold to Matthew Howells, gentleman, of Montgomeryshire, Wales. Soon after his arrival here his wife, Maria, gave birth to a son,

Samuel, and died that December when the infant was about three months old.

'On the 12th of August, 1756, Josiah Abelson was buried. Since there's no earlier pattern of August deaths, I am assuming him to be the first victim but I confess that he does perplex me somewhat. If he really was Jewish, what was he doing in Llantathan? Ideas, anyone?' I stopped and looked around.

John and Adam shook their heads but Marina said, 'In the 1700s the Jewish population of Britain was tiny but by about 1730 there were communities in Swansea and Gloucester. Take your pick. Maybe Josiah belonged to one of these groups but, since he appears in a Christian burial register, I'd guess that he was the child of a mixed marriage. How he got here we'll probably never know, but does it matter? Go on, Steph.'

There was a murmur of assent but I waited while Marina poured more coffee for us.

'Well, other victims followed annually until January, 1782 when six children were buried between the 4th and the 6th. Matthew Howells was buried on the 10th of January but the actual death dates would have been earlier.'

'What's the connection, Stephanie?' Adam asked.

'I don't know. All I can say is that each time an adult male Howells dies, so do six children. The burial dates imply that the children died first, and a sample I checked from a later period, when registration of deaths was compulsory confirmed this.' I lit a cigarette and went on. 'I don't know,' I repeated, 'but let's leave it for now.

'Samuel Howells inherited his father's estate and somehow acquired a baronetcy, and he also inherited whatever role his father had played because on the 13th of August, 1782 we have the burial of George McClaren aged 16. We know that Samuel married at some stage because his wife's burial is recorded, along with three infant daughters born between 1805 and 1810. In 1811 she gave birth to a son, James, and she died six months later. But who she was... who any of the wives were, apart from Penelope Vine, is a mystery.'

'Don't the registers have any details?' John queried.

'Beyond their first names, nothing,' I told him. 'The registers here don't record any marriages for the Howells family. Well, it's customary for a wedding to take place in the bride's parish, but there are no banns records either. I've ransacked every source I can get at, and paid for searches with no success.'

'Are you implying that there are no marriages? Adam asked.

'No. There would have to be legal marriages for inheritance purposes. But the one we do know about made me wonder. James Howells married Penelope Vine in a high-profile London ceremony. Given who she was he would have found it impossible to avoid that. I'm only guessing but perhaps with that one exception, Howells men married girls of absolutely no consequence and that the marriages were for form's sake. I thought of Fleet weddings but Hardwicke's Marriage Act made them illegal in 1754. Gretna weddings would be OK but they're pretty well documented from the late 18th century. No trace there, but there were other forms of Scottish irregular marriage which would serve to satisfy the girl, be legal, yet leave no record. Alternatively, they took place abroad, or perhaps in Ireland where documentation is problematic.'

No comments or suggestions were forthcoming so I pressed on. 'Now, the Howells children. All born and baptised in Llantathan. Registration of births became compulsory from 1837 but apart from Penelope's child, there's not a single local record. They will have been registered but where is anyone's guess. If I could find the records, I'd have the mothers' maiden names but it would take a trip to London and a lot of searching to get at the information.

'What's clear now is this: no Howells marries young but all the wives are very much younger: teenagers, as far as I can judge from their ages at death. No Howells wife survives longer than a few months after the birth of a son, and there are no second wives. Three wives produce daughters before sons but none gives birth to a girl after a boy. There is never more than one son, and no son dies in infancy though all the daughters do.

'I've tried to get more information about the first Matthew Howells and about the present one and so far, I've made very little headway. At the moment all we know for sure is that this one isn't yet married.' I looked round. 'Let's hope he's in no hurry.'

We stopped at that point so that Marina could answer the telephone. I took the opportunity to bring glasses and whisky while Adam and John read over the first pages of my summary. Neither said much. When Marina returned, I began again.

'I've also looked at the village families,' I said. 'This was easier: being pretty static they tend to be reasonably well documented. They all turn up on census returns but, incidentally, no Howells ever does.

'Patterns here too. In 1755 there were around twenty other families in Llantathan as well as the current twelve. All the families were intermarrying to some extent, and also marrying outside the village. And the rates of childbirth and infant mortality were typically high. Everything just what you'd expect. But from 1756 you start to see a shift. Families disappear until only the twelve are left. Then new names appear at all the farms which are leased to the incomers. And now the twelve only marry eachother and the numbers of their children are just enough to maintain this arrangement: one boy and one girl per family per generation. There are other children, but none which survive to adulthood.

'Where I've been able to look at occupations, I've found that the key jobs in the village have never been held by other than the twelve families, with one exception which I'll come to in a minute. Thus you find that the doctor is now Richard Reece. Before that it was his father, Clayton Reece. The constable is Neil Griffiths. Mrs. Tudor is the local nurse-midwife and the undertaker is Eifion Jones. The Williamses keep the Cross Guns and the Pritchards the post office. John Evans is a solicitor; his wife teaches and Peter Lewis is the land agent who deals with the Howells estate. The rest farm except Robert Powell, but Bowen is a magistrate and Davies is a local councillor.'

'But Stephanie, how can they maintain this?' John demanded. 'One can't just *be* the local constable. What you're saying isn't possible.'

'The evidence says it is,' I replied.

'The rest of it,' he said, 'How can that possibly work? What happens if someone dies unexpectedly? Who, for instance, will replace Anne-Marie? And what if a son dies? Stephanie, this is just too far-fetched.'

'I know,' I agreed. 'But there it is. They do it somehow. Given the past pattern, Paul Williams won't marry because there is no-one to take Anne-Marie's place. However, he needs a son and a daughter to maintain the balance and continue his family line. So some unfortunate girl destined to be the wife of one of the other younger men will bear his children as well as those she is supposed to have.'

Adam made a sound expressive of his disgust.

'Yes, it's sick. But I've found three instances including our good friend Elwyn Pryce. He and his sister were fathered on Richard Reece's mother before she married Clayton. If a son died, they would have a harder problem to overcome but as it happens, they never have lost a son after the age of 14. Thereafter the sons lead charmed lives and it isn't uncommon to see four surviving generations in one family. Clearly, they always need to maintain the full complement of twelve adult males to carry out the functions for which they were bred, and they need rising generations to take over.

'Now, about that key job exception. It's yours, John. Until the beginning of the century the living of Llantathan was in the gift of the lord of the manor, so a Howells could appoint anyone he wished. The first Howells replaced the incumbent rector in May of 1756, installing one Siriol Bevan. He was a bachelor, holding the living until his death in 1814.

'Most of Bevan's successors were around for years, but three who weren't are interesting. Pryce Humphries was appointed in 1822 and stayed for two years. He moved to Celyn in mid-Wales in 1824 where he married and had a daughter, but in 1829 he locked himself in his vicarage and shot his wife out of a window. He would have killed the little girl too but a servant got her to safety. Then he shot himself. The account in the newspapers said that Humphries left no explanation. He was described by his servants as a good vicar and a kindly man, but much troubled. I think we might draw some conclusions there.

'David Lloyd was around for less than a year. In 1866 he set off from Llantathan to attend a deanery meeting in Newport and was never seen or heard of again. Thought to have fallen in the Usk and drowned during a snowstorm. Or not.

'By the time your predecessor was appointed, John, the Church in Wales was disestablished. Times had changed and the Howells family couldn't place the living as it wished. In spite of objections a young clergyman, Alun Harris, arrived in Llantathan in 1925, staying for only six months before resigning after a huge row with his Vestry. Some of this got into the papers and it seems that the village obstructed everything he wanted to do. I tried to trace him or, more likely, any descendants but he never married. He went to Kenya as a missionary and died in the Mau-Mau uprisings of the 50s.

'After that the Church backed down and gave in to Howells' pressure. William Blayney arrived and under him parish life was cut back to the bare minimum. He may have had his own strange agenda but if so, it suited Llantathan to encourage it. Services were strictly according to the Prayer Book, and there was a complete rejection of any modernisation, which is still the case.'

'Ah, but Stephanie,' John interrupted, 'most of Wales has tended to reject revision of the Prayer Book. There have been attempts to replace the 1662 version since the 1950s. We'll finally get the new one this year.'

'Which, no doubt, Llantathan will refuse,' I smiled. 'The significant point is that because there is no requirement to have harvest festivals and carol services, there were none. Even the Sunday school was replaced by a catechism class. Technically, Blayney was doing nothing wrong and had the village's support, so the bishop couldn't do a thing. I think the diocese must have reckoned that Blayney was dotty but, given his age, wouldn't last much longer. Then, when he died, he could be replaced by someone reasonable.

'In the event, Blayney hung on until 1981, by which time he was almost certainly insane. He could still function enough to carry out his few duties but I'm told that otherwise his behaviour was quite scandalous. Even Angela doesn't know the whole of it but she did say that he was picked up in Newport roaring drunk more than once. He died in hospital of a stroke, certified by a Newport doctor. Nothing odd about it. Is there anything you can add to that, John?'

John shook his head. 'Only that he'd infuriated a succession of bishops and archdeacons. I did know of Blayney's drinking and I was warned that Llantathan needed a good shaking up. But, no... I heard nothing else.'

'You knew that when you were appointed Howells lodged an objection which was supported by the village?'

'Oh yes. Howells claimed that Llantathan wanted a Welsh clergyman. It wouldn't stick, though, because I was born in Wales: in Llangynog, and my mother was a Thomas of Bala.'

I nodded. 'Well, that just about concludes it except for one curious little sidelight. Have any of you ever looked at the war memorial?'

Heads were shaken.

'Look at it next time you go past. There aren't many names and those which are there are of incomers. The village men didn't go to war. Not one. Reserved occupations.'

There was something about Llantathan and the war which had bothered me before. I was trying to remember what it was when Marina, who had been making notes, asked, 'What puzzles me is that for all this time the women have been allowing it to go on. Not being a mother myself, I don't *know*, but I can't imagine me allowing a daughter to be forced into marriage let alone giving up a child to be murdered, which is what they must be doing whenever a male Howells dies.'

'No,' I agreed. 'Obviously they're conditioned from birth. Remember that until they're 13 they attend school here, taught by members of their own families. After that it seems to be private education, boarding during the week. They grow up with very limited contact with the outside world. On top of that they must be terrorised into compliance like Anne-Marie. Anne-Marie is an indicator that the conditioning doesn't always hold, and there's something else which makes me think that the women are the weak link. It's the fact that Llantathan has a slightly higher than average death rate for adult females between the ages of 35 and 50, and I wonder if that's concealing suicides. You don't find it amongst the teenage girls so most marriages may not be cold arrangements. Or the kids grow up knowing that they're going to marry X, Y or Z and just accept it. Usually. Either way, Anne-Marie's engagement to Paul Williams was probably a mistake.'

Marina nodded. 'OK. Now what about Anne-Marie? According to Reece she had a heart complaint. That could have made childbearing dangerous so why was she being made to marry Williams?'

'I think the heart complaint was a fabrication,' I said. 'It would make sense for Reece to have a false set of medical records for every single villager so that he can always claim a long-standing condition and so avoid a post-mortem.'

'I can see that he could get away with that a lot of the time,' Adam put in, 'but not, surely, with six child deaths in one week. In the past, yes, but the last time was – when?'

'1966,' I supplied. 'Yes, I did check that. It was in Clayton Reece's time. The children: three girls, three boys, were aged between four and 12. All died on the same day: 15th July. According to the papers they were attending a birthday party at the Tudors' farm.

'The kids were playing hide-and-seek and the ones who died had gone to hide in the barn. No-one knew how the fire started but it was speculated that one of them: perhaps the little Davies girl, had got hold of the matches used to light the birthday cake candles. Whatever... the barn was a timber building half full of hay and it burned to the ground. And of course a port-mortem on ashes will inevitably be limited.'

John winced.

'A cover-up,' Adam said. 'If they know they can't avoid a P.M. they make sure that the real cause of death is impossible to find. And I suppose if it is ritual, the real cause has to involve bloodletting. If it didn't, they wouldn't have to go to so much trouble.'

'I expect they didn't, in the past,' I said. 'It's only since the advent of modern forensics and, of course, modern policing, that they've had to take such care.'

Marina wanted to know about the illegitimacy rate. 'Anything unusual there?'

'Yes. Very. Except where girls have died leaving the village one childbearer short, there just isn't any illegitimacy. I'm not saying that this implies that there is, with that one exception, no extramarital sex, but if there is, it doesn't produce results which get into the records.'

'OK.' Marina thought again. 'What do you suppose happens if someone proves to be sterile?'

'That's something the records can't tell me,' I said. 'But I can think of solutions. If a woman was incapable of having children a surrogate mother would be found, much as if a childbearer had died. But if the man was infertile, I can only suppose that his function devolved to another male relative. It may never have happened but if it did there's no way we can tell.'

'But after over two hundred years of what amounts to inbreeding, shouldn't the village be crawling with congenital idiots?' Adam asked.

'Maybe it was, at one time,' I replied. 'I don't understand much about genetics but I did look into it and it seems that after several generations the gene pool cleans itself. Weak traits are bred out. And if the gene pool isn't clean yet, now they can detect physical conditions before birth and deal with them. What they do about mental defects I don't know.'

'They're all insane,' Adam growled. 'They have to be.'

'Socially and morally insane, yes,' Marina said. 'But legally insane?'

'Does it matter?' John demanded impatiently. 'What we need to know is why? What's behind all this?'

'Something for sure,' I said. 'This must be why the registers were hidden. Take over a century's worth out of circulation and the chances of anyone discovering the patterns are virtually nil. But John, I still don't think it's Satanism. Satanism recruits. Llantathan keeps whatever it's got to itself. The only outsiders are the Howells wives and the rectors. The wives don't live long so we can assume that they don't participate. What the rectors gain is anyone's guess. It isn't money. Blayney left only a couple of thousand.'

'Where do the rectors come into it anyway?' Adam wanted to know. 'They can't be involved in the rituals because it's gone on since John came here.'

John thought part of it was the need to preserve an illusion of normality. 'They don't want anyone looking too closely at the village,' he said. 'In that respect Blayney came close to sinking the ship. He only got away with it because he was regarded as mad. But even Blayney kept up the normal services which were, so I'm told, always well attended. And you'll have noticed that except for the boycott, my congregations aren't small. They know that if numbers fall, there'll be a parish amalgamation. They can't risk that: it would bring outsiders in.

'Their real need, though, is a clergyman whose faith is non-existent. They don't want a force for good in the village. The Church has enormous spiritual power. I'm not talking about the earthly organisation. I mean the Church Eternal. If Llantathan's rector is without faith, without the indwelt Holy Spirit, then in effect there is no Church in Llantathan. So the fact that these people attend services, are baptised, married and buried by the church is meaningless.'

'Yes, I see,' Marina said. 'But what about confirmations? Aren't they performed by an outsider?'

'They are, but what would the bishop be confirming? Only empty promises. I don't think that would change anything.'

She nodded. 'Well, at least you can take their rejection as a compliment, John. They must actually be afraid of you.'

'In which case, sooner or later, they'll try to get rid of you,' Adam warned.

'I know,' John said simply.

'But not, perhaps, until they've got rid of the rest of us.' That was Marina, musing. And no-one disagreed.

I can, now, look back to that evening and know that we had all the data we needed to deduce the basic truth about Howells. What we lacked was imaginative thinking. And, of course, the will to believe the unbelievable. We were not in a position even to begin to work out the means by which Howells could be stopped, but the essential 'why' was there to see, and we missed it. We can't be blamed for that. I know that if *I* had seen it then I would not have been able to accept it. It was hard enough for me to accept what my precious data said. But even I couldn't rationalise that now. Even I had to admit that there was no ordinary explanation.

XI

It must have been years, centuries perhaps, since the church had been the focus of so much activity. As soon as the excavation had ended, the workmen moved in. Lorries and vans came and went. Skips filled and were replaced. All kinds of building materials and tools accumulated along the church walls. For the duration, the quiet of the High Street was broken by purposeful noise and welcome movement. Then, with the restoration work well advanced, the archaeologists returned for the churchyard excavation, and the attempts to get rid of us began soon after.

In the expectation that trouble would be directed at the excavation, Adam had taken every possible precaution against vandalism. The site had been fenced and screened: a legal requirement anyway when exhumations are involved, and the facilities made available at the rectory obviated the need for site huts. Adam never relaxed his vigilance, following security routines meticulously. Perhaps because of that, when the attacks came, they were not directed at the site or the team but at Marina and me.

It was a distressing episode but it didn't last and it could have been worse. Some extremely offensive anonymous letters to Marina focussed on her Jewish heritage, then we both had letters stigmatising us as filthy perverts. Dead rats were left on our doorstep and, finally, Marina's car was vandalised: tyres slashed and its bright red paintwork daubed with yellow stars of David.

'What on earth can we do?' I asked. It was Saturday morning and John had run Marina to Newport to collect the hire car she would use until her own was repaired and resprayed. In her absence I was at the rectory having coffee with Adam.

'It ought to be a police job,' he told me. Anywhere else it would be, but what can you do when the village constable almost certainly knows about it, condones it, and may even be one of those responsible? This is the kind of thing we were talking about in February.'

It was: the impossibility of involving outside authorities. If I hadn't grasped it then, I certainly did now. I could see exactly how the village, denying everything, could portray us as troublemakers and make Marina look neurotic, implying that she was doing it herself.

Marina looked ill and though she never admitted it, I knew she was afraid of a more personal – physical – attack. 'How do they know? How can they possibly know what we are? What I am?' She demanded. It was Easter Saturday and we'd been looking forward to a long weekend doing nothing much. Marina was knitting and I was messing about with some fabric.

'They can't but they can make educated guesses,' I said, putting the fabric aside. 'We know they watch us. They must have seen enough to realise that we're more than friends.'

'But how do they know I'm Jewish?' She sounded exasperated. 'Does a Jew go to an Anglican church?'

'I don't know, love,' I said, 'but maybe the spies have seen the menorah.'

'Oh Lord!' she sighed. 'I expect you're right.'

Last winter, on the last day of November, Marina had set the ornate candlestick in the window and lit the first of her Hanukkah candles. 'One of the celebrations I still like to keep,' she smiled, her face lovely in the pool of pale golden light.

Afterwards, Marina had polished the menorah and put it back on the window ledge amid Christmas greenery and later still, when all the festivities were over, it remained because it seemed to belong.

Logically it had to be the explanation and we looked no further. I would have been satisfied: the more I thought about it the more reasonable it appeared, but I could sense that Marina wasn't, quite. As if she knew that there was something more: something beyond logic.

As to why this was happening, that was obvious. They were trying to intimidate us into leaving. Probably they'd assumed that once the church excavation had finished, we would go, but the second dig tied us up there for an indefinite period.

'But,' pondered Marina, 'are they trying to get us out because of the excavation or because they don't want us around by August?'

'Maybe both,' I replied. 'But they have to try to get us out because the longer we stay the more chance there is of us seeing and hearing something we shouldn't, and of spotting the patterns. If they did know how much we've pieced together I think perhaps we'd have been disposed of by now.'

Marina frowned. She stuck her needles into the ball of sage green yarn and put her knitting aside. 'Hang on a minute, Steph. I've just thought of something. You said that the longer we stay the greater the chance of spotting the patterns. Yes? A good reason for wanting us out. If that's the case how come the outsider families don't spot the pattern? I think that if I was... oh... Mrs. Jackson at Maes Coed I'd be rather worried by now.'

I sat down. Stood up. Wandered round the room. She was right and I'd never thought about it before. The Jacksons had been at Maes Coed for three years. They had two girls and a son just turned 13. They couldn't fail to be aware of Brian's death. Andrew's too. Maybe more. If things went on unchecked there would be another this August. Yes, if I was Mrs. Jackson I'd be wanting out. 'They wouldn't know just how many,' I pointed out. 'Three or four... You could probably rationalise that.'

'You'd try,' Marina agreed. 'Anyone would. But you'd be jittery. Yet they do stay, and I think it might help us to get hold of one of these people and see if we can find out why. Then there's Miss Vine. She can't have lived here for all these years without knowing. Steph, as soon as I can I'm going to have a little talk with Angela. If anyone can tell us about these incomers and where any of them have gone, she can.'

'Yes, do that, love. But I don't believe that if we can track any of them down, we'll get much joy from them.'

'No, probably not,' she sighed. 'Inducements. What people will do for money.'

'Or fear.'

'It might not be any one thing,' she suggested. 'It might be whatever will work best. Everyone has a weakness to be played upon. Perhaps we should start looking at our own.

If we're not going to be frightened out of Llantathan, what will they try next?'

'They'll try to stop the dig,' I said. I sat down again, on the rug, leaning against Marina's chair. 'I'm sure of that. No... Wait a minute. Let me think.'

She waited, her hand playing gently with a strand of my hair. Ideas revolved in my mind and another piece of the puzzle fell into place. 'No,' I announced. 'No, they won't try to stop it. They want to, I'm sure, but they're realistic. The degree of sabotage needed to stop it permanently would put Llantathan under the microscope. Far too great a risk. Yes, they want us out as soon as possible, but the main thing will be to prevent us finding out whatever secret's bound up with this second dig. Don't you see?'

She didn't, so I explained. 'They objected to the church excavation because it would bring outsiders to the village and, perhaps, because it gave them an opportunity to hassle John. But as soon as the local paper picked up on it all objections ceased. It was preferable to endure a few strangers for a while than to attract wider attention. I don't believe there was anything about the excavation itself which troubled them.

'If the same reasoning is applied to the second dig, you'd expect them to put up with it because it isn't going to go on forever. Yes, I know I said that the longer we're around the greater the chance that we'll find things out, but the work will be finished by October and the team will be gone. They might expect that we'll leave too. John will stay, but for how long, given the hostility? Sitting it out would make far more sense, so the fact that they're prepared to attract outside attention has to mean that this excavation holds some threat for them. Something they know will come to light if it goes on.

'That has to be prevented. They can't stop the work and if they don't realise already that getting us out is virtually impossible, they soon will. Their only option then is to destroy whatever it is they don't want found. I assume that since the site hasn't yet been vandalised, whatever it is must be in the parts scheduled for digging later.'

'I see the reasoning, Marina admitted. 'And I can't better it, but what on earth can be in the churchyard?'

'Hitherto unsuspected evidence of what they're up to, I suppose. I don't know, but whatever it is must be under the ground, not on it. We've had the run of the place for months.'

'You're recording the grave stones now. Spotted anything odd?'

'Not really. There's no plot for the burying or scattering of cremation ashes. Probably just another of Blayney's hang-ups. Otherwise, nothing. Typical groupings and horizontal stratigraphy.'

''You mean they start burying people in one place and put the next body alongside the last, and so on? It can't be that simple, surely?'

'No, it isn't,' I agreed. 'To start with the land's been reused any number of times since God knows when. Look, if you're interested let's go down there now. There'll be enough light for an hour or so and I wouldn't mind a walk. I'm too restless to settle to anything much.'

'OK. Who knows? We might even spot something interesting.'

'Oh yeah,' I drawled. 'Elwyn Pryce doing bad ninja impressions behind a yew tree.' I threw her jacket to her. 'Come on. Let's go and say hello to the nasty sod.'

She laughed. 'You spend too much time with Adam,' she said.

'I beg your pardon?'

'You've picked up quite a lot of his less elegant terminology. Still, I can't disagree...' She locked the door: new security locks since the attacks started. John and Adam both had spare keys.

'Steph, what's the date today?' Marina asked as we set off down the drive.

'The 21st,' I said. 'Why?'

'That's all right. I've got that follow-up appointment at the well-woman clinic but it's not for a couple of weeks. With all this going on I lose track of where we are.'

We turned into School Lane and she said, 'If it's almost May we've not got long. I wonder when Howells will come back.'

'Not yet,' I replied. 'Oh Lord! It isn't long, though, and still so much we don't know.'

'I wish I knew what the villagers get out of it,' she said, returning to her earlier thoughts. There must be something.'

'John believes that the basis of Satanism is power,' I said. 'By harnessing the supernatural they gain power which they use to obtain whatever they want. Usually it's wealth and influence.'

'But you don't believe it is Satanism, do you?'

'No, but I believe they must be using the supernatural. Or they think they are.'

She said nothing and I went on, 'One of the reasons why I don't believe this is Satanism is that, for the leader of a coven, Howells doesn't seem to spend enough time here. Ten days a year at most. And if this is was a true coven, they'd all have some degree of supernatural power or at least ability which is independent of the group. They don't seem to have it. To know what they do about us they have to use spies.'

Closing the churchyard gate, she turned to stare at a figure lounging by the porch. Pryce. He stared back then spat and turned away, hands in pockets, strands of thin, reddish hair straggling from under his cap.

She bent her head to me. 'Whatever he gets out of it, it isn't good looks and charm,' she said softly, grinning as she watched the ex-verger slide off round the church. 'Right, Steph. Now tell me about this horizontal stratigraphy. Where does it start?'

'I've no idea,' I replied. 'All I can say is that the oldest surviving stones are these which are early 1700s.' I gestured to the rows of eroded, tilting headstones flanking the main path. 'Otherwise, the earliest visible phase is on the south side. It starts at the west end with a few mid-18th century memorials, and the dates progress as you move east. With exceptions the most recent burials are here towards the east end of the church.'

'The exceptions being?'

'The village families. They all have their preferred places. You've got Pritchard, Evans and Griffiths to the left of the path, and Pryce, Lewis, Reece and Powell to the right. On the south side Davies, Jones, Williams, Bowen and Tudor.'

'Given the nature of this place I'd have thought there'd be no-one else buried here,' she commented.

'More than you'd think,' I said. 'Those rectors who died in office for a start. And remember that when the first Howells arrived there were a lot of other families. They're represented too, along with some incoming tenants and people connected with the Allington estate. A few others whose connections with Llantathan I can't imagine and, of course, all those boys. Two hundred and twenty odd there alone, though most aren't marked.'

'You're forgetting one other family.'

'No, I'm not,' She followed me along the path round to the south where I stopped in front of the tall slate headstone bearing the name Howells.

'The burials here are from the 18th century to the 1870s,' I said. 'Later ones are on the north side.'

'Do all the names correspond with the registers?'

'Yes, apart from a couple of infants. Nothing odd about that. Very young children often were omitted, usually when they'd died years before the stone was put up.'

'Doesn't it bother you having to spend so much time here?' With the light fading, she was beginning to cast longing glances towards the rectory.

'Sometimes,' I admitted, but I didn't elaborate. Sometimes it bothered me a lot. Not then: the violet shadows and the softness of dusk made it the epitome of the romantic country churchyard. Nor did I mind the early mornings when a damp mist wreathed the stones. Eerie, yes, but it smacked too much of overdone Hammer horror to impress me.

We were into a spell of exceptionally warm weather for late April and, pleasant though it was to be working outside, the times I really hated were those afternoons when the sun bleached the sky and created sharp-edged shadows. Sometimes, then, sounds from the church and the site seemed to fade and a curious, dusty stillness settled over the place. My sensitivity heightened and I would become aware of what I thought of as the hot spots: areas in the churchyard which seemed to give off vibrations, auras. It disturbed me. I hated having to work with my back to one of these hot spots. It was too much like being watched. And the worst was the Howells stone on the south side. Wherever I was in the churchyard I was conscious of that one. It had to be fanciful. Nothing to do with what lay beneath. I'd seen any number of skeletons during the church excavation and had been surprised by my lack of response.

It was one afternoon last autumn when the excavation had uncovered over 50 inhumations in the body of the church. We were watching Dawn photographing one of the skeletons. 'There's nothing deader than dead,' Adam remarked. Well, obviously, but I knew what he meant: if the life once vested in those remains continued after death, it did so elsewhere.

So, knowing that what rested under my feet was no worse than anything I'd seen in the church, why did I have these fancies? Why, if dead was so very dead, was I still plagued by this childish unease? Because, I suppose, I suspected that Marina was right and that all the fears of childhood are based on reason: obscure, perhaps, but surely there. Marina believed this and that was why I didn't tell her about the hot spots. She had enough to worry about.

DARKNESS

1984

Let's talk of graves, of worms and epitaphs;
Make dust our paper, and with rainy eyes
Write sorrow on the bosom of the earth;
Let's choose executors and wills

William Shakespeare

I

Adam, looking distraught, let us in by the kitchen door. 'John should be back before long,' he told us. 'Miss Vine...' In answer to our unspoken question, he nodded.

Marina, eyes glistening, went through the motions with the kettle and the three of us sat with mugs of tea and cigarettes, not saying much. Then I remembered that if Miss Vine died intestate Matthew Howells would inherit. Had Marina or Adam heard anything about the will?

'No,' Marina said. 'But she wouldn't let there be any possibility of Howells getting his hands on her property. I'd guess it will all go to Angela.'

I hoped so. If it did, we could negotiate with her to carry on renting our house. Maybe even buy it. It seemed unlikely now but, sometimes, I felt that if only it was sorted out, Llantathan might be a nice place, one day. Oddly, though I'd questioned our theories and whether we could put a stop to Howells' activities, I never doubted that if we did, all would be well. Llantathan would wake from its long bad dream and its inhabitants, released from whatever hold Howells had over them, would be transformed, perhaps with a little gentle counselling from John, into good and happy people. There's a fairytale for you. It never occurred to me then that Llantathan might not be able to cope with release.

We decided to wait for John and filled in the time regaling Adam with my latest hypothesis. 'Oh great!' he complained. 'You say they're going to vandalise something in the churchyard but you don't know what and you don't know where. Stephanie, apart from the archaeology, that churchyard contains nothing but burials so if you're right, which of the one hundred and sixty four plots in the planned area is it going to be?'

'Calm down, Adam,' Marina urged. 'Give us time to work on it.'

'OK. OK. Yeah, I suppose it's good news in a way, assuming you're right. But if you don't know what it is we're not supposed to find, how can you work out where we're not supposed to find it?'

Marina dealt with that briskly. 'By a process of elimination,' she said. 'We can rule out all burials of people whose connections with the village are slight or unknown. Likewise incomer adults and members of families which died out or moved. What does that leave us with, Steph?'

'Some of the teenage boys, three of the rectors, parts of the known Bowen and Tudor groups, and the Howells plot,' I said, 'but I'd need to check the plan to be sure.'

'Plus any number of unmarked burials. What about those?' Adam demanded.

'I don't know,' I confessed. 'But I know how you might narrow it down. My money's on the Howells grave if only because everything else centres on that family. Have you got any spare fencing and screens, Adam?'

'No, but I could get some.'

'Well, screen another area not including the Howells grave and see what happens.'

'What if you're wrong?'

'If I'm wrong, they'll do something. They know I've recorded the stones and they didn't interfere. Whatever it is, it must be underground. If you set a watch, you can stop them before they start. And if nothing happens at all, we'll know it's probably the Howells grave.'

He thought about it. 'I can do it,' he conceded, 'but I'll have to give Alan some sort of explanation or he'll think I've flipped. What bothers me is that all this is based on a chain of assumptions and even if you are right, we'll still have to deal with an attempted destruction and God knows what else. And another thing: suppose we manage to keep them out and we do find whatever-it-is. If they don't stop us finding it, aren't they going to stop us using it?'

'Yes, if they can,' Marina said calmly, 'but we'll handle that as and when. Let's concentrate on making sure that we can get to whatever-it-is first.'

'And what if we don't recognise it when we do find it?' Adam wanted to know.

'If there was a possibility of that they wouldn't try to stop us,' she replied.

John came in soon after 10, tired, sad but, curiously, a little excited. Miss Vine, he said, had suffered a stroke that afternoon and died in hospital soon after. Angela had sent for him and he'd driven her back to Allington where he'd spent the last couple of hours discussing practical matters including funeral arrangements.

'She did make a will,' he said. 'So Howells won't benefit in any way. And as you know she had no other surviving relations.'

'So it all goes to the cats' home?' Marina smiled.

John shook his head. 'There'll be provision for Angela and other bequests. I doubt the cats will get a look-in. Anyway, the will's being read after the funeral next week. Angela says could all of you come, please: to the funeral and afterwards.'

'Well, yes,' Marina said, rather bewildered. 'Naturally we would want to attend the funeral, but why afterwards?'

'Something to do with your house, I believe,' John replied. 'Meanwhile...' He took up a brown paper package which had lain on the top of the fridge since his return. 'Angela asked me to give this to you both. No, I've no idea what's in it, but just before she was taken ill Miss Vine said that you were to have it as soon as possible.'

Mystified, we surveyed the small parcel. It was sealed with Sellotape and a small white label bore our names in Miss Vine's elegant script. Marina made no move so at last I picked at the tape and unfolded the brown paper to disclose a book bound in dark blue cloth. Tucked inside the cover was an envelope which I handed to Marina. I turned a few pages of the book. It looked like a journal.

Marina slit the envelope and withdrew several sheets of heavy cream notepaper. Slowly, she read:

'My dear friends,

Despite my isolation I am not unaware of your aspirations concerning the village of Llantathan. John Holmes has, no doubt with the best of intentions, declined to confide in me, but he has conveyed more than he realises. I need not stress the gravity of your situation but I do not believe that you are foolish, nor are you cowards. Because I was both, I shrank from making use of such knowledge as I had acquired through my half-sister's marriage to James Howells. To my eternal shame I dismissed Arthur Vine's statements as the ravings of a senile old man and because of that, Llantathan's curse continues.

Since my incapacity Angela Morton has been invaluable to me, gathering what information she could and enabling me to follow the events which occur in Llantathan with such appalling regularity. Nevertheless, I always felt that what I knew was never quite enough, and as my infirmity increased, action became impossible. All I have been able to do, in recent years, is pray for others to come to the village: others who would see what I have seen and would not be afraid to take the necessary steps. I believe that my prayers have been answered.

You, I know, have seen a pattern to the activities of the Howells family and I have no doubt that you have reached the same terrible conclusions as I. I am entrusting Penelope's journal to you in the hope that it will add to your store of information and lead you closer to a resolution.

Penelope was 20 years my junior, my father's daughter by his second marriage and the darling of the family. Our father died when she was still a child and her mother, not appreciating our family's aversion, allowed her marriage to James Howells.

She died soon after the birth of her son Matthew in circumstances which were not explained to my satisfaction and I was never permitted to have any contact with her child. He was, after the custom of the family, raised and educated abroad, probably in Switzerland, since that is where my sister met her husband and she alludes to it in her journal.

My late uncle, Arthur Vine, deplored Pen's marriage which, he believed, was an attempt to acquire the Vine estates. Over the years there have been other attempts by various means and in recent years there have been moves on his son's part to "persuade" me to will my lands to him. I, however, am far less malleable than my sister.

After Pen's death Arthur Vine became increasingly obsessed with the Howells family. I know that he attempted to discover its origins and that he collected a good deal of information over the years. He confided in no-one but it was clear to me that he was deeply troubled.

In the last years of his life he declined rapidly. I believed that he was losing his mind and that he suffered from fantastic delusions regarding Howells. When we are afraid, we will always tend to choose comfortable explanations.

I now believe that my uncle knew much more than I, and meant to halt Howells' activities. What he intended was, I am convinced, in some way connected with his plans for the commemoration of Pen's death.

I have no idea why my uncle should have chosen to perpetuate Pen's memory by means of a bell, but his stated intention was to have the old treble bell taken down and recast and, on re-hanging, a peal rung in Pen's honour.

My uncle's scheme gained the agreement of the archdeacon and work began in 1951. The tower and the belfry were renovated and the bell recast with additional metal. In 1952 the bell was blessed and dedicated by the bishop but it was only in the face of considerable opposition from the rector and from James Howells that the bell was hung. The planned peal on the anniversary of Pen's death was abandoned when ringers invited from another parish were forcibly prevented from entering the church by the rector and a number of the villagers.

I should mention that before the bell was made my uncle died suddenly and I undertook to execute his wishes. Also, in accordance with his will, I have ensured that although Llantathan's bells have been silent these many years, they are in perfect working order.

With regard to Pen's journal, I am sure that James Howells was unaware of its existence. If he had known, I might not have been left in relative peace.

I have made provision for your occupancy of Vine Villa within the terms of my will and I trust that you will enjoy a deservedly happy and long life together there.

With gratitude and sincere good wishes, and with my prayers,

> *I am your friend,*

>> *Imogen Vine.'*

Marina folded the letter and placed it on the table beside the diary. No-one said a word. We were all looking at that dark blue book. It might have been a bomb, and we might have sat there forever if John hadn't moved, brought glasses and his good sherry. He didn't say so but I knew that it was meant to be a toast of thanks and a farewell to a valued friend.

'Do you think it'll help?' Marina asked later, as she undressed.

'Miss Vine thought so,' I replied. 'But yes, I do. How else could we get a glimpse into the Howells household?'

'A past Howells household,' she murmured, 'but I take your point. I only wish we could see into a few other households round here.'

'So do I. One can only deduce so much from the outside. I'd like to know how prosperous these people really are.'

'If Pryce is anything to go by, not very. He looks as though he buys his clothes from jumble sales.'

I laughed. 'But his car's new.'

'Doesn't prove a thing,' she declared. 'And even if we could see inside the houses, we could only make guesses. Lots of people with expensive possessions are in debt up to their eyes. Some live in squalor with a fortune under the mattress. What they own might be suggestive but we'd need to see their bank accounts.'

'I'll ask Pryce next time I meet him in the churchyard.'

She grinned and climbed into bed, confessing to extreme tiredness. Since February, though Marina and I had talked through our disagreements, I knew that we had lost something. She knew too and though neither of us said anything, we both passed it off as tiredness, preoccupation with work and worry. It would come right again one day, when the nightmares stopped, when term ended, when... whatever. And so I fell asleep against the warm comfort of her body, unaware that that night signified the end of my peace.

* * *

Over that Easter break I worked on the journal, fascinated as names and statistics took on life in its pages. Penelope Howells, née Vine, was a lively writer though she did confuse me with abbreviations and a good many references to people and events of which I could have no knowledge. Still, that's in the nature of journals, as is bias.

The journal gave an impression of a young, excited girl – 18 when she married James Howells – dazzled by a much older man and by the idea of becoming Lady Howells; superficially sophisticated, yet far more naïve than a teenager of today.

Her married life began when Europe was on the brink of war. For the duration they lived at Llantathan Hall, but apart from a reference to James Howells' annoyance about that, Pen hardly ever alluded to the conflict. I guessed this was because what was happening to her seemed far more important for it was soon apparent that Pen was not happy, writing of broken promises, of changed attitudes, of coldness, lies and loneliness.

In one long passage she described Llantathan and her intense dislike of it, expressing a longing for the war to be over so that they could go to Switzerland. *Even being bombed in London would be better than this,* she wrote.

And in July, 1941: *J. perfectly beastly. He's arranged for me to go and stay with Muriel and Leonard for August. Again! He knows how I simply loathe them. We had a row exactly like before. I said that if I had to go anywhere, I would go to Mother or Imogen. He told me it was already arranged. I asked why did he always send me away for August. Estate business. Interminable explanations about sheep. I stopped arguing. It's hopeless when he's been drinking. I do wish he would stop. He never drank so much when we first met.*

In September Pen was back at Llantathan Hall. *Nothing much seems to have happened while I was in Dorset. J. says that the Wilsons will be giving up their farm soon. There was an accident about a week after I left and Joe Wilson was killed. His parents don't want to stay now. I suppose it's too sad for them.*

In October Pen wrote of her mother's sudden death and funeral and then, at the end of November, she reported that she was pregnant. *J. is very pleased. He seems to think that everything will change once it's born and I'll be more content. Naturally he wants a boy. I don't. I don't want any baby yet, but I'd rather have a daughter.*

At Christmas Pen complained of sickness and the dismal atmosphere. *The rector doesn't agree with Christmas and I don't think J. does either. But it was beastly anyway. I had a fearful row with J. about some Jewish refugees in Yorkshire. Imogen wrote about meeting them and how they escaped from Poland just before Hitler invaded. I told J. about it and he said they should have stayed where they were.*

I ought to have known better than to answer back. J. was in a vile mood. He always is when he drinks. So I suppose the row was my fault in a way, but I was simply furious and terribly upset. At last he said that he was sorry I was so offended. He couldn't help the attitude he'd inherited from his father. He explained that his family had always been wary of Jews because there was an old saying about the family's wealth: 'It came with a Jew and it will go with a Jew'. I called it superstitious nonsense.

In June, 1942 Pen's baby was born. She wrote that her husband was delighted with his son who was to be named Matthew after the first Howells to own Llantathan. *J. was very pleasant. He sat with me for ages this evening and told me about this ancestor of his. He said that the first Matthew was born very poor but he was clever and hardworking. As a young man he'd taken a position with a Bristol merchant who rewarded his faithful service by leaving him a fortune in his will. J. says it was probably not that much but it was enough to buy Llantathan because the estate was in such a poor way. J. says that M. H. made a lot more money and put the estate to rights and every year on the 8th of August, the village held a big celebration for his birthday, to thank him for what he'd done. I said it sounded like a fairy story. I can't work out where the Jew comes into it. Perhaps the rich old man who left M. H. the money was a Jew. I'll ask J. tomorrow if he's in a good mood.*

But presumably Pen never did. The last entries in the book were patchy and recorded only that she felt tired and ill. Her final words stated that she was no better and that J. had arranged for her to go away to recover. *But first I'm to spend a weekend with Imogen. How I look forward to that!*

On the next page, in a hand I recognised as Miss Vine's, I read: *My sister Penelope was sent to a convalescent home in Lincolnshire at the end of July, 1942. A letter from her reported that she continued to feel ill. A fortnight after this I was informed by James Howells that she had died. The cause of her death was given as acute anaemia. She was buried at Llantathan. After the war the child, whom I had never seen, was taken out of the country and did not return to Llantathan until he inherited the estate on the death of his father in 1966.*

I closed the book and sat for a long time wondering what Marina was going to say. So far, she had left it all to me and had asked no questions, but she would want to know what it told us and she would certainly read it for herself. *It came with a Jew and it will go with a Jew...* How was she going to react to that?

With a very robust cheerfulness, I found. And with a sense of relief I couldn't share. 'That's why they're trying to drive me out,' she said. 'They're scared in case I'm the Jew!'

'Don't crow,' I warned. 'It isn't an omen. They may have disposed of dozens of Jews over the years.'

'Well they won't dispose of me,' she declared. 'I'm here to stay.'

'So they're sacrificing teenage boys to commemorate the birthday of Matthew Howells I,' Adam said when I shared the journal gleanings with him and John.

'No. They're continuing a rite established by Matthew Howells. I suppose that if it has to be a fixed day a birthday is as good a date as any.'

'Don't forget the other murders,' John put in. 'The ones associated with the Howells deaths.'

'They're random,' I reminded him. 'No fixed date. 'Well, you couldn't have a fixed date, could you?'

'No, but... I don't know Stephanie. Sometimes I think that the answer's there if only we could look at it all from the proper angle.' John's expression was both perplexed and annoyed.

'Yes, I feel like that too,' I said. 'But if it is there, I can't see it. I need one more piece of the puzzle.'

'What piece is that?' Marina asked.

'I wish I knew,' I replied.

II

On the Tuesday morning Marina didn't get up. 'It feels like flu,' she said. She was weary and shivering, didn't want breakfast, just paracetamol and quiet.

Term hadn't started but college was open and I was going in to do some more work on the Normans. Before I left, Adam phoned. 'Would you ask Alan if he'll bring out some more screening, Stephanie? And picket fence. Whatever's in the store.'

'Sure. Do I give him any explanation?'

'If you can think of one. It was your idea.'

'OK. OK. I'll come up with something.'

Alan frowned when I relayed the request. 'Adam's surely not planning to open up another area yet?'

'No. It's just a ploy to fool the village.' I gave him the modified explanation I'd thought up on the way in, adding, 'The team's getting very jittery not knowing if the villagers are going to do anything. Please...'

'If you really think it'll help, I'll take it out this afternoon. By the way...'

He passed a carrier bag across his desk. 'I don't know how useful this will be but there's some Llantathan stuff in it, and a couple of old estate maps which you may need for the Llanfair project.'

With that folder came the bit of the puzzle I'd wished for the previous day. Only I didn't recognise it.

A note in the carrier said that the contents had been passed to Hafren by a Mrs. Parsons of Newport whose late father had collected items of local interest.

Collected, but not collated, and there was a lot of material. I sorted everything into files relating to a dozen villages between Newport and Caldicot and put side a small pile of Llantathan items to examine more closely.

A Short History of Llantathan was a thin booklet published in 1924 by one Freda Fairford. Although it contained no new facts, it did report two traditions I hadn't come across. According to Fairford the land on which the rectory was built was said to have been called the Mint Field and she wrote of having been told of a well in the churchyard which was believed to have magical properties. A footnote added that this information came from a Caerleon resident whose ancestors had lived in Llantathan.

A substantial book on Monmouthshire bellringing published in 1961 had a chapter on Llantathan's bells. Something to read later: it might explain the village's failure to ring after the war.

More obviously interesting were a number of newspaper cuttings. One, from August, 1956, reported a serious car accident on the Usk road. The driver, a Mr. Sidney Bowen of Llantathan, had escaped uninjured but his passenger, 15 year old Tommy Barker, also of Llantathan, was trapped in the burning car and died before help arrived. I put it aside. It was one more confirmation but it didn't take me any further forward.

The other cuttings were from illustrated periodicals, each reporting some event involving a member of the Howells family. Two were obituaries: George in 1921 and his son James, in 1966. Both featured formal studio portraits of the subjects. The remainder, spanning 16 or so years, were all to do with Matthew Howells and the quality of the accompanying photographs was variable. One had certainly been abstracted from a group and another enlarged from a distance shot. But they were all good enough to be recognisable as the same man, and the family likeness was unmistakable. I put the one of James next to the best shot of Matthew: Penelope Vine's husband, and the son she'd only known as a tiny baby. Although his face looked broader than James's, Matthew certainly took after his father, and his grandfather too. The distinctive Vine features: aquiline nose and high forehead, which recurred in portraits at Allington were completely absent.

The stories accompanying the pictures of Matthew were of a society nature. As a rich, enigmatic baronet, he was of interest. Matthew Howells inspects latest tractor at agricultural show. Matthew Howells at London nightclub with mystery beauty. Matthew Howells flies to Europe where he is believed to have extensive business interests. Hmm.

Up to that moment I don't think I'd quite believed in his existence, but I could believe in a man who bought a new tractor and who danced till three in the morning with a laughing, fabulous blonde. That was real, ordinary, believable, though I couldn't imagine dancing with the man in the photograph. I had an impression of self-indulgence but it was, I supposed, an attractive face in its way.

I took the new material home with me. Marina was still in bed. She'd slept for most of the day, felt a bit better and thought she could manage some soup. I gave her the cuttings to look at while I made up a tray for her and when I brought it, she commented on the close resemblance between the three men.

'They're quite good looking,' she said, 'but not nice.'

'Yes, but is that because we expect face to reflect character.'

'It might be.' She picked up the best of the Matthew cuttings. 'Hard and soft at the same time. If I knew nothing at all about him, I still wouldn't like that face.' She put the papers aside and took the tray. 'Oh well, it's hardly evidence.'

Having eaten enough to make me think she really was much better, she turned back to the cuttings, remarking that although the obituaries said little, the snippet about the Howells racing stables in Lincolnshire was interesting. 'The only indication we've seen that he has interests in Britain other than Llantathan.' Then: 'There's something...' She sounded puzzled. 'Stephanie, do you have a magnifying glass around?'

I did, and brought it, watching while she pored over the photographs, examining each one several times. 'Steph, when you first saw these, what did you think? About the family likeness?'

'That it's very pronounced, obviously.'

'Yes...' She lifted her head from her examination of the pictures. 'How closely did you look?'

'Well, not as closely as you're doing.'

She handed me the magnifying glass and the picture of James Howells. 'Look at the left side of his forehead just above the eye. What can you see?'

It took a moment before I was sure that what I saw was not a printing flaw. 'It looks,' I replied, 'as if he had a cut at some time. It's a bit like a glassing scar. She nodded and passed me the picture of George, and then the best of the photographs of Matthew. And then we stared in silence at eachother.

'No...' she breathed at last. 'No. I'm not going to believe it. I *can't* believe it. It just isn't possible.'

'Isn't it? I wonder...'

She was inordinately distressed. I can't say that I was happy but I was excited by the possibility that we'd found the answer. When she fell into an exhausted, troubled sleep I crept down to the study and, after some thought, I phoned John.

'I think we know what it is,' I said, and heard the sharp sound of indrawn breath. Choosing words carefully – we'd long ago agreed not to speak openly on the phone – I went on, 'Marina has flu. She's not at all well.'

'Oh dear. How are you? What are you up to?'

'I'm fine. Just reading Oscar Wilde, and putting up a new picture.' Would he make anything of that? 'What about you? Busy?'

'No. I was only doing the *Mephisto* crossword. Shall I come and cheer you up?'

So he had made the connection!

* * *

I checked on Marina. She looked more peaceful now, but pale, ethereal. 'Asleep,' I told John when he arrived. 'She seems totally washed out.'

'These bugs do that but most of them don't last long.'

'I don't know where she picked it up. No-one else I know has it. She's been run down for a while: since all the trouble started. I was surprised that the well-woman examination didn't throw up anaemia.'

'So, Stephanie,' John said. 'It's Dorian Gray, is it?'

'Sort of. I had to tell you something and that was the nearest allusion I could think of. No, I'm not absolutely sure, but it fits everything. And there are the photographs and what you can see in them. Come into the sitting room and I'll show you.'

I spread them out on the coffee table. 'Yes, I see what you mean,' he murmured. 'What a pity there aren't any of the previous generations.'

'Probably are, but we're unlikely ever to see them.'

I passed him the magnifying glass and waited in silence as he inspected each picture. Finally he looked up and nodded. 'You say that everything fits. Could you give me a rundown, Stephanie?'

'I'll try. I haven't had time to think it through properly so it's a bit rough and ready, but let's suppose that Matthew Howells wanted to go on living. That somehow he made a pact with the devil, and the deal involved the sacrifice of a boy every year on his birthday. He takes to himself the vitality of the boy and it gives him renewed life.

'The photos show that he does age, but when he reappears in the guise of the next heir he's rejuvenated. That must account for the six sacrifices each time a Howells dies. John, we should have realised from that pattern alone what might be going on. Those children died *before* purported Howells deaths. They couldn't have predicted *when* a Howells was going to die.'

'No, but what if they were propitiation sacrifices meant to try to avert death?'

'Hardly, John. You don't go on killing your children in a ritual which doesn't work. And if they were meant to be company on the journey to the afterlife, they would have been killed afterwards.'

I thought for a moment and went on. 'But, leaving that aside, there's Howells' problem of maintaining the appearance of normality. If he's going to reappear as his son and inherit the estate, there has to *be* a son, with witnesses and evidence. Even in the 18th century some records were kept. But no Howells has married within the lifespan of his father. Because I've only got James's age at marriage, I've had to calculate the others from the births of children so they're not accurate but as far as I can tell, none of them married under 40. That fits too. It means that by the time he's ready to stage his death he can come back as a young man.'

'But Stephanie, there are sons. What...' John put his head in his hands. 'He's murdering his own children,' he muttered.

'Yes, I'm afraid he probably is.' I reached over and took his hand. 'John, I don't know what happened to them but according Miss Vine, Pen's son was taken out of the country at the end of the war. Switzerland, she thought, and the journal mentions Switzerland too. I think that's likely. If you're rich enough and you know what you're doing...'

Poor John. He looked so pained, so confused. 'Stephanie, I can't see how anyone could get away with this.'

'Easily, I should think, before there was a real policing system and no forensic science. Especially if you move around a lot and if you marry someone who has no family to enquire, and if you have a complacent clergyman at home to do the necessary. If you have money and power. And John,' I added gently, 'it doesn't stop there. Remember that no Howells ever had any daughter surviving beyond infancy or a wife who lived long after bearing a son. I'm sorry, but there's no getting away from this. He could not afford to let them live: there must be no relations who might discover his secret. And it may be, you know, that this was the price he had to pay.'

'The whole village would appear to know his secret,' John said bitterly.

'Yes. He needs the connivance of the village because he has to have one secure base. Somehow, he tied the twelve families to him at the beginning. What they get out of it I don't know, but it must be worth having. Or they must think it is.'

John shook his head slowly. 'What can be worth this?' How many times we'd all asked that question – and how many more times was I going to hear it?

I said, 'John, I'm in the way of seeing these people as monsters without feelings, but they're not. At least not the women. The other day Mrs. Griffiths was playing with her baby on the lawn. That's not a sight you see often here. It was obvious that she loves her child. And remember Mrs. Pritchard and the others who put flowers on Anne-Marie's grave every week? All these women know what they've had to do, what life has in store for their children. Conditioned and terrorised as they no doubt are, they still experience maternal bonding, so they have to believe that the deaths are necessary.'

John passed his hands over his face. He looked very tired. 'I can see that, Stephanie, but necessary for what?'

I sighed. 'If we're right, all we can say is that it looks like it's for the perpetuation of Howells' life, but I don't think that's the only reason. Marina suggested money but how many women would countenance the murder of children solely for material gain? Or for power? But if you look into the history of religion, you do find many instances where children have been sacrificed to various gods for the good of society. So I suppose a woman *might* give up a child if she thought that by doing so, she was saving her community.'

'Is that what you would do?'

I stood up and went to put a match to the fire. 'No. I'd run with the kids. Which makes me think they're held by more than threats.'

'If Howells has so much power – if he does deal with the devil – then it could be that running would solve nothing.' John was doubtful. 'He may have the ability to strike at a distance.'

'Yes, but aren't there ways of obtaining protection? Anne-Marie must have believed that.'

'Anne-Marie trusted *me*. And even I, knowing how to go about helping her, wasn't quick enough. It isn't a case of running into the nearest church and shouting "Sanctuary". How would you go about it, Stephanie?'

'Deviously,' I replied. I sat down again and curled my feet under me. 'Once I'd decided, I'd make some plan which would allow me time to get myself and the kids as far from Llantathan as possible before I was missed. I might well take sanctuary somewhere – some monastery, say – but what I'd really be doing would be throwing myself on the mercy of God.'

John said nothing. I thought for a moment then went on, 'John, there are lots of things we can't know. We might never be able to discover everything including the nature of Howells' hold on the village. All we can say is that it's there and it's very strong. Strong enough to induce the villagers to do whatever he wants including ensuring that what is or isn't in his family grave is never discovered.'

'Does that matter now?'

'It would be a confirmation. My guess is that all this hostility is directed at getting us out before we stumble on something, but they must still be assuming that we're largely ignorant. Once the Howells grave is opened, though, and if, allowing for a reasonable degree of preservation, we find an unaccountable lack of bones, then whatever they think we do or don't know, they'll expect us to start probing. I must talk to Adam first thing in the morning. We need to work out how to deal with this grave. Oh God, I hope he believes all this!'

'Do you want me to have a word with him first?'

'It might be as well.' I looked up at him. 'You believe it, don't you, John?'

He considered. 'It fits the facts we have. And my instinctive reaction is that you're right. But reason revolts. I don't want to believe it. I don't want to believe that God has allowed such evil to exist and flourish.'

I bit my lip, groping for words. 'Don't imagine that I'm accepting this any easier than you,' I said. 'I'm not, and what keeps tripping me up is the supernatural element. If, instead of this, we'd found that Marina's pagan ritual idea was the truth and that a succession of Howells men had been carrying out these murders to propitiate some obscure god, then although I'd deplore what they were doing, I would be able to understand why. It would still be evil, but evil arising from misguided notions.

'But if the Matthew Howells we expect to arrive in Llantathan in a few weeks is the Matthew Howells who bought the estate in 1755, that brings in a dimension which defies all rationality. The medieval mind could cope with it but we're the products of the age of reason. We may not have killed God but we've certainly abolished the devil and all his works.'

With the fire nicely alight I knelt to add a couple of log segments. Over my shoulder I said, 'I don't want to believe this, John. Marina's scared and so am I.' I dusted my hands on my jeans. 'If Matthew Howells can live for over two hundred years what else can he do? And if he can do it, others can. If he's tapped into a power strong enough to defy death, how are we supposed to stop that?'

'With the help of a greater power we can break the continuity of his filthy ritual.'

'Do you think so? John, what if it doesn't work? What if we thwart him this year and he goes on?'

'Then we go on thwarting him.' John sounded confident now. 'As much as it takes for as long as it takes.'

I reached into my bag for a tissue and blew my nose, trying not to cry. 'When I knew this had to be the explanation, I felt relieved,' I said. 'It all seemed cut and dried. Stop another killing and Howells would disappear in a puff of green smoke, or fall to pieces before our eyes. You know. Like Dracula. Then everything would be all right again. But we've no idea if it will work. It might not matter if he misses a year. Or two or three. And if it doesn't kill him, we'll all be in terrible danger. We've got one shot, John. It's got to be right. We have an advantage now because they don't know how much we've guessed, but as soon as we make a move, we lose it. And what move do we make? There are two boys who might be potential victims. Even if we can protect them isn't he just going to go out and snatch some kid from the streets of Newport?'

'Stephanie dear, don't distress yourself.' John's voice was warm with comfort. 'Listen to me. The records show that there's been a death every year since 1756. Now tell me something. Have any of those boys come from any place but Llantathan parish?'

I shook my head. 'No. Even the first one was registered as a resident in the parish.'

'Exactly. Now doesn't that suggest that boys from elsewhere won't do? Especially when you remember that in the 18th and 19th centuries it would have been so much easier to pick up a boy from a town.'

John was right. How much simpler to avoid awkward questions by luring away an unemployed lad who had gone to the town looking for work. And who would miss him at a time when so many drifted around seeking livings from the coal- and ironmasters? Murdering the sons of his own tenants was a big risk. The fact that he did it with such consistency had to be significant. 'But why?' I demanded. 'Why does it have to be these boys?'

'It could have been one of the conditions laid upon him. Or perhaps he thought that despite the risk he could ensure a constant supply of healthy young males. The towns may have been teeming with potential victims but I wonder how many would have been suitable at a time when there was so much malnutrition and disease. Sacrifices always have to be healthy. These are possibilities but I don't think we're ever going to know a lot of the whys. If we wait until we know everything more lives will be lost. Yes, my dear, I know we take an enormous risk but I will not bury another boy this August.'

Well, I sniffed some more and blew my nose again, and made supper. Marina still slept and John and I talked on until late, discussing ways and means. And, increasingly, I saw the enormity of what we planned.

III

When John left, I knew I ought to go to bed but I was restless and I didn't want to disturb Marina with my wakefulness. There was something niggling at the back of my mind: something about Lincolnshire, but trying to think got me nowhere except more worried so, in the end, I curled up in Marina's chair with *The Bellringers of Monmouth*.

It interested me more than I expected. I read of the long history of bells and how they are cast, hung and tuned; of the development of change ringing and the various, to me incomprehensible, methods: Stedmans, Grandsire, Kent, Norwich.

Superstition attributed to bells power over evil spirits: they rang to frighten the spirits away from newlyweds and drive them from the dying. Even in recent times bells were named and consecrated and, sometimes, anointed. Occasionally they had been 'baptised': sprinkled with holy water, clothed in white and decked with garlands of flowers.

Apart from changes, bells could be rung singly or in pairs to inform the community of important events. The best known examples, I found, were the passing bell and the tailors – or tellers – rung on the tenor bell. The passing bell tolled when a parishioner lay dying, and the strokes of the tailors: nine for a man, six for a woman and three for a child, followed by one for each year, announced the status and age of the newly dead. In the 19th century it was, apparently, still believed that until the tailors had been rung the soul could not leave the body. For these solemn reasons the tenor bell's inscription was often a reminder of mortality.

Examples of famous bells and their details were less interesting so I turned to the chapter on Llantathan. There, the book said, the angelus bell of the Augustinian priory, given by Reynald Devigne in 1131, was the earliest known. I sat up. This was something new: the first time I'd come across the Devigne family in the medieval period. I'd made a point of looking out for the name and its variants and though there were plenty of references from the 16th century on, when it had become Vine, I hadn't, so far, been able to substantiate the family tradition of Norman origins in Llantathan. This looked good if I could trace the source of the reference.

I read on. Some of it I already knew. Some looked useful provided I could check it. I reached for the morning paper, tore off some edge strips to mark pages and yawned, and skimmed through a familiar account of the Dissolution. Then, yawning again, I launched into an account of the rise of change ringing in Llantathan.

In 1799 Hubert Vine celebrated his marriage to Miss Henrietta Cavendish by causing the angelus bell donated by his ancestor to be recast. The new bell became the treble of the first ring of eight at St. Michael's, a tenor bell having been given by the Cavendish family. The new bells were, however, the cause of a fracas in the village when the lord of the manor refused to allow the bells to be rung...

I rubbed my eyes and blinked. 1799? That couldn't be right. The trouble over the bell had been in 1952. I read the paragraph again, frowned, read on. *Thereafter, although St. Michael's retains its ring of eight, the teams have rung only on the middle six, excluding the treble and tenor...*

I skipped some stuff about the technicalities of this, and some more about method, and reached the 20th century, discovering that six of the bells had rung a peal to celebrate the end of the First World War and that ringing had continued until 1939. OK. I knew that.

After the war, however, it was discovered that the timbers of the belfry had become infested with death watch beetle and ringing ceased...

How very prosaic, I thought. And in those days, there wouldn't have been the money around to put it right.

An attempt was made to revive ringing in 1952 when the treble bell was again recast at the instigation of Arthur Vine who was also responsible for the restoration of the belfry and tower. The new bell was consecrated at a special service but history repeated itself when the owner of the Llantathan estate objected to ringing. Ringers invited to the church had intended to give a peal of Kent Treble Bob Major but were turned away by the rector, the Rev. Arthur Blayney. It is a curious fact that while St. Michael's possesses what must be a ring of outstanding quality, it has never been fully heard. No ringing now takes place at Llantathan but the bells are maintained in working order by the Vine family and we must hope that...

A sudden noise made me jump: I'd dozed off and dropped the book. I felt cold and stiff and the fire had gone out.

In the morning Marina was still sleeping when I got up. I showered and dressed and went back to her. She opened her eyes, attempted a smile and asked for a glass of water.

I brought it and asked her to let me send for the doctor.

She shook her head. 'It's only flu,' she whispered. 'Better soon.'

I left her to sleep again and went downstairs. No work today. I couldn't leave her like that. Only I'd have to. I needed to see Adam. Oh hell!

Two cups of coffee cleared my brain sufficiently for me to make decisions, and I phoned John. Would he sit with Marina for an hour or so? Yes, by all means, but not until 11.

I filled in the time with some overdue ironing, looking in on Marina at intervals, but she didn't wake. By the time John arrived her face had lost some of its hectic colour and she felt cooler. Perhaps she was over the worst.

Adam was checking context sheets in the dining room at the rectory: the unit's temporary H.Q. 'Hang on a minute, Stephanie.' Cross-referencing, he flicked through the files, then: 'OK. Let's go for a walk.' He locked up and we crossed to the site to hand over the keys to Joyce Sanderson, the finds supervisor. Then we headed for the ramparts, away from possible eavesdroppers.

As we paced the track I went over the theory. He'd already heard it from John and I was prepared for disbelief: Adam could accept the murders but never, I thought, would he believe that the murderer was over 200 years old. He did, though, and with none of the conflict the rest of us experienced.

'It is a bit mind-stretching,' he admitted, 'but the evidence suggests that he's done it. The fact that *I've* never come across it doesn't mean it can't be done. I've never come across a pygmy shrew but I believe they exist.'

I laughed. 'Well, there is good evidence for shrews.'

'There's evidence for this too. Plenty of medieval accounts. And later. The only difference between this and shrews is that believing in them doesn't cause conflicting feelings and fear. There's no reason not to believe in shrews but who would choose to believe this?'

'I don't think we can do otherwise.'

'Nor do I. Not unless you've made some mammoth cock-up with the data and that's even harder to believe. So you think we're going to open the Howells grave and find a shortage of stiffs?'

We'd stopped by one of the remaining portions of the medieval wall. Brambles had all but taken it over and it looked in danger of crumbling. What consolidation had been done in the past hadn't been particularly effective. Adam lit a cigarette.

'Yes, that's what I think,' I told him. 'There are burial records for three male adults who, if the wording on the headstone is to be believed, should all be in that grave. If I'm right, they won't be.'

We walked on in silence for a while. 'You realise that we might not find them anyway?' he said. 'Preservation's very variable.'

I frowned, bothered by something. 'Adam, Bert Tudor is the sexton. He must know about the soil conditions and how variable preservation is. It's so variable that kicking up a row and putting Llantathan in the spotlight wouldn't be worth it. There has to be something they know that we don't. Something that would tell us that the bodies were never there in the first place.'

'A bit speculative, Steph, but I see what you mean. Well, if you are right, the excavation's safe until we move into Area G.'

'That's the part with the Howells grave? How long before you have to?'

'Beginning of July, but it depends. I can move on to the southern strip which should indicate another side of the cloister, or Area G which I hope will demonstrate the junction of the western cloister range and the church.' Everything adjacent to the south wall of the church has to be cleared anyway because of the problems with the damp and the foundations.'

'Given the choice what will you do?'

Adam had no doubts. 'Area G,' he replied. 'It'll give me the best return as things stand now.'

'OK. So no worries for the time being, but when you do start on Area G, can you leave the Howells grave until the very last?'

He shook his head. 'It's within the area we're clearing back for the damp problem. Why is it so important, Stephanie?'

'Because once we know about the missing bodies, they'll move against us. The longer we can keep our heads down, the better.'

Adam wasn't sure but he suggested opening up a much smaller patch where he wanted to clarify the relationship of some wall footings. 'There's something odd there and I think we've got traces of an earlier structure. That would mean another week or so before we do anything serious around the Howells plot.'

'Would you?' I pleaded.

'If you really believe it'll help. But that won't engage the whole team. I'll have to put some of them into Area G to start the preliminary work.'

I heard the church clock strike the quarter. 'We'd better go back. Look Adam, shall we discuss it with John and Marina? There are a lot of things to decide.'

'Sure. When?'

'As soon as Marina's well enough. I'll let you know.'

We turned and began to retrace our steps. 'Is Marina very bad? John said it was just a flu bug.'

'That's what it looks like.'

He stopped, kicked the toe of his boot at a tuft of thistles, seemed about to say something but didn't and we went back, he to check the site and I to Vine Villa, hoping to find Marina improved.

She was: sitting up in bed with tea and toast. But my relief didn't blind me to a curious tension I felt from John. 'I must go now,' he said and I followed him downstairs. 'I'm due to see Angela about tomorrow.'

Miss Vine's funeral. I'd forgotten.

'All that sleep must have done some good,' I remarked. 'She's a lot better.'

'Stephanie...' He stood in the sitting room, car keys dangling from his fingers. 'After you left, she became much worse. She was delirious. Rather like those nightmares.'

'But she seems fine now. John, what are you saying? What happened?'

'I sat with her and prayed. I... er... took certain steps and the... affliction went. She woke and as far as I could tell, she was perfectly well again.'

'What steps?' I stared at him in bewilderment.

'Marina hasn't been suffering from flu.'

My mind raced. 'Possession?' I whispered. I felt cold.

'No. Not possession. I'm almost certain that someone has been interfering with her mind.'

'How?'

'I've no idea. I've read about such things but I've had no experience.'

'What steps, John? What did you do?'

'Prayed, mostly.' He looked very embarrassed. 'As an Anglican priest I'm not supposed to believe that objects... crosses... relics... have any intrinsic power against evil. They're just symbols. But... well... A friend brought me a souvenir, a bottle of Jordan water from the Holy Land. It's been in my car for ages. So I blessed it and sprinkled her with it.'

'And it worked.'

He sighed. 'All this is turning my notions of faith upside down. I need to think.'

'Yes, of course.' I tried to sound soothing. 'Will it be a permanent effect?'

'I don't know. In case it isn't I've left the bottle on your dressing table.'

'But would it work for me? It's really faith, isn't it?'

He smiled wanly. 'You'd think so. But when I did it, it was desperation.'

'Does Marina know?'

'Some of it. Stephanie, I'll come back this evening with Adam if that's all right. There's a lot we need to discuss.'

I watched him walk to his car. This was doing him no good at all. He looked permanently tired; older too, and the grey in his hair hadn't been there last year.

Closing the door I stood in the hall trying to assimilate this latest development as the sound of John's car faded. The engine sounded clattery: no doubt he'd forgotten to do a service recently. Hardly surprising. An unposted letter on the hall table told me that I was forgetting routine things too.

Could anyone do what John had suggested? Interfere with Marina's mind at a distance and to the point where she became physically ill? It was as difficult to come to terms with as Matthew Howells' longevity. Worse. The possibility raised a flourish of questions and I had no answers. I don't know enough, I thought. I can't cope unless I *know*. I sat down on the stairs and, frightened, I began to cry.

* * *

Later, when Marina had had a bath and come downstairs looking as if she'd never had a day's illness in her life, we sat in the kitchen with coffee and walnut fudge cake. She said, 'John told you, didn't he?

'Yes, but...'

'I knew before, love. It's all part of trying to get us out of Llantathan. The vandalism and abuse... that was unpleasant but it stopped pretty quickly. Why bother with that if, as John thinks, you can interfere with a person's mind to such an extent. I've been trying to fight it but I think I would have died today but for John. What did he do, exactly? He was rather vague when I asked him.'

When I told her she said she had more faith in his prayers than a bottle of water.'

'So have I,' I agreed, 'but the fact that it did work upset him a lot.'

'I bet.' She dabbed up cake crumbs on her finger. 'So where do we go from here, Steph?'

'John's coming with Adam this evening,' I replied. No decisions until we've talked everything through.'

'Does John know about Matthew Howells? The photos... the scar?' she asked.

'I told him,' I said. 'And he thinks it's probable. So does Adam. What about you?'

'I've got no option but to accept it. It's all of a piece. I can't deny the reality of what they've done to me. If one's possible, so is the other.'

IV

Adam arrived first saying that John would be along shortly. 'Some old guy on one of the farms. Never goes to church or anything but now he's got bronchitis and thinks it's a judgment for his sins.'

John told us more. 'Old Albert,' he said, settling himself into a chair. 'He's a bit of a fraud. No, he's not seriously ill. But,' his smile faded, 'He's Robbie McArthur's grandfather. Visiting Albert means that I'm getting to know the family. It could be helpful.'

It could. Robbie was 15 and one of the two possibilities – the other was Nathan Clough – Howells could choose from come August. John's introduction into the household was one small point in our favour. If only he could get into the Clough house.

'I'm working on it,' he assured us. 'I'm giving Mrs. Clough a lift into Caldicot tomorrow afternoon.'

Settled with drinks and a snack supper, we showed Adam the photographs. 'You're right,' he said. 'It looks remarkably like a glassing scar.' And then we talked, wasting no time on whether we believed that Matthew Howells and his ancestors were one and the same person. We did, and that was a relief of sorts. It meant that we were all, at least theoretically, prepared for an encounter with an opposition which might use supernatural forces.

'Which has already been done,' John pointed out, nodding at Marina. 'We countered that successfully but there's no knowing whether they'll try again.'

'How do they do it?' I appealed to John. 'And who does it? Is it Howells, or someone in the village?'

'I don't know,' he said. How I hated that statement! 'We can only accept that it can be done and we must bear in mind that someone other than Howells must have enough ability to use supernatural means. After all, Marina's nightmares started months ago.'

'Yes, but this is Howells,' Adam said flatly.

'Any particular reason?' Marina wanted to know.

'He's back.'

That made us sit up. 'Since when?' I demanded.

'Not sure. I noticed a car outside the Hall last week. It wasn't one I knew so I did a bit of snooping and watching. I managed to get close enough today after work to overhear someone talking to the gardener and from what he said there's no doubt.'

'This is very early for him. Does it mean a change in the pattern?' John wondered, but Adam shook his head. 'Not from what I heard. The guy was saying Howells was back to sort out some business problems.'

'I don't think I like the sound of that,' I said.

'No,' John agreed, 'but we might be jumping to conclusions. One would assume that Howells does have business difficulties sometimes.'

It was a good try, but even John didn't really believe his own optimism, and Adam wiped it out completely when he pointed out that the start of Marina's illness coincided pretty well with Howells' return.

For some time there was silence as we absorbed this. Taken with what had happened to Marina, I could only see it as the marshalling of the big battalions. Adam looked none too happy either.

'So how can we protect ourselves?' he wanted to know. 'If Howells has come back to take mental pot-shots at us, what do we do? Sprinkle each other with Jordan water?'

John looked uncomfortable. 'There's so much I don't understand,' he said quietly. 'If I'd happened to be a Catholic, I'd probably have a lot less difficulty with this. But as an Anglican I have, or am supposed to have, no belief in the ability of crosses, medallions, holy water, relics or even the Communion bread and wine to protect, cure or in any way alter man's condition. They're just symbols. Faith is all, and the use of objects is little better than shamanism.'

'Yet look what happened when you sprinkled Marina,' I said.

'I know. And it's causing me a great deal of worry. For one thing, it shouldn't have worked. For another, I should never have thought of it. Water, even if it was from the river Jordan, which I doubt, shouldn't be able to accomplish what faith cannot.'

'Not in itself,' Marina agreed. 'But maybe God, aware of your weakness, used the water as a channel for his power. Isn't it possible? God can, after all, use anything he wants.'

John smiled. He always enjoyed Marina's theological forays. 'You mean that God could allow symbols to work like magnifying glasses for weak faith?'

'Yes. Why not?'

'There could be a psychological angle,' Adam put in. 'Think about all those Dracula films where Peter Cushing shrivels Christopher Lee with a cross. Does it work because Dracula believes it works? If you believe an object or an action will harm you avoid it.'

'Hmm. Yes. Phobias. Something evil would have an inordinate fear of a symbol of good. There might be something in it,' John agreed. 'But it rather depends on whether Dracula is based on real laws of action and reaction or whether Bram Stoker made it all up.'

'Well, the vampire does have a history,' I said. 'Whether you believe it is another matter. Shrews again, Adam.'

He laughed. Marina and John looked bemused. While Adam explained I went round closing curtains and switching lamps on. It was dark enough now to justify what had become routine at our gatherings.

'Anyway,' I said, sitting down again, 'if it is faith, is it the faith of the individual? John, you blessed the water, didn't you? As a priest you made it sort of official. So did you, in doing that, somehow join your faith to the faith of the Church Eternal? Because, if so, that's an entirely different matter. It's faith on another plane.'

Adam looked blank while Marina appeared to be contemplating the contents of her glass. What she thought of the Church Eternal I never knew, but John left us in no doubt as to his views.

He leaned back and proceeded to give us the theology of the Church Eternal: that innumerable host of Christians from the beginning to the end of time: dead, living and as yet unborn; whose faith exists eternally and in perfection. 'Difficult to grasp,' he said, 'but just about possible if you can accept that eternity has no past, present or future. So, in eternity, the first Christians are happily coexisting with those who will witness the end of the world. And every Christian now alive is there too. *And...*,' here John paused, laughing a little because Adam was so obviously agonised, '...and they always have been there and always will be.'

'Try thinking of it as a parallel universe, Adam,' Marina murmured helpfully.

'Thanks,' he muttered, unconvinced. And: 'All right, John. So you've got this endless, timeless congregation out there on some plane waving palms and singing hymns. What good is that to us?'

'It's the real Church,' John said. 'The Church perfected. And, being perfect, its power is infinite. What does it mean for us? It means, I trust, that the perfect faith of the Church can be called on by all temporal Christians. Yes, Stephanie, perhaps you've got something. Perhaps it wasn't the Jordan water but faith after all. Not mine, but the faith of the saints. Though Marina's magnifying glass idea is just as possible.'

Having worked this out – whether it was true or not – John seemed happier. Not so Adam. This was one shrew in which he couldn't believe. He refilled his glass. 'That's fine for you three. But what about me? I'm not a Christian. I'm not anything. You know that.'

'Nor am I,' Marina countered. 'Not in any accepted sense. Steph is, sort of, but hardly committed. We are, therefore, all heading for hell. Isn't that so, John?'

John nodded. 'According to scripture and the teachings of the Church, if you do not accept Christ as your saviour then, yes, you are damned.'

Marina objected to that. 'If salvation is only through Christ, what about all the people who lived before his message and all those who've never heard it? What about babies who die? All damned because they never even had a chance?' You can't say that and then claim that God is a loving father! And,' she glared at John, well and truly going now, 'don't give me all that crap about God moving in mysterious ways and his ways not being man's. If he wants men to follow him then he'd better make his way plain from the start and not change the map halfway through. This is life, not a bloody magical mystery tour.'

John was amused. 'The Church can refute everything you've said, Marina, but its answers often sound pretty empty even to me. No, personally, I don't believe that anyone who does God's work is damned whatever their faith or lack of it.'

'All right,' Adam said. 'So we're OK and God's OK. What next? Do we go on as we are, or do we try to make them show their hand?'

'How? By concentrating on the Howells grave?' I asked.

'Look, I told you, Stephanie, that there'll come a point when I have to do it regardless,' he said. 'I can delay it a bit, but unless something entirely unforeseen happens, that grave will be excavated well before the 8th of August. If you don't want that, I suggest that John starts praying for snow.'

'Considering that you're absolutely paranoid about vandalism on site,' Marina said, 'you seem remarkably keen to invite it, Adam.' She leaned forward to take the cigarette he offered. Behind her back John threw me an amused glance: trust Marina to point out contradictions, it said.

Adam glared. 'I may want to invite it, but I've no intention of letting it happen,' he snapped.

'I don't see now, if our hypothesis is correct, you can avoid it once you focus attention on that grave.' Marina was unruffled.

'I agree,' John contributed. 'You can't watch over the site every minute of every day.'

Adam knew that but he was on the defensive and likely to explode. Time, I thought, to put in my two penn'orth. 'What about stalling tactics? Adam, if you put up interim reports on the church notice board, Pryce will read them even if no-one else does. Rundowns of work done and what you plan to do next.'

'I get it,' he said thoughtfully. 'When we do start on Area G, we tell them that although we're going to be removing the gravestones and stripping back, excavation's a slow process and we don't expect to start exhuming before whenever... Yes, it might work. That's if we want to go on playing softly, softly.'

'It gives us something of a choice,' I stressed. 'Especially if you can make it sound and look as if you won't be excavating the Howells plot until well into August. Don't screen anything until you have to and use that small area you mentioned to emphasise the impression that you're in no great hurry to get into Area G. I think they'll hold off if you do that, but you'll still have the option of moving in on the grave if it seems the right thing to do.'

'I suppose it's the best thing we can do,' he conceded, still obviously dissatisfied.

We ended up with a compromise. We would go on as before with Adam delaying work on Area G as long as possible, and posting interim reports, but if pressure of any sort was increased, he would, as he inaccurately put it, go for the bones. Meanwhile, John would continue to ingratiate himself with the McArthurs and the Cloughs. That way he might at least get a clue as to which boy Howells wanted. Then, perhaps, we could find a way of getting him out of Llantathan. If not...

'If not, we'll have to snatch him and hang onto him until it's too late,' Adam said. 'Maybe both kids because if they can't get hold of one, they'll go for the other.'

'You make it sound so easy,' I complained. 'We walk up to this kid and grab him, or worse, we drag him away from Pritchard or Powell or whoever. Just like that. A kid who won't want to go with us but who will most likely want to go to whatever little get-together he's being lured to. Supposing we do that. Supposing Neil Griffiths isn't there to arrest us for kidnapping, where can we go? We'd never outrun them. None of our cars could outrun a pair of roller skates. And they might not even have to chase us. A bit of mind-bending and they've got us. So at the very best, we can only hole up in the village and I don't imagine that either this house or the rectory could withstand a siege.'

'No, but the church could,' John offered. 'The fabric's proof against anything except bombs and bulldozers.'

'Yes, that's true,' I agreed. 'And the fact that it is a church may help.'

'Just how secure is it?' Marina wanted to know.

He considered. 'The only weak points are the vestry door, the boiler room door and the windows.'

'Not so bad,' Marina said. 'We can deal with that.'

By the end of the evening we had a rough plan. If both boys couldn't be got out of Llantathan we would – somehow – get them into the church. We would barricade ourselves in the tower and this would allow us to retreat to the ringing chamber and, if necessary, to the bell room. As Marina pointed out, we would have all the advantages of medieval castle defenders. All we'd need to do would be to hold out until the team arrived next morning.

Adam made a list. Bolts and bars, 'And I can electrify the window grilles. No more lethal than a cattle prod, but a good deterrent.' And, because I was worried about being trapped by fire in the belfry, he agreed to rig up a system of ropes to get us down to ground level.

'John, I know you don't care for all this,' Marina said, 'but it may save lives. Call it sanctuary if you like. We won't use more force than is necessary but you must understand that if we have to, we will use considerable force. They won't hesitate to damage us so we have to be prepared to damage them to keep those boys safe. Whatever it takes.'

'I understand, Marina,' he said quietly.

'One other thing,' I added. 'The aftermath. What's going to happen if we don't succeed? And what if we do?'

V

The decisions we'd made were good as far as they went, but I fell asleep feeling as if I was embarking on a complicated journey to an uncertain destination with out of date maps, conflicting guide books and inadequate baggage. By any standards we had to be out of our minds, yet if we were to prevent another murder, we had no choice. But I slept well and felt better when I woke to the distant sound of Marina clattering breakfast things in the kitchen. I peered out of the window. Hazy, but it was going to be another fine day. Miss Vine's funeral day.

After breakfast we dressed as soberly as our wardrobes would allow and, remembering that we had to go to Allington later, we went down in the car.

There was still work to be done in St. Michael's, but there had been a simple ceremony of reconsecration the week before and, for now, the workmen were gone. John met us at the church door, his white surplice fluttering a little in the breeze. 'Adam will be here in a minute or two,' he said. He stepped from the porch to look up at the clock. 9.25.

As John moved forward the modest cortège pulled into the layby in front of the gate. Just the black motor hearse, the sun glinting wickedly on the flawless polish of its bodywork, and one car.

We watched as the coffin was carried through the gate. Angela in a plain black coat, a neat hat set on her curly hair, followed with a tall, thin man who might have been about fifty. The little procession passed us, out of the sunshine and into the shadows beyond the porch. From the interior came quiet music: *Jesu, Joy of Man's Desiring*. John had managed to borrow an organist from a neighbouring parish. Marina, Adam and I straggled into a pew three or four rows from the front.

The coffin: plain, small and unadorned, rested on the bier before the chancel steps. Angela, her back very straight, stood at the front with the unknown man. I supposed he must be the solicitor. Just the five of us, and John, to witness this passing ritual for the last of an ancient line. The music ended and the service began.

...in the midst of life we are in death... How little we believe that! Even then, in Llantathan where death was an invited guest; even then I didn't believe it. Do we ever? I felt both glad and sad – that I had known Imogen Vine, but had never had the chance to know her well. I was sad too for John and Angela, and grateful for Miss Vine's kindness to us. But many of my thoughts were wholly conventional: she was old and ill, and my high-heeled shoes hurt.

Angela welcomed us to Allington and one by one we exchanged a few words with her as we passed from the hall to the breakfast room where a buffet had been laid out. She thanked us all, expressing her particular gratitude to John for everything he'd done. 'Now,' she finished, 'Mr. Curtis will read the will. No, no, Adam!'

Adam had made excusing gestures but he was persuaded to sit down with us. 'I feel like an eavesdropper,' he grumbled softly to me.

From a shabby briefcase Mr. Curtis produced a document tied with pink tape. Without haste he unfastened the bow and opened the stiff folds of the engrossment. He said, 'Miss Vine finalised this will not long before she died and it represents her wishes as to the disposal of her estate. It was drawn up after much consultation with me, and with Miss Morton. I confess that I found some of the reasons for the disposition of the estate somewhat surprising...'

Oh dear, I thought, it is the cats' home after all, and he doesn't like it. But then the solicitor smiled at us and added, 'However, I have long been aware of Miss Vine's determination to pursue her cultural interests in spite of her infirmities. Moreover, she placed a high value on loyalty and friendship and she was a generous woman who enjoyed giving pleasure to her friends. So...'

He began to read the preamble, again without haste. I waited with vague interest. If not the cats' home, what?

The first surprise was the extent of Miss Vine's property and wealth. As expected, Angela received a bequest, but the size of it made me blink. She was also to have the London house and its contents. Her face told me that this was no news to her. There was mention of retired servants, and a sum to be held in trust for the maintenance of the church bells. Mr. Curtis paused. That couldn't be it, I thought. What about Allington? Vine Villa? Then: 'To my dear friend John Martin Holmes...' I felt Marina stir. Adam turned his head and we all watched John's face as he became possessed of Miss Vine's main property, Allington, and its contents, together with the associated estate, and the sum of two million pounds net.

Angela beamed: she was fond of John. He looked completely dumbfounded. 'I expected a token,' he said later. 'Not this.'

Mr. Curtis had paused again. Now he coughed to regain our attention and dropped another bombshell. 'To my friends Stephanie Margaret Hargreaves and Marina Judith Graham jointly I leave my house known as Vine Villa, the properties known as Eastwood Farm and Pentre Farm, and the sum of one million pounds each net in recognition of their valuable services to local history and the community...'

Shock is shock whether it's nasty or nice, and I felt the blood drain from my face as Mr. Curtis moved on to his next surprise.

'To the Hafren College of Higher Education I leave the sum of five hundred thousand pounds net for the purpose of establishing and maintaining an efficient local history archive. It is my wish that this project shall be under the direction of the said Stephanie Margaret Hargreaves and of Adam Pembury. I further bequeath the sum of one million pounds net to Adam Pembury personally, together with my house known as Cavendish Hall and its associated estate situated near Caleby in the county of Lincoln in recognition of his work in local archaeology and in gratitude for his kindness...'

There were predecease clauses and something about the residue but I don't think any of us heard it properly. Later, when the will was executed, we, the beneficiaries, found ourselves further enriched by the division of that residue.

Curtis folded the engrossment and relaxed. He told us that Miss Vine had made more than adequate provision to ensure that we were in no way burdened with Capital Transfer Tax and then he remarked that perhaps we would all benefit from a glass of sherry.

'I must say that I never knew Miss Vine took such an interest in local history and archaeology,' I heard him say to John.

Angela pressed sandwiches on us and nodded at the girl who had come in to dispense tea and coffee. Adam pulled at his tie. 'Can we smoke in here?' he whispered.

I glanced round and saw ashtrays on a side table. 'Yes, please do,' Angela said in reply to my request. 'I can see that Adam is very surprised, but I do hope he's pleased.'

'I'm sure he is. We never imagined this.' I hardly knew what to say but she seemed to understand. She patted my arm. 'Miss Vine had her reasons. She knew what she was about. Now go and give Adam his ashtray. He's beginning to look desperate.'

As the shock started to wear off, constraint eased. We talked, made some inroads into the buffet and tried to collect our wits. Adam said nothing. Knowing, as I did, the financial limitations of archaeology I wondered how he felt now.

'I can't believe this,' Marina murmured under cover of the general chat.

'I can't get my head round the amounts,' I responded.

'No. But, Steph, I'm pleased for John. He'll need this house.'

I looked a question.

'He won't stay in the Church,' she opined. 'I think he's more at odds with it than he's showing.'

There was no opportunity to discuss that. Curtis came to congratulate us, offering assistance, should we need it, to deal with these legacies. 'We'll need it,' Marina said later. 'What on earth will we do with two farms?'

The journey back was rather tense, the mood strange. We wanted to talk but were, I think, too overwhelmed to know what to say, let alone how to say it. Does anyone ever know how to react to gifts that come through a death?

Marina and I had a quiet evening pottering in the garden and, over supper, we played around with the idea of a holiday. In August or September. Afterwards...

Then, quietly but with utter conviction, Marina told me that she wanted to be baptised and confirmed into the Anglican communion. 'I still hold to my belief that no one religion has a monopoly of the truth,' she said. 'But I just feel that this is something I have to do.'

Was it, I wondered, a way of avoiding the implications of her Jewish heritage? 'No. I am what I was born. I had no choice about that and I accept it, but I can choose this, and I do. And, yes, John knows.'

And so, after several instruction sessions with John, Marina was baptised. Then, by special arrangement with his bishop, John took her to Newport Cathedral to be confirmed on Ascension Day. Adam and I were there, both of us a little bemused but, as Adam said, nothing much surprised us anymore. John, delighted, took us all out for lunch afterwards. He presented Marina with a prayer book and the first rose from the Ena Harkness bush in his garden, and came the nearest I'd ever seen him to being drunk.

* * *

At home, we enjoyed the remains of a rare sunny day. The exceptionally fine weather of April hadn't lasted and May had been patchy. Tomorrow it would be June. We sat outside until the light faded and Marina said she thought she would go to bed.

'You're tired?' I asked anxiously.

Her eyes danced. 'Not at all.' Her smile was an invitation, a provocation. Something missed for so long. In the gathering dusk she was a ghost again, a lovely, laughing ghost, her pale oval face a compulsion. 'Oh Marina...' I said softly, and went to her.

Marina had put John's rose in a bud vase on her bedside table. Its scent filled the room but already the petals were falling.

'Nothing lives forever,' she murmured.

'Nothing?'

'Perhaps... love...'

'Do you love me, Marina?'

She gathered the rose petals and crushed them in her hands. 'Yes, I love you,' she replied. 'You'll never know how much. Oh God, Stephanie!' As she turned to me the broken petals fell like crimson confetti unheeded from her fingers. 'I never thought so much love was possible. I never thought I could keep you. I never want it to end.'

Marina... filling my heart, my mind... My pale ghost, warm with life, sweeping me from the world on the tide of her love. Hands, rose-scented, halted time with their touch. Reality was here and now in the softness of her body and the caress of her fingers. Reality was the red, swelling flood of need which, breaking its bounds, bore us, lost and beyond control, to some strange, unknown, eternal place. And all I knew was an exquisite blending of love and passion so sweet that it might have been pain.

Poets talk of oneness with the beloved. How many, I wonder, have ever truly experienced it? That night I was no-one and everyone. I was the dark and the night, the moon and the garden. I was the rose and the essence of the rose, infinity and eternity, earth and the universe. And I was Marina.

I remember falling asleep in utter contentment. At that moment Llantathan didn't exist. I felt unassailable. Nothing could touch me; nothing could hurt me. Then, when I woke... I knew. As soon as I saw her, I knew it was too late.

* * *

The alarm dragged me from a sleep as heavy and clinging as treacle. I was cold and the sheet, crumpled beneath me, felt clammy. With my head informing me that it would soon start to ache, I struggled into a dressing gown, supposing vaguely that it must have been the wine we'd had at supper, on top of the lunchtime drinks.

Marina, curled up like a baby, still slept. I put my hand on her shoulder. Cold. Dreadfully cold. I called her name and shook her until her damp hair flew. A sound, very faint, and a trace of movement. I felt relief, then the quick escalation of fear, and I ran for the phone.

Let her be all right. Please. *Please!* I prayed frantically as I waited for John to answer. When he did, I was almost incoherent. He made sense of it, ascertained that I'd called 999 and promised to come as soon as he could. 'The Jordan water, Steph!' he said before I hung up. I raced back upstairs.

She lay exactly as I'd left her, cold, yet drenched with sweat; the marks of my fingers on her shoulder were mauve against her white skin. For a moment or two, as I showered the Jordan water on her, I believed that I would see a miracle, that she would wake, sit up and smile. She never moved.

Forcing calm into my mind and my hands, I felt for a pulse, listened to her heart and caught the faintest movement of breath. She seemed colder by the second. I dragged the counterpane from the foot of the bed and wrapped it round us both, trying to warm her against my body. And I prayed with the repeated words of abject desperation.

John arrived, dishevelled and scared and, almost simultaneously, the ambulance. I was detached from Marina and made to tell what I could before John drew me gently to the window. Time distorted as we watched the crew trying to get some response. It seemed to take an age yet everything rushed past me like a train. One of the paramedics beckoned. I returned to the bedside and looked down at her, hardly hearing what was being said. Something about hospital, about possible heart failure. He faded into the background and John took his place. Gently he held Marina's hand and began to pray, his voice no more than a whisper.

My fingers rested on her arm. I was beyond praying then. I heard the distant clatter as a stretcher was unshipped from the ambulance. Footsteps on the stairs. Slowly I bent and kissed her. And walked out of the room where rose petals still lay like splashes of blood.

In a little while they would come and tell me what I already knew. Nothing lives forever. Once I might have said that love goes on though we do not, and I might have quoted Dylan Thomas. Now? No. Marina was dead, and all her love died with her.

John took me back to the rectory. A doctor came, said things I don't remember and left a prescription for sedatives. Tea was put before me and removed untouched. I sat in the kitchen, still in my dressing gown, and learned that if joy can seem infinite, despair is boundless.

VI

There were things to do, to arrange. People to inform. John and Adam, hardly less shocked than I, carried out a multitude of tasks which, in the first couple of days, I couldn't begin to tackle.

But funeral arrangements couldn't be made until I had a death certificate and that had to wait until after the post-mortem on the Monday. Adam and John did their best to distract my thoughts from that but neither their efforts nor the sedatives could stop the mental images. I slept little, and fitfully. My dreams appalled me but waking to granite truth was worse.

The result of the post-mortem was clear: sudden, massive heart failure. Natural causes. Heart trouble? How could that be? How could she not know that? She who, only a week or two before, had been pronounced perfectly fit, for the second time, by the well-woman clinic?

Mistakes somewhere, but Adam's vociferous anger and John's gentler though obvious disbelief scared me. Hadn't Marina herself had believed that they were trying to kill her? Hadn't John thwarted an earlier attempt? 'No,' I contradicted. 'The clinic must have missed something. Mixed up her tests. The post-mortem result was unequivocal.' If it hadn't been, if nothing had been found, all doubt would have evaporated, but I had another two days of misery to endure before I was able to find relief in rage.

The night before we buried her, Marina's body rested in its simple pine coffin at the foot of the chancel steps in St. Michael's. In a letter stating her wishes, given to John as one of her executors, she'd requested an Anglican burial at St. Michael's with John officiating. 'You'd think this was the last place she would have wanted,' Adam said but John shook his head and read a bit of the letter, in which she wrote that in spite of the problems, her loved ones, her friends, her happiness: all were here.

Dealing with the undertaker was an ordeal I coped with only by being brisk, businesslike: brushing aside his professional sympathy. Knowing that Marina deplored ostentation, I chose a plain coffin and stipulated no fuss or frills, no cortège or bearers. All I required, I said, was that she should be dressed in the silk nightgown I'd made for her: 'Not one of those hideous plastic shrouds' and that the coffin was to be taken to St. Michael's. 'Before that,' I said, 'before you close the coffin, I'll come and see her.'

And so, in what they called a chapel of rest, I gazed down at her dead, bloodless face. This was the body which, warm and living, had given me the greatest joy I'd ever known. There is nothing deader than dead. Nor so utterly unreachable. If, in looking at all I now had of her, I hoped to grasp again some shred of what she'd been, I was disappointed. What I saw had less reality than a cheap plaster effigy.

How long did I stand there in the cool, deadened quiet, in the muted sunlight filtering through the coloured glass of a small, high window? I don't know, nor do I recall much of what I thought. I rearranged the drapery to uncover her mottled hands: hands which had given me hot coffee on a snowy morning, and tea in a Gloucester attic. Hands which had lifted strands of my hair, written cards, held my hands, caressed, clung, comforted.

Into those hands, waxen, stiff and cold, I forced a few crimson roses from John's garden. It looked as contrived and as trite as any sentimental image of St. Theresa, but I found I didn't care. She died amid red rose petals. Let her be buried with red roses. Let all the red roses in the world go with her to the grave. I would never see another without remembering.

In all the time I looked at her that afternoon I felt little, but those overblown crimson blooms drifting their sweet, heavy scent into the still air had more power than the dead thing I came to see. I couldn't weep over this travesty of my darling, but the roses... the memory of that last night... All the way back to Llantathan in John's car, tears ran unheeded down my face onto hands clenched tight around a few broken petals.

* * *

I didn't know what to do with myself. Adam sat with me in awkward silences punctuated by equally awkward snatches of conversation. 'Would it help to go into the church,' he suggested once, and flinched at the look I threw at him.

'Why? Sitting next to a box of rotting flesh isn't going to help.'

If I wanted to beat myself over the head with the facts that was my affair but this was inexcusable. I said dully, 'I'm sorry, Adam. I don't mean to be nasty. Oh God... It hurts so much!' And so the tears began again, soaking the shoulder of his shirt as he held me, and my eyes ached, shrunken in a face swollen with weeping.

In the end I did go. Through the pierced oak screen of the old Lady Chapel I could see the soft, steady glow of the tall candles burning around the coffin and, on his knees, John, motionless in prayer.

I didn't, couldn't pray. The one thing I wanted was past praying for. John, no doubt, asked his God to give me comfort and peace and saw, perhaps, no conflict in that. But I did. God had permitted this death. Was I then to ask him to comfort me? It would be like a battered child asking solace of a violent father.

Yet I did find a small measure of comfort there. The subdued light was gentle on my sore eyes; the rich colours and textures around me, and the clean coolness conspired to still my mind and relax my body. Unaware, I ceased to be conscious of place and pain, drifting in a timeless limbo which may have been sleep.

Then, gradually, from this nothingness, I emerged to a different light, an unknown place. A room, it seemed; and I saw a piece of paper white against the dark wood of a desk top. Hands, big-boned, fleshy and male, took up a pen and wrote. And I read: '*MARINA JUDITH GRAHAM*'. The pen was laid aside, the paper folded twice, firmly, and placed onto the green baize lining of an open drawer. Then the drawer was closed and locked. As the scene began to disintegrate, I heard a voice, clear, warm and calm. Where it came from, I couldn't tell. From within the remnants of the image? From my own mind? 'And that is how it was done,' it said.

With that I moved to full wakefulness feeling none of the disorientation which often follows vivid dreams, just certainty and a cold, raging hate. Quietly, so that John wasn't disturbed, I went swiftly from the church to find Adam.

There was a light showing under his door and he was far from sleep. 'What is it, Stephanie?' He was alert, sensing my altered mood. 'Sit down. Somewhere...' He swept some plans from the other bed.

I told him about the dream, the voice. 'If that is how it was done,' he said, considering, 'it's something akin to sympathetic magic, but I've never heard of it before. Have you?'

I shook my head.

'Stephanie, you know that it might be nothing?' He looked embarrassed. 'Your mind could be playing tricks and it wouldn't be surprising.'

'Yes,' I told him. 'I do realise that given the state I'm in I could imagine all sorts of things. But I've never been one to see messages in dreams. And I'm not even sure that this was a dream. I have to say, though, that if Howells is capable of mind bending other, better, forces must be. It doesn't matter anyway. I don't suppose we'll ever find out for sure how he killed her. I only want to know if it could have been done this way. Because however uncertain I was before, I do believe now that Marina's death wasn't natural.'

He nodded and I went on: 'Marina used to say that all it took for evil to triumph is that good men do nothing. Sometimes I would have been more than happy to do nothing, and right up to last Friday I think I still half expected it just to go away. Well, Matthew Howells may not have put a foot wrong in 200-odd years, but he's done it now. Whatever it takes... but I want to see him dead. *It came with a Jew and it will go with a Jew.* Damn right.'

I was still up when John came in. One in the morning on the day of Marina's funeral, with all that lay before us, was no time to be accosting him, involving him in yet more impossible speculation. In my grief and now my anger, I was selfish. As soon as I came down the steps and saw him standing in the hall, I knew he was exhausted but it didn't stop me. And he, may his God bless him, never complained.

Like Adam he gave my story a cautious reception. How many tales of significant dreams he must have heard when comforting the newly bereaved! 'Have you ever heard of such a thing, John?' I demanded. 'I haven't, and neither has Adam.'

'Killing by writing a name on a piece of paper and locking it in a drawer? Yes, Stephanie, curiously enough, I have. Wait a moment. Let me make us a hot drink and then I'll tell you about it.'

He put a pan on the hob and poured milk into it. While he was setting out cups Adam pushed the door open. 'May I come in? Couldn't get to sleep.'

John added more milk and another cup and soon we were all sitting round the table drinking hot chocolate while he told us about the silly yet frightening episode he'd been involved in at Cambridge.

It had been towards the end of his first year when he and three friends, in hopeless pursuit of four English Lit. second years, went out to drown their sorrows. I couldn't imagine a 19 year old John chasing girls, but it was a diverting notion.

'The Eagle was packed so we went up the street to the Bath Hotel and sat over our pints being maudlin. Then Peter suggested trying magic to influence the girls. All you had to do, he said, was concentrate the appropriate thoughts as you wrote down the name of the person you wished to influence. Then you put the paper in a drawer and waited for the happy result. According to Peter you could produce any effect you wanted using this method as long as your will was strong enough.'

'Did it work?' I asked.

'We didn't try. We were tempted but finally we agreed that it wasn't the right thing for would-be clergymen to do. I didn't think any more about it, but Clive must have, because when his sister's Pekinese chewed up the only photo he had of the girl he was mad about, well... you can guess what he did.

'I'd seen this dog. Fluffy... Flossy... something like that. It was a horrible specimen, overfed and asthmatic, so it might have died anyway, but Clive did write the animal's name on a bit of paper and put it in a drawer, and the dog dropped dead of a heart attack.'

At the end of this recital Adam fixed John with a hard stare. 'Are you trying to wind us up?' he demanded suspiciously.

'No. No, really!'

'What happened to Clive?' I asked.

'Oh, he's a rural dean now,' John told us. 'It is a true story, however silly it sounds, and it was pretty frightening.

Clive really believed that he was responsible for the dog's death and, at the time, so did I.'

'Not now?'

'I don't know. I'd forgotten about it until tonight. Perhaps the action of writing the dog's name focussed Clive's hatred of the creature. A symbol as a magnifying glass again. So, yes, I have to think it's possible that Marina's death could have been caused in the same way.'

Adam got up to rinse his cup. 'It sounds ridiculously easy,' he remarked over his shoulder.

'Frighteningly easy,' John agreed calmly.

Adam put his cup on the drainer and turned round. 'I hope you're wrong, John,' he said. 'Because if it's that simple it won't be long before someone else's name goes into the drawer.'

* * *

We buried Marina in the morning with Ravel's *Pavane* and the rites of the Anglican Church. Adam, Alan Foster and two history lecturers carried her coffin to the grave. I followed, the full skirt of my white Indian print dress, always her favourite, stirring in the soft breeze. I would have no mourning black, I had decided. John walked beside me, good, solid comfort. Behind us the team, Fred Denton, Dr. Taylor, Marina's colleagues and students, Angela Morton and Mr. Curtis.

There were tears at the graveside, but not mine. John stood apart to read the committal, and Adam took his place, grasping my hand as the coffin was lowered. His hand felt awkward, hard and unfamiliar to me, used to holding Marina's slim, delicate fingers.

Earth to earth...

Adam let go and I stepped forward to sprinkle soil from her scented garden onto the coffin. And then one of Marina's students donned his kippah and read the El Malei Rachamim: *God, full of mercy, Who dwells above, give rest on the wings of the Divine Presence...*

The last amen died away and I took a small box from my bag. Careful of the breeze I removed the lid and let the contents fall in faded red drifts into the grave.

Nothing is that is...

MATTHEW HOWELLS

1984

The strength of women's hands isn't worth anything,
but what they've got in their heads
will carry them as far as they need to go.

May Belle Mitchell

I

When the mourners were gone John, Adam and I sat in the kitchen, amid the debris of plates and glasses, drinking tea, both of them trying to persuade me to stay longer.

'John, you can't go on camping in your study,' I told him. 'I'm so grateful to you – both of you – but I have to go home and get it over with.'

Home.

Vine Villa hadn't been touched since that terrible morning. I'd collected what I needed, and the rose petals from the bedroom, but I left everything alone, and refused offers of help. If the bedroom was as it was when she died, it was also as it was that last, incredible night. It was for me to deal with. Only me.

* * *

On the Monday after the funeral I went back to work. I had to be active, to have distraction, a purpose, or my life would slide into chaos, and I was as composed as I was going to be for some time. Perhaps, having killed Marina, Howells imagined that I, at least, might be scared enough to leave, but I was going nowhere. For the time being Angela was still at Allington. John and Adam were entrenched in the rectory. Whatever the significance of that triple grouping of Vine properties, I wasn't going to break the triangle.

* * *

No-one could have had kinder friends. Grieving themselves, they gave me so much support. At the end of that first day back at work Adam walked up School Lane with me. Using his key, he opened the front door and did a quick check round inside. Mail on the mat looked like more condolence cards, and I put them aside with all the others, still unopened, on the dining room table.

'Are you OK for shopping, Adam asked. 'Bread? Milk? Just say if I can do anything.'

It set something of a pattern. At lunchtime, if he wasn't too busy, he would keep me company, sometimes with John, in my upstairs room, or he would suggest taking our sandwiches out onto the ramparts somewhere. And, always, it was as it had been when we were in York: undemanding companionship and conversation that had nothing to do with Llantathan. Then at the end of the day, when the team left and Adam had checked round the site, he walked back to Vine Villa with me, talking of this and that: nothing very much. As often as not he would stay for a while, chatting over coffee. Occasionally he brought the makings of a simple meal and cooked it for us, or he would persuade me to go back with him to the rectory for the evening, and afterwards, he took me home again.

Alone at Vine Villa when Adam had gone, when the silence surged back... that was hard. There was so much I needed to do and I had little inclination to tackle anything. That first day after the funeral, buoyed up by anger and determination, I'd dealt briskly with the bedroom, cleaning, clearing, rearranging. The following day I bagged up all her clothes. I had a task before me and a life to live somehow, but I would be fit for nothing if I kept running into all the tangible evidence of what Marina had been to me: all those little, personal bits and pieces so redolent of her and of our life together. So I began to strip the rest of Vine Villa of everything that could catch me unawares and set off those dreadful storms of helpless, furious weeping.

In the evenings, I did what I could: the absolutely essential notifications such as the DVLA, the DHSS, the Council, and I opened the heap of condolence mail. There were cards and letters from Gwent friends and colleagues, from our old history department and from Marina's Cambridge contacts. All would have to be acknowledged, even, I supposed, that trite little note from Alison Prentiss. No. Not all. There was one...

I told Adam about it at the weekend on the way to the supermarket in Caldicot. 'A sympathy card,' I said. 'Quite plain, and all that's written inside is "So sorry". It's signed "Rose". I don't know anyone called Rose, but there is a Rose in Llantathan. Anne-Marie's mother. Rose Pritchard.'

'How likely is that?'

'On the face of it, not very but... it's a Newport postmark. And another thing. Someone's put fresh flowers – carnations – on Marina's grave, and it isn't me.'

Adam inched the car into a space at the supermarket, killed the engine and we sat in silence for a few moments. Then: 'Didn't you say that the women are probably the weak link?'

'Yes,' I agreed. 'And even if there was only one, I'd put my money on Mrs. Pritchard.'

'But why would she do this, Stephanie? She, of all people, knows the consequences. Her daughter...'

'That might be the reason,' I replied. 'Since we came to Llantathan I haven't known a week when there haven't been fresh flowers on Anne-Marie's grave. It's noticeable because they're not big on grave tending. Marina pointed that out. It might be that those flowers are a statement. Grief, certainly, but maybe defiance. I don't know, but for sure I can't ask.'

We dropped my shopping off first then went on to the rectory for lunch with John. I put together a salad with cooked meats and cheese and Adam opened a bottle of cider. Over the meal I related the mystery of the card and the flowers.

Saying nothing at first, John listened and, when I fell silent, he urged caution.

'Well, yes,' I replied. 'The slightest acknowledgment could be catastrophic for her. As likely as not the women are watched. Well, we know they must be. Anne-Marie...'

John was frowning. 'That's one reason, but what if it isn't all it seems?'

Adam caught his meaning faster than I did. 'Bait to lure us into the open?'

'What's called an invitation to treat in contract law,' John went on. 'An offer to negotiate with no intention of being bound by acceptance of the offer.'

'But I might do no more than thank Mrs. Pritchard,' I objected. 'In fact that's what I would do in normal circumstances.'

'Yes, but what if you found a hint of friendliness? A suggestion of support? Might you not be drawn to that?'

'I rather think I'd be suspicious,' I said. 'But I see what you mean. If they think we're onto something they might use Mrs. Pritchard as a plant, especially if they assume, as they must, that we know about Anne-Marie. She would be the perfect person – in fact the only person – with whom we might be tempted, as you put it, to treat.'

'And if it's not a lure?' Adam asked. 'What if it's genuine and we miss our only chance to have insider assistance?'

'What if it's a plea for help?' I added.

We all looked at eachother. I saw John's distress, Adam's exasperation, and supposed that my sense of helplessness was just as evident to them.'

John rose and filled the kettle. 'Let's not rush into any decisions,' he said.

I turned from collecting up our plates. 'Rush, John?' I said. 'I don't think I could decide what to do about this if I had ten years to do it.'

'The first thing,' Adam mused, 'might be to watch and find out who is doing the flower thing.'

I ran hot water into the sink. 'That probably means you,' I told him. 'Before this boycott Anne-Marie's grave was tended after Sunday morning service but since then I think the flowers are changed while we're in church. So...'

'OK,' he said. 'I'll find a convenient place.'

'Meanwhile,' John put in, 'what, if anything, should Stephanie do about the card?'

'In practical terms, I can't do anything.,' I said. 'If it is from Rose Pritchard, and I can't imagine who else it might be, I can't say anything to her about it. I might get an idea from her attitude, body language. I could go to the post office and try, I suppose.'

'If you did get some sort of indication, what then?' Something in Adam's tone made me look round at him and I saw in his face what had been in his voice: concern, fear. And, in his eyes, not the affectionate kindness of a friend, but the sudden, harsh blaze of love.

John's voice broke in: 'No,' he said firmly. 'You do nothing, Stephanie. We can't take risks on the strength of a card and a bunch of carnations.'

'I wouldn't,' I assured him. 'But nor would I close off future possibilities. It's not something I could decide unless and until I was in that situation. I wouldn't go beyond conventional responses, but I don't think that, if I sensed sincerity, I should shut it down with ice. We haven't much going for us. We can't afford to waste even the tiniest thing in our favour.'

'If it is...' Doubt still wreathed John's face and the concern in Adam's voice was amplified when he spoke.

'Stephanie, promise that you won't go beyond what you said. Please! Even if you think you see more opportunities.'

'I won't go beyond what I said. And I promise, too, that if I do see any chance to improve the odds in our favour, I won't do anything until I've spoken to you both.'

'He nodded and seemed relieved, but John wasn't. When Adam went up to his room he said, 'You didn't promise absolutely, did you, Stephanie? You didn't promise not to act if we disagree.'

'No, I didn't. But I can't imagine wanting to go against you both for the sake of something – some advantage – which was outweighed by the danger of following it up. Don't worry. It's not likely that any of us is going to be given any chance to improve our odds, is it? So whatever I did or didn't promise is neither here nor there.'

Determined to make a start on all the cards and letters, I went back to Vine Villa leaving John in his study once more, marking the relevant lessons and collects for the following day: Trinity Sunday, and Fathers' Day too. In the churchyard Adam was setting up some screening for the morning's flower-watch. He offered to walk back with me but I declined. I had to start getting used to going into the house alone. Adam's company helped to cushion me against that first, miserable sense of emptiness, but I would be the better for knowing that I could cope without it.

He might be the better too. At the time, I hadn't taken Marina's outburst about Adam seriously but, the evening we had the air-clearing session, as we talked across the table, I'd caught a glimpse of something in his expression which made me wonder and which, disturbingly, had sparked some very confused, conflicting emotions in me.

What I'd seen today: that fierce look of love and, yes, of desire, had more than justified Marina's assertion that, to Adam, I was "a damn sight more" than just a friend. How had she known? What had she seen, intuited, that I'd missed? And why on earth had her reaction to that York weekend been so extreme?

Thinking of the night before she died, of her fear that she could never keep me, I realised that she, unambiguous in her sexual orientation, must have wondered whether she was taking a huge risk in her commitment to a woman who was not. Might it be possible that, one day, some man would come along and prove more attractive than she was; offer what she, naturally, could not? But I didn't care about labels. I loved Marina. And as she feared to lose me, so had I feared to lose her. Not to a man, obviously, but another woman with a more measured approach to life; someone less impulsive, more practical than I was, maybe. Yet I had, after all, lost her to a man who had destroyed her because she was a potential threat to his vile, unnatural life. If anything kept me going during my hours alone at

Vine Villa, it was the thought of this and its corollary: that Matthew Howells was going to pay for what he had done to her, to me.

The hall had that utter emptiness one never feels in a house where the other occupants are just away for the day, and I wished that, after all, I had let Adam come with me. Selfish and wrong, I told myself. It wasn't fair to take advantage of his kindness, especially since I'd seen how he really felt about me. So much made sense now: York; "Stephanie love"; all the time he'd given me even before Marina died.

I was ashamed to remember how I'd talked about her and how, during those first, terrible days, he'd held me when I cried, sometimes, it seemed, for hours on end. Well, I still cried. I was crying now. But I wasn't going to inflict my misery on anyone else, and certainly not on Adam. I would have to try not to need the comfort he offered. But, as I sat down with the correspondence, with packs of note cards and a box of tissues, I found myself wishing that I was back in York, away from everything. In that little bubble Adam created for us that weekend.

That night, overtired and unable to sleep, the thought of Marina, underground and insensate for all time pursued me. Lamplight dispelled those images but others, of Adam, replaced them. A dozen times I tried to settle, with the light on, with the light off until dawn came and I fell into a heavy morning sleep waking with half an hour to go until church.

John was calling on the congregation to say the general confession as I slid into a pew towards the back. A childhood of churchgoing enabled me to join in until I found the correct place in my prayer book in time for the psalm. *Plead thou my cause, O Lord, with them that strive with me...* So much of that psalm, of that whole service seemed to be preternaturally appropriate. *Let a sudden destruction come upon him unawares...* Yes. Though I'd raged against God for letting Marina die, I could pray for that: for the destruction of her killer, with a whole heart. In front, and a little to my right, Angela turned, smiled, and gave a slight nod. As John's tiny congregation warbled its way through *Holy, holy, holy Lord God almighty* I felt a little comforted by that implied complicity.

Afterwards, leaving John deep in conversation with Angela, I walked to the rectory the long way round, instead of cutting through the churchyard to the side gate. Looking back from the lych gate I could see the profusion of mixed flowers marking Anne-Marie's plot and, yes, a fresh but different arrangement at the head of Marina's grave. Interestingly, though the previous week's blooms had been removed, my own posy, very dead now, was untouched. I should, I supposed, go and remove it. Perhaps get more flowers. But I couldn't bear the thought of being so close to what had been Marina and, now, was not.

In the rectory kitchen, where the scent of roasting chicken hung in the air, Adam was peeling potatoes. 'Staying for lunch, Steph?' he invited.

'A bit hot for a cooked lunch, surely?

'It is, but we're sick of lettuce.'

I put my bag and prayer book on top of the fridge. 'Yes, I'll stay, thank you. Can I help?'

He put down the peeler and rinsed his hands. 'John will finish up,' he said. 'He's on his way across now. Let's get out for some air.'

Avoiding the village, we made for the western rampart. 'They're getting too used to seeing us walking that bit down to the south-eastern corner and along past the motte,' Adam explained. 'We shouldn't be so predictable.'

This section of the bank was overgrown, the track rarely used. Having been to church, I wasn't really dressed for this and as Adam held out a hand to help me up to the top he apologised. 'I didn't think,' he said.

'Doesn't matter,' I replied, and ignored the fact that, as we set off, he was still holding my hand. After a few paces he let go and we strolled on to the north-western angle. Here, the remnants of a corner tower provided us with somewhere to sit, and an excellent view, across a couple of fields, of the back of Vine Villa.

Perched on some rough stonework, with cigarettes and no-one around, I was reminded of when we'd done the same sort of thing in York. It may have reminded Adam too for he asked about my mother.

'She says she's well,' I told him. 'Chatty enough when I phone. I've suggested going to see her but she always tells me to wait until I'm not so busy. Besides...'

'If you need to go, don't hesitate, Steph,' he broke in.

'I wouldn't, but... Adam, Mum doesn't know the truth about Marina and me, and I don't want her to know. She's not stupid and if she saw me at the moment...'

He knew what I meant. 'You're not sleeping or eating properly, are you?' Useless to deny it, but I headed him off by asking what he'd seen in the churchyard that morning.

'Nothing at first,' he told me. 'It was a while before they turned up. But you were right, Steph. Mrs. Pritchard and a couple of the other women. One of them had a blonde ponytail and a kiddie in a pushchair.'

'Louise Griffiths.'

'Well, they gathered round Marina's grave. With the excavation area fenced off they can't get to the outside tap at the back of the church so they had a bottle of water. Mrs. Pritchard left your posy alone but she replaced last week's carnations with some daisy-looking things. Then one of them said something and they all left pdq. I thought they'd spotted me but in a couple of minutes along came Pryce.'

'Did he see what they were doing?'

'I don't think so. It looked to me as if they'd posted a watch who warned them. There were three at the grave, but when I saw them walking back down the High Street, there were four.'

There seemed to be nothing to say beyond the speculations we'd already shared. We sat on a while longer, then Adam said that we'd better get back. He held out his hand again and, wondering at that, and at myself, I took it, stood up and walked back with him to the rectory.

'If it's a put-up job,' I said over lunch, 'it's a very elaborate one.'

'Wouldn't it have to be, if they think we suspect even a little of what's going on?' John was still very dubious, but we all were.

For the life of me I couldn't begin to fathom it. I was no more willing to trust it than John and Adam, but nor could I dismiss it. It could be genuine. I said as much, adding, 'I think that all I can do is wait and see what, if anything, happens next. After all, they might have expected me to throw their flowers away in disgust. I haven't, and I won't. They can interpret that as they like.' I smiled across at John. 'It's *my* invitation to treat, if you like.'

'As long as you don't *do* anything.' Again, briefly, that blazing look from Adam.

'I don't know what you imagine I could, or would do,' I replied. 'March into the shop and invite Mrs. Pritchard to come and join us? Hardly.'

With that he had to be satisfied, though he didn't look it. John took the conversation in a different direction:

something about Angela's future plans, and, willingly, I stopped worrying at this card and flowers puzzle. Adam didn't, though, and when he walked back to Vine Villa with me that afternoon, he returned to his concern that I might be drawn into some sort of village plot.

'I won't be, Adam. I promise.'

'You say that,' he said gloomily, 'but what if you think you see a chance? Something we might use?'

'Then I talk to you and John.'

'If you have to make a quick decision?'

'I temporise. And talk to you and John.'

'Promise?'

'Promise.'

He unlocked the door and did his usual check round, staying long enough to drink a mug of coffee and chat about nothing much. 'I was thinking of going to Caerwent next weekend,' he said. 'Would you like to come with me? We could have lunch somewhere afterwards and do the shopping on the way back.'

'I'd like that,' I agreed. 'I've never been to Caerwent. Not properly.'

'Funnily enough, nor have I,' he told me. 'Never seemed to have had the time.'

'So why now?'

'Because there's an excavation kicking off there next month. I want to have a look round before it starts, and drop in a couple of times once it's under way. That's my personal interest. Beyond that, I want to organise a visit for the team. Alan thinks that if it's still going when term starts in September, he'll put on a trip for the students. So I need to see what parking's like and whether the pub there can cope with parties.'

'Even Llantathan managed when I came with Marina's field trip a couple of years ago.'

'That was the first time I saw you,' he said quietly.

'No! How...?'

'You came into the churchyard. I was there with John discussing the possibility of excavating in the church.'

A sudden, vivid, snapshot memory fell into my mind. 'I remember!' I exclaimed. 'It was very hot and there were two people standing out of the sun under that big yew tree. That was you and John?'

He nodded. 'You said hello to us.'

'And then I went back because Marina had caught up with me. She and I had cheese sandwiches in the Cross Guns. How very odd that the four of us should have been together in Llantathan like that. Almost a year before we really were.'

'I wonder...'

'Meant to be, you think?'

'Marina would have thought so.'

'You made it very clear at the interview that you didn't want me to get the job though, didn't you, Adam?'

'I did.' A pause, then: 'Stephanie, that's past. Let's not go there. Just tell me what time I should pick you up next Saturday.'

I wanted to say more but I caught the thread of tension in his voice and, instead, suggested that around 10 would be a good time.

II

There seemed no end to the warm evenings so, thinking that I might sleep better if I had physical activity, I used them to tackle the garden. Marina, a better gardener than I, had had ambitious plans: for a vegetable plot as well as her scented border. I just wanted to get it tidied up.

Adam thoroughly approved. Since the rhododendrons by the drive had been considerably diminished there was little cover for anyone wanting to spy, but it wasn't too difficult to get into the back garden from the adjacent field as, he pointed out, he had done. I accepted his help gladly and together we got rid of everything close to the house which might screen a watcher. We neatened the hawthorn hedge but didn't reduce its height, and we cleaned out the pond.

By the end of the week, the only bit of wilderness left was the big bramble patch behind the garage. And, by the end of the week, I was aware of an indefinable shift in my relationship with Adam – and his with me.

On Saturday morning Adam arrived armed with the official Caerwent guide: one of the Department of the Environment's blue book series. One day, perhaps, there would be one for Llantathan.

'Not a blue book,' Adam said. 'I think in future they'll be produced by Cadw and English Heritage and they won't look like this.' He opened up the plan in the back on the kitchen table and pointed to the temple site. 'It was excavated in 1908,' he told me, 'But now the National Museum of Wales and Cadw are having another look as part of a larger programme of work.'

I gazed at the complex plan of the known remains of the Roman town. 'Do we have any idea of what there is in Llantathan?' I asked. 'Roman, I mean.'

'Well, nothing like this,' he replied. 'We have a fort, known from bits of rampart and cropmarks, and a medieval itinerary mentions a few standing ruins. Unless we can excavate, though, we're never going to know more than that. And if we don't stop Howells, that's not going to happen.'

'No... Adam, could there be more than a fort?'

'You mean some sort of settlement?'

'I don't know. But I've come across a reference to a possible mint. The land the rectory's built on used to be called Mint Field.'

He frowned. 'I doubt it. Roman mints are rare, late and tend to be associated with usurpers.'

'So part of a medieval herb garden then – mint sauce for all that Welsh lamb.'

He laughed. 'Come on, Stephanie. Let's go and look at some real Roman remains.'

Bypassed by the A48, as is Llantathan, Caerwent straddles the Roman road connecting the legionary fortresses of Glevum and Isca at Gloucester and Caerleon. West of Chepstow much of this road is assumed to be overlain by the A48. 'But,' Adam told me, 'This isn't certain. I wouldn't be surprised if the east-west road through Llantathan turned out to be Roman in origin.'

We left the car next to the Coach and Horses where Adam was assured that parties would be no problem, and walked up the main street to the temple site. According to the plan, it was immediately east of the forum, close to the centre of the Roman town.

From the viewing point the layout of the building was clear, the preserved remains of its foundations pale against the grass, and the size of it surprised me.

'In Romano-British terms Caerwent was a big town,' Adam said. 'And religion was important in the Roman world. We don't know which deity was being worshipped here but it was almost certainly a local one which the Romans conflated with one of theirs.'

He went on to tell me about a similar temple complex at Lydney, dedicated to Nodens who, he said, seemed to be equated with Mars and Neptune. 'It's about 10 miles the other side of Chepstow. We'll go some time and, if you like, we could go on to Gloucester and...'

I cut across whatever he was going to suggest with a sharp 'No!' Then, more gently, 'Lydney, yes, but not Gloucester, Adam. I couldn't.'

His expression was impassive and he said nothing, from which I assumed that he understood. That silence ought to have told me more than it did, but I didn't grasp then what that understanding was costing him.

We spent a good while looking at the preserved remains on Pound Lane and opposite the Baptist Chapel, then walked back to the church. There were inscribed Roman stones in the porch, and we found information about the church's association with St. Tathan to whom, with St. Stephen, it is dedicated. And after a turn around the churchyard we did what we'd done so often in Llantathan: we walked along part of the rampart.

The area enclosed was, I thought, about the same as that at Llantathan but here the defences were Roman, not medieval. 'Interesting, isn't it, Stephanie,' Adam commented. 'So similar, yet so different.'

Very different. This village looked lived-in, real, and the people we passed smiled and said hello.

'Lunch in Chepstow, Stephanie?' Adam asked as we headed back to the car.

Another car had parked a couple of spaces from Adam's Golf: a dark blue Daimler Sovereign. 'I've seen it before somewhere,' he remarked, frowning, as he slid into the driver's seat. I opened the passenger door then paused a moment. A man: apparently the owner of the Daimler, passed, nodded and said, 'Good afternoon.' I managed some sort of response before I got into the car and slammed the door. As I tried to fasten my seat belt, I realised that I was shaking.

'What is it, Stephanie? What's the matter?' Adam would have cut the engine but I told him to go.

'Home, please!'

'Yes, sure, but...'

'Adam, that man...'

'Who? The Daimler guy?'

'Yes. Adam, that was Matthew Howells!'

Swearing under his breath, Adam drove us back, not to Vine Villa but to the rectory where John was just making a sandwich for himself. 'I didn't expect you,' he began.

'Doesn't matter,' Adam replied abruptly. 'Sit down, Stephanie. John, get the brandy, would you?'

The two of them seemed to whirl around me. Adam pushed me onto a chair by the table and John put a glass into my hand: a hand which was still shaking.

'Don't put that bottle away, John,' Adam warned. 'I think you might need it in a minute. I know I do.'

John poured more brandy and I, calmer now, explained.

'She's right, John,' Adam confirmed. 'I'd seen the car before, parked at the Hall, but it didn't click.'

'Was it coincidence?' John wondered. 'Or did he follow you?'

'I would have noticed if he had,' Adam said. 'It's not an anonymous sort of car. I think it was just chance. After all, even Howells must like to get out and about sometimes.'

'He does,' I agreed, 'if the society pages in magazines like *Country Life* are anything to go by.'

'So... He goes out for a bit of a ride round,' John said thoughtfully. 'He sees your car parked by the pub. No doubt he knows all our vehicles. Curious, he stops and wanders about, waiting for you to come back. And strolls by to have a closer look at you.'

'It could have been exactly that,' I agreed. 'He may have seen us earlier, but we didn't see him. He certainly wasn't flaunting himself. And when he did walk past, he behaved exactly as you'd expect a casual passer-by to behave.'

'And you're absolutely sure it was Howells?' John asked.

'I am,' I told him firmly. 'I haven't stared so long at those pictures for nothing.' To Adam I added, 'I'm sorry I freaked. It was the shock of coming up against the reality. All we know, all we've heard, all we've conjectured... But none of us had ever seen him. He was...sort of...mythic. Give me an hour, and I'll half believe I imagined it.'

III

My Monday morning work schedule: the documentary evidence for the priory, was scuppered the instant I set foot in the rectory when Joyce Sanderson called me to look at a series of small metal objects spread out on the trestle table. 'You might know what they mean,' she said.

'Can I touch?'

'Yes. They're not fragile.'

I picked one up: a flat, oval plaque about five inches by three with a screw hole at either end, silver and badly tarnished. On one side I traced an engraved design. I put it down and selected another. Virtually identical. They all were. 'Some sort of coffin plate?' I hazarded.

'They must be. They don't have inscriptions but they always turn up in association with conventional plates.'

'But not with every plate?'

Joyce shook her head. 'No. I haven't had a chance to plot them but Adam thinks you should do it. Said he thinks it's more your area.'

The task was more intriguing than I expected, and not difficult. It was simple enough to produce a scatter diagram matching the coffin plates to grave cuts, and the cuts to headstones. The conventional plates were always brass and at least semi-legible, so it didn't take me long to see that those accompanied by the silver plaques were associated only with the inhumations of male members of some of the twelve village families.

That the plaques had been attached to coffins I didn't doubt but when I examined one under a lens, I noticed a curious fact. The outer side – it had to be that for the screw holes were countersunk in that way – was blank, but the reverse had a design made up of interwoven plants. Even with the lens it was difficult to make out enough to identify the leaves and flowers. I'd need a cleaned plaque, a desk magnifier and a botany book for that. Very pretty, though, and very strange. Why go to so much trouble for something which was never going to be seen?

They were all nearly identical. Stylistic variations, of course, for they spanned several generations, and that suggested a tradition. Not a general local tradition but something pertaining strictly to one section of the village community. I'd never heard of anything like it before. Very puzzled, I opened my door and called to Joyce downstairs.

She ran up, drying her hands on a grubby old towel. 'What is it? Anything interesting?'

I showed her my findings so far. 'Yes,' she agreed. 'It is odd. But you can argue that a lot of work goes into a coffin and no-one expects to see that again either.'

'No. Not once it's in the ground. But at the time we're dealing with there would have been a lot of display. Fond farewells, last respects. The coffin, its trimmings and the corpse would have been highly visible. The engravings on the back of these plaques wouldn't.'

She nodded slowly. 'Well, I could give one or two a basic clean here if it helps,' she offered. 'But I don't have a more powerful lens. I can bring one out tomorrow. Best I can do.'

'Yes, please. Oh, and can you tell me the positions of both the name plates and the plaques in relation to the skeletons?'

'No, but you could look at the plans. A pity we haven't yet had any turn up attached to coffins but we've not had any coffins. Not outside.'

'And the ones inside only had the usual brass plates. Hmm... Well, perhaps something will turn up in Area G.'

'Not unless preservation's much better. How's it going out there? I saw you talking to Adam at lunchtime.'

'Not about work,' I told her. 'I left that strictly alone. He seemed pretty ratty.'

'So what's new?'

I took my work folder home with me to grapple with such documents as had not been translated: some charters, largely formulaic, and a list of gifts to the priory. This last included small parcels of land, revenues from various commodities, items of plate and vestments and, given by Reynald Devigne in 1132, *a fine bell that did call the brethren to prayer and the people to the mass...*

Reynald Devigne, described as pious and faithful, became a novice canon of the priory in 1144 when, his wife being dead and his sons grown up, he was free from family responsibilities and able to devote himself to the service of

God. His entry to the priory had been marked by a gift of *that portion of land between the priory garth and Badger's Close where, in antiquity, the lords of this town struck their coinage...'*

There it was again: the source, probably, of the reference in Freda Fairford's *History*. But who were the 'lords' in antiquity? Not the Romans, Adam had said, and I thought he was right: educated medieval men knew about the classical world and if the writer of this document had thought the lords were Roman, he would have said so, notwithstanding that reference to antiquity. Welsh tribal leaders?

Meanwhile... Reynald Devigne was something else. I'd noted him in my jottings when I came across a reference in that ringing book I'd been reading when Marina was ill. I'd forgotten most of it now but wasn't there some connection between Reynald's bell and the bell Arthur Vine commissioned in 1951?

I recalled Miss Vine's letter: there was a suggestion there that her uncle's insistence on the bell as a memorial was closely associated with his scheme to rid Llantathan of Howells. And he and Reynald had not been the only ones associated with bells. Germs of an idea began to grow but if there was any sense to be had from this bell information, I needed to tabulate it all first.

I yawned and looked at my watch, surprised to see that it was almost eleven. No point in starting it now. All those sleepless nights were coming home to roost. I tidied up and went to bed.

* * *

Tuesday was another hot day. I listened to the weather forecast at lunchtime on John's radio hoping for no immediate change: as long as it stayed dry the team would make good progress, though Adam was beginning to think that the reverse was true. He muttered about having to wet down the site all the time, about the need to allow heat breaks, about lack of concentration when the temperature climbed in the afternoons. It was, he said, becoming a nightmare.

Even for me, in the rectory, the heat was a distraction, but I made headway with the plaques. With the big lens I was able to see that the delicate engravings represented seven plants: ash, hazel, rowan, yew, rosemary, hypericum and wild garlic. Identifying them – I was no botanist – was only half the problem. Now I had to discover why these particular plants had been chosen. Garlic was supposed to repel vampires and rowan kept witches away. That was the limit of my folklore knowledge, but it had to be something like that.

Trying to get information from the positions the plaques might have occupied on the coffins was hopeless: they'd all been found, like the name plates, in the upper parts of the graves, most usually somewhere near the head, but whether they'd been attached to the lid, side or end, inside or out, was impossible to tell. The only thing that could be said was that none had been found under skeletons, so not on the coffin bases.

It was a nice little problem within the context of my job and I was going to enjoy the research it raised, but could these plaques tell me anything significant about Llantathan's private rituals and about the twelve families? Or were they merely a sidelight: interesting, but not helpful? In the end I took the problem to John and, to my surprise, he became quite excited.

'Yes, I think it is important,' he said. 'You say these have only been found in village family graves?'

'That's right. Others may turn up in Area G, but none of the burials from the church had them. As far as I can tell, no-one from a village family was buried inside.'

John looked thoughtful. 'Well, as I see it, this suggests that the village men have more power than we've tended to think.'

'Their own power rather than what they have as Howells' cats-paws?'

'I think so. Listen. This is something I know a little about because my mother was rather keen on folklore. There are seven plants depicted. Rowan and garlic are obvious deterrents of evil but why do you suppose yews are planted in churchyards? Not just because they were thought to absorb poisons from the soil. They were supposed to drive away devils. Hypericum – that's St. John's wort – guards against evil spirits. Ash, hazel and rosemary: more of the same.

'Now, seven itself was considered magical in pagan times and, in biblical numerology, it's important. There are a lot of references to seven in the Bible. It's the number of Christ, made up of three: the number of God, and four: the number of man. And Christ is God made man. Do you see?'

'But would that have any significance? These people aren't Christian.'

'No, not the men. Not the women either, perhaps, but who knows? In the light of what Mrs. Pritchard has been doing, we may have to keep an open mind about that.'

'Hmm. But where does this get us?'

'Think, Stephanie! The countersinking of the screw holes tells us that the side with the plant symbols must have been face down on the coffin, as you've noted, not facing out. So as a talisman against evil, it was meant to protect the living and not the dead. It was to keep evil in, not out. Which, in turn, suggests that whoever was responsible for these plaques believed that these men really did have power. If the power the men had was derived solely from Howells it would die with them, and the families wouldn't bother.'

'Wouldn't it die with them anyway?'

'These suggest that they believe it doesn't.'

'So are these things the equivalent of what they used to put on witches' tombstones? What was it?'

'God grant that she lie still,' John supplied. 'That's what you mean, isn't it?

I nodded. 'It sounds like bad news for us.'

'It's not good, but better to find out now than later.'

'Talking of later, have you any news about the boys?'

He grinned wryly. 'Well, one of them thinks of nothing but being another Nigel Mansell when he grows up, and the other wants to be David Bellamy. A Formula One race meeting in a jungle would be the very thing to get them both out of Llantathan.'

I laughed. 'Never mind. So I suppose you've no idea which one Howells wants?'

He shook his head. 'But logically it would be the 16 year old. That would leave the other one for next year.'

Seeing his expression I said, 'No next year, John. There isn't going to be a this year.'

In the end, the decision to move the team into Area G was taken out of our hands by the Clerk of Works who, with unforeseen logistics problems for September, wanted to get in to Llantathan to see what was going on with the damp and subsidence as soon as possible.

So Adam did what he'd wanted to do all along. Leaving Paul and Dawn to finish up the peripherals, he moved everyone else to work on that section of the churchyard which contained the Howells grave. He gave no warning and didn't advertise his activities by putting up screens until he had to.

'It'll take time,' he warned me. 'Don't expect anything until well into next month.'

'So long?'

He displayed a touch of impatience. 'Damn it, Stephanie, it's not long since you were telling me to leave it alone.'

'I know. I'm sorry.' I left my table and joined him at the window from which we could see most of the southern portion of the churchyard. The area already excavated to the east had yielded the foundations of part of a range of monastic buildings and now Adam was proposing to dig that portion – Area G – which, according to logic, might be expected to contain the opposing range with the cloister gateway. The Howells plot was located to the east of the line of what Adam expected to be the inner face of the cloister wall, and about two metres from the south wall of the church.

At the moment all activity was centred on the removal of memorial stones. 'And that,' Adam informed me, 'will take us until the middle of next week. It's potentially dangerous and it can't be rushed.'

Watching two of the team manhandling a discoloured white marble kerb stone onto a sort of stretcher arrangement, I believed him.

'I'm doing the best I can,' he went on. 'But I'm short-handed until Glyn and Janet finish up at Mellyn. I've got Ceri and Phil plotting the graves ahead of the removal team and we're fortunate that most of the stones aren't composites: there isn't too much dismantling to do. But it's heavy work: you can't force the pace, especially not in this weather. I don't want people going down with heat exhaustion and I certainly don't want injuries.

'And when we've cleared the stones, we have to strip back and plan again. I can get that started at the church end while clearance is still going on to the south but you're looking at... oh, say two weeks today before we've cleared and cleaned back and planned the whole area. Then we can start digging. And that's assuming that the dry weather holds. I told you we should have done this sooner, Stephanie.

'OK. Now let's see what happens in the next couple of weeks. If they try to do anything to that grave, we've got confirmation of its importance. And if we do have a shortage of bodies I for one will be a lot happier about going after Howells. I think we've reached the only conclusion the evidence will allow but it is still circumstantial and there is just the very remote chance that we're wrong. Oh no, not about what Howells does, but whether there's one or half a dozen. And frankly, Stephanie, I'd rather it was one. I know it means we're up against things we don't understand but I feel better about trying to get rid of someone who should have been dead two hundred years ago.'

We talked a little longer. Adam seemed preoccupied: anxious about the site, I supposed, but then, hesitantly, he asked me if I'd like to go out with him for a drink that evening. 'I've got a few ideas I'd like to discuss with you.'

I said that I would and then, oddly, considering how busy he was, he hung around for another ten minutes saying nothing very much. I sat for some time, thinking about that, about his awkward invitation and about my instant acceptance. Though I questioned the fairness of spending so much time with Adam, I knew that as long as he invited, I would accept.

IV

John, on his way to Allington, dropped us off at the Tredegar Arms in Shirenewton, noted for its wide range of malt whiskies. 'So what are these ideas, Adam?' I asked when we were settled in the bay window with Laphroaig, a malt I'd never tried before.

He lit a cigarette, and mine. 'I'd like to scare the shit out of Elwyn Pryce,' he announced.

'What! Why?' I stared at him. 'I mean, so would I, but haven't we got enough to do without getting sidetracked?'

'Not for laughs, Stephanie,' he assured me. 'I've been thinking about this for a while and wondering if there's a way of gaining some sort of advantage. We can't risk trusting Mrs. Pritchard so whatever we do has to be of our own devising.'

I nodded, but I had no idea where this was leading.

'Look, given what's been done to us, they must be feeling pretty confident. Howells has been playing his games for two centuries and as far as we know no-one else has ever come close to touching him. Right?'

I nodded again.

'OK. So we come along. We may not know anything but we're enough of a risk for him to take action. Maybe the fact that Marina was Jewish worried him and the excavation certainly does. So he acts and he's absolutely secure in the knowledge that we can't retaliate. Even if we could, John's ethics wouldn't allow it. As far as he knows, we haven't an ounce of supernatural ability between us, and that's true. If we had we might not have lost Marina. John couldn't save her so Howells probably doesn't rate his hotline to God either. We may be potentially a little more dangerous than most, but still just an inconvenience.'

'If we're no more than that,' I asked, 'why take such extreme steps to get rid of us?'

He said, choosing words with care, 'I think we should consider the possibility that we've placed too much significance on Marina's death. No, wait. Don't misunderstand me, Stephanie. Of course to us, especially to you, it's a terrible thing. But to Llantathan murder isn't terrible: it's the right thing to do, either for Howells or as protection. I've always thought that we've overestimated our importance to them. We may see ourselves as being on a mission, but to them we're probably nothing more than a nuisance. I don't mean that they won't hesitate to sweep us out of their way, but on the basis that we're mice, not lions.'

'So what are you saying, Adam? No. Hang on a minute.' I stood up. 'What will you have?'

With two glasses of Lagavulin on the table, I invited him to go on.

'Right. Now, if you were Howells, nice and safe and secure, how would you react if you found that these little pests could bite?'

'He's going to discover that soon enough,' I said.

'Sure. But what if we start to shake his confidence now? Give him some of his own back.'

I looked up at him, frowning. 'Adam,' I said, 'either you're not explaining this very well or I'm thick. You've already said that we can't do anything. We don't have the ability and if we had John wouldn't let us. So what are you suggesting?'

'It doesn't matter that we don't have any real supernatural power. We can make him think we have. Listen, Stephanie. We can't get anywhere near Howells. His turning up at Caerwent had to be coincidence. We've never seen him apart from that, and we're not going anywhere near the Hall. But it's a safe bet that whatever Elwyn Pryce sees and hears is reported back.'

'Yes. Pryce does seem to be the go-between.'

'More than that, I think. I'd say he's Howells' deputy, with a lot more clout than we've credited him. And, possibly, some degree of supernatural ability.'

'Those plaques certainly suggest that. In which case, isn't trying to scare him somewhat risky?'

'Yes, but it might be worth it.'

I had to admit that it would give me much pleasure to see Elwyn Pryce shaken. 'But how, Adam?' And when Adam told me, I was amused.

'But will he be fooled? It all sounds like the appearance of the demon king in pantomime. Stage effects.'

'Yes. That's exactly the sort of thing, and though it might startle you, it wouldn't fool you for a minute. But what if you'd been steeped in magic since the day you were born? What if you'd been party, all your adult life, to rituals, and the results of rituals, which we can barely imagine? Wouldn't you tend to see a supernatural explanation for uncanny happenings rather than an ordinary one? If you were a total and absolute believer in it, wouldn't you think magic normal?'

'I suppose...' I saw what he meant but I wasn't sure that Pryce was so stupid.

'No. He's not stupid. He just has a completely different view of these things. He can't rationalise as we can. Or, if you prefer, his form of rationalisation is the exact opposite of ours.'

I thought about it while Adam went to get cigarettes from the machine. I didn't believe that Pryce, any of them, couldn't rationalise at all but I knew how one year in

Llantathan had altered my perspective. A lifetime of it... well... yes, Adam had to be more or less right. So when he came back, I told him: 'OK. I'll buy it provided John agrees.'

Adam got us a taxi and we said nothing more until we were back at Vine Villa when I raised a query. 'Adam, I love the idea, but do you think it would be wise to do anything yet? Wouldn't it be better to save it all up for August and give them one hell of a shock then?'

'We'll do that anyway,' he replied. He sounded confident. 'But a few tricks beforehand might well shake them. Make them doubt their assessment of us.'

'It could make things harder,' I pointed out. 'As long as we look harmless...'

'True, but we're in trouble already. We may be no more than irritating pests but they're going to kill us if they can. I don't doubt that for a minute. And they'll believe it will be as easy as killing Marina. Having a go at Pryce can't put us in a worse position, but it just might make them stop and think. OK. Maybe it won't, but it could push them into acting before they intended, and if they do that, they're more liable to make mistakes.'

While I made coffee, he wandered around the house checking the security of doors and windows. 'I wish you weren't here alone,' he told me.

So do I, I thought, but I said that I was all right. He looked into my face.

'You're not,' he stated. 'Stephanie love, I admire the brave front, but you don't have to keep it up all the time. Not with me.'

I sat down in Marina's chair. 'Leave it, Adam,' I warned, my voice brittle.

'OK, but...'

We talked for an hour or so. Mostly we discussed the setting up of the Local History Archive which would occupy us over the winter. Llantathan was hardly mentioned and perhaps because of that, because we were talking about what I thought of as the real world, the world beyond the village, I felt as I had in York. Normal.

It was so reminiscent of that February weekend that I was unsurprised when, leaving, Adam bent to kiss my cheek. What did surprise me was the sudden, clear wish that he would stay, a wish that prompted me to reach one hand up to his shoulder. Then, realising the implication, I dropped it and the blood rushed to my face.

* * *

I was aware, next morning, of a change: the end of the beginning? It might not last but, reviewing Adam's ideas as I ate breakfast and made a packed lunch, I felt better: more controlled, and the possibility of gaining even a small advantage seemed increasingly attractive. But before anything could be done it was essential to get together with John and try to plan out the coming weeks.

'Of course, Stephanie,' John said when I arrived at the rectory. He was just finishing breakfast so I sat down with him and accepted a cup of tea.

'Is Adam around?'

'On site, checking the hoist. He worries about sabotage. By the way, you kept him out very late last night.'

'I didn't think it was all that late.' Nor was it. I'd been in bed by twelve.

'Past two. I'm surprised to see you here so early.'

'Well, you know...' I replied vaguely, aware that he was too wise to probe, but wondering what Adam had been up to after he left Vine Villa.

John brought his diary from the study and leafed through it. 'Let's see... I'm trying to keep it as clear as I can which isn't difficult as far as the parish goes. Yes, Stephanie, we really do need some better plans, don't we? Would this evening be too soon?'

I found Adam plotting memorials in Area G, and looking rather the worse for wear. He was sitting on a low, sandstone grave marker with a drawing board across his knees, a mug of cold coffee by his foot.

'John said you came out to check the hoist,' I remarked, crouching beside him. He didn't look at me and his only reply was a grunt. I took it to be an affirmative. Undismayed – I'd had many such grunts from Adam – I went on, 'I think we ought to meet tonight to make some plans. John agrees, but is that OK with you?'

Now he did lift his head and I saw just how tired and drawn his face looked. 'Does it have to be tonight?'

'No, but I don't think we should delay much longer. Tell me when and I'll set it up, but no later than Friday.'

He pushed his pencil behind his ear, rubbed his eyes and began, awkwardly, to feel in his pockets for his cigarettes. The drawing board slid off his knees and I put out a hand to stop it. I took it from him and rested it against the next headstone.

'You don't look well,' I told him, and as I said it worry began to stab at me. He looked exactly like someone about to come down with flu. Oh God, not another name in the drawer!

'I'm tired, that's all,' he replied shortly and, to himself: 'Where the fuck are my cigarettes?'

I gave him mine. 'Are you sure that's all it is?'

'I'm not being hexed if that's what you mean. I'm just bloody knackered. Look, Stephanie, make any arrangements you like, but not tonight. I've got to get some sleep.' He retrieved the board and started work again. It was a dismissal.

Adam's on-site moods were nothing new but this was a mood and a half and it contrasted starkly with his amicable frame of mind the previous evening. John was probably well aware of it so beyond arranging supper for the three of us at Vine Villa the following evening, I said nothing and went upstairs to work. But from time to time the question of what Adam had been doing until two in the morning returned to niggle like toothache.

* * *

It was while I was endeavouring to transform dry facts gleaned from charters and chronicles into readable narrative that Joyce put her fair head round the door. 'Adam says could you come onto site please? A visitor's turned up and he wants you to talk history to him.'

I made a face at her. I hated talking to visitors. 'Who is it this time?'

'No idea. Probably another church bloke.'

Cutting through the gate into the churchyard I could see the two figures at the far end, their backs to me: Adam giving the standard site tour to a youngish-seeming man in jeans and a pale blue casual shirt. Not my idea of a cleric but you never knew these days.

Not wishing to interrupt Adam's flow I waited on the edge of Area G where Dawn was plotting the last of the gravestones.

'Who's the visitor?' I asked her. She took off her glasses, and turned her head to look.

'Oh, is he still here? Adam must be giving him the full, unexpurgated version. I don't know. Something to do with Llantathan Hall, Paul says.'

No. No. Surely not!

I left Dawn to her plotting and went to stand by the church wall where it was slightly cooler. Adam and the visitor paced slowly along the perimeter path to the southern extent of Area G, Adam talking and answering the occasional interjected question. He looked all right.

Now that I had a better view, I saw that the stranger was older than I'd first thought: somewhere in the forties. He was a shade below Adam's height but broader, fleshier, thickening slightly at the waist. His hair was black and glossy, discreetly fashionable in cut, like his jeans. I knew him. Matthew Howells.

Adam, noticing me, called me over. They were standing now next to the Howells memorial looking so normal, so ordinary. I joined them feeling that every step I took carried me further from reality. The visitor watched my approach with an expression of polite anticipation on his tanned face.

'Stephanie,' Adam said, 'this is Sir Matthew. He thought he recognised us in Caerwent and now he's come to see how we're getting on. Sir Matthew: Mrs. Hargreaves, our Field Historian.'

My hand was shaken as, murmuring a conventional greeting, I looked up into the face of Marina's murderer. God knows he was only moderately good looking, but his smile was surprisingly charming.

He let go of my hand. 'Mrs. Hargreaves,' he said. 'I'm very pleased to meet you. I've heard so much about your work.'

Have you now, I thought. Before I could reply Paul, having trouble with a marble angel, claimed Adam's attention. He excused himself and, with a look to me that said, *Watch it!* he went to Paul's rescue, crossing the site in long strides.

'I understand that you're writing a complete history of Llantathan,' Howells said. 'Rather dreary, I should think.'

'It's like all history,' I replied. 'Times of great interest and significant events, and long periods of relatively mundane activity. A lot depends on how good the documentation is. Too many gaps can distort the picture.'

'And do you have too many gaps?' I heard teasing in his voice.

'Historians always think there are too many gaps,' I responded, 'but Llantathan is really very well documented, and this excavation will give us more information which can't be obtained in any other way. I only wish the community could be persuaded that it's a good thing. It is their heritage after all.'

'Llantathan is very conservative,' he replied.

'And you, Sir Matthew?'

'I?' His surprise looked genuine. 'I assure you Mrs. Hargreaves that I am not at all conservative. I always wanted to do a great deal for the village but I've found it virtually impossible to break down the resistance to change. No. No. Please don't imagine that I'm the instigator of their protests. I think all this,' he made a sweeping gesture, 'is tremendously exciting and I hope we'll have more.'

His voice was warm, persuasive. If I hadn't known what I did I would have believed him. Even with the knowledge of what he was it was difficult not to.

He glanced up at the church clock, checking it against his watch. 'I'm afraid I must say goodbye or I shall be late for my next appointment.' He took my hand again. 'I've enjoyed our chat, Mrs. Hargreaves. Would it be impertinent to suggest that we continue it over dinner one evening soon?'

This was becoming farcical: to go out to dinner with a 200-odd-year-old multiple murderer? Yes, if I could turn it to our advantage. I said, 'I don't have a great deal of free time, Sir Matthew, but I think I might have a clear evening soon. Perhaps if you phone me at the rectory in a day or two...'

'Of course. Now I really must be going. Please say my goodbyes to Mr. Pembury and thank him for his time.'

I walked with him to the church gate and watched him drive away up the High Street. Before the turn for the Hall took the dark blue Daimler from sight, he put one arm out of the window to wave.

* * *

'It was bizarre,' I said. 'Utterly bizarre...'

Lunchtime, and I was eating my sandwiches with Adam and John on the little terrace at the back of the rectory. 'John, I do wish you'd been there.'

'Yes,' he said, but without conviction.

'I simply could not believe it,' I went on. 'He was so... so ordinary and... and... quite charming in a way.'

'Well, what did you expect? Adam demanded crossly. 'Fangs and a long black cloak? Steph, you already knew what he looks like.'

'Yes, but even that didn't make him seem entirely real. It's the ordinariness. Jeans. Desert boots.'

'Oh, for God's sake, Stephanie! He lives in the 1980s not the 1780s. It's exactly what he would wear.'

'OK. OK. No need to snap. Weren't *you* just a little bit freaked?'

'Yes, by the fact that he turned up. Not by what he looks like. But then, *I* never expected Bela Lugosi.'

But for John's hasty intervention it would have degenerated into the pettiest sort of squabble. He asked, 'Why *did* he turn up? Not simply a social call.'

'That was the impression he tried to give,' I replied. 'And to make it clear that he had nothing to do with the protest.'

'Which is a patent lie,' John stated. 'What else did he say?'

'To me nothing much,' Adam said. 'I don't think we talked about anything but the excavation. What about you, Stephanie?'

I recounted the conversation as accurately as I could. 'I thought he was playing games. Some of his questions could have been applied to our private research. But I played innocent. Naturally.'

'Anything else?' Adam screwed up his crisp packet and stuffed it into his pocket.

'Yes. He asked me to have dinner with him.'

'What!'

'Stephanie...'

I looked from Adam to John and back again. John's face was all worry. Adam's expression was far less easy to read. Anger, yes, but fear too. 'I hope you told him what to do,' he said.

'I did what I promised,' I replied calmly. 'I temporised. I told him to give me a ring in a day or two.'

'You did what?' Adam.

'Stephanie, dear...' John.

'I didn't say I would,' I pointed out, 'but it might not be a bad idea.'

'You must be out of your mind!' Adam raged. 'How can you even consider it?'

'I'll tell you why tomorrow evening. John, if Howells phones for me before then, will you tell him I'm out or something. I don't want to set anything up until we've had a chance to discuss it.'

'Discussion be buggered!' Adam fumed, almost dancing in his fury. 'You're not going to set anything up. You must be crazy if you think we'd even let you go to the end of the road with that devil. Right, John?'

Poor John began to make pacifying noises but they were lost when I rounded on Adam.

'I'm not losing my mind, but you're not using yours. Look Adam, I'd go a lot further than the end of the road if it brings us closer to stopping Howells. I'm not going to do anything without a proper discussion, so will you stop being so bloody... proprietorial.'

Without another word he walked off the terrace into the house.

Oh Lord!' I sighed. 'I'm sorry, John.'

'Don't apologise to me, Stephanie,' John replied with a touch of sharpness. 'Go and say you're sorry to Adam. My dear,' – gently now – 'he's only concerned for you and too tired, I think, to be tactful. Or to think very clearly.'

'I suppose... You can see the possibilities though, can't you?'

'I can see something of what you're thinking but I agree with Adam: it would be very dangerous.'

'We're playing a dangerous game.' I shrugged. 'Right. I'll go and make my peace with Adam. John, try to make him go to bed early tonight.'

Adam and I did call a truce, but not before we had another flare-up. He was with Dawn and Phil in Area G where the first of the vegetation was being stripped off.

'Later,' Adam said curtly when I asked him if I could have a word. 'I'm too busy now.'

'Now, please,' I insisted. 'You can spare me five minutes.'

'OK. Five minutes.' He tapped his watch. Infuriated, I glared at him, turned and walked back to the rectory.

He caught me up at the front door. 'Stephanie, look, I didn't mean... What was it you wanted?'

'Are you sure you have the time?' I was still angry.

So was he. I saw his fingers curl into tight fists. His face was grey. 'Yes, I have the time,' he said, teeth clenched on his temper.

'Adam, I wanted to say that I'm sorry I snapped at you.'

'Thanks,' he muttered. 'Does that mean you're going to give up this stupid idea? No? Then from here on count me out.'

I looked at him, wondering how serious he was.

'All right,' I said. 'Consider yourself counted out. At least I'll have room to manoeuvre without you telling me what I can and can't do.'

I reached to push open the door but he grasped my arm and swung me round. 'Room to get yourself killed. Christ Almighty, Stephanie! How can you be such a crazy bitch?' His voice was low, savage. His fingers gripping my arm hurt. I looked up into his eyes and my anger died. I knew desperation when I saw it, and I knew the cause.

'Adam, please, *please* listen. I am not committed to this, but I can see ways forward for us if I can use it. If, when I've explained it to you, you and John still disagree, I won't do it. All I'm asking is a fair hearing.'

Some of his tension eased. He let go of my arm. 'I'm sorry,' he said tonelessly. 'Did I hurt you?'

'It doesn't matter. Will you come tomorrow evening?'

'Yes, I'll come. I'll give you your fair hearing but I can't imagine what possible good can come of it.'

'You will. You'll see.'

'I'll tell you what I see, Stephanie: you, in a box.'

'No. No, Adam. Don't worry. And please don't let's argue anymore.'

He closed his eyes, sighed. 'No. I'm sorry, Stephanie. I'll be there tomorrow.'

* * *

Nothing had been discussed since Marina died. Our ragbag plans hadn't been refined and now we were in a worse position. Now we were only three, with Howells already on the doorstep, and thrusting himself under our noses. It would have been nice to imagine Marina in heaven having personal audiences with God to plead our cause but I wasn't that mawkish, and I was none too sure that God cared. The extent of my faith at that time was that God *might* help those who helped themselves if he could be bothered to notice. Tonight, when John and Adam arrived, I was going to see that we did help ourselves. I wanted use made of the miniscule advantages we possessed.

Six weeks today and it will be all over. That was the one real thought in my mind as I prepared supper that Thursday evening, shredding lettuce into the colander. All over, one way or another. I remembered Thomas Hardy's Tess recognising, suddenly, that the date of her own death was concealed in the calendar and passed over, unknown, year after year. Tess had wondered when it was. I wondered too: what the date on my calendar, circled in red, would prove to be. Well, six weeks today, I thought, and I would know. Or I would be beyond knowing. Six weeks today either Howells would be finished, or we would.

I said as much to John and Adam over supper, adding: 'And unless we sort out exactly what we're going to do, unless we use the few advantages we have, it'll be us, not Howells.'

Adam began to look mutinous: he knew what was coming, and he was right. I went on: 'I see Howells turning up as a plus for us. Being asked out to dinner is another.'

'Short cut to a premature burial more like,' Adam grumbled. I ignored him.

'All along, the thing we've lacked is any kind of handle on Howells. Until last Saturday we didn't even know for sure what he looks like. For all we'd seen of him he might not have existed. I know you disagree, Adam, but I don't believe that having dinner with him is all that risky. I do believe, though, that if I did, I might at least get an idea of how he rates us as opposition. With luck I might learn more. Who knows what he might say?'

'Is that likely?' Adam was scornful.

'No, but possible,' I replied coolly. 'It depends on why he issued the invitation. Yes, to try to find out about us but, without being conceited, I think he just fancies me.'

John's expression was considering, while Adam displayed all the signs of a child about to throw a tantrum.

'Adam, listen. I know a *come-to-bed* look when I see it. And although it may be years ago, I also remember what a man's like when he's trying to get a woman there.'

Adam said, 'If you've got some daft Mata Hari idea...'

'No. For one thing I can't dance. She was some sort of spy, but did she actually sleep with anyone?'

'I don't bloody well know. And I don't care.'

'Neither do I. Now listen and tell me something, Adam. If you had a secret... Say you knew where a fabulous hoard of archaeological treasure was buried, when would you be most likely to give the location away? Before, during, or after sex?'

Adam laughed reluctantly. 'OK, Stephanie. Go on. Explain.'

'Well, you wouldn't be likely to blurt out the grid co-ordinates in... let's call it the throes of passion. Physical and possibly emotional sensations would override thought and coherent speech. Yes?'

He admitted that probability with a slight nod.

'And afterwards you'd fall asleep?'

He admitted that too, ruefully.

'But beforehand, when you've got your sights fixed and you're doing your damnedest to please the lady so that she'll take off her clothes? You know? When things are getting cosy and confidential? I'm not saying you would, but isn't that the most likely time?'

'Likely but not certain,' he said. 'I can't imagine telling anyone however much I fancied her. And if I fancied her a lot, I wouldn't be thinking about grid co-ordinates at all.'

'No, but don't you think that if she asked the right questions in the right way, at the right time you might just say more than you intended without realising you'd said it?'

'Yes. All right. I see where you're coming from. But what you're thinking of will only work at a pretty advanced stage of the game. And I don't think that in this case you've a hope. Howells must know every trick in the book by now.'

'But what we tend to forget is that he's still human,' I persisted. 'He can make mistakes.'

'Not so far.'

'We don't know that,' John put in. 'He might have made plenty of mistakes over the years.'

'Granted, but he's still gone on, and I'd guess he rectifies mistakes pretty ruthlessly.'

'Sure,' I agreed, 'but we're aware of that, and I don't plan to be rectified.'

I got up to clear our plates and serve the pudding. John helped while Adam sat staring morosely at his wine glass. Eventually, halfway through the apple pie and ice cream he said, 'OK, suppose you do agree to have dinner with him, what safeguards have you got? How are you going to make sure you don't end up dead in a ditch?'

I'd thought about this. 'For a start by ensuring that plenty of people know where I am and with whom, and that I'm remembered at the restaurant, which I will choose.'

'Fine, but how will you get home again?'

'In his car, or mine. I haven't decided yet.'

'Risky,' Adam thought. 'Especially if it's his car.'

'That's the only risk,' I told him. 'But I think I have to take it. If I do otherwise it'll look contrived and might suggest that I'm suspicious of him. Besides, that's one of the times when he could give something away. Look, as long as he's aware that people know I'm out with him I reckon I'm safe. If I disappeared, he'd be number one suspect. And it wouldn't be Llantathan where people would lie for him. It would be Newport. Well, what do you think?'

John pushed his dish away and leant on the table. 'Yes,' he pronounced. 'With care you should be safe, and it might be a valuable exercise. Adam?'

'I'm not convinced that it would be valuable at all,' he said, 'but you're obviously set on it. OK, Stephanie. Go ahead, but be bloody careful.'

The next item on the agenda was Adam's plan to, as he'd put it, scare the shit out of Elwyn Pryce.

'Give me an example,' John requested. He looked interested: even saints must have their weak moments.

Adam, distinctly happier now that he was on his own ground, poured himself another glass of wine. I'd heard this before so I did the washing up while he entertained John with his ideas.

'It occurred to me as a way of scaring Pryce from the site,' he began, 'He seems to spend most of his evenings in the pub but he always ends up in the churchyard, wandering round the excavation. How much sense he can make of it is anybody's guess but I suppose he's keeping an eye on how close we're getting to the Howells plot. OK. So I thought that one night I'd sneak out, lay a trail of petrol across his path, and put a match to it as he approaches. Can you imagine how you'd react, John, if you were suddenly confronted by a line of fire?'

'I'd be startled, naturally,' he said. 'In the right circumstances I might be very frightened.'

I tidied up and went through to the sitting room to close the curtains and switch on the lamps. In a few minutes they drifted in, still chewing over the possible reactions of the ex-verger. There wasn't much doubt or disagreement here: we were all keen to sting Pryce a little and, if Adam was right, we might go into conflict with Howells with our confidence enhanced and his shaken.

'As long as you don't actually hurt him,' John concluded.

'If he's damaged it'll be his own mind doing it,' Adam replied. 'This is a schoolboy trick. Most people would see through it at once or work it out soon after. But Pryce might not. I'm hoping he'll jump to conclusions, and if I'm careful to remove all traces, maybe he'll start to wonder whether we have some power after all.'

With those two matters out of the way we went on to make what further plans we could, but it wasn't easy. Adam agreed to put in hand the fortification of the church, and John promised to do all he could to find some excuse to get the likely victims out of Llantathan. Failing that, though, we were still locked into the problem of keeping them and Howells apart. Whatever else we did or didn't do, that was essential. With only one approach open to us, it seemed impossible. There had to be a better way, and I could only hope that it would present itself before August.

V

Because the good weather held, work on Area G progressed faster than Adam predicted with the excavation proper expected to start the following Monday. The day before my dinner date with Matthew Howells.

Howells hadn't phoned as quickly as I expected and I thought, half disappointed and half relieved, that he wasn't going to bother. When he did, apologising profusely for the delay, he wanted to know whether I would be free to have dinner with him at the weekend.

Hoping that I sounded genuinely regretful, I declined. 'I've too much to do this weekend, I'm afraid. No, I'm sorry but I can't... Not until Tuesday... Yes... the 10th.'

Tuesday it was, and that suited me: I was going to be in college for the afternoon. I would work late, use the gym showers and change there – and ensure that my destination and intentions were known in the department.

Howells had been, I thought, unenthusiastic about my choice of restaurant, but he'd acquiesced with grace. That was good. At Papa Gino's I was known: Marina and I had often eaten there. It was small: family run, and I could be certain of encountering someone who would later, if necessary, remember me. But, to be absolutely sure, I phoned and had a word with Gino's son Mario who ran the front of house. And, too, I wanted to let him know about Marina.

It would be difficult. I knew that on Tuesday I would look up from my plate, or over my glass, wanting to see those green eyes gazing at me with love and the promise of love, and I would see, instead, her murderer, but not for the world would I miss an opportunity which I believed would bring me that much closer to the witness of his end. For Marina, this. Only for Marina. All those dead children counted for nothing against that one death. By then, stopping Matthew Howells before he could kill again was almost a secondary consideration. My motivation was revenge, and the power driving me was hate. She would have been ashamed of me.

Working over the weekend was no empty excuse. By Saturday lunchtime I'd finished my piece about the founding of the priory leaving the afternoon free to deal with other matters. First, some letters: to a mid-Wales local history society enquiring about Matthew Howells' origins, and a subscription to a news cutting agency with a request for anything to do with him and his 'father'. With those out of the way I settled down to attack the matter of bells and bellringing in Llantathan.

On two separate, but strangely similar, occasions the ringing of a bell given by a Vine had been forbidden by Howells and physically prevented by the village. It had to mean something, but what? The sitting room floor was littered with notes and books but I still had no answer when John called in around four.

'Perhaps Howells doesn't like the sound of bells,' he suggested. 'Some people just don't, you know.'

I shook my head. 'It can't be that because the trouble only started when the ring was increased to eight at the end of the 18th century. And ringing continued after that on six bells until the last war.'

'Yes. I see...' He offered to make tea and disappeared to the kitchen leaving me puzzled. John was invariably willing to explore any avenue concerning Howells, no matter how unpromising but not, apparently, today.

When he returned with the tea tray, I wondered whether to try again. Perhaps not: he looked mildly disturbed. Preoccupied. Once or twice he seemed about to say something, yet didn't. Not until I mentioned Adam.

'I'm becoming rather concerned about him,' he confessed.

'Why? What's wrong?' Sudden anxiety made my voice sharp.

'He's not getting the sleep he should. He has very disturbed nights.'

'You don't think it's...?'

'No, Stephanie, I do not.' The firmness of John's rebuttal was comforting.

He peered into the teapot then poured two cups. I took one.

'I think there are a number of things worrying him at the moment. He isn't going to bed until very late. Sometimes he doesn't even come in until two or after.' He sipped his tea and took a biscuit. 'Of course occasionally there's an obvious reason, such as the evening you and he went out.'

'No,' I said thoughtfully. 'That wasn't my doing. Adam can't have left here later than 11.30. Maybe earlier. Is he out every night?'

John nodded. 'Sometimes only for an hour or two but more often than not he'll go out around 10 and not come back until the early hours.'

'Haven't you any idea, John? You're usually pretty good at working out things like this.'

His expression told me that he had a very good idea. 'I think he's worrying about you,' he admitted. 'It's making him restless.'

'You mean this dinner with Howells?'

'No, it can't be that because this was going on before that came up. I don't know...'

I thought he knew more than he was telling, and said so.

'I'm not sure...' He hesitated, clearly wondering whether to come clean. 'No, that's not true. I'm as sure as I can be, but I don't think it's something I ought to discuss with you. Adam would, I think, be deeply offended.'

'John, if you're trying to drop hints about Adam's feelings for me...'

His face betrayed sudden relief. 'You know?'

'A bit belatedly but, yes, though I'd had... sort of suspicions for a while. Marina knew, didn't she?'

'She did,' he told me, but didn't elaborate, and I didn't probe. In any case my concern, at that point, was the matter of the bells.

John looked too tired to be of help. Watching him sitting there, almost nodding off over his cooling tea, I felt a rush of belated guilt. I'd relied on him heavily, making demands which were excessive and unfair. And now he had this additional worry. I could, perhaps, ease the burden at least for one night. So I asked, 'John, is Adam busy this evening? If he isn't, would you mention that I need a hand with all this?' I gestured at that paperwork. 'A sounding board...'

John nodded. 'I expect he'll be pleased to help.'

'The thing is,' I went on, 'it might turn into a late night session. If it does, I'll tell Adam that he's welcome to stay.'

'Are you being devious, Stephanie?' John looked amused.

'Only a little. He might worry less if we're under the same roof. And you might get some sleep too.'

It was after 8.30 when Adam arrived, apologising for being so late. 'I needed to finish reading the metalwork analysis from the church excavation,' he explained as he put a bottle of Grenache in the fridge to chill.

'Have you eaten?' I asked, watching him from the kitchen doorway.

'Yes.' He turned and looked at me as if trying to assess my thinness through my loose, floating frock. 'Have you?'

'Yes, but I'll make supper later.'

He didn't reply, but continued to look at me until, growing uncomfortable under his gaze, I turned and went through to the sitting room. And as he followed me, I felt unusually aware of him. Not quite safe. Strange, that, because I'd come to regard him as very safe indeed. He and John had become my bookends: ill-matched but serving the same purpose; bracketing and supporting me with an easy, fond friendship I never questioned. I'd sensed changes: after we did the gardening, and since the evening at the Tredegar Arms, and if I'd given more thought to my reaction to him then, I might have understood but, with other things to think about, I'd pushed it aside. Now, though, I felt it, and it made me nervous.

He picked his way through the papers spread on the floor and sat down in Marina's chair. I folded myself up on the hearthrug and took a cigarette from the packet he held out. If he noticed that my hand wasn't steady, he made no comment, beginning, instead to describe the preparations he'd made so far for the fortification of the church.

'Can you do it all in time?' I asked.

'Yes, I think so. The tricky job is the grilles: getting the wiring through the windows without causing any damage. Don't worry. I'll work it out. Now about these bells, Steph...'

I nodded and sighed. 'I'm sure it's important,' I said, 'but I can't seem to make connections.'

'You'd better start at the beginning,' he advised, 'because I know sod all about it.'

So I told him about Reynald Devigne's gift of the first bell in 1132. 'And after the Dissolution it seemed to have been used as a summoning bell until 1799. In that year Hubert, a direct descendant of Reynald, with his name simplified to Vine, married Henrietta Cavendish. No connection with the Chatsworth Cavendishes but, like the Vines, prosperous gentry. Incidentally, Adam, your Lincolnshire inheritance became part of the Vine estates through Henrietta. The marriage was celebrated with a very costly gesture: Hubert had the old bell recast as a treble and his wife's father commissioned a new tenor bell to augment Llantathan's existing ring of six.'

I explained about the methods of change ringing and the greater flexibility which eight bells gave. 'Ringing was incredibly popular,' I said, 'and Llantathan's ringers seem to have been enthusiastic, but they wouldn't ring eight, which is very odd.'

'Would it be harder to ring more bells?'

'Maybe, but experienced ringers would learn quickly, and the extra bells would open up a whole new range of changes. Logically they should have been falling over themselves to thank Hubert and Cavendish.'

'Hmm, but ordinary logic doesn't apply in Llantathan,' Adam said. 'What happened?'

'Well, the bishop came and the bells were named, sprinkled and dedicated to God's service. So far, so good. But then Howells kicked up a fuss. First he tried to prevent them being hung but the bishop was having none of that and the bells went up. So Howells told the village ringers to leave the new bells alone, and they did. The bishop tried to bring in ringers from some other parish but the rector barred the church door and there was a fight in the High Street. It must have been a pretty scandal at the time.'

He grinned, obviously picturing the brawl. 'But it doesn't make sense, does it?'

'No, but sense there must be if only I could see it.' I shook my head in frustration. Adam stood up.

'I'll get the wine,' he offered. 'Hang on a minute, then you can tell me the rest.' In the doorway he stopped and turned. 'From what I've heard so far, I think you're right, Steph: this is important.'

He disappeared to the kitchen leaving me both fretted and relieved. I was beginning to be obsessed by this bell problem and it was good to know that Adam shared my view of its importance. What importance, though? What was I missing?

Settled again with glasses of cold Grenache, Adam sat back in the chair and I resumed my story, telling him that ringing had continued on six bells until the start of the war in 1939. 'Of course at that point all ringing stopped,' I said, 'except after Dunkirk and Alamein. But the government lifted restrictions in 1943 and when the war was over victory peals were rung up and down the country. Llantathan didn't ring because according to this...' I tapped the cover of *The Bellringers of Monmouth*, '...the belfry timbers had death watch beetle. It's not true though because I asked the diocesan architect and he told me that although renovation work was carried out in the belfry in 1951 the timbers were in good condition. So it looks like Howells or Blayney or both putting a stop to ringing altogether.'

I shifted some papers so that I could stretch out my legs. Adam lit two cigarettes and passed one to me. 'Go on,' he invited.

'Yes... well... then we come to Arthur Vine's memorial to Penelope. I'm sure he was on to something,' I said. 'And I can almost see the connections. There's the old bell given by his medieval forefather which is recast by his Georgian ancestor and which he causes to be recast again. And Howells won't let it be rung. Then there's the tenor bell given by Cavendish in 1799 and that's banned too. Now why?'

He topped up his glass and mine. 'You said that when the bells were blessed the bishop dedicated them to God's service. Wouldn't that upset Howells?'

'It might if the other bells weren't blessed,' I replied, 'but they were, so it can't be that.'

'OK. Is there anything else about these bells which makes them different from the others?'

'Well, the treble predates Howells. At least part of it does. It incorporates the original bell metal and what was added was paid for by other members of the Vine family. So it's almost a personal bell.

'The Cavendish bell was new, donated after Howells established himself here but, like the treble, it had nothing to do with him, and a lot to do with the Vines. It must be important too, but I can't help thinking that it's the Vine bell which really matters.'

He nodded. 'Who paid for the other bells?' he asked. 'Howells?'

'The village, with a donation from Howells.'

He nodded again. And the Vine bell and the Cavendish bell bracket the six...'

'Yes, numerically, but the bells are hung in a square, two to each side, so they're also next to each other, though I can't remember just where.'

'Oh yes, you had to go up there to record the inscriptions, didn't you?'

I shuddered. 'Don't remind me! Yes, right at the beginning when you lot were still hacking at the plaster. Marina was curious and went with me. Even then I was petrified.'

'I've been up several times. Can't say it bothered me.'

'It bothers me plenty,' I said, remembering the eight heavy, brooding presences. 'I know it sounds silly but those bells seemed alive.'

'Hostile? Sinister?' he asked. 'Some people feel they are, and there are quite a few horror stories featuring bells.'

'No... judgmental. I could well believe that if the bells didn't like us... Oh, it's nonsense. Forget it.'

I drank some wine and, realising that I felt cold, put a match to the fire. It was high summer but fires at night were a comfort.

'Was Marina afraid of the bells?' Adam wanted to know.

'Not a bit. She clambered around them looking at the mechanisms. It's all in excellent order. The Vines made sure of that. Miss Imogen had the lot remounted with new bearings when Arthur's bell was installed.

'I must say, though, that the treble does fascinate me. It isn't the original priory bell, but it contains that bell, and Hubert's bell too. All those centuries – so much history carried forward in that one object. Nothing lost because it's been made and remade. Oh, just fanciful ideas but...'

'No, maybe not so fanciful, Steph. That bell goes on rather like Howells. Almost a parallel, and each time it returns it takes to itself something of the Vines who are a part of Llantathan. The good part. If bells do have power that one must have God's amount...' He lapsed into thought. I poured more wine and looked at my watch. Time to make a snack if I was going to. I went into the kitchen and left Adam to his musings.

There was quiche in the pantry, and a dish of tomatoes: the fruits of Marina's efforts in the greenhouse. Ham too, and some nice rolls. Plates, cutlery, butter, chutney. I was loading the trolley when Adam drifted in. 'Didn't you say that the bells were named?' he asked.

I glanced up. 'Yes, all of them. And they all have inscriptions and dates.'

'Can you remember any?'

'Oh Lord! It's ages since I did it. Let's see...' I pushed the trolley through to the sitting room. 'One's called Briton, and there's Titan...'

Adam moved some papers to make room. 'What about our two bells?'

'The Cavendish bell is Timothy from *Timor mortis conturbat me*. The fear of death troubles me. But, unusually, it has a second inscription. A canting motto – a sort of skit – on the Cavendish name: *cave diss*. I thought at first it meant beware of God, but diss is an abbreviation for *dissolutio* which can mean destruction. They're the kind of quotes you'd expect to find on a bell that's used to toll for the dead.'

'And the treble?' He helped himself to quiche as he spoke and, pointedly, passed me a plate.

'It's an odd one, that.' I took some ham and a roll. 'Hubert Vine called his bell after a character he'd seen depicted in a painting in Italy when he was doing the Grand Tour. A biblical scene, but I don't know which one. I don't think it can have kept the same name when it was recast in the 1950s, though, because Arthur called his bell Judith, and I can't think of anyone in the bible with that name. Can you?'

He couldn't but that, he said, meant nothing, his knowledge of scripture being patchy. 'Let's leave it for tonight, Stephanie, or we'll start going round in circles.'

I didn't object: I'd thought of bells all day and I'd probably dream about them. So I tidied the books and papers onto the side table, ate a piece of quiche and suggested watching the late film.

I switched on the television set and went back to sit on the floor again, hoping that Adam wouldn't want to discuss my dinner date with Matthew Howells. I'd already told him what arrangements I'd made and he'd seemed satisfied, but since then I'd had John niggling at me with his worries. I couldn't see anything in Adam's manner to be worried about, though. He didn't look all that tired. Slightly preoccupied maybe, but that was understandable.

Thankfully he made no mention of Howells or anything connected with him. Until the film started, we chatted about cars. Adam was thinking about buying a new one. We had coffee and I opened a bottle of Islay malt.

The uneasiness I'd felt when Adam arrived was forgotten now. I was relaxed, anaesthetised by whisky and warmth and friendly conversation. When the film began, I turned up the volume and instead of returning to the rug, I sat with my back against Adam's chair. It seemed the natural thing to do, and far more comfortable. I'd done it dozens of times when Marina had occupied that chair. Adam knew that. It never occurred to me that he might find it disturbing.

When the film ended, at about 1.30, I switched the set off and Adam stood up.

'Coffee?' I suggested, but he shook his head.

'It's late. I'd better go.'

I felt disappointed. It had been a full evening. Full enough, almost, to make me forget. 'It's Sunday tomorrow. You don't have to get up early.'

'Don't worry, I won't. No Stephanie, I'll be off now.'

'You could always stay here,' I said, knowing that there was more behind the offer than my wish to ease John's concern.

He stood very still for a moment then he came and rested his hands lightly on my shoulders. His expression was grave. 'Do you mean that?' he asked.

I nodded.

'I wonder why...' Then he turned to the door. 'Goodnight, Stephanie,' he said, and was gone.

As the front door closed behind him, I knew. Finally I knew just why Marina had exploded last February. At some point the friendship Adam and I shared had tipped into something else, and though I might have been blind to the fact, she wasn't. I was aware – painfully aware – that in spite of all she and I had been to eachother, and in the face of this terrible, consuming despair, I was attracted to Adam. And that attraction was not something borne of my loneliness since Marina died. It had been there for months, and he knew it.

Sunday was not a good day. Not with the memory of the previous night accusing me, and face-up-to-it Monday just ahead. The only thing I could do was go on treating Adam as I'd always done with, perhaps, a little more circumspection. Because if I didn't, there might come a time when all the forbearance, the kindness and affection I took for granted would fly out of the window. I had sense enough to recognise in Adam a model for that still waters cliché: stepping out of the framework of our friendship might well involve more than I bargained for. And that, I have to admit, was a possibility as intriguing as it was unnerving.

But such embarrassment as I had the grace to feel was forgotten when, on Monday morning in John's kitchen I put the radio on for the news and froze. Adam, dropping slices of bread into the toaster, turned and we listened in horror to the Today newsreader talking about a catastrophic fire at York Minster. Neither of us said a word, but there was an odd complicity in the look we exchanged. A remembering.

Over the course of the day we spoke only of work and the prospect of being able to investigate the Howells grave during the next week. When it came to it, we could both be professional because that's what we were; but I knew that our relationship was never going to be the same. There had been tacit admissions last night and again this morning of something between us. And behind all this there were other truths too far away, buried too deep for me to grasp.

VI

Before I left work on Monday evening, I had a brief chat with John who assured me that he would be at the rectory all the next evening should I need to contact him. 'And if I should be called out, Adam will be here.'

I didn't ask, and he didn't say, but I knew that while I was dining with Matthew Howells, he would be reminding God of my existence. Maybe God didn't care much, but if John pestered him enough... At that point God and I weren't on speaking terms.

Not entirely true. As Tuesday wore on, I made more than one serious advance towards the Holy of Holies. What had looked easy last week began to seem reckless. Now I thought I was neither clever nor guileful enough to succeed. Nor was Matthew Howells fool enough to let me. At best this was going to be a waste of time. At worst...

I was about to get some tea when John phoned with news.

'Two things, Stephanie. First a message from Adam. He said to tell you that it's a vault...' I caught my breath. '...and please say nothing about it. Details when you get back, and he sends his love.'

'Tell him much appreciated.'

'Now the second matter. I've just spoken to Angela. Yes, she's fine. Stephanie, she was trying to contact you about something she found when she was clearing out the attics. She thinks it should go into your... archive.'

The slight pause suggested volumes to me. 'How urgent is it? I don't think I can do anything until tomorrow.'

'That's all right. She'll call in here tomorrow morning.'

I got my tea and sat gazing out of the window across the parched college lawns, an inexplicable concern growing in my mind. Tomorrow. Would I be there tomorrow? Yes, tomorrow I would be at work in the rectory with this evening already a memory. The safeguards I'd built into it would ensure that. I would be there to receive from Angela Morton whatever it was that she'd found. Something whose importance to us I didn't question. But would Angela be there to give it? That question sneaked into my mind at a tangent.

I reached for the phone, got an outside line and dialled the Allington number. It rang and rang. Well, if Angela was clearing attics perhaps she wouldn't hear it. I left it fifteen minutes and dialled again, tapping the handset with impatient fingers. Still no reply. I tried the rectory and eventually Joyce answered, telling me that John was out but would be back by four at the very latest. Over an hour! When I asked for Adam she was incredulous. 'Are you kidding, Steph! Only an idiot would go within ten feet of Adam with a request like that just now.'

The Howells grave – no, vault. Of course. Adam would be hyped up as hell.

'Joyce, listen. This is important. The instant John comes in tell him to go straight to Allington.'

She promised faithfully, but she could have no idea of the urgency I felt: a minor crisis on site and she might well forget.

I lit another cigarette and sat, tense, trying to make up my mind, wondering if this was real intuition or merely overheated imagination. Wondering how wide Matthew Howells' net was cast and whether Angela knew enough to avoid it. No. If something was wrong, John might not get to Allington in time. I had to go. One more check, but the Allington phone rang on unanswered.

I ran along the corridor to the office, digging in my bag for the car keys, and left a message with Kate, the secretary. 'I'll be back,' I promised. Whatever happened, I had to get back.

It was too early for home-going traffic, but there were plenty of holiday motorists to hold me up. Once clear of that, though, I made some speed, reaching Allington faster than I expected.

The frontage of the house with its sweeping carriage turn looked much as always: pristine and quiet. As I parked the car at the foot of the wide steps John's Saab came nosing along the drive. He pulled in behind the Escort and jumped out, his face strained, his expression almost angry.

'What is all this about, Stephanie?' he demanded. 'I had to cancel an appointment...'

'Did Angela call you from here,' I asked. He nodded. 'Was she in any way explicit about what she'd found?'

'No. She merely said that she'd been going through old papers and thought she'd discovered something which would be valuable to you.'

I looked soberly at him. 'We don't know – we've never known – if it's safe to speak openly on the phone,' I began, but I didn't need to say more. John's mystified crossness turned to comprehension, and he bounded up the steps to set the old-fashioned doorbell pealing. Twice, three times he pulled at it but no-one came.

The kitchen courtyard betrayed signs of recent activity: bags of rubbish stacked by the wall of the old vegetable store, and a mop, upended, was propped against a drainpipe to dry in the sun. John disappeared inside, calling, but he was soon out again. 'No sign,' he said, 'but she can't be far. I'll go and see if she's still up in the attics. You look round outside.'

I nodded, very tense now. This quiet was too much. It reminded me of those afternoons when I was recording in the churchyard: that sense of being watched.

None of the outbuildings yielded a clue and I wondered where, in Allington's spreading gardens, to look next. Running along worn brick paths between clipped hedges I tried the rose alley and the sunken wet garden then, drawing a blank, I took a path behind the poplars bordering the old croquet lawn. It brought me back to the walled kitchen gardens but there was no access on that side. In a moment or two, breathless, I found myself in the orchard. I also found Angela.

She was lying like washing on a Monday morning. A ladder beside her on the grass and an overturned basket of cherries told an obvious tale. Crisis calm, I knelt and put my fingers on the wrist of one outflung hand, waiting to be sure that what I felt was real and not hopeful imagination. Vague on all but the most basic principles of first aid, I stuck to the one I was certain of. I made sure she could breathe and left well alone.

Racing back to the house I almost collided with John coming round the end of the vegetable store. Pausing only to tell him where and what, I dived inside, remembering that there was a phone extension in the kitchen. Angela needed an ambulance. That done I took a big old coat from the vestibule and hurried back to the orchard.

'I think there's blood on the back of her head,' John said softly. 'Should we...?'

'Better leave alone,' I counselled. 'I can't see enough to suggest that she's bleeding to death and if we move her God knows what damage we might do. I'll go round to the front and wait for the ambulance. You stay here and see if you can spot anything odd. It might have been an accident but again, it might not.'

He gazed at the tree and the ladder. 'It looks straightforward...'

'So did Andrew Mason. So did Brian Bennett. We'll only know for sure when and if we find whatever it was she wanted to give me. If it's still in the house this was an accident.'

The two-tone screech of the ambulance cut the late afternoon silence. It would be at the house in minutes. Indeed, before I reached the carriage turn it came into sight and behind it, P. C. Griffiths' patrol car. Oh joy!

Alan Foster was leaving for home when I met him on the half landing of the Arts staircase. 'I got your message,' he said. 'What's going on?'

'Miss Morton at Allington had an accident,' I explained. 'She was companion to Miss Vine who left us the money for the archive.'

'Oh yes. What happened?'

'Fell off a ladder picking cherries. She's in the Royal here in Newport. John's there.

'Bad?'

'It could have been worse.' If there was irony in my voice, he missed it.

'Well, let me know how she goes on. I'll get Kate to organise some flowers.' He picked up his briefcase. 'Anyway, what are you doing here now?'

'Work,' I told him. 'I've got a dinner appointment later so I'm making use of the time between.'

He smiled. 'I'm glad you're getting out. Who's the lucky person?'

I put on a you'll-never-believe-it face. 'Matthew Howells.'

He stared. 'Good God! He really exists then?'

'Large as life and twice as natural.' I laughed and thought how the cliché took on extra meaning when applied to Howells.

Alan shook his head. 'Funny,' he mused. 'That man's caused endless trouble yet I've never quite been able to believe in him.'

'Oh, he's real enough and he seems to want to smooth things over. So I'm doing my bit to help it all along.'

'Good for you.' He felt in his pocket for his keys. 'Well, have a nice time. If you're on site tomorrow, would you tell Adam that I won't be out until later in the week? Friday, probably.'

He went down and I turned to mount the stairs. From the tall windows I could see the clock on the tower of the Engineering block. Twenty-five past six, and I was meeting Matthew Howells in the bar at Papa Gino's at eight. I wasn't scared now. Pausing, I leant on the brass banister rail, watching the big black minute hand of the clock advancing in stiff, measured jerks towards the half hour, and mentally re-ran the afternoon's events.

There wasn't an atom of proof that the ladder hadn't just slipped but it was a mighty big coincidence. And coincidence in Llantathan usually meant Matthew Howells. Yet another convenient accident. But this time you got it wrong, I said to myself. This time the victim lived. You're not infallible. That being so, I might succeed. A man who makes one mistake can make another. As the big hand of the clock reached half past, I ran up the last few steps and along the corridor to my office. I should be able to finish the re-draft I'd barely begun when all this intervened. And then it would be time to get ready.

Before I left, I phoned the Royal and was encouraged by the news that Angela's injuries were not serious. She'd regained consciousness and, despite stitches in a scalp wound and some cracked ribs, was reported to be comfortable.

John, by virtue of his dog collar, would certainly have been allowed time with her and might well have already ascertained the situation regarding Miss Vine's papers. Worrying about it then was pointless, and I didn't. I sat still for a few minutes, breathing deeply, stilling my mind. Then, confident of my appearance, confident of my ability to twist Matthew Howells round my little finger, I went out to meet the man who had killed my lover.

VII

Howells was already there when I walked – five minutes late – into the bar. He looked impatient, uncomfortable. Obviously Papa Gino's wasn't his sort of place. The click of my high heels caught his attention. He turned and I notched up a small advantage. Here was a man who was definitely keen, waiting for a woman who, in every respect but one, wasn't keen at all. He came forward to greet me, smiling. 'Mrs. Hargreaves, how lovely to see you again. May I get you a drink?'

Smiling, I asked for a white wine spritzer and perched myself on one of the high bar stools wondering if I should have worn a short skirt. I had no idea how susceptible Howells might be but at least my frock was low cut. It might be helpful. Adam would be furious if he knew that I was considering such flaunting tactics. And then, another thought. *He sent his love.*

I sipped my spritzer. Howells had whisky and it wasn't his first. Unless he had a very hard head he wasn't going to be capable of driving me home. Of course a drunken Howells might be more to my advantage...

'You look very thoughtful,' he remarked. 'Or is that an obligatory expression for historians?'

'We tend to acquire it, I suppose. It's a demanding discipline.'

'Only if you make it so.'

'No,' I contradicted. 'There are no half measures with history. It isn't a nine till five job. Only a fool would enter the profession with an office hours mentality.'

'And you are not a fool.' It was a statement to which I made no reply so that he was forced to provide the next contribution. 'With such an attitude you'd make an excellent businesswoman.'

I shook my head. 'I've no talent at all in that direction. Strange, since both my parents had plenty of business sense.'

'Really? You surprise me. I should have said that you come from an academic background.'

He was prodding, probing. Fair enough. Give a little to get a little. I said, 'My father was craftsman cabinet maker.'

'And your mother?'

'Very hard-headed lady. She ran the office.'

He finished his drink and ordered another. I shook my head.

'So, Mrs. Stephanie Hargreaves,' he said, 'tell me more about yourself. Where do you come from?'

'Yorkshire,' I answered truthfully but vaguely. There's a lot of Yorkshire.

'Do you miss it? I believe Yorkshire folk are very... chauvinistic.' He used the word correctly. That interested me.

'I miss the countryside,' I allowed. 'But I've no ties there now.'

'No family?'

'No,' I lied, and closed that avenue. Nor did he get far with a tactful reference to my marital status. I agreed that I was divorced implying mendaciously that the subject was painful and not to be discussed.

What he might have tried next I don't know. He didn't get a chance: Mario, smiling his pleasure, came to usher us through the trellis arch to our table in the restaurant.

Showing us to an alcove where climbing plants made a picturesque frame, Mario flicked the merest hint of a wink at me. Go on, Mario, I willed silently. Do your bit. He had a somewhat flamboyant line in Latin flattery and it was exactly what I needed to fix the attention of the other diners on us.

'La Signorina Bella!' he exclaimed delightedly if inaccurately. 'Signorina Stephanie, where have you been all these weeks!' His flow was enhanced by a series of extravagant gestures causing heads to turn as we were seated: not everyone who ate at Papa's was given the Mario treatment, and even those who were, including me, had never had it larded on like this. He was a star that evening.

He burbled on, praising my frock, my hair, my eyes. There was a flourish of menus, a kissing of fingertips, a final 'Bella!' and he was gone. Howells had a face like thunder. So much attention, and not at all to his taste. It suited me though: in the unlikely event that I was found dead in a ditch – and to be fair I didn't believe Howells had any such designs – at least two dozen people would remember La Signorina Bella and her angry-looking companion.

Displeased Howells was but he made no comment. He read the menu and the wine list and when Mario returned, more decorous now, gave our orders in fluent Italian. It was an obvious ploy intended either to show Mario up as a fake, which he wasn't, or as a kind of one-upmanship. I was delighted: he could be stung into retaliation. A mistake, that, for Mario took it as a nice gesture and made more of a fuss of us than ever.

The food was, as always, excellent. If Howells had expected the kind of stuff which often passes for Italian *cucina* he must have been pleasantly surprised. This was the real thing and the standard of the wine Mario served us matched the food.

With the antipasti Howells' black looks gave way to grudging appreciation and his good humour returned, suggesting that my first impression of him was accurate. The self-indulgence I'd suspected was evident, but held in check, at least where food was concerned. Alcohol was another matter. The wine he ordered was the Brunello di Montalcino, a rather special red. It was too heavy for me and I drank less than half a glass. I remembered Pen Vine's frequent references to her husband's drinking, linking it to his vile moods. Worth bearing in mind. So far, though, he seemed, apart from during Mario's histrionics, pleasant enough.

Recalling Pen's journal brought on that weird sense of unreality. More than once I glanced up at Howells' face trying to connect him with the man who had married Penelope Vine. That they were one and the same I believed, but it was an academic belief forced upon me because logic permitted no other explanation. Nor did the marks on his forehead. The scar which was visible in the photographs had gone but, pale against his discreet tan, faint traces suggested plastic surgery. Oh yes, my thumbs pricked all right, but I was back to the old problem of rationalisation. It is all but impossible for the mind to accept that one is in the company of a man looking no older than the 42 he purported to be, yet of whom I had read, albeit in another guise, in a journal begun before the war. Pen Vine would have recognised him instantly as the man she married in 1938 who, according to the records, died in 1966. Encompassing that was hard; trying to see in this man the Matthew Howells who arrived in Llantathan in 1755 was enough to induce instant lunacy.

'Thoughtful again.' His voice called me back to 20th century Newport. 'Still history?'

'I'm afraid so.' I smiled wryly. 'I'm sorry to be such poor company but I'm so busy now that it's hard to stop thinking about work.'

'Problems?' His voice was sympathetic and once again I was aware of his immense charm. If he hadn't been Matthew Howells I might, perhaps, have liked him.

'Not really,' I replied. 'It's all fairly straightforward but... Oh never mind. You can't possibly be interested.'

'Oh but I am,' he assured me. 'I don't believe I ever met a historian before. Certainly not one as lovely as you.'

I made a deprecating gesture and tried to change the subject but he persisted. So, as we waited for the next course, I said, 'My contribution to the excavation report will include a survey of Llantathan's history but, as you know, I've also been given the task of writing a comprehensive history of the village.

'Naturally much of the survey concentrates on the medieval period but the history's another matter. The scope's much wider and I must give a flavour of life in Llantathan through the ages. Atmosphere. I'm happy enough until the early 18th century but frankly, once past the Stuarts, trying to imbue the later history of Llantathan with atmosphere is like... like trying to make a dentist's surgery look cosy.'

It was bait. Would he take it? Before he could Mario was hovering again with the main course so it was some time before Howells replied. 'I wouldn't have thought that such a stagnant little hole would have any history worth mentioning...'

'Oh, come on!' I protested. 'You must know about its medieval heyday!'

'Certainly,' he replied coolly. 'But after that what is there? It became a backwater, an anachronism on a road to nowhere, and that's what it is today.'

'Then it hasn't changed much in your lifetime?' That was a tricky question. Would I get away with it?

'Llantathan will never change,' he said shortly, and the bitterness in his voice surprised me.

I looked up in what I hoped was a frank and candid manner. 'I know what you said when you visited the site, that you're not conservative but – and please forgive me if I'm wrong – I've always been led to understand that much of Llantathan's insularity stems from your wishes and those of your ancestors.'

Howells' pale eyes were hard and I was afraid that I'd strayed into very deep waters. His fingers gripped the stem of his glass until I was sure it must snap. But, slowly, he relaxed and favoured me with a tight smile.

'Your impression is correct, Mrs. Hargreaves,' he said, his voice harsh. 'But the facts are otherwise.'

When he didn't elaborate, I asked how long he was planning to stay, and that question appeared to displease him too, at first. 'I would prefer not to have to visit Llantathan at all,' he said. 'The place is... sick... rotten. And believe me, there is nothing even your good Mr. Holmes can do to change that. Llantathan does not want change. It likes itself as it is, as it has always been.'

'And you?' I prompted softly, wondering... wondering...

'I detest it!' There was venom in his voice. 'I wish to God I'd never set eyes on the place. But, since I'm saddled with the estate, I must administer it. I come, as you will know, once a year to consult with my agent, speak to my tenants, deal with necessary business. And as soon as that is done, I go. Beyond that I have no reason or wish to stay.' Then he smiled and the coldness gave way to charm. 'But perhaps this year will be different,' he went on. 'Perhaps this time there is a reason to stay.'

I raised my eyebrows. 'Is there?'

Another smile. 'Who knows, Stephanie? You might be a very good reason.'

So I might, and if I had my way he would be staying –
six feet down in a box – but I didn't think he meant that.
He might have meant that I was a problem to be dealt with
after the 8th, if he hadn't managed to do it before. Playing
innocent, I responded with a pleased if slightly surprised
smile. And I let the use of my Christian name pass without
comment. 'Aren't you here rather earlier than usual,
though?' I asked. I put my head on one side and produced
what I hoped was a teasing look. 'If you hate the place so
much...?' I let the question hang in the air. Flirtation.

'Ah well, I'd heard so much about the excavation. And
about the beautiful historian. I simply had to come back
and see for myself.'

I bet, I thought. And what of the beautiful historian's
lover? Did you come back specially to wipe her out? I
pushed the thought down. I had to know more and if I
thought of Marina I would become morose which would
not appeal to Howells. I wasn't even sure now that physical
attraction was going to produce results. That angle had
brought, so far, only nauseating flattery. Direct questions
were risky, but they'd won me the best response so far.

Howells had spoken of Llantathan with bitterness
and hatred: a reaction I never anticipated. Every scrap
of evidence pointed to the village being his possession,
his existence, his raison d'être; yet he claimed to detest
it. I could have understood if he'd been dismissive,
contemptuous, patronising. But how could he hate what
he made? And what of his assertion that it was not his writ
which ran in the village. That, surely, was an out-and-out
lie. *Sir Matthew says* was Llantathan's litany. But could I
really ask him direct questions about all that?

Mario returned with dessert menus and we deliberated
the merits of the various puddings on offer. I chose one of

the house confections of raspberries and sorbet. Howells declined such frivolities and called for the cheese board. Coffee was served, and grappa or limoncello offered. I refused both but Howells ordered a double grappa and that decided who wasn't driving me home. He looked in reasonable shape but I wasn't taking any chances.

'If you dislike Llantathan so much, why don't you sell the estate?' I suggested, and waited to be blasted.

'I wish I could,' he replied with every sign of sincerity. 'Unfortunately the way it's tied up makes that impossible. Do you understand entails?'

I nodded. Entailed property was a feature I'd encountered often enough in documents. I let him talk about the restrictive terms in the will of Matthew Howells I, and enjoyed listening to him making a mistake. It is always a mistake to imagine that a historian wouldn't know that entails could be broken and, since 1833, broken quite easily.

It was my belief that anything Matthew Howells told me – anything at all – could be useful but his apparently genuine dislike of Llantathan had to be probed. So, when the subject of entails was exhausted, I remarked on the awkwardness of working in a hostile atmosphere.

'Yes, it must be unpleasant,' he replied. 'And I'm sorry for it but I'm afraid I can do very little to help.' He leaned forward, his expression earnest. 'Please believe that this is not my doing. I can make my feelings known but I have almost no control over the actions of the community. It is not, and never has been, my wish to cause trouble.'

He really was doing his damnedest to dissociate himself from it all and I half believed him. There was something... something... Nothing I could formulate at all: just that he wasn't what I expected. Evil could and often did wear a fair face: wasn't Lucifer supposed to be beautiful? This was nowhere near so obvious, and it was going to need a lot of thought.

It was after 11 when we made moves to go. While Howells paid the bill, I tried to think of a tactful way of refusing to allow him to drive me home. I'd wanted to use that journey but not after the amount of alcohol he'd consumed. To my relief, however, he asked Mario to call a taxi to take us back to Llantathan.

Obviously, there wasn't going to be any possibility of confidences in the back of the car: this wasn't a nicely partitioned London cab; but I didn't mind. I had every chance of reaching the rectory safely and unless I was mistaken this wasn't going to be my sole opportunity.

The roads were quiet and the journey time short. We made polite, nondescript conversation from which I gleaned that Howells had a house in Switzerland which he disliked, preferring his holiday home in Italy. Then the village sign came up on our left and I told the driver to drop me at the rectory.

'I must call in to see Adam Pembury about work tomorrow,' I explained. 'I have a message for him from the unit director.'

'But surely it's rather late?' Howells protested. Had he been expecting an invitation for coffee at Vine Villa?

'No, he'll be around,' I replied and, as the car drew into the rectory drive, lights in the house vindicated me.

I climbed out, turning to say goodnight and thank you but Howells followed me. 'Wait, driver,' he ordered. 'I won't be long.'

And so I was escorted to the front door where I said my party piece, shivering a little. 'Thank you, Stephanie,' he said softly. 'It was a delightful evening.' A pause, then: 'May I see you again? Soon?'

'I don't know,' I told him. 'It depends entirely on pressure of work. I am very busy but...'

He took my hand. 'I'll call you before the end of the week.'

I thought he would go then but he still held my fingers in his. 'I don't know if I should mention this,' he said diffidently, 'but will you accept my condolences. Your friend, Dr. Graham...'

A tide of fury rose in me but before I could do or say anything he went on, 'I've been backwards and forwards to London, and I had to fly to New York so I only learned of her death when I saw my agent yesterday. I was very grieved. I'd hoped to meet her, and I'm truly sorry...'

The only thing which prevented me from giving vent to the boiling rage inside was a note of real regret in his voice. He sounded as if he meant it and that made me pause just long enough not to blow it all. I came so close to pouring out all the hatred; blasting him with threats. And then it would have been all up with us. But the sorrow – yes, sorrow – I heard when he spoke saved me from disaster. Either Howells was a liar to his fingertips or... what?

'You're getting cold,' he said, leaning across to ring the bell. 'Goodnight, Stephanie. I'll call you soon.'

My hand was kissed and released, and as the door opened spilling light across the drive, he swung himself back into the taxi and slammed the door. I lifted my hand in lieu of the goodnight I never said, and went inside.

John closed the door behind me as Adam came bounding downstairs, relief writ plain on his face. Relief was my principal emotion too and, suddenly, I felt like crying, like being held and hugged and babied.

'Stephanie, you're frozen!' John exclaimed. 'Come into the kitchen and let me get you a drink. Adam, find Stephanie something warm to put on.'

And so, cuddled in one of Adam's better jumpers, I sat by the Aga sipping whisky and smoking, revelling in warmth and safety, in being able to talk freely without playing games. The evening had been harder, more stressful than I ever imagined. How I valued John and Adam then, not least because I was made so aware of my value to them.

'How's Angela?' I asked. 'I did phone earlier and they said comfortable.'

'She'll be fine,' John assured me. 'But... it wasn't an accident. And I'm sorry, Steph: the papers intended for you have gone.'

I wasn't surprised, only sorry that Angela had been hurt, and glad that it wasn't one of Howells' best attempts. 'It can't be helped,' I sighed. 'I don't suppose she can remember what the papers were about?'

'No, not in detail, but she told me that they were written by Arthur Vine.'

'They would be! Probably the very thing we needed.'

'Steph dear, don't despair,' he said. 'I'm seeing Angela again tomorrow and I'm sure she'll tell me all she can remember. Don't distress yourself. Be comforted by the fact that your reasoning almost certainly saved her life. If you hadn't been so quick-thinking she might have lain there helpless all night. Maybe longer, and she would have died of shock and exposure.'

'Howells 258. Hargreaves 1,' Adam muttered. Now that he was reassured by my safe return he'd lapsed into his former disapproval exacerbated, no doubt, by my frock. 'No wonder you're bloody freezing,' he hissed at me when John was getting the whisky. 'You might as well not be wearing it. I hope it was worth it.'

Oh, I'd been tempted then to make some snide remark about jealousy, but I could see what lay behind the snappiness and I hadn't the heart to do it.

'No! No, Adam!' John was saying. 'Can't you see what a victory this is for us?'

'Yeah, I suppose. But it's pretty pathetic isn't it?'

John was shocked. 'Pathetic? To have saved a life? To have prevented a murder?'

I intervened hastily. 'John, I know what Adam means. Yes, it is a victory and the first real break we've had, but there's still so much to do. Please don't be upset if, sometimes, we're rather disheartened.'

He apologised adding: 'You don't look disheartened Stephanie. How did you get on?'

It was late and I was very tired. Too tired to think properly now, and any analysis of the evening was beyond me. Eventually I said, 'Hard facts? I can tell you that Matthew Howells has houses in Switzerland and Tuscany and speaks fluent Italian. He drinks heavily and dislikes being noticed. He can exert considerable charm if he chooses, and he's a liar. He prefers cheese to puddings, is capable of bad judgment and he wants to see me again.'

'And that's all you managed to find out?' Adam was disgusted.

'You didn't expect him to tell me his true life story, did you?' I snapped irritably. 'Look, I think there's a lot more to this than we know but I need time to think a few things through. I'll go home now and let you two get to bed. If I can borrow your sweater, Adam, I'll walk...'

'I'll take you home,' Adam interrupted abruptly. 'Come on. No Stephanie, you are not walking back at this time.'

John added his voice to Adam's and, too tired to argue, I trailed outside to Adam's car.

It was less than five minutes' drive to Vine Villa so Adam's silence barely mattered. He parked the Golf outside the front door and turned off the engine. Wearily

I climbed out, scrabbling for my door keys, lost as usual at the bottom of my bag. Not waiting until I found them, he used his key, turned on the hall light and told me to stay there. I listened to him checking round the house. It made sense: with me safely out of Llantathan for a whole predictable evening Vine Villa was a target for anyone who wanted to snoop or worse.

'OK,' he said, and went along the passageway to the kitchen. I followed. What was he doing now? Boiling a kettle. 'Go to bed, Stephanie,' he said. 'I'll bring you a hot drink in a few minutes.'

I didn't argue and the tea he brought up was welcome.

He hovered, not speaking but wanting to. I told him to sit down and he did so, hesitantly, on the edge of the bed. 'Stephanie, you are all right, aren't you?' His earlier brusqueness was gone. I heard concern, tenderness and a hint of fear in his voice and I was sorry. I put the mug down and reached out to hold his hand.

'Adam, I am all right. Really. I don't think Howells had any plans to get rid of me this evening but if he had he would have found it very difficult. I promised I would be careful and I was.'

He didn't look at me. 'I didn't mean...'

'I know. I know what you meant.'

His hand, passive in mine, turned then, and held. 'Stephanie, I accept that this is a God-given chance to find out as much as we can about Howells but it's not worth...'

Once I would have hit him with what he couldn't say. Not now. I said, 'Adam, Howells may be trying to find out what we know. He may want to see me off, but I'd be a fool not to exploit his interest. Only... please... please don't ever think that I would allow this to get out of hand. Never mind what I said before. I didn't mean it and it was never part of my plan.'

I don't think it lessened his worry: he had too much imagination. I had imagination too, and it was my undoing. Feeling for him, wanting to reassure, I put my hand on his shoulder and, leaning forward, I kissed him. In the circumstances that was the last thing he needed.

'What was that supposed to mean, Stephanie?' He stood up. 'Kissing me better, like I'm a hurt kid? Fuck that!'

He flung himself out of the room, out of the house. I heard the front door slam and then his car engine. And silence.

THE VOICE OF THE BELL
1984

Held we fall to rise, are baffled to fight better,
Sleep to wake.

Robert Browning

I

I was just leaving for work next morning when Adam came up the drive. 'I needed to see you before we start work,' he said. 'We're opening the vault, if all goes well. It's going to be a long day if it's straightforward, and a bloody nightmare if it isn't, and whatever it is I'm not going to have much time for anything else. Look, last night... I didn't mean... Put it down to reaction. It was a hell of a time waiting for you to get back.'

'It's OK, Adam.' I wanted to say more but there wasn't time, so I locked the door and we set off down School Lane, neither of us much inclined to chat.

In the rectory drive Paul, Dawn and Joyce were unloading boxes from the back of the site van. Adam asked Paul something about additional equipment then, to me, 'I'm not sure yet if our lifting gear can cope with the sealing stones. Come and have a look.'

All activity in Area G was now centred on two massive stone slabs rather longer and wider than normal ledger stones. The hoist was being positioned and Simon was busy with tools on one of the slabs. As I drew closer I could see that iron rings had been let into the stone and that the iron had corroded, bonding it into the circular grooves.

'If all those rings can be freed we'll manage it without too much trouble,' Adam told me. Simon's loosened two already and I think they'll hold. The corrosion's superficial.'

'How long, do you think?'

'To get the slabs up? If we can use the rings, by tea break. If we can't we'll have to bring some more gear out. In that case probably not today.' He drew me a little apart. 'Steph, I may need some help tonight. That little matter of Elwyn Pryce... With so much activity concentrated in one small area he's bound to come and see what's going on.'

'I'll be there. What are you going to do?'

'Remember what we talked about that evening in Shirenewton? I've not finally decided because it depends on how much progress we make. I'll let you know.'

It was, technically, coffee time, but Adam and the team were still working. Dawn, flying in to take some of her 35mm film from the fridge, said that things were going well, and they expected to be able to stop soon for a break. Before they did John, just back from the hospital, told me that Angela had been able to tell him a great deal.

It seemed that while she was tackling the accumulated junk in the attics Angela had discovered some brown paper packages in a box of items which had belonged to Arthur Vine. One contained newspaper cuttings mostly to do with unfortunate accidents, and there was a list of births, marriages and deaths...'

'Ah! So Arthur Vine really was on Howells' tracks.'

'Exactly,' John confirmed. 'What Angela said suggests that he must have pieced together quite a lot of evidence.'

'And the other?'

'Everything to do with the memorial bell.'

I sat there poised between hope and despair. 'Did she read it all? How much can she remember?' I sounded as desperate as I felt: like bashing my head against the wall.

'Well, some of the documents were quotes for the work involved, accounts and so on. There were notes about the history of the bell and about traditions and superstitions. The rest of it, she said, was written so oddly that it didn't make sense to her, but it seemed to be about a bible story, a song and a painting.'

'That would have been to do with Hubert's bell,' I said, disappointed. 'Unless there's more that Angela can't remember, it doesn't sound as if there was anything new.'

Soon after the team's belated break Joyce put her head round the door. 'The sealing slabs are up,' she reported. 'Come and see, and bring a hard hat.'

I ran downstairs and across to Area G where Phil and Paul were assembling a scaffolding catwalk to enable Dawn to take overhead photographs. Adam was in the vault. He steadied the ladder and I climbed down.

The vault was about the size of a typical third bedroom in a standard semi; brick construction, with a massive cross-member to support the sealing slabs. Along one side ran tiers of deep stone shelves and on the shelves coffins: warped – some gaping in places – mouldering, foisty, but intact. Big coffins, sad little boxes. And on the single cross shelf at the end, the one I most wanted out and opened. Matthew Howells: 1717 to 1782.

'I can't!' Adam protested when I urged this action. 'We've got to make a schematic plot and photograph everything first.'

Oh God, yes. It would take ages. 'Can't we open it *in situ*?'

He poked experimentally at the lid with the point of his trowel. Not this one,' he said. 'Let's have a look at the others.'

I could have wept with frustration. Those coffins looked as if they would crumble to dust at any moment yet the lids were tight.

'Steph, I'll do what I can. I want to know as much as you, remember? But I still have to do my job. I'll get someone onto the schematic as soon as we've got the first photographs and we might be able to lift this bugger during the afternoon. We'll have to be quick anyway. Word will soon get out.' As I climbed out he added softly, 'You were right, Stephanie. This is what we weren't supposed to find.'

Just before lunch Joyce brought a message from Adam. 'We're working late,' she informed me. 'He wants the vault cleared.'

'Can you do it?'

She shrugged. 'We'll have to try. It's claustrophobic and a bit unnerving, and no-one can stand it for long so we're working in relays. Oh yes, and he wants you to be around when they move the coffins. He's going to open one before it goes into the lab with the others. We don't often get to see that sort of post-excavation work so Adam thought we might benefit from the experience. It's a bit of a risk, though, because we don't know what will happen once the air gets in.'

'Hmm. But surely those coffins aren't airtight. It's not going to be a crumble-to-dust-before-our-eyes situation.'

She grinned again and leaned against the table. 'No, but some of the adult ones are lead-lined so soup's more likely than dust. It's masks all round and... That's another thing. If it is soup it could be messy. Adam said to tell you to go home and get something old to wear. Something you don't mind burning afterwards. And do you have anything I could use temporarily? To go home in?'

'And people think archaeology's romantic!' I laughed. 'Yes Joyce, I think I can find something.'

'Thanks, Steph. John says we can clean up here afterwards if necessary.'

'Where is John?'

'Gone out again. He didn't say when he'd be back.'

At the mention of John her face acquired a pinched look and I watched her as she turned away to look at the scatter diagrams of the plaques pinned to the wall by the door. She was what used to be called Junoesque. Graceful and attractive. I could imagine her, a few years hence, with a brood of children, the epitome of the earth mother, the source of unfailing, uncomplicated love and common sense sustenance, the pivot and mainstay of a full and happy home. I hoped she got the chance she wanted. Joyce had never admitted it but Dawn and I both knew that she was in love with John and since last winter, whenever we could, we'd been trying to edge him in her direction. 'The trouble,' Dawn said, exasperated, 'is that he's too unworldly to see what's under his nose.' It wasn't just that, of course. Afterwards, though, perhaps...

Afterwards. Everything was afterwards. What would I do – afterwards? When my need for revenge had been satisfied and there was nothing to sustain me? There would still be Adam and what would I – could I – do about him?

At half past four Adam sent everyone off site for a break. I found him sitting on the plank edging laid down round the vault making some notes. 'We haven't a hope of finishing today, Steph,' he told me. 'Whatever Alan says, I'm going to have to leave some of the coffins here overnight.'

'What can you get out?' I sat down next to him.

'The three females from the top shelves, and as many of the kiddies as we can get at easily, and I'll move Matthew Howells' coffin no matter what.' He was confident about that. 'Unless there are unforeseen problems we will get to see inside that one and for our purposes that's all we need. The buggers will still come and try to smash things up though.'

'That would be pointless once we've seen inside that coffin.'

'Oh yes. *We* know that, because we know just about everything else. It depends on what they think we know. Without all the other information one empty coffin would just be puzzling but more than one... If they're still doubtful about what we know, and if we only get to see inside one, they might think they can limit the damage by wrecking the rest.'

'But will they know that the only other ones you're getting out today are the wives and children?'

'They might if they know how the vault's arranged, but even if we don't get the other males out today, we will tomorrow and they can't take the risk. So... any ideas, Steph?'

'There's your deterrent,' I suggested. 'But apart from that, set a watch. A relay.'

'Who? I can't ask any of the team to sit up half the night in a graveyard.'

'You'd do it.'

'I've got a personal interest.'

'I'd do it. So would John.'

'Can't have anyone watching alone. We'd need someone else.'

'Ask Joyce.'

'Joyce? Why Joyce?'

'I rather think she'd have a personal interest too. Let her take her turn with John.'

He gave me a quizzical look. 'Well, OK. I don't know what you're playing at but I'll go along with it. As long as you do the asking.'

Joyce looked apprehensive. 'What if there is trouble?' she asked. I don't think I'd be very useful.'

'I doubt they'll do anything if they know we're around,' I assured her. 'Look, why don't you go home and get Gladstone?'

Gladstone was Joyce's German Shepherd dog. 'I'd have to anyway,' she said. 'I couldn't leave him all night.'

'Right. So you will?'

'Go on then. Anything for a laugh.'

When John returned I steered him into his study and roped him in too. 'And if you don't mind, would you run Joyce home to get Gladstone?'

He would. 'This is very dramatic, Stephanie,' he said. 'Do you think they will come?'

'Pryce almost certainly will. Beyond that, I don't know, but Adam's very worried.'

There was no time to discuss it further with Joyce telling us to get ready for the soup. The first coffin was coming out.

'Me too?' John asked, standing up hopefully.

'Yes, but get changed in case it's messy,' Joyce ordered. 'And hurry up.'

He gazed after her retreating form. 'She's always snappy with me,' he sighed. 'I don't think she likes me very much.'

What should I say? Leave it, I decided. A few hours together in a dark churchyard might break more ice than I could.

Out on site Adam was directing the lifting of Howells' coffin. I held my breath as the hoist pulled it up from the vault on its supporting board to be guided manually onto a big dust sheet spread on the ground. When Dawn had taken her photographs Adam told everyone to put on masks.

Then: 'Joyce and Stephanie over here, please. The rest of you at the other side, well back.'

We shuffled around, arranging ourselves, and Adam began. 'Right,' he said, 'This coffin contains, according to the plate, the mortal remains of Matthew Howells who was the ancestor of the present owner of the Llantathan estate. He was 65 when he died in 1782. As you can see, his coffin is well made and has fittings and decorations typical of the period, and in keeping with his status. From its weight, and from what we can see where the wood has cracked, we know that it has a lead lining. The construction of the coffin suggests that the lining is just that and not a separate, soldered inner. If that's the case it may not be completely airtight. But if it is, the condition of the body is likely to be unpleasant. Soft tissue may have liquefied and there could be a build-up of gases. However carefully we remove the lid some liquid may come out under pressure, though I wouldn't expect it to be as dramatic as the incident in York several years ago which you may have heard about.'

'What if it isn't airtight?' Paul asked from the back.

'Less predictable. All kinds of variables come into play here including the cause of death. Some liquefaction seems possible, but less pressure. Be prepared for the worst.'

Who would have thought that Adam, no less than I, expected none of this? He gave his talk with a perfectly straight face and was so convincing that when the process of removing the lid began, I moved back just in case.

The screws were eased in series first. It took time and several careful applications of WD40. Then they were eased again before removal. This easing was to allow any pressure to escape slowly, but the lid was on so tight that I didn't think it helped. Next Adam used a thin blade between the lid and the tops of the coffin sides. Again we all stepped back as the lid moved. Nothing happened.

'Seems OK,' he grunted, and beckoned Paul, Phil and Glyn to come and help.

Together they grasped the edges of the lid, lifted it and set it down on the dust sheet. For a moment there was silence, then an uproar of questions in which all but John, Joyce and I joined. I sat down on the grass to make notes and John, detaching himself from the crowd around Adam, inched his way towards me.

Joyce, watching him, took off her mask. Then she turned to me. 'You knew,' she said softly. 'You weren't a bit surprised and neither was he.' She inclined her head towards John.

I was saved from replying as Adam lifted his voice. 'Look, shut up all of you,' he said wearily. 'I don't know of any decomposition process which could account for this, so we have to consider that there was no body in the first place. Stephanie, have you found anything in your researches which could throw any light on it?'

Thanks, Adam, I thought, scrambling to my feet. Trying to look authoritative I said, 'I haven't found any direct evidence, but I have picked up hints that Matthew Howells was rather eccentric, and this,' I gestured at the coffin, 'may be a confirmation of that. Although he settled in Llantathan and did a great deal for the village, he had associations elsewhere. Perhaps, not wishing to cause offence here, where he was held in very high regard, he let them think that this was his burial place when, in reality, he'd made other, secret arrangements.'

'Did people do that?' Dawn looked doubtful, as well she might. Over her shoulder Joyce's face told me exactly what she thought. Undeterred, I pressed on.

'They did much weirder things than that!' I told Dawn cheerfully. 'Look at Jeremy Bentham... Iron-Mad Wilkinson...' I hoped they wouldn't: they were hardly fitting comparisons but I was struggling. Adam intervened hastily.

'Stephanie's got a point. It's strange, but it's not the mystery of the century, and more research will hopefully come up with an answer. Come on. Let's get some work done.'

The team dispersed. Adam rubbed his eyes and gazed down at the coffin. 'Who the hell was Iron-Mad Wilkinson?' he demanded.

II

By the time the light was beginning to go all the adult female coffins and most of those pathetic little boxes had been transferred to the college's big equipment van and driven away by Paul and Phil, followed by a very weary team. They'd done the best they could and if Adam was dissatisfied, he didn't say so. The empty coffin was a problem though.

It would have to go to Newport when Joyce had photographed and drawn it, taken samples and done whatever else she wanted. She was all for getting it into the rectory dining room and onto a trestle, 'At least for the time being' but, understandably, John vetoed that.

'It's got to go somewhere,' Adam grumbled and before he became too irate and Joyce too mutinous, John allowed it to be moved to the church boiler room.

John and Joyce returned with Gladstone as I was packing sandwiches and a flask of coffee into a basket. With full darkness almost on us we couldn't afford to sit around in the rectory, even to eat, and we still had to sort out a roster. So, for the first hour, we all watched, picnicking by the light of a nearly full moon and a couple of candles in jam jars.

Joyce suggested a staggered four-hours-on-four-off system. 'John and I do two hours, then one of you – Adam, say – comes out and John goes in. Two hours later Steph comes out and I go in. In another two hours it's John's turn again, and so on. That way we have changes of company and conversation, and both watchers aren't dead tired at the same time.'

Adam said that he wanted to be reasonably awake in the morning so would prefer to sleep from two to six. 'In that case, Joyce told him, 'You'd better start it off. Steph, are you OK for now until midnight?'

Knowing that Adam might have private plans I said that I was.

We agreed some practical details about fresh coffee, food and, because it would be chilly later, blankets, and with Gladstone to escort the in- and outgoing watchers, everything was settled. Joyce gathered up the remains of our supper and went in with John. Adam and I moved to a better position: in the angle of a buttress with Gladstone at our feet.

We talked very quietly: although we were deterrents rather than spies Adam preferred not to advertise our presence. No-one had seen Pryce that day but he was convinced that the ex-verger would turn up soon. 'Then we'll try the... what did you call it? The entrance of the demon king trick. If you're still up for it.'

I said that I was and Adam went on to describe Pryce's near nightly routine. 'He follows the west path from the front of the church then cuts across the site at an angle from the tower. Going back, he heads straight to where the west path and the Rector's Path meet, and pokes around in the rectory garden before he leaves. He can't get round this side any other way because of the spoil heap so when he does come, we'll see him but he won't see us unless he walks directly in front of us.'

'Which he will, if he goes to the vault.'

'Yes, but by then we won't be here. As soon as he appears you go round the far side of Area G and end up where the west and south paths cross. OK? There's plenty of cover all the way. East of the screens you can follow the barrow run to the south path, and it's clear. I made sure. While you're doing that I'll go in the opposite direction, and we'll be at each end of the western extent of Area G.

'Pryce never hurries and he always stops somewhere on the site to light a cigarette. You can tell where he's been by the footprints and the fag ends every morning. Lately he's been coming out around half past 11, give or take ten minutes. So in a bit I'll go and lay a trail of petrol along the edge of Area G.'

'Won't it evaporate or soak into the ground before Pryce gets here?'

'No, because while John was ferrying Joyce around and you were inside I cut a narrow channel and lined it with half sections of those brown plastic tubes the builders left when the church was finished. That'll hold the petrol and tomorrow, when Pryce comes snooping again, there won't be a sign.'

'He'll smell it, surely?'

'He might, but the hoist machinery's by the corner of the church and it stinks of petrol. He'll think it's that.'

'So what next?'

'As soon as Pryce turns to leave Area G and gets within a foot of the edge, we both light the trail. The rest takes care of itself. But remember, Steph: you're lighting the vapour above the petrol, not the petrol itself.'

'What about Gladstone?'

'I'll see to Gladstone. Don't worry. You can't miss your end of the trail, by the way: I stuck a grid peg next to it. Anything else?'

I didn't think so.

'Good. You've got a lighter?'

Gladstone heard Pryce before we did, lifting his head, ears pricked. Adam put a warning hand on the dog's collar and we both stared into the darkness beyond the screens. Adam's voice was the merest whisper. 'Go Steph!'

I went, sure that Pryce must hear every footfall, certain that my nervous breathing must be audible. Yet it wasn't difficult. I reached the south-west corner of Area G and crouched in the shadow of a big yew. From its shelter I could see Pryce's bulky form, a black shape in the darkness pinpointed by the red glow of his cigarette. Adam was invisible but once I caught the gleam of Gladstone's eyes.

With my eyes fixed on Pryce's cigarette end I felt in the pocket of my jeans for my lighter. To my left, about a yard away, the grid peg stood out as a dim white dot. I moved closer and caught the smell of petrol. Until then I hadn't noticed it.

The red glow dropped. I heard a soft crunch as Pryce trod on it. Yes, he was moving, sauntering in his usual arrogant manner back towards the west path. And he was whistling. A bonus. Enough to cover the scrape of my lighter. He was about two yards from the western perimeter of Area G. Two more steps. One... The vapour exploded, fire blooming up around my hand, and I dropped the lighter. Flaming fuel splashed up onto the sleeve of my jacket, and I flung myself back behind the tree nursing my hand, but the effect was all we could have desired.

Our timing must have been near perfect. Two lines of flame leapt chest high, streaking along the channel to meet at the point where Pryce would have crossed. He yelled and fell back, arms raised against the fire. At that moment there was a horrible, unearthly howl. Gladstone. I heard another yell as, stumbling, Pryce looked for a way out. Belatedly I saw that he would have to make for the south path.

Probably he would never notice me but I couldn't risk it. I rolled across the path into the deep unmown grass by the wall, burying my face in my arms, mentally reciting times tables to kill a wave of nausea. I'd reached five nines when I felt Gladstone's nose nuzzling my ear.

'Stephanie?' Adam called softly. 'Where the hell are you?'

I lifted my head. 'Here.' And struggled to my feet. Everything swam and I crouched down again.

'Oh God! Steph, what happened?'

I stood upright and took several deep breaths. 'OK now,' I said. 'Let's go back round the other side.'

By now the wall of flame had died and acrid fumes of burnt plastic hung in the air. I sat down in the angle formed by the screens and one of the box tombs in the unexcavated area. 'We did it,' I said with satisfaction. 'That was absolutely brilliant, Adam.'

'Pretty good,' he allowed. 'It would have been all up if Gladstone had barked. As it was, the howl was perfect. But what happened to you?'

I told him. 'And of course it isn't just grass. It's nettles and brambles and God knows what. And I burned my hand...'

'Right. Let's get you inside.'

'No! It's not that bad. We can't both go in and I can wait until midnight. It's not long.'

'Stephanie, don't argue. Go in now and send Joyce and John out, then I'll come in and look at it. We can go back to the roster when I've had a look at the damage. Go on.'

I did as I was told, feeling less reluctance than I'd shown. The hand hurt a lot now and one side of my face felt raw with nettle stings.

'Christ, Steph!' Joyce shrieked when she saw me. 'What's going on?'

'Not a lot. Can you both go out to Adam? It's a bit early. I'm sorry.'

'No, it's all right. I'm ready anyway.' Abandoning her magazine she reached for the basket of sustenance. 'I'll get John.'

She stopped by the kitchen door. 'You are OK aren't you?'

'Everything's superficial,' I assured her.

'It doesn't look it.'

No, it didn't. I saw my face in the hall mirror as I passed through and understood the horror in Joyce's expression. John was horrified too but the explanation cheered him. 'Adam's coming in to patch me up,' I finished. 'It's mostly nettle rash but I think I got too close to some brambles when I rolled across the path. So if you could go out with Joyce for a short time...'

'Let's see it, Stephanie,' Adam ordered, and I held it out. 'Shit!' he muttered. 'This is a mess.' Melted bits of my jacket sleeve were stuck to my hand. 'I ought to get you to a doctor.'

'No way!'

He sighed and filled the sink with cold water. 'Stick it in there. It's probably too late but it'll feel better. I suppose it got nettle stung as well.'

'I expect so. The other hand did, but it's not bad now. And my face will be all right soon.'

'Oh sure, but you've a graze as well, and a bruise coming up on your forehead.'

'That must have been the brick...' I started to shiver.

'Shock,' he said. 'Sit down. I'll find a quilt or something and get you some tea.'

He enveloped me in a pink blanket and though he was careful, it hurt. 'I'm sorry. I'll sort the scratches in a minute. Yes, you can take it out now.'

I rested my hand on a freshly laundered pillowslip. It looked horrible. Funny: I couldn't remember it being so bad at the time. Adam stared at it too. 'You'll be lucky if it's not permanently scarred,' he said gloomily. 'How on earth did you do it?'

I explained and ended, 'Don't tell John. He'd be very upset.'

'No. Steph, I'm going to run some fresh water and get some ice. Let's try to cool it down some more. The rest of you will have to wait.'

So I sat there drinking hot tea with my hand freezing in the iced water. It ached with the cold and I felt thoroughly miserable. But at last I was allowed to take it out. He teased off the bits of fabric then patted it dry as gently as he could. It was so numb now that I felt nothing. When I'd demonstrated that I could move thumb and all fingers he smeared it with Acriflex and wrapped it lightly in a gauze bandage.

Rolling across the path had dragged my jacket and teeshirt up and I had some grazing, and one bad scratch across my left side. 'It could be worse,' he said when he'd cleaned it up. 'If that's the lot, go to bed now. The other one in my room's made up. Get some sleep and if you don't feel like taking your next turn, don't.'

'I'll be fine.'

I bundled up the blanket, climbed the stairs to Adam's room and set his alarm. Then, awkwardly, I semi-undressed, turned the lamp off and crawled into the spare bed, glad to be there even if I wasn't comfortable. Very soon I heard John come in, then nothing more. In spite of my myriad hurts I slept.

Adam's return at two disturbed me briefly. I lifted my head from the pillow, blinking at the sudden light from the landing before it was cut off as he closed the door. I heard him struggling out of his top layers of clothing. Everything's all right?' I murmured.

'Everything's OK, Steph. Go back to sleep.'

The other bed creaked as he climbed into it. For a while I listened to his breathing and knew that he was wakeful then time and place drifted and my next awareness was of the alarm's insistent bleep.

* * *

Dragging myself out of bed at a quarter to four was murder. I shut off the alarm before it woke Adam and reset it, and crept out with my clothes to dress painfully in the bathroom. Then another flask of coffee and a packet of biscuits, all I could find.

The changeover went smoothly. Nothing at all to report and Joyce thought it a waste of time. 'And it's cold,' she yawned. 'Go on, before John falls asleep.'

That watch too looked set to be uneventful. Wrapped in travel rugs John and I kept each other awake comparing childhoods and schooldays. Dawn came grey and slightly misty at about five, and the half-light was far more disturbing than darkness. To my tired eyes things seemed to be moving. For minutes I watched a white object in the unexcavated area, convinced that it was wavering from side to side.

'Yes, it looks the same to me,' John said when I pointed it out. 'A trick of the light.'

'Are you sure, John?' I asked, because I wasn't. What I thought was the Owen memorial looked now like a tall column of dense mist and now like a thick nebula of smoke. 'That's not a trick of the light,' I insisted. 'It's something atmospheric, surely?'

John had cast aside his rug and was on his feet. 'Wait!' I grabbed his sleeve. 'Let's see what it does.'

Standing now, I could see that the mist column or whatever it was had formed a little to the west of Area G, near the big, multi-stepped memorial commemorating one of the former rectors. Though a thin haze wreathed the whole churchyard, this was a steady concentration which didn't billow and dissipate.

I shivered in the dawn cold. The light was growing, but slower than it should have been and the sky, which had been clear and starry, looked overcast.

The column of mist became denser, growing and thickening, and then it moved. I thought it turned into an advancing wall. Later, John described it as a tidal wave rolling towards us in slow motion. At that point we were more intrigued than afraid. Weird it was, but it was so obviously mist.

It came on towards us diagonally across the site, still not spreading or dispersing, and moving far faster than we realised. As soon as that white wave hit us, I knew that this was no natural phenomenon. It was hot. Scalding. Blinded, and squealing with surprise and pain, I flung out a hand, feeling for the rough stone of the church wall, pressing myself against its coldness. I heard John's voice and caught his words: '...*not fear the terror of the night... but* it *will not come near you... give his angels charge...*' The 91st psalm.

'*He shall give his angels charge over thee,*' I echoed, '*to keep thee in all thy ways.*'

There was an almighty bang like that sharp, cracking thunder which sounds rendingly destructive. At once I felt a rush of cool, fresh air and in an instant all was normality. The fog was gone, the morning mist evaporated. John and I stood side by side against the church wall blinking in the growing sunlight under a cloudless sky. An early butterfly investigated Gladstone's nose. The dog shook his head and snoozed again, completely unaffected. We stared at each other.

'I think the show's on the road, Stephanie,' John said. 'Look!'

The vault.

The screens and the picket fence lay flat. The vault's covering of boards, canvas and polythene had gone. A few melted shreds of plastic clung to the fragmenting sides. I went as close as I dared: close enough to see that the walls were cracked and unstable. All was shattered brick and stone and splintered wood. Wisps of dust rose and I caught the smell of burning though I could see no fire but, through the cracked cement floor, water was seeping in a thin stream. The lost magical well? Of course. Where else could it have been?

'I'll get Adam,' I said. 'Come in, John. There isn't much point in staying here now.'

We picked our way across the site carrying all our paraphernalia with Gladstone at our heels. John glanced back once. 'It's going to take some explaining,' he said.

III

'You're not kidding!' Adam exclaimed when he'd seen it for himself. 'It looks like someone dropped a bomb in it. You say you think lightning, Steph?'

'It sounded like it but I couldn't see anything. We were completely enveloped in the fog. Oh, I don't know what it was but it wasn't real.'

'What's happened to my site is real enough,' Adam raged. 'God! We might as well have not bothered guarding it if this is an example of what they can do.'

'We already know what they can do,' I said. 'They can kill.'

'They can probably turn the church upside down and balance it on the tower.' Adam was impatient. 'I don't care. I don't need proof to know they're dangerous. What I need right now is an explanation.'

I shook my head. 'You don't. You go out at your usual time, discover it and deal with it as you would if you didn't know a thing.'

John nodded agreement but Adam looked derisive. 'And we didn't hear anything during the night? We slept through an explosion?'

'Well, you did, didn't you? Yes, we all did. We'd stayed up late talking, had a meal and some wine. We slept. OK, it's flimsy, but who knew that we were going to keep watch? Did you tell the team, Adam?'

'No. Joyce might have. And what are we going to tell her? That a heavy mist conveniently came down and under cover of it someone wrecked the vault? Oh yeah!'

'Perhaps we should tell her the truth,' John suggested. That was a surprise.

'She'll think we're insane.' Adam got up, put the kettle on and began to organise breakfast.

'She does anyway. There's no bread, Adam. It'll have to be cereal. I'll bring the milk in. It ought to have arrived by now.'

While Adam set out cereal boxes, bowls and spoons on the kitchen table, I brought in the milk. Ordinary. St. Michael's clock struck the hour and the post van passed. Ordinary. How could all this ordinariness exist in the same world as scalding fogs and thunderbolts which weren't there? Ordinary, now, seemed abnormal. If Joyce thought we were crazy she might just be right.

Adam and John were still arguing about Joyce when I put the milk bottles on the table. I sat down and gazed with distaste at the cornflakes in my bowl. I felt vile, my hand was sore and I needed sleep. 'I say tell her,' I announced. 'It doesn't matter whether she believes it, as long as she backs up our story.'

'I don't suppose we've much choice,' Adam conceded. 'Who's going to do it?'

'I will,' John offered, 'and if you've got to go out and be convincing at half past eight, we'd better get her up now.'

'I'll go.' I pushed the cornflakes away with relief and went to wake her.

She peered blearily at the clock. 'You're not supposed to be here,' she complained. 'What's going on?'

'Do you mind getting up, Joyce? I'm afraid we lost the vault after all.'

She sat up. 'Oh no! What happened?'

'You'll never believe it,' I told her heavily. 'Come down as soon as you can. There's a lot to sort out.'

'Wait!' She threw back the duvet and scrambled into her clothes. 'Is everyone OK? When was it?'

'We're all fine and it was soon after dawn. Come on. Adam's going spare.'

'Why didn't you wake me?'

'You couldn't have done anything. No-one could.'

I gave her coffee and left her to John. Adam had gone outside and I found him leaning on the garden wall, smoking. 'You all right?' he asked.

'Tired, that's all.'

'How's the hand?'

'Sore, but not too bad. John saw the dressing and asked about it but I said I cut it on something in the grass.'

He nodded. Then: 'The fog… What was it like?'

'Unbelievable now,' I said. 'I think I was more shocked than scared. Panicky because I couldn't breathe. It can't have lasted more than a minute or two though, and I can imagine worse things.'

He looked at me curiously. 'You're very calm about it.'

'No point in being anything else. It may have hurt but it didn't damage us.'

'Just the vault.'

'Better that... And we couldn't have prevented it, Adam. I know it makes things difficult, but from our point of view it doesn't matter, does it? We already got what we wanted. And frankly, I'm not impressed. They've already done their worst as far as I'm concerned. They can't hurt me more than they have.'

'No, but they've barely started on the rest of us. Losing Marina was bad but there's worse they could do to me.'

I looked up at him and his face told me what his worst was. He finished his cigarette. 'All right, Steph. Let's go and play silly games.'

By feigning total ignorance and sticking to our story we got through it. P. C. Griffiths made no appearance but the Newport police turned up in force because John told them it looked like a bombing.

On the heels of the police came the press. That was easier. They were referred to Alan Foster who gave a brief, nondescript statement similar to the one issued by the police, and everyone else declined to comment. At last, bored, they went to harass the villagers. Judging by the accounts we read later, Llantathan said a unanimous 'No comment' too.

Once the sides of the vault had been shored, Adam worked with one of the police forensics people sifting the mess. And it was a dreadful mess: although the seepage from the well didn't accumulate it soaked into the debris creating a sort of mud layer. John shut himself in his study, Joyce did her thing in the dining room and I tried to work upstairs. It was a tacky day and everyone was relieved when home time came. I went back to Vine Villa, had a bath and a cheese sandwich, fell gratefully into bed and slept for almost twelve hours.

* * *

'Thank God it's Friday!' Joyce was in a state of early morning collapse when I arrived at the rectory.

'I'll do my thanking at half past four,' I said. 'Any tea?'

She pushed the pot across the table with a weak and feeble hand. 'Help yourself.'

I did, and sat down. 'I take it you stayed over last night.'

'I stayed for supper. John would have run me back to Newport but he was shattered and I all but fell asleep once I'd eaten. So Adam offered me the other bed in his room and I wasn't going to say no.'

'Don't blame you.'

'Well, you're looking better,' she remarked. 'I heard what you and Adam were up to.' She paused and turned over a page of the morning paper to a centre spread: photos of the devastation in York. 'I also heard a lot more.'

I nodded, but made no comment.

'Quite honestly, Steph, I can't believe it. Not all of it. Well, how can I? I've seen nothing. I only know what I've been told. It's obvious that you three are all wrapped up in it but I'm not and I wonder if you've let your imaginations run riot.'

I took a deep breath and didn't say what I thought. Instead I suggested that an open mind might be useful adding, 'You did see the empty coffin. And the vault.'

That made her frown. 'They do add colour to your story,' she admitted.

I was in no mood to attempt to convince her. As long as she kept her mouth shut and didn't get under our feet...

'Is John about?' I asked. 'Adam?'

'I think John's still asleep. Adam's around.' She pushed herself to her feet. 'I'd better move. The team'll be here in a minute.'

With patent reluctance she removed her presence to the dining room, Gladstone padding at her heels. I sat on with a pen and notebook making lists: one concerned with work and a second – a much longer one – of all the loose ends I felt must be tidied up before the 8th of August. It was now the 13th of July. Which meant that we had less than four weeks to sort everything in a way which would give us the best possible chance of still being around on the 9th.

There was too much to do. I was going to lose valuable time for all kinds of reasons: mundane things like shopping, getting my car back from Newport, seeing Mr. Curtis on Monday about the house and Marina's will, and getting my own will rewritten. Had Adam and John had sorted theirs? I made a note to mention it to them. Then there was my mother. Should I try to fit in a flying visit to Scarborough?

And still there was the question of the bell. I couldn't see any parallel between Hubert's version with its scriptural and artistic associations, and Arthur Vine's improbably named Judith. Without more information there seemed to be no way forward.

My to-do list grew, covering two and a half pages. It was time for another heads-together session, but I was reluctant to organise that before I'd seen Matthew Howells again.

I had meant to share my thoughts about Howells with Adam and John but now I was less sure. There'd been no time to assess that evening or to follow through any of the ideas his statements had suggested. As it stood, I wouldn't be able to present a credible case for examining Llantathan from new angles, so it was best left alone until I had something more definite. But there wasn't much time and so far, I'd heard nothing from Matthew Howells.

I studied the calendar in my diary trying to calculate how long I could afford to wait and decided that I had very little leeway. If I hadn't been able to meet Howells again in the next 36 hours I would be forced to put forward such half-formed ideas as I had no later than Sunday, and with very little hope of persuading the others that they had any validity at all.

'Steph, it's almost 10. Aren't you ever going to start work?' Adam stood in the doorway, a new roll of Permatrace in his hand. He sounded at least half serious.

'I could, but if it's all the same to you I'll take today as holiday.'

He came into the kitchen and took a can of Coke from the fridge. 'This weather...' he said. 'Feels like a storm's coming.'

It was very close. Oppressive, muggy, and horrible to work in.

'Take today in lieu,' he suggested. 'You've plenty in hand. Save your holiday for later.'

'Whatever. I don't mind. I've no real holiday plans so it doesn't matter.'

'It might, afterwards, but it's up to you. And maybe, after, when we can think about holidays you might come with me to see what sort of estate I inherited.'

That prompted me to remind him about a new will. 'And another thing,' I said. 'What about Joyce? She doesn't believe anything and I can't help seeing her as a problem.'

Adam didn't think so. 'Yesterday, after you went home, we told her all we know, and John showed her some of the parish registers. She can accept that Matthew Howells is a multiple murderer but not that he's the same Howells as James, George et al. Well really, Steph, you can't blame her for that. It took us months of involvement to get to where we are. Still, the empty coffin shook her more than she's willing to admit. And then the vault.'

'I should hope it did. Even so, I still think she's a problem if only because she may be giving what credence she does because of John.'

He looked so blank that I had to laugh. 'Oh Adam! Haven't you noticed? She's dotty about him!'

He went back onto site and I sat on thinking of our pathetic little plans. As they stood, we didn't have a hope of thwarting Howells. Success depended on two factors: being able to keep Howells and his victim apart; and knowing what it took to destroy him. Fulfilling the first requirement might be all that was necessary but I didn't think so. It couldn't be that simple and though I had no firm evidence to the contrary there was a corpus of strong suggestion that I could not ignore. Arthur Vine had worked it out somehow. If he could, I could. I had to.

Just before lunch I fielded a call for John from the archdeacon. I took a message and hung up, frowning, realising that I hadn't seen John all morning. Joyce said that he was sleeping late. Understandable, but this late? No, not John. He must have gone out, but without at least a cup of tea? Without being noticed?

Chances were that, under pressure after the last few days, he'd gone for a long walk, or he might be over in the church praying. I decided to eliminate that sensible possibility before I let myself worry.

John was not in church and Adam, checking plans on site, denied having seen him since the previous evening. I was walking back to the rectory when Joyce came flying out, fear contorting her face. Frantic, she grabbed my arm, dragging me towards the house. 'John... I took a cup of tea up for him... Steph... Oh Steph!'

I found myself plunged instantly into terror. John lay comatose: cold and sweat-drenched, barely breathing. Exactly like Marina. Another name in the drawer.

* * *

I'd seen all this before and I wasn't going to waste time. I told Joyce to get an ambulance. 'Fast as you can.'

I'll say this for her: she was very fast, and the instant she'd sent for the medics, she collared Adam.

The three of us stood round the bed scared and helpless. Beyond trying to warm his icy body there was little we could do. Joyce, no doubt sensing that the tension Adam and I shared was beyond the ordinary, whispered, 'Stephanie, what is it?'

'The same as Marina,' I told her shortly.

She stared at me, disbelieving. John would have told her about that too. 'But Marina died!'

I heard the wail of the ambulance siren. Dear God, how sick I was of that sound! 'Go and let them in, Joyce,' I told her, keeping my voice steady.

Almost before we knew it, John was being stretchered into the ambulance. I bundled Joyce in too, with her jacket and bag, promising to join her as soon as I could. 'Phone when there's news,' I said. The doors closed and they were gone.

I listened to the siren dying away in the heavy air and, knowing it to be beyond the ramparts, exhaled deeply and turned back to the hall. As I closed the door drops of rain as big as old pennies began to dot the step. In the distance the first ominous rumblings of thunder broke the silence.

Adam followed me into the kitchen, ill-looking and shocked. 'Is there any chance?' he asked.

'I hope so. If we got him out of Llantathan in time. There's just a possibility that distance might weaken the effect.'

'Do you believe that?'

'I don't know. But I do know the hospital will do everything to keep him alive. Whatever it takes. If we can only find a way to break it...'

He made an impatient gesture. 'Like what?'

I shook my head. I hadn't the faintest idea, but there had to be a way.

In this Adam wasn't going to be any help. At the moment he was so shaken that he seemed incapable of doing anything much without being told. So I told him: to put the kettle on, to send the team back to Newport, and to get the keys of the church.

Meanwhile I phoned the archdeacon to let him know situation and that I would keep him informed.

Before I left the study I closed the sash window. The rain was heavier now, bouncing up from the flagged path under a leaden, louring sky. I heard the site van start and pull out of the drive, then the slam of the kitchen door as Adam returned.

He was brewing tea when I went to him. 'The keys are on the table,' he said. I picked them up and took John's old Burberry from the back of the door. 'I'm going over to the church,' I said. 'I won't be long.'

With the coat over my head like a cloak I ran through the downpour to the church porch. Lightning flashed blue as I unlocked the grille. Automatically I counted seconds until I heard the thunder. Miles away yet.

Inside, the light was almost non-existent. I found the panel of switches and flicked them all on. I didn't mess about being careful and reverent. I didn't expect people to tiptoe around my house and I hardly thought God gave a damn either way.

Up to that point I wasn't entirely sure of my intentions. Even then, I made it up as I went along. John would have suggested that I was led. Maybe. Considering the whole crazy business of Llantathan I'm not prepared to say that I wasn't.

My favourite corner of the church was the old Lady Chapel but I didn't go there. Instead I made for the tiny oratory which, with the vestry, was all that remained of the priory church's north transept. Known as the Michael Chapel, it had room only for a small altar and two kneelers. But – and it was for this reason that I chose it – it was before this altar, so the cartularies said, that Reynald Devigne had been buried. And in later centuries other members of the family had come to dust under the same floor.

What I was doing might have been some form of sacrilege but I refused to worry. God, if he cared at all, would look at the intent, not the outward appearance. Or so the bible said. I found matches in the vestry and lit the candles on the little altar. Then, from the cupboard in the tower room, I brought another candlestick with the biggest candle I could find. I set it in the centre of the altar and lit that one too. And all the time, as I handled that tall, wax cylinder, I willed into it a sense of John, of his identity, his goodness, and my intention that he should recover.

It was magic, pure and simple: just a variant of the name in the drawer. The difference was that my motive was saving, not destroying, and I did it with God as my witness.

Kneeling, I prayed. I prayed aloud with a fluency I never dreamt I possessed. And I surprised myself by adding a request – no, a plea – for the assistance of Michael, the warrior angel, in our battle against the darkness.

Very odd. The whole performance was, considering that I had never been much more than a conventional believer, and hardly that since Marina died. Yet I carried it through with absolute confidence, certain for once that God was looking my way.

When I left the church, the storm was overhead. I shed the wet Burberry in the kitchen and sat down to drink the tea Adam poured for me. 'No news yet?' He shook his head. He still looked quite dazed and very unhappy. I said, 'That's all right. As long as we don't hear it means that John's alive.'

He nodded, disinclined to talk, and I didn't try to distract him with pointless remarks. There was too much to think about anyway. For the moment, I believed, John was safe. I'd done what I could to give us a breathing space, and who could say that it wasn't more than that? But I was totally ignorant of the countering means by which John could be released. There was only one sure way of securing his complete recovery. The hex had to be lifted by the person who was responsible for it. As simple as that, but short of marching up to the doors of Llantathan Hall and demanding of Howells that he remove John's name from the drawer at once, I didn't see what I could do.

The phone rang. I jumped. Adam's face drained. As long as we don't hear... 'I'll go,' I said, and scrambled for the study to snatch at the phone.

'Hello, Steph?' Joyce, against a background of hollow clattering and voices.

'Joyce! How's John?' I held my breath.

'They say he's stable. He came round about ten minutes ago but he's not really with it. They're doing tests. The doctor told me it might be a virus.'

'That's fine, Joyce. If that's what's wrong they'll be able to sort it out. Can you stay there?'

'Yes. They don't seem to mind. But will you come soon?'

Adam hadn't moved. I think that from the start he'd regarded this as a no-hope situation. Marina had died so it was inevitable that John was doomed. I'm sure he expected me to come back from the study with the worst possible news. He looked up at me, the question in his eyes, and his nervous fingers went on shredding the edges of the morning paper.

'John's regained consciousness,' I told him. 'He's said to be stable, and they think it's a virus.'

Hope flared in his eyes. 'A virus? Something normal?'

'It could be. It is possible that John's just ill and we jumped to conclusions.'

Before I could say more the phone rang again. Assuming that it would be Joyce with further news, I was totally unprepared for Matthew Howells' smooth voice in my ear, burbling greetings, apologies and general inanities.

I cut him short. John ill, possibly dying, by his will and he wanted me to have dinner with him? As neutrally as I could I said that this would be impossible. 'What!' His exclamation of shock when I explained sounded so genuine that again I was forced to consider that he might...*might* not be all we assumed. 'What's wrong with him? You say it's serious?'

'We don't know what it is. He's in hospital and stable but it looks very bad.'

'Was this sudden?'

'Yes. He was perfectly well yesterday.'

'Wait. Hold on a moment, Stephanie.'

I heard a clunk as he put the receiver down, and sharp footsteps on a hard surface. His voice indistinct, calling. Footsteps again.

'I'm sorry, Stephanie. No, of course you won't be free. I understand. Now will you please let me know how Mr. Holmes goes on? Perhaps it won't be as bad as you fear.'

'I hope not,' I replied, and that sense of the surreal was there again. 'Yes, when I have any news I'll let you know.'

He gave me the phone number. I said goodbye and so did he, but I didn't put the receiver down straight away: I was still scribbling his number across John's blotter. And because of that I heard, before he hung up, his voice bawling: 'Get that idiot Pryce up here now. Even if you have to...' And a click as the line went dead.

I stood for a long time staring out of the window at the drenched garden. The storm had passed and the oppressive atmosphere was gone. By evening the skies would be clear and tomorrow the sun would shine again. *Get that idiot Pryce...* I thought over Howells' words and knew that those half-formed, half-believed notions of mine were right. Howells was not the complete liar he seemed, nor was he responsible for John's illness. That being so, it followed that he was almost certainly not responsible for Marina's death.

Pryce.

Elwyn Pryce all along. The creeping, slimy dogsbody. The arrogant cat's-paw. The man we all loathed but whom we'd misjudged and underrated from the beginning.

I stood so long, thinking about the possible ramifications, that Adam came to find me, speaking my name hesitantly from the doorway. When I turned I must have looked very strange to him: later he told me that for a moment he was convinced that the phone call was to tell us that John had died. He approached warily, obviously uncertain about what to say. 'I suppose that was Joyce again?'

'Joyce? No...' I was still thinking furiously, my brain reorganising ideas and plans like a set of file cards. 'No... sorry, Adam... It was Matthew Howells.'

Before he could give expression to the anger I saw in his eyes I said, 'I've just discovered something new. Completely new. I think it may change everything. And...'

I moved at last to the door. '… and I'm sure that John's going to be all right.'

My return to the kitchen was purposeful, energetic even. Adam followed and I told him to sit down and listen. Then I went over the details of my evening with Matthew Howells, repeating the conversation as nearly verbatim as I could, particularly those remarks Howells had made about Llantathan.

'So?' Adam said when I reached the end. 'It's just what you'd expect him to say. As for sincerity, he's had plenty of time to learn to act.'

'That's what I thought at first, and there were times when he was definitely lying. The unbreakable entail, for instance. But unless he's incredibly stupid he wouldn't phone to ask me out knowing that John was in extremis.'

I shook my head and went on: 'He's not stupid. I'm sure he knows that if we're not already a threat to him, we will be. We're virtually predisposed by our jobs to catch on eventually. Seeing me is, I think, partly to try to pin down how much we've worked out. When he talked about the entail I believed he was making a mistake in assuming that because I'm a historian I wouldn't know about law. I'm more inclined, now, to suspect that it was one of his probings. He must know that I've seen the original will and that I'm familiar with the law as it applies to land holdings. I played innocent, but someone who was bona fide would have pointed out to him that the entail could be broken. That's probably given us away, to some extent, but it also says something about him…'

Adam looked better now that he had something to think about. 'OK. Let's accept that some of the things he said to you were true: about hating Llantathan and so on…'

'And about Marina's death,' I added.

'That's pushing it, but yes, all right. How does that change anything? He might well want to blast Llantathan off the face of the earth, but he needs it so he's not going to. He might not have wanted to kill Marina but he felt he had to. He could do it and still be sorry for the necessity. No doubt he was sorry to hear about John.'

'More than that. He was shocked.'

Understandably Adam looked sceptical. 'Maybe he was shocked because John's still alive.'

'Adam, I would agree with you but for one thing. I didn't say anything to you and John about other possibilities because I wasn't sure. I could see that if my suspicions were correct we might find ourselves with a very different scenario come the 8th, but I needed confirmation. And now I have it.'

I told him what I'd heard in the seconds before Howells put down the phone. He stared at me unable, initially, to grasp the implications. Then, slowly, 'So if what Howells said wasn't merely for your benefit – meant to mislead you – then he really didn't know about John and couldn't have been responsible.'

'Right. He was demanding Pryce's presence and Adam, he sounded furious. So it's Pryce or, at a push, one of the others. But my money's on Pryce.'

He nodded, thinking hard. 'So Pryce hexed John without Howells' knowledge or consent. Yes, I see your reasoning now, Steph. Probably Pryce who killed Marina. Also without Howells' agreement. But if that's the case what set-up do we have now? This doesn't alter the fact of all the killings or that Howells goes on living as a result. There's just too much evidence.'

'No, it doesn't change what happens but might it not mean that we've been wrong about who's in control? All this time we've assumed that when Howells moved in, he perverted Llantathan for his own ends. But it looks to me as though either the village perverted Howells or at some stage it gained the ascendant so that now he's in their power.'

'There's some sort of symbiosis. Each party gains.'

'Oh yes, but haven't we always seen Howells as the one with the real gains paying off the village for what it does for him? Haven't we always wondered how? Damn it, Adam, we've even hypothesised that he's controlling Llantathan through fear. But when you look at Elwyn Pryce, at Reece, Williams... any of them... do you see fear?'

'No. You're right! The one word I'd use to describe any and all of them is arrogant. They're scared of nothing. The men at any rate.'

'Well we never did think that the women have much to do with this apart from what they're told.'

'It still leaves a lot up in the air, Steph. And in practical terms what does it mean for us?'

'For a start we have to be bloody careful where Pryce and the others are concerned because they probably have a lot more clout than we've credited them with. It might even be that they have all the supernatural power and that Howells has little or none at all beyond his charmed life. It means that come the 8th we've got to be able to deal with them too, not just Howells. In fact, getting rid of him is only part of it if their power doesn't derive from him. God, I should have realised just how important those coffin plaques are. They were a hell of a clue.'

'This is one tall order, Steph.'

'I know, but at least we found out now. If we'd never known we wouldn't have stood a chance.'

'We don't stand much of one as it is.'

'Better than we might. Look Adam, I'm going to have to get off to the hospital. I've booked a taxi so I can pick my car up from college. Whatever the state of affairs at the hospital I'll be back later and if you don't mind, I'll stay here tonight.'

'No, I don't mind. Will you ring when you know how John is? If you're right about all this and Howells was able to make Pryce take the name out of the drawer, John ought to be ready to come home.'

'Fingers crossed. Yes, of course I'll call you. And I do think that Howells will insist on Pryce reversing the hex. Even though he may be controlled by the village I believe he has the power to do that much.'

'Christ, let's hope so!'

'One thing, Adam. I lit candles for John in the Michael chapel. Would you check them and if they burn down too far, get some more from the cupboard in the tower room. Light the new ones from the one in the middle.'

'Trying your hand at a bit of magic?'

'Why not?' I gave him the church keys and gathered up my bag and sweater.

'I don't think John would approve.'

'I'll make my confession later,' I replied, 'and do penance if necessary, but for now I'm sticking with it.'

IV

Joyce fell asleep in the car on the way back. It wasn't late but she'd had a frightening time on top of a difficult and draining 48 hours. But, like me, she was happy. Before we left the hospital we had the satisfaction of seeing John awake, alert and confounding the staff with the rapid pace of his recovery.

I had little chance to talk to him but it could wait. As long as he continued to exhibit every sign of health he would be home tomorrow. If necessary he would discharge himself so could one of us bring clothes for him, please. The ward sister said she didn't think they would keep him in. None of the tests they'd done had shown the slightest abnormality and though she mentioned a possible insulin irregularity, she spoke without conviction. Before long I hauled Joyce off to the car with John's approval. 'The poor girl's dead on her feet,' he said. 'Take her home, Stephanie. And thank you – all of you – for what you've done.'

We were almost at the door of the rectory before Joyce woke. She yawned and muttered something about work. 'It's Saturday tomorrow,' I reminded her, pulling on the handbrake. 'No work.'

'Thank God!' Still half asleep she lurched into the hallway where Adam stood, holding the door. I followed, realising that I, too, was tired. Joyce went on to the kitchen to make a fuss of Gladstone, but I hung back to bring Adam up to date.

'So it looks as if you were right, Steph. Does she...' He nodded towards the kitchen door. '... does she know anything?'

'No. There was no chance to talk at the hospital, and she fell asleep on the way home.'

'John?'

'I think he knows the cause and that something positive was done but nothing else. He'll be home tomorrow so I'll tell him then. All OK here?'

He nodded. 'Very quiet. I checked your candles and had a look at the site. No sign of Pryce so far.'

'I'd like to think that Howells broke his neck. Adam, do you have any more plans to... upset him?'

'A few. I'd need to get hold of some special stuff first though. But I'm having second thoughts. Look what happened last time!'

I shrugged. 'They must always have intended to wreck the vault so that would have happened when it did anyway. John? I don't know. The trick worked so perhaps Pryce did assume some supernatural force. OK. Let's give John the final say.'

Adam volunteered to cook supper while I sorted out the few outstanding matters standing between us and an early night. I left a message for the archdeacon then went over to the church to pray again and to substitute a little sanctuary lamp for the candles: safer for overnight. When I locked up it was almost dark, the air fresh again after the day's rain.

The air in the kitchen was anything but fresh. Adam was swearing inventively at a grill pan of spitting sausages while Joyce, giggling, struggled with burning toast. I left them to it and went to the study to phone Matthew Howells.

'I'm delighted,' he said when I told him that John was better. 'Do you know when Mr. Holmes will be allowed home?'

'Tomorrow. Provided, of course, that he doesn't relapse.'

'I'm sure he won't. Now I've no doubt that you're going to be busier than ever over the weekend so I won't add to your burdens. May I call you? Monday probably, or Tuesday?'

I said that that would be fine and thanked him for his concern.

'I wish I could do more. Please give my kind regards to Mr. Holmes and tell him that I'll be along to see him during the week.'

What would John say to that, I wondered as I hung up. It sounded so normal. You would expect the lord of the manor to visit the rector after an illness. But not here. Howells had never before shown any interest in John except to protest at his appointment. And even that was open to question now. Howells? Or Pryce and the others, taking Howells' name in vain?

After a supper of sausages, eggs and tinned tomatoes on toast – all Adam and Joyce had been able to find in the pantry – I went to sort out sleeping arrangements. John's bed had to be changed and the spare in Adam's room was none too inviting. My efforts emptied the airing cupboard and I made a mental note to do the laundry first thing in the morning.

Going down for coffee and a cigarette I remarked to Adam that living in a real horror story was nothing like any I'd ever read. 'It's like living in a surrealist dream and that just adds to the horribleness of it all.'

'Talking of dreams...' He looked across the table at Joyce, fair head on her arms, fast asleep. 'What are you going to do with her? Because I'm not having that dog in my room again, scratching and snuffling all night.'

'Then it'll have to be me,' I said gravely, leaning over to give Joyce a shake. She lifted her head and blinked.

'Bed, Joyce. All of us.'

'Where...?' She staggered to her feet.

'John's room. Come on. And don't worry about getting up early. I'll let Gladstone out for a run.'

I crossed the landing to the bathroom, washed quickly and cleaned my teeth. Downstairs Adam was turning lights out and locking up. Before he came up, I was in bed and asleep in minutes, too tired to worry about the wisdom of sharing his room.

* * *

Saturday started well. The alarm woke me at six. Adam stirred, turning onto his back, one arm outflung, but he slept on. I showered, dressed and brushed my hair feeling, as I plaited it, awake and efficient. As proof I loaded the washing machine with bed linen, set the programme and went upstairs again to let Gladstone out for a walk round the churchyard. Leaving him by the porch I made a brief visit to the Michael Chapel to check on my little lamp.

By 7.30 I'd had breakfast and put in a second load of laundry. I took the basket of clean sheets and the peg bag and went out to the garden. An early morning haze had cleared: it was going to be hot again.

During all this dry spell John hadn't mown his lawn, declaring that it would withstand the drought better if it was left uncut. He'd been right but the grass was looking rather wild now, and strewn with rain-bruised rose petals. The bushes had taken a battering from yesterday's storm. It may have been the roses which turned my mood. I tend to forget, now, that little more than six weeks separated the day Marina died and the day John came home. Memory distorts time especially when that time is crammed with events. Looking back at myself on that Saturday in July, I'm surprised to remember how fragile I was then, and how easily the sight of those petals broke me.

I left the washing line and walked to where the deep-drowning crimson of Ena Harkness lay fallen on the damp grass. Not one bloom had survived the storm. The denuded heads drooped, ugly as old whores on a Sunday morning. A prospecting bumble bee wove an erratic flight path through the stems and, disappointed, lifted its impossible body high into the air, droning away over the wall to richer pickings in the churchyard. I saw muddled symbolism, felt the sharp ache of loss, and the crimson carpet blurred.

That bush would flower again over the next weeks, a glory of colour and scent, but I did not want to see it. I went to John's potting shed and found a spade. Later that morning I phoned Harkness Roses and put a cheque in the post. John would have another bush, but it wouldn't be Ena Harkness, and it wouldn't be red.

Silly, destructive emotionalism achieving nothing. Ena Harkness was one of the most popular roses ever bred and the sight and scent of it would never fail to summon the memories even if the pain eased. But the bush which had produced the petals strewing our bed, her deathbed, would grow no more. It was about as futile a gesture as killing the bearer of bad tidings.

Thereafter the day fell to pieces and all I did seemed bedevilled by hitches and problems. I snapped at Joyce, wishing she would go home, irritated – unfairly – by her struggle to believe. She was clutter under my feet yet I could not sweep her out of the door. John wanted her there.

Adam watched me with quiet amusement. 'PMT, Steph?' he asked when I tripped over the vacuum cleaner, a remark that provoked a pseudo-feminist rant.

'Look, pack it in. Joyce is sitting in the kitchen twiddling her thumbs. Let her do something. Leave it alone and come and have lunch with me. No, don't say you can't. Joyce can hoover as well as you. We can go and have a pub lunch and collect John this afternoon.'

'I have to go home and pick up my post,' I protested. 'I'm expecting something important. And shopping... There isn't enough to feed a hamster...'

He sighed. 'We can do all that. Right? Good.'

So we did, and it helped. I reflected that I should not be lunching alone with Adam but it didn't seem to matter now. As a problem he was shelved like the week's milk bill on the day the quarterly telephone account arrives. It wouldn't always be so: bills can be temporarily forgotten but they never go away and what was between us was no different. I hadn't missed his expression when I said that it would have to be me sharing his room. After the 8th, assuming we survived, there would be a reckoning.

'So what's bugging you, Steph?' he asked.

'One of those days,' I said. The waitress hovered, pencil poised. No time for much deliberation: it wasn't that kind of place. We chose, she scribbled and went away. 'Time's running out and I can't seem to get on. I still haven't made any sense of the bells... And Joyce seems like one more problem.'

Cutlery folded in paper napkins arrived, and then coffee with wrapped sugar lumps in the saucers. I ate mine, dipped in coffee, and Adam's too. 'That probably has some significance,' he observed.

'What has?'

'Eating sugar cubes. Do you do it often?'

'Since I was a kid. But cubes are getting rare. Mostly it's little packets of loose sugar. Not the same at all.'

'Poor Steph,' he mocked. 'I'll buy you a box.'

Our food came. Adam, smothering his chips with tomato ketchup, told me not to fret about the bells. 'I've a feeling that'll all fall into place. As for Joyce, don't you like her?'

'I do, but that's not the point. She isn't committed and that makes her a liability.'

'I think she believes a lot more now.'

'But not enough. Adam, John seems to want her around and she seems to want to stay, and from one angle I'm glad of that, but we must keep her out of Llantathan on the 8th.'

'Don't you think she might be useful? After all, we're not over-blessed with manpower. Tonight, if John's up to it, let's rehash everything for her benefit and discuss new developments. See which way she jumps. If she comes back for more then I think we make use of her.'

'OK but I still think she might be dangerous. She might get in the way or hesitate...'

He put down his fork and looked at me. 'So might I. Or John. And do you know how you'll react when it comes to it? Let's face it, Steph: we don't know what'll happen. We can't begin to imagine. For all your commitment, which I don't question, you might still freeze with fear. Now, would you like a pudding or were the sugar lumps enough?'

I had to admit that Joyce had done a far better job than I could have managed that day. She'd ironed the sheets, changed John's bed again and even found enough ingredients to bake a cake. I hoped that John would notice her efforts just as I hoped he wouldn't notice the absence of Ena Harkness until I'd had a chance to confess. As soon as he went to his study to look at his mail I followed and closed the door.

As I expected, he wasn't annoyed about the rose bush but the church thing was something else. I didn't care what the authorities decreed but I did care about offending John.

'Sacrilege, Stephanie?' He looked mildly amused. 'Hardly that.'

'Well, I don't know,' I replied doubtfully. 'I did it in a Christian context but it was still magic of a sort.'

'Terminology. You lit some candles and prayed for me. Some would regard that as... hmm... Romish, shall we say... but it's only symbols again. No worse than Jordan water. And, it would appear, much more effective.'

I bit my lip. John still didn't know just how the reversal had come about. He had accepted my assurance that what had been done was permanent and now he'd jumped to the conclusion that it had been my candle performance.

'John, there's a lot more to it than that.'

He became serious. 'What else did you do?'

'Nothing.'

'So it must have been your prayers.'

I shook my head slowly. 'Your name went into the drawer, John. The man who put it in was made to take it out again.'

'By whom?' Poor John! He looked so bewildered. 'You? How...?

'By Matthew Howells. It's Howells you owe your life to. Not me.'

When I was small – an only child and lively – I drove my mother mad, sometimes, with my badly timed demands for attention. 'Stephanie, you'd try the patience of a saint!' was my mother's frequent, exasperated lament. I certainly tried the patience of my particular saint that afternoon when, having shell-shocked him with my announcement, I refused to explain until we'd had the meal Joyce was now cooking. 'We've a lot of ground to cover,' I said. 'I don't want to have to do it twice. One straight telling after we've eaten. I couldn't do more than give you an outline now and that still wouldn't satisfy you.'

He looked every bit as exasperated as my mother. So exasperated that he actually swore: the only time I remember him doing so in those days. Adam, putting his head round the door to call us to eat, missed it by seconds. A pity. Even the mildest expletive from John would have entranced him.

Well, the meal being on the table there was nothing John could do but acquiesce. Conversation was general, though John did mention that before we'd collected him, he'd visited Angela. 'She'll be out on Monday,' he told us. 'I did ask her if she could remember anything else.'

I looked up hopefully.

'She said there was something about sanctification by the laying on of hands. Does that make any sense, Stephanie?'

'It might. I'll need to think about it.'

Joyce, listening to this with patent incomprehension, stood up. 'Well think about it while you wash up. I'll have to take Gladstone out.'

Adam raised his eyes to the ceiling. 'Nagging women!' he said, exaggeratedly longsuffering.

'Rather harsh, Adam.' John was amused. 'Joyce doesn't nag.'

'You don't work with her.'

The subject in question batted Adam with a folded tea towel. 'You see?' he said. 'I'd watch out if I were you. You'll never have a minute's peace.'

John may not have understood but Joyce did, removing herself and Gladstone with telling promptness. Adam flung the tea towel at me. 'I'll wash,' he stated. 'It might get the last of this grease staining off my hands.'

He explained that he'd been doing some security work while I was at the hospital. 'I've sorted the locks and bolts and put up some brackets so that the doors can be barred, but I'll need some thick planks and a transformer for those grilles.'

John suggested an agricultural supplier near Newport. 'I know the place you mean,' Adam said. He emptied the bowl and dried his hands. 'And there'll be a few other things to attend to during the week but I'll have a better idea after this evening.' He nodded towards John who, making a note on the calendar, didn't notice. 'I've thought of something else too, Stephanie, but I'll need your help. Well, mostly your agreement.'

'I'll agree to anything that'll give Pryce nightmares.'

'I don't know... I'll think about it some more. It wouldn't be easy to do and I'd have to keep it for the 8th.'

Gladstone bounded in then with Joyce following more sedately.

'OK folks,' she said. 'Do we get to talk now?'

'I think we do,' John said, and his glance in my direction heavy with significance.

'The floor's yours,' John said to me when we were seated but, to his chagrin I didn't start with the explanation he wanted. Instead, for Joyce's benefit, I did a concise recap of the evidence which had led us to believe that Matthew Howells was cheating death, and how he did it. I took it as far as the destruction of the vault but omitted any reference to my dinner with Howells and his phone call of the previous day. Nor did I say much about the Vine connection and the bells. That would come later.

Joyce listened closely, stopping me once or twice to clarify points, and when I paused to give her a chance to speak, she said only that the evidence certainly suggested that murders were being committed. 'Howells looks like the killer,' she agreed, 'but I still find it virtually impossible to believe that he's been around since God knows when. Yes, I know the coffin was empty. You expected it to be. I know the vault was wrecked. That goes quite a way to substantiating your theory. I can't disbelieve what you and John say about the burning fog, but I'm bogged down by the supernatural bit. Things like this just don't happen.'

'That's what we thought once,' I returned, relenting towards her as I remembered my own determination to find an ordinary explanation. 'I didn't want to believe it either, but in the end, no matter what I did with the data, it came out the same.'

'Fine,' she said, 'but your stats only suggest there's been continuity since 1756. They don't necessarily support the theory that Howells himself has continued.'

'Up to a point they do, but there's other evidence. You haven't seen the photographs for a start.'

'All right. I'll keep an open mind. Try to.' She frowned then. 'Besides,' she added, 'there's Marina... and you, John. Marina died and from what I saw of you yesterday, you ought to be dead too. Yet the doctors can't find a thing wrong.'

'There isn't anything wrong. Not now.' John confirmed. 'Stephanie?'

'Right. I've given the picture as it was until this week. The day Howells visited the site he invited me out to dinner, and I did that last Tuesday.'

'Considering what you believe about him, that must have taken some doing,' Joyce said.

'It did,' I agreed, 'but it seemed a good opportunity to find things out. In terms of hard, useful facts I discovered very little but the way he spoke about his connection with Llantathan made me wonder whether the picture we'd built up was true. Oh, I don't mean the killings or the complicity between Howells and the village. I couldn't quite pin anything down though, but Howells was denying things which we'd taken as fact from the start.

'At first, I assumed that he was lying either to ingratiate himself with me or to put us off the scent. The trouble was that I felt he really meant it when he said he wished he'd never set eyes on Llantathan. And again when he told me how sorry he was that Marina had died.

'You can imagine how I felt about that. Spending an evening with the man I believed had killed her was hard. Listening to him telling me how sorry he was... Except that there was sorrow...'

John was very thoughtful as he spoke. 'I suppose even a man as deep in wickedness as Matthew Howells might sometimes regret having to perform what he sees as a necessity.'

'I suggested that,' Adam put in.

'And I would have agreed,' I went on, 'but for what transpired when he phoned me yesterday.'

I relayed that telephone call, including Howells' final words, and sat back, my eyes fixed on John's face. Disbelief, understanding, horror: all warred in his expression.

'Pryce? Elwyn Pryce? *He* killed Marina? *He* tried to kill me?'

'And might have succeeded except that Matthew Howells appears to have forced him to rescind the curse, the hex or whatever you wish to call it. John, Matthew Howells did not want you to die and I'm certain, now, that he never had a hand in Marina's death either. Pryce acted on his own initiative. Add to that another piece of evidence. Those silver coffin plaques which you, John, saw as an important clue. What does all that suggest?'

'That it's the village controlling Howells and not the other way about,' Joyce supplied. 'That Matthew Howells is as much a victim as anything else.'

John started. 'No!' he protested. 'How can you...' Then he subsided as he saw the possibilities implicit in Joyce's suggestion. 'Not an entirely innocent victim,' he amended.

'No, hardly that,' I agreed. 'I would imagine that he is, technically at least, the killer of all those children, but I do wonder how much choice he had about it and how far he's responsible for the other deaths: the wives; his own children.'

'Wait!' John held up his hand. 'Let me think!'

Adam lit a cigarette. Silently Joyce rose and went out, returning with coffee and biscuits. I gave her a grateful smile and took a mug from the tray, and we all sat still and quiet until John spoke again.

'If your theory is correct, Stephanie – that Howells is controlled by the village – why would he act against Llantathan to save me? And if Pryce has the real power, how could he be made to back down?'

'If Howells is, somehow, a victim, then he might well want to hit back at the village.' I replied. 'I don't know what he could have done to influence Pryce but perhaps by reminding him that he could have all of us together on the 8th. Or at some other time. I just don't know. But I'm willing to bet that Matthew Howells is snarled up in something he detests but can't get out of and will take pleasure in crossing swords with Pryce now and then. It could even be that he made those huge donations for the church restoration, just to annoy the village.'

'None of this changes the basic premise, however,' John said slowly. 'Howells must be stopped on the 8th. Are we still safe in assuming that by preventing the annual sacrifice we destroy him?'

'As safe as we ever were,' I replied. 'But...'

'No. Wait. What has changed now is that we can no longer take it for granted that, when Howells dies, the power we associated with him dies too.'

'The plaques turning up cast doubt on that,' I said, 'No. We're going to have to stop Howells *and* the village.'

'But how did it start?' demanded Joyce. 'And why? I can see what Howells gets out of it, but what does the village get?'

'I think,' I began, 'that when Howells came here, he was just a self-made man determined to go up in the world. But weak, perhaps. Some element in the village must have been into witchcraft or some such thing already and Howells was drawn in with the usual promises of power and riches. And, in this case, endless life.

'Why would the villagers do that? I think it must have been protection. Remember that when Howells arrived these were very poor tenant farmers living on a seriously impoverished estate, and poor means powerless.

'Elevating one of their own wouldn't have served. Rather the reverse. Poor, mainly illiterate, farmers who make money tend to be scrutinised and they've never wanted outsiders probing. Nor would money alone have brought real power. They could have made a Pryce or a Pritchard... any of them rich but they couldn't turn him into gentry. Today that wouldn't matter but it really did in those days. To be well-born was everything.'

'But Howells wasn't,' Adam objected.

'Howells was a mystery. We know a little of what he did because he told Penelope and she put it in her journal. He wouldn't have advertised humble beginnings in the 1750s or for a long time after, but as it happens, he came from excellent stock.'

'You traced him?' Adam asked in surprise. 'You didn't say anything.'

'The information only came in the post I picked up today. I contacted some mid-Wales family history people who tracked him down. He was born in a village called Trefeglwys and his fortune came to him as a bequest from his employer, Samuel Owen. They sent a photocopy of Samuel's will, and one of Howells' family tree which shows him to be descended from the princes of Powys. So although that might not cut much ice in England it was good enough for Wales. John, you can verify that, I suppose. Your mother was Welsh.'

'Yes, and it still means something to be able to establish your place in a kinship group. A royal connection, however distant, would confer prestige even on the poorest of men.'

I smiled my thanks. 'There. So in Matthew Howells they have the ideal candidate. His bloodline's good, he's capable, land-owning and ambitious and maybe, by the time all this began, nowhere near as rich as he was, because going up in the world doesn't come cheap.

'He needs to invest in the land: improve it and introduce the new farming methods which are beginning to permeate the country. Then his tenants demand roof repairs, drainage, fences. He has to contribute to the upkeep of the church and its rector, and maintain a lifestyle appropriate to his station. His kids have to be properly educated and launched into society. And he'll want the estate he leaves to be worth inheriting. He's taken on more than he knows and when he realises, he's devastated. He wants his dreams to come true but he can't afford it. And on top of all this, his wife dies and his chances of remarrying well must look pretty slim. What has he got to offer?

'Then along comes the 18th century equivalent of Elwyn Pryce with proposals that could make all those dreams reality. Whoever that man was, he must have read Howells right and given him very little indication of what he would have to do. Perhaps, when he killed his first victim he didn't know what he was doing: drunk, drugged, hypnotised, bewitched. But, having done it, he was caught. Llantathan had a hold over him and every year he was in deeper.

'You can bet your lives that he signed a pact with the devil and believed that if he reneged something horrible would happen to him, and his soul would be damned for all time. Llantathan would have shown him enough serious magic to convince him, so he was trapped. They cheated him of course but technically he got all he was promised. He acquired a title and accumulated huge wealth: Jamaican plantations and slaving, perhaps. Every enterprise prospered and he gained the necessary entrée into fashionable society. Later, when trade no longer carried social stigma, he built a business empire.'

I paused and looked at my companions. Joyce's expression was the one I'd seen when she was listening to The Archers. What that said for my narrative I'm not sure. Adam's face was, perhaps, a better guide: neutral concentration. That was all right.

'Discovering anything much about the modern Matthew Howells and his business dealings is almost impossible. What's in the public domain is mostly gossip column speculation: plenty of innuendo and very little substance. But... thanks to the snippets of information in one of the news clippings, I've been able to put a few things together and, I think, solve a puzzle which has bothered me for ages.'

I paused, then: 'John, Adam, have either of you ever wondered how, if Howells lives abroad, he can come back to stage his death in Britain and also arrive for the funeral as his son?'

John shook his head. 'I never thought of it,' he confessed. Adam's expression was tense. 'We ought to have thought of it,' he said. 'It wouldn't be difficult before passports, customs and whatnot, but...'

'Yes. But... I think I know how he's done it at least once, in 1962. Here, in James Howells' obituary you have James and Matthew returning from Switzerland to visit their racing stables near Market Rasen, during which visit James is taken ill, is admitted to a Lincolnshire nursing home, and dies there.

'Howells is more than rich enough to be able to obtain any amount of false documentation, including passports so someone arrives with his entourage who carries the necessary paperwork in the name of Matthew Howells and looks enough like the person he's supposed to be. That establishes James and Matthew in the country together. They go to Market Rasen where James stages his illness and books into the nursing home, leaving Matthew at the stables. James then leaves unobtrusively to go and be rejuvenated in Llantathan, returning equally unobtrusively to the stables where he takes over as Matthew. The stand-in Matthew? Who knows? If he's lucky he gets a passport in another name and goes home. I wouldn't necessarily put money on that, though. Then the real Matthew rushes off to the nursing home to be with his dying father. Shortly after, he accompanies the coffin to Llantathan for the funeral before heading back to Switzerland.'

John frowned. 'Yes, but... Stephanie, what you're suggesting implies collusion on the part of the nursing home.'

'I know,' I told him grimly, 'and I don't think it was the first time. Remember that Pen Vine died in a Lincolnshire nursing home? I got copies of her death certificate and James Howells' and they both died at Astral House, North Willingham, about three miles east of Market Rasen.'

'Maybe it's just coincidence, or it's a very good nursing home,' Joyce suggested, trying hard for the rational.

'It's good for something,' I agreed. 'Now it isn't easy to get reliable information about Matthew Howells in any of his incarnations but what I have discovered indicates that he's fabulously wealthy and he makes charitable donations. Enormous donations, but to very obscure organisations. So far, I've found five, three of which are British. There may be others.'

'What are these organisations?' John asked. Now he looked concerned and I knew he had a good idea of the theory I was going to advance next.

'One of the British ones is The Society for the Promulgation of the Alternative Gospel which promotes a humanist rather than a religious interpretation of the teachings of Christ. Another calls itself The New Era Society. This one purports to favour the salvation of mankind through, and I quote, *the indissoluble conjunction of the heavenly and earthly landscapes.* The third is a federation of communes going under the banner of The People of Caprius.

'They all claim humanitarian aims but apart from the New Era people, it's hard to discover what they really do because they don't advertise widely or seek publicity. However, Astral House is owned and operated by The New Era Society and their very discreet adverts in quality magazines suggest that they have other similar establishments.'

'Are they registered as charities?' Adam asked.

'New Era is, and has been for years but I don't know about the others. I haven't had time to find out more than this. John, if you know of anyone in the Church who studies dubious organisations, would you ask if these have ever come up for scrutiny?'

'Yes, of course. They are, I take it, not what they purport to be?'

'I've not a shred of proof that they're not,' I said, 'but I'd guess that they're all in some way connected with what the witchcraft manuals call the Left Hand Path. I owe you an apology, John. I think you were right after all. Howells may or may not be involved beyond what we know, but I'm sure that Llantathan is up to its collective neck in Satanism. Howells is the paymaster and, given these so-called charities, Llantathan must be part of a massive set-up. I don't know very much about this kind of thing and I don't suppose it's easy to find out but we'd be wise, I think, to proceed on the supposition that while Llantathan is autonomous it has affiliations to other groups. Is that reasonable, John?'

'I think so, but I understand that there's just as much disagreement between Satanists as there is between the various Christian denominations.'

'But what do the people of Llantathan gain?' Joyce demanded again. 'They live controlled lives, not free to marry as they wish or even leave the community. The women produce kids to order and whenever Howells stages a come-back some of those kids get killed. They don't even seem to be particularly well off. So why do they do it?'

I smiled, but shook my head. 'We've been asking ourselves that for months, and I can't give you anything more than hypothetical reasons. The women, we think, may not be directly involved. They do as they're told because they're too conditioned and terrified to do otherwise. Joyce, I can't overstress that. We cannot imagine what it's like to be Mrs. Pritchard, Mrs. Griffiths... any of them. It's very easy for us to say that we'd never let anyone force us into marriage or that no-one would get away with murdering our children, but we didn't grow up in Llantathan where all this is the norm.

'They know that other places are different but that's other places, other people. It's like us knowing about the lifestyles of the rich and famous. Nice, but our lives can't be like that. And you have to remember that they believe in supernatural power with a fervency we usually associate with saints. They *know* it's real and what it can do. They're aware that their fathers, brothers, husbands, sons have or will have access to this power and that if the men who control their lives choose, they can let loose the most unimaginable torments on them. Finally they know that they can be subjugated in more mundane ways.

'Anne-Marie Pritchard was supposed to have died of a heart attack, and I think she did, but one produced with an empty syringe. An air embolism. The men of Llantathan are probably very restrained in their use of the supernatural but with Dr. Reece and P.C. Griffiths to cover for them, they won't hesitate to use other means.

'So the women conform because they can't do otherwise. With the men it's more than that. They're conditioned too, of course, but haven't you noticed that while the women are all pretty retiring, the men, without exception, behave as though they rule the world. They're confident, supercilious, arrogant. Don't they always make you feel as if they're sneering at you?'

There was general assent. 'They're so bloody superior,' Adam said.

'Exactly. That's the way they see themselves. They've got something few others have. They can do anything they like and they're untouchable. They feel like gods. They've never known a moment's insecurity in their lives. Just think about that. We all have insecurities: emotional, financial, intellectual. Whatever. They don't. No wonder they sneer! To them we're just a bunch of losers.'

'OK,' Joyce said, 'but that doesn't apply to the women.'

'Some of it does. They never want for anything. No worry about new shoes for the children. No hand-me-downs. No having to refuse when the kid asks for a bike. No wondering how the bills are going to be paid.

'Then, too, they know that they're never going to be separated or divorced. There never has been a divorce in Llantathan. Whatever goes on here, some of these couples must at least like each other. Some may regard themselves as happily married.'

'So they're domestically secure,' Joyce mused. 'But I'd have expected them to be a lot better off than they are.'

'Than they *seem* to be,' I amended. 'They probably are but that's something I can't check. They certainly don't have to work very hard. Look at Pryce. He spends more time leaning on the church wall than he does tending his pigs. Not that he keeps many. Pritchard doesn't do enough trade in his shop to keep it going and the Cross Guns is hardly the social hub of the village. It's only when you look very closely that the anomalies become apparent. But here's a clue. The pram Mrs. Griffiths had for her little girl was a high coach-built Silver Cross: the Rolls Royce of baby carriages. New. Have you any idea how much those things cost? You'd have no change out of £500. Now she's got a state-of-the-art pushchair. On a village constable's pay of around £12,000 a year gross? We can barely see the tip of the iceberg but I wouldn't be at all surprised if you told me that Pryce and co. are multi-millionaires.'

'Even so, would that – with all the other benefits – be enough to override their feelings for their children?' Joyce persisted.

'You have to remember, Joyce, that it isn't for straightforward gain. It's all part of something much, much bigger. Llantathan is, in effect, a committed religious community. It will do whatever that religion demands of it. If one of those demands is the sacrifice of children, so be it. If that hurts, well, sacrifice is supposed to hurt. They do what they do because they believe they are right.'

'They must know they're not!' Joyce protested. 'They're not isolated. They're aware that the rest of the world doesn't live like this.'

'Wait a moment, Joyce,' Adam intervened. 'You're underestimating the power of faith. The Jonestown people knew that the rest of the world didn't live as they did but that didn't stop them killing their kids and themselves with cyanide-laced Kool-Aid. Almost a thousand people died because Jim Jones said so. People who truly believe in something will give up a lot more than personal freedom. Nuns and monks, for instance. Isn't that so, John?'

'I see what you mean, Adam, but it's very hard to equate the evil here with a vocation to serve God. Conditioning... fear...'

'John, listen,' I said. 'Suppose that Llantathan was the opposite of what it is. Suppose that it was a perfect example of a truly Christian community where children were brought up from birth to believe in and serve God. A community in which Christian married only Christian and the outside world was largely ignored...the Amish, for instance... What would you have to say about conditioning then? Nothing, I suspect. And nothing about fear either despite the fact that it would be a brave soul who tried to run contrary to the rules of the community. Yes, of course Llantathan is evil and it has to be stopped, but we have to understand it to achieve anything.

'It's not going to be easy. Far harder than we ever imagined. Because when we've seen Howells off and dealt with Pryce and the others, Llantathan will fall apart. I don't know what will happen but I do know that there'll be one hell of a mopping up job. The village is going to be as devastated as if it had been hit by a disaster.'

'Aren't you going a little melodramatic, Stephanie?' John asked.

'No, I don't think I am. We're going break this community's mainspring; take away everything it lives by and for. The village doesn't know any other way of life and it won't be able to cope. If it was Howells who controlled them it mightn't be so bad but as it is, expect the worst. Long before Christmas Llantathan will be crawling with social workers.'

While they thought about all that I made fresh coffee. Waiting for the kettle, I wondered what Joyce's standpoint was now. Still not convinced, probably, but definitely wavering. Mostly, though, I fretted about the magnitude of the task before us and the horrid feeling of inadequacy. Taking on Howells successfully was one thing. Difficult but possible. But a whole village? Arthur Vine had discovered some of the truth about Howells, but did his solution include the village? And what solution could possibly encompass not only a man who didn't die but a community whose social fabric was a web of evil? Men motivated by utter devotion to that evil, who could summon the kind of power we only knew as Hollywood special effects.

We moved onto ways and means and, making no progress, we were becoming exasperated. 'If it was vampires we'd know where we are,' I said, half seriously. 'Wave the cross, waft the garlic, bash in the stake. Sorted.'

Everyone laughed. Adam said, 'I'd really love to see you stake a vampire, Steph.'

'Oh, you know what I mean. Nothing about this is predictable because we don't know what they can do.'

'We've seen some of it,' he said. 'Presumably they can do a lot more than summon fogs and thunderbolts. That's going to make it very difficult getting to the church from wherever we are when we snatch the kids. And we've no guarantee that we'll be safe inside the church.'

John thought we would. 'The reconsecration wasn't a meaningless performance. It was a holy event which I believe will prevent the seniors getting in and protect us from supernatural attack. The younger ones might be able to stage a physical attack but from what I've seen of your preparations, Adam, I don't think we have much to worry about once we've secured the building.'

'Let's hope so, John,' Adam said. 'But meanwhile we've got to get two boys into the church, under protest, and pursued by the hounds of hell. There has to be another way.'

'Wait,' John said. 'I think you're misunderstanding the nature of the power they have.'

'You saw it! Steph saw it! It doesn't leave much room for misunderstanding.'

'No, not the manifestation, but that kind of display must take some preparation and effort. I doubt that it can be done on the spur of the moment.'

'So you're telling us that if we surprise them, they won't be able to do anything?'

'Probably not in the way you mean. As Stephanie pointed out, they've always opted for natural methods wherever possible. It's easier and less risky.'

'I shouldn't have thought so,' Adam objected. 'If they can mumble a few incantations or just write a name and get their filthy work done for them...'

'It may be a lot more than a few incantations to harness the degree of power that wrecked the vault. It might have needed all of them together which can't always be possible. Then, too, performing any sort of magic would leave the one who channels the power exhausted. They wouldn't chance that on the night when they need all their powers for whatever it is they do with Howells. And if all I've read is right, there's the risk of rebound. If you use supernatural power against anyone, the force you've raised must be spent. If you fail and your intended victim repulses it, it will turn on you because you summoned it.'

'What else can we do?' I asked. 'Can you do anything special, John?'

'As myself, no more than you,' he replied. 'But I intend to go into this as a priest representing the Church and with all the trappings of the Church. We still don't know the value of symbols but I'm not inclined to leave out anything which might be useful.'

Into the silence which fell as we digested that, Joyce dropped a provocative question. 'If you're so convinced about Matthew Howells, wouldn't it be easier just to kill him? Remove the threat?'

John began to explain that however much we might feel like it, we couldn't do that. 'That would be to descend to his level. We can't take his life. We can only cause the evil he's perpetrating to turn back on him.'

'But...'

I stopped listening. I was watching Adam's face. He looked back and lifted his eyebrows. 'I'll get supper,' I said. 'Adam, give me a hand, would you?'

He followed me into the kitchen. 'She's right, isn't she, Steph?'

I began to assemble sandwiches. Adam took cutlery from the drawer and opened the wine. 'Yes,' I agreed. 'But so is John. And we don't know that it would be possible to kill Howells by ordinary means. But if we could somehow snatch him instead of the boys... It would be bloody difficult.'

'Virtually impossible, but we ought to consider it. Is that everything?'

We carried the laden trays into the study where Joyce was still arguing for direct means and John was beginning to look exasperated.

'Does it matter if you do descend to his level as long as you stop him?'

'Yes. It would be murder.'

'But you're planning to murder him anyway.'

'No, we are not!' John stressed. 'We're planning to stop him murdering. If, as a result, he dies, that's because the natural order of things will have reasserted itself, not because we killed him.'

I handed plates and Adam filled glasses. 'Joyce, John is right. However, I think we should consider your idea,' I said. 'No, calm down, John. No violence. But it would be easier if we could work from the other end: keep Howells from the boys instead of the other way about. I know it would be difficult but look at the advantages. If we have Howells there's no possibility of him killing anyone.'

'I see that, but I don't see how. We'd never get near him.'

'We could,' I said slowly. 'I could...'

In the slow-motion silence they stared at me. Joyce's face held dawning excitement, John's anxious doubt.

Adam? A trail of wistaria by the window brushed against the panes. Joyce eased herself into a different position. The plate on her knee wobbled, and her fork fell to the floor with a soft clatter.

'No!' Adam exclaimed. 'Stephanie, there is no way I'm going to allow you to do it. Seeing him at all is bad enough but this would be idiotic.'

Seeing fear and love behind his anger, I had no inclination mention proprietorial attitudes. 'OK Adam,' I said. 'If not that way, how? If there is another way I'll be happy to go along with it.'

He was expecting confrontation but I meant what I said. I could see as well as Adam the risks I would be running in trying to decoy Howells. To get him out of Llantathan Hall on the evening of the 8th I would probably have to make him an offer he couldn't refuse. That would smack of desperation and give the game away. At the very least I would fail to persuade him to go anywhere near the church. At worst he would kill me or have me killed. With regret, no doubt, but he'd do it. Oh yes, I could understand why John was worried and Adam angry, and they were right to be. But, unfortunately, I couldn't see any alternative.

'Hang on,' Joyce put in. 'Need it be a big risk?'

'Too bloody big,' Adam growled.

'Depends,' she went on. 'I don't think Steph should go anywhere near Llantathan Hall...'

'No,' I agreed. 'I wouldn't at any time. But what if... No, let me think...'

'Think all you like Stephanie, but I still won't agree. John, tell her she can't!' Adam was beginning to sound desperate.

But John shook his head. 'I can't order Stephanie. I can only advise.'

'Advise then!'

'I will, when I've heard her ideas. If she can find a safe way...'

'How can there be a safe way? John, Matthew Howells may fancy her like hell and he may not be the totally evil sod we thought, but he's not going to let anything stop him on the 8th is he? And if it's the village in control of this, they're going to be on the qui vive for any potentially threatening move on our part. Howells might not harm a hair of her head, but they will.'

'Well, Stephanie?' John asked.

I put my plate and glass aside, leaned forward in my chair and thought a moment longer. 'Pryce and the rest will have plenty to do that evening,' I began. 'Remember last year? The 8th was the day that Marina and I found the old parish registers. And while we were looking at them Pryce came calling. That was early evening and he was all dressed up. Adam, you saw them arriving at the Hall that night and the last to get there was Reece. Bringing Brian Bennett. It suggests that they're all pretty busy all evening.'

'We were still watched,' Adam pointed out.

'Oh sure, but apart from you, we weren't doing much. And the one who followed you was pretty useless, wasn't he? So, come the 8th, let's make sure that we, and you, are still doing nothing very much, as if we don't know anything. John, you're going to have a bad cold that week. Go to the shop on the 8th, buy some Lemsip and tell whoever serves you that you're going to bed as soon as you can to nurse your cold. Rub an onion under your eyes to make it look real.

'Adam, you get out of Llantathan, but not too far. The King's Arms at Llanfair, say. Park your car, have a drink and come back across the fields. They'll never know.

'Joyce? Well, love, what you do depends on what you want to do.'

'Oh me? I'll be on the town in Newport. Will that do? Or should I be nursing the sick?' We grinned at each other. She was in.

'No. Best if we're all separated. If they think we're up to something they won't expect that, and far as we know they've never followed us beyond Llantathan because once out of the village we cease to be a threat.'

'Right then, Stephanie,' Adam said. 'We're all scattered. Where are you?'

'In Newport, having drinks or some such thing with Matthew Howells. Perfectly safe because Joyce is there too. Oh, not with us. But close enough to keep an eye on things. That possible, Joyce?'

'As long as you go to a place that'll be busy enough for me to lose myself. It'll be a Wednesday. Not a big clubbing night. But I think Aphrodite's Bar should do. I'll have to borrow a car, but I can do that.'

'This is all very well, Stephanie,' John objected, 'but even if Howells agrees to meet you on that evening – and it seems very unlikely – you can't seriously hope to keep him there until after midnight.'

'No. That's not my intention,' I assured him. 'If I can get him there – and I agree that it is a big if – he will insist on being back in Llantathan well before midnight. That's fine. I'll make sure he runs me back and I'll ask him to drop me here so that I can check on the sufferer. Being courteous, he'll see me to the door. While he's doing that, Adam will sabotage his car.'

'Me!' Adam squawked. Stephanie, I can't do anything effective in, what? Five minutes tops?'

'Yes you can,' Joyce contradicted. 'You stick a potato in the exhaust pipe.'

'You'd know, I suppose...' He was sarcastic.

'Yes, I would. I did it to our neighbour's car when I was a kid. My dad had to pay for the repairs. He stopped my pocket money for months.'

'All right! All right!' Adam said heavily. 'But this is a Daimler Sovereign with twin exhausts. I can't do it in seconds, and not with him feet away at the front door. You'll have to get him to take you round to the kitchen door. And what then? All he'll do is call on someone in the village to give him a lift to the Hall. Or walk, for that matter. It's not far.'

'If we let him.'

'I don't really see how we can prevent him,' John said.

'Bash him on the head,' Joyce suggested. She saw John's expression and added, 'Not too hard, of course. Then we carry him into the church and slam up the shutters for the night.'

'That's probably the only way,' Adam agreed. 'Unless you think you can persuade him to go in of his own accord, Stephanie.'

'Don't sneer, Adam. No, not even my charms will stretch that far. But there is another possibility. What if Joyce smuggles herself back into the village unseen and starts screaming rape and murder in the church porch? Naturally we go and investigate. And I shove him inside.'

'That's better,' John conceded, but he still looked doubtful.

'It's the best you'll get,' I told him, 'And if that doesn't work we will have to hit him. I'm sorry. I know you want to avoid violence. But it might be the only way.'

He nodded, forced by his own realism to accept what I said.

'It's ramshackle,' complained Adam.

'It's better than anything we've come up with so far. Trying to keep the boys from Howells wasn't on, you know.'

He sighed. 'Yes...'

'So you agree?'

'I don't have much choice, do I?'

I felt a quick rush of sympathy for him. After all, would I have allowed Marina to do what I was suggesting without protest? 'I will be very careful,' I promised.

'So what happens when we've got him in the church?' Joyce asked. 'Is that it?'

'We don't know,' I admitted. 'All the information we have suggests that he must make his sacrifice on that one day but whether failure to do so means that his life is immediately forfeit or whether he just ages a bit faster, we've no way of telling. I think it must be the former because he's been absolutely consistent about it, and the sacrifices may have more significance than just keeping him young and beautiful.'

'What if you're wrong and he's still there after midnight?'

I don't intend him to be,' I told her with more conviction than I felt. 'Keeping Howells and his would-be victim apart is necessary obviously, and it may be enough to kill him, but I'm sure it needs more than that. Remember his family's saying? *It came with a Jew and it will go with a Jew.*'

She nodded uncertainly.

'The Jew it came with must be the first sacrifice, Josiah Abelson. The big question is the identity of the Jew who ends the Howells family fortunes. Any Jew, or one in particular? An actual person or something symbolic? We don't know. It may be very complex.'

'Haven't you any idea at all?'

'Yes and no. They were obviously worried by Marina, and Marina herself was convinced that she'd been chosen to do it. They killed her, so she was obviously wrong, but it does suggest a person, doesn't it? Arthur Vine, though, appears to have been following a different line.'

I summarised what I knew about Vine's plan to deal with Howells, his preoccupation with the bells and the loss of his papers following the attack on Angela Morton. 'So we know that the treble bell and perhaps the tenor must be very important,' I finished, 'but we don't know which bible character Hubert was so hooked on, nor do we know whether it was something Arthur took into account. If we did, we might be able to understand what effect the bell was supposed to have. The inscription on the treble might be a clue because inscriptions usually relate to the functions or supposed characters of bells. But I can't remember what it is. It's nearly a year since I did the recording and I can't find the notes I made then.

Joyce shrugged. 'So go up and look at the bell again.'

'I will if I have to.' I would, and the thought of it made me feel sick. It was a nightmare I wanted to avoid at all costs. Going up to the ringing chamber was hard enough: I could feel the presence of those bells above me, waiting. Superstition? I could call it that or anything else, but I couldn't dismiss the notion that the bells were something more than lumps of metal; that they were personalities.

I remembered how easy Marina had been in the belfry: unafraid, fascinated, her hands resting on the sound bow of the treble with all the confidence and amity of an old friend. Hadn't Angela remembered something about the laying on of hands?

Joyce was speaking again. I dragged myself back to the present and caught: '... meant his bell to be rung, didn't he?'

'Yes,' I agreed. 'He invited a team of ringers.'

'So isn't the answer to ring the bell? All the bells if necessary?' Practical Joyce again.

'It must be, but why? And when?'

'Does it matter?'

'I think so. Arthur Vine wanted his bell rung on a specific day: the anniversary of Pen's death.'

'Which was?'

'Early August, but not the 8th. If it had been I'd say yes, let's do it regardless: it must be the means of despatching Howells. But it wasn't, so I need to know what he had in mind.'

'Who cares? Let's ring them.'

'Joyce, we can't if we don't know what's supposed to happen.' I relished her enthusiasm but her fools-rush-in attitude was worrying. She had to understand that this was no game. We were either right or dead. I said so and she became a little more restrained.

'Or in gaol,' Adam contributed. 'Wouldn't that sort us out nicely?'

That subdued her completely. Being dead was scary but unreal – it can't happen to me. But being in gaol... yes... that was imaginable.

'Well, get on and work it out, Steph,' she grumbled. 'It can't be that difficult.'

V

If only she knew! Marina's death excepted, I lost more sleep over those wretched bells than all the rest put together. The frustration of it gnawed at me and a couple of grim dreams helped to turn fear into phobia. What I should have done, of course, was tell John or Adam and ask for company if I had to go up there again. Neither would have regarded it as a matter for ridicule but I did and it stopped me seeing sense. So... After wasting Sunday morning going through my files for the notes I made last year, I pinned my hopes on the very remote chance that I'd left the notes at college. Meanwhile I tried to use the remainder of the day. Yet again I set out every scrap of information I had and tried to see what Arthur Vine had intended.

As symbols, bells had always been regarded as powerful. In monasteries the ringing of the bell was, in effect, the voice of God, demanding instant compliance. And in medieval times ordinary men and women obeyed the call of the bell to attend mass. And was it significant that, despite the Anglican denial of the effectiveness of symbols, Catholic churches had not, for a long time, been permitted to have bells? Yet despite the iconoclasm which had been an integral part of the spread of Protestantism, bell lore, and the old beliefs, survived. Bells continued to exert a fascination and, in time, ancient customs crept back. Puritanism is, perhaps, no real part of the British psyche. As a nation we enjoy ceremonial and value tradition. Thus it was that new bells began to be installed with varying degrees of pageantry and with the blessings of the established church. The Vine bell had, in its various incarnations, been consecrated three times, the last time in an elaborate ceremony of baptism by the then bishop. Similarly, the Cavendish bell had had an episcopal dedication.

I gnawed at a thumbnail, thinking hard. Thanks to the rows kicked up by the village over these two bells I had a pretty detailed picture of their inaugurations. In each case

I could put names to the clerics who had given the bells their dedications. By comparison I knew next to nothing about the other six. They had been paid for, and rung, by Llantathan people, but who had blessed them?

My mind trailed back through a thicket of recollections to the evening when I'd first revealed the results of my researches. What had been said then about the complaisant rectors of St. Michael's? Men of straw, we'd agreed. Spiritually bankrupt. The only sort Llantathan would tolerate so that the village was without any true Christian influence, without the opposition of a force for good. If that was so, Llantathan would naturally not want some outsider – some Christian outsider – coming in to bless its bells. Because such blessings would not be the empty words its own pastor pronounced, and those bells really would be dedicated to God.

That being so, I could make some sense of Llantathan's ringing history. The Vine and Cavendish bells, truly consecrated, had never been rung. The other six had, until the war at least, which suggested to me that they'd received the meaningless benediction of a fake Christian. I remembered what Adam said about the Vine bell being thrice blessed. I remembered the charters which praised the bell's originator, Reynald Devigne, who was good and pious and holy and who had dedicated his life to God, living by the sound of the bell he had had created.

Oh yes, if all that meant anything at all, it meant a lot. John, Adam and I might question the power of symbols and I had precious little faith in anything, but I could see the significance of the Vine bell. No wonder Llantathan wouldn't let it be rung. If... if... an inanimate piece of metal could be imbued with spiritual force then that bell was the most powerful object in the village. And if I, sceptic that

I was, could not shake the feeling that the bells were not inanimate, if I was frightened of them, what must their effect be on Llantathan? If Elwyn Pryce ran in terror from a trail of fire, what would he do when he heard the Vine bell ringing?

I made myself a mug of coffee. It was mid-evening now, and just beginning to rain. As I waited for the kettle to boil, I watched a couple of half-grown rabbits bouncing around on the grass beyond the shed. The rain became heavier. The rabbits disappeared and I closed the curtains against the growing darkness. I was feeling pleased with myself, and excited. There was a lot to do but I had made progress.

Monday was a fretful day. Matthew Howells hadn't phoned by the time I had to leave for a 2-o-clock appointment with the solicitor. John promised to take and convey messages if he called while I was away but I didn't like the idea of it being out of my hands. Time was too short now to lose control of this situation, but there was nothing I could do.

I was just getting into the car when Adam stopped me. 'I could do with some help again if you don't mind. Pryce.'

'Tonight? No problem.'

'Thanks, Steph.' He looked at his watch. 'Got to go. Have a nice time with the law.'

I suppose it was nice being given confirmation of how much I was worth, but it was still unreal. I gave instructions to Mr. Curtis for my new will and made another appointment to sign it.

'Could you make it Wednesday the 8th?' I asked. 'I'm going to be pretty busy between now and then.'

Mr. Curtis agreed, and I was pleased. A late appointment gave me an excuse to be in Newport and to meet Matthew Howells there. If he agreed. And it was essential that he should. I shook the solicitor's thin, dry hand and headed to college to begin another futile search.

My office was not large. Adam called it the Local History Research Cupboard. But it did have, apart from a desk, two tall, grey filing cabinets and shelves upon which I was accumulating reference books and box files. A few plants and posters made it look comfortable; some maps and date charts gave, along with the books and files, an illusory impression of activity: for the moment it was more convenient to work in Llantathan and I came into college once or twice a week at most.

Only one cabinet was in use and the box files contained nothing but local guide books. Little here had anything to do with Llantathan but, faced with the increasing certainty of the belfry, I had to be sure. My desk drawers contained nothing but the usual office stationery and a photograph wallet holding prints of Marina and me taken on a weekend trip to North Wales the previous autumn. I put them in my bag and went home, depressingly aware of more time wasted.

At home there was a note on the mat behind the front door.

I've got the gubbins sorted. If you're still interested could you be at John's by 9? Will manage otherwise. A.

I had no idea what he was planning this time but I wasn't going to miss it and I arrived at the rectory soon after eight.

'What are we going to do?' I sat down with Adam at the kitchen table. Of John there was no sign and Joyce had gone home.

'Dry ice. It's what you use to create stage fog. You pour hot water on it and it just boils out like steam. I've got the ice in one of John's big Pyrex bowls in an insulated container and a flask full of nearly boiling water down in the vault. Along comes Pryce, and out comes the fog. See?'

'Yes, but where do I come in?'

'I'll have to be hidden in the vault with most of the covering in place well before Pryce is likely to arrive so I won't be able to see him coming. I need you out there to signal when he reaches the site.'

I lit a cigarette. 'OK, but don't ask me to be an owl.'

He grinned. 'I never thought of that. Look, I've rigged up a length of mason's line from the vault to the screens where we were before. All you have to do is pull the string. Easy.'

'Yes, but there's a gap now between the spoil heap and the church wall,' I reminded him. 'What if he comes that way?'

'He can't. I blocked it this afternoon. He has to come the same way as before, so you'll be able to see him as soon as he comes round the end of the church.'

I pictured it. Yes, it was all right, but since the last time, some of the screens had been moved. As Pryce advanced into Area G towards the vault, he would see me.

'No problem,' Adam assured me. 'You pull the string as soon as you see him. It'll be tied to my wrist, by the way, so don't pull too hard. Then you drop the line and move back right up to the wall of the church. By the time Pryce reaches the point where he'd be able to see you, you'll be in the angle of the wall and the buttress. You know? And by then he'll be too preoccupied with the vault to bother about anything else. You stay where you are until he's gone. Which should be no time at all.'

'This had better be foolproof,' I warned. 'Last time...'

He reached across the table and took my hand – the one I burned. 'You're going to have scars. It should never have happened.'

'It doesn't matter. Forget it.' I knew he wouldn't.

He glanced at the clock. I did too. Ages yet if Pryce stuck to his usual routine. 'Where's John?' I asked.

'Gone to see someone in Newport. Another vicar. I think it's to do with your bells. Any progress there?'

I pushed back my chair. 'Some,' I told him. 'In fact, quite a lot.' I related the thoughts of the previous evening and my conclusions, and was pleased when he agreed.

'But you still don't know whether Arthur was perpetuating Hubert's biblical association in any way?'

'No,' I admitted and, to change the subject, I reminded him that he was supposed to be talking to me about future special effects.

'Oh yes...' He passed me a cigarette. 'I have an idea for something. Another stage device really, but done well it could freak Pryce like nothing on earth. Trouble is, it might upset you. If it would I'll drop the idea.'

'Well, tell me,' I said impatiently.

'I want to project a picture of Marina in the churchyard. Look, if you think it's tacky... in bad taste... whatever, say so and I'll forget it.'

'No... But I don't understand how or why,' I confessed.

'The how is fairly easy. It would be a back-projection onto gauze with a rheostat and timer so that it appears gradually and fades again. If I can get the projection right, how do you think Pryce would like it if he saw – apparently – the ghost of his victim hovering in the churchyard? Especially on the night of the 8th when funny things are happening anyway?'

I nodded. It was like the fire trail, the dry ice. A trick, but to one for whom the supernatural was as much a part of life as a pint of beer, potentially terrifying. Yes. Marina was dead, but let her image play a part. It couldn't hurt me.

'I'll need a slide of her or a photo I can make into a slide,' he said. 'Full length. Full or three quarter face. Preferably something with a neutral background though I could fog that out if the image was right. And if possible one in which she's wearing something pale and dressish... floaty. You know...'

Something ghostlike. 'I don't know,' I said thoughtfully. 'Floaty wasn't her thing, but I'll look. If there is anything suitable it'll be a print. We only used slide film for places and things. How soon would you need it?'

'Pretty quick. I'll have to try it out. No, not here, but somewhere similar. John says he'll get permission from his vicar friend to use his churchyard.'

'Where do you intend to set this up?' I asked. 'When it's for real, I mean?'

'Over Marina's grave,' he told me. 'If you don't mind. I think it's feasible if I vandalise the street light by the church gate so that the gauze isn't visible.'

'I don't mind,' I said. 'Do anything you like.'

I looked at the clock again. Still half an hour before we needed to move. I made some coffee, adding a third mug when I heard John's car in the drive.

'I've been picking Nigel Faringdon's brain about bellringing,' he told us as he hung up his jacket behind the kitchen door. 'Nigel's church has a team and he's a keen ringer himself. I thought he might know something about the Vine/Cavendish debacle. He'd read about it, but he couldn't add anything new. I'm sorry, Stephanie.' Then he mentioned that Angela thought that the scriptural character was a woman in the Old Testament.

'Oh Lord! There are any number who might feature in a famous painting. We could rule the bad ones, like Jezebel and Delilah...'

'I'll give it some thought,' he promised.'

Adam said, 'We'd better think about making a move soon, Steph. Are you going to be warm enough like that?'

'I'll have to be. I don't have a dark jacket now. I wrecked it when we did the fire trick.'

'Oh, yes, you're off to play games again. Adam told me. You can borrow one of my black jerseys,' John offered, and went upstairs to get it.

'OK?' Adam said. 'You know what to do?'

'Yes. Got all you need?'

'Everything's out there already.'

John passed me a big woolly jumper and I pulled it on. 'Let's go,' I said. 'John, if you leave your window open you might just hear Pryce's screams.'

Adam had predicted a pushover, and it was. We sneaked out to my hiding place and Adam put the end of the line into my hand. Then, with that silence and invisibility I envied, he melted away into the darkness. I heard a single, soft scuffling sound as he climbed down into the vault, then the slack of the line was taken up.

Waiting was the worst of it. In itself the churchyard didn't bother me. I was well past the childhood fears Marina had talked about: to me this was an archaeological site first and a burial ground second. What did bother me was the discomfort. In spite of John's jumper I was cold, and though it wasn't raining there was dampness in the air.

The church clock struck the quarter hour. A car passed and from the sound of its engine I knew it was Richard Reece's E-type. Then there was quiet again: only the usual night noises, the rustlings and scuttling of leaves and hedgehogs and whatever else moves in the dark.

Then... something that wasn't hedgehogs or leaves: a stone skittering under a boot. Pryce, rounding the corner of the tower. I pulled the line, let go and shrank back into the deep darkness of the wall.

But I could have stayed where I was. Pryce would never have noticed me if I'd danced a tarantella on a table tomb.

From the cover of the buttress I watched a thick white cloud billow from the vault and spill onto the ground, rolling along, low and sinister. I could see little of Pryce but I heard one strangled imprecation, then the thud of his boots as he pounded back round the church and away. Moments later Adam climbed out of the vault carrying the box and the flask.

In the rectory kitchen warming up in front of the Aga, we shook our heads in a kind of awe: that we had produced such a result with so little effort.

'Will he guess, do you think?' I asked.

Adam shrugged. 'Maybe. He'll probably go back at some point and have a look under the covering, but there's nothing to see. Thanks, Steph,' he said, and then he hugged me. And I hugged back.

We looked at eachother. And, in silence, we moved apart. 'I'll walk you home,' he said abruptly. 'It's late.'

* * *

Over breakfast I decided to take another lieu day. The house needed cleaning. Really cleaning. If I did that, I thought, perhaps those notes might still come to light. Anyway, it was raining. It would clear up by lunchtime, so the weatherman said, but for now the rectory would be full of people processing finds and inking plans. John liked such days, enjoyed having his house full of noise and bustle, but I found it a distraction.

I phoned Adam and told him. 'No problem, Steph,' he said, 'but do you have the scatter diagram of those plaques? The one you had pinned up on the wall.'

Yes, I did, I told him. 'Has something else had turned up?'

'No. I'm just organising all the paperwork and plans for that area.'

'Oh. Well, I've written my piece on the plaques if you want that.'

'Great. I'll come up some time this morning and collect everything if that's all right with you.'

There was nothing urgent about my documentation on the plaques. I knew that, just as I knew that he could have handled last night's spooking without me. I said yes, come up any time, and reflected that, in some obscure way, Adam and I were playing games.

By lunchtime, when Adam arrived, I was halfway through the cleaning. I gave him tea and he sat at the kitchen table to eat his sandwiches asking, pointedly, if the cream crackers and cheese I brought to the table indicated a light lunch.

I ignored that. 'You've come for the plaque stuff, I suppose.'

'No. I just felt like walking up here to eat my lunch.'

I looked down at his remaining sandwich. It was squashed, unappetising. 'Fitting surroundings for your gourmet feast,' I replied, my voice waspish.

'I suppose you're in a lousy mood because you still haven't found those notes.'

I glared at him as I buttered a second cracker.

'Well, have you?'

'No,' I snapped. 'Not yet.'

'It's the belfry, isn't it?' There was concern in his voice and my irritation collapsed.

'It's very silly...' I tried to laugh at myself but it sounded more like crying.

'No sillier than being scared of spiders.'

'Joyce would think so. She isn't much given to the fanciful, is she?'

He didn't reply to that. I offered the cake tin but he refused, lighting a cigarette instead. 'Is there any chance that those notes will turn up?' he asked.

'A chance. Not much more. Unless Marina tidied them away somewhere or they've fallen down the back of the bookcase, I think they must have been destroyed accidentally.'

'Surely not. You're more careful than that.'

'I can't be or they'd be in the right file.' I sighed. 'Well, if they don't turn up today I'll do the recording again.'

'I could do it, Steph.

I shook my head. 'No way. I lost the bloody things so I've got to make good.'

He didn't offer his company as and when. That could be taken as read. But I wouldn't ask him. If I had to do it I would do it alone and prove to myself that the fear was within my control.

By the end of the day I had a spotless house and a feeling of sick misery because there was nowhere left to look. It says much about my obsession that not once did I think about Matthew Howells. I'd left for Newport the previous lunchtime fretting that he hadn't phoned, but since then he hadn't crossed my mind. Nor did he, until John phoned at teatime.

'Howells rang,' he said. 'Apologies for not phoning earlier and would I let you know that he'll be in touch as soon as he can. It seems he's going to be away for a few days.'

'That's all?'

'Apart from some very polite enquiries about my health. You're right, Stephanie: he does sound quite charming.'

I ate tea, watched part of a TV retrospective on Lillian Hellman who had died the previous month, and went to bed early. Early for me. Lying in the dark, listening to a rising wind, I wondered if, by reconstructing the day I did the belfry recording, I might remember what happened to the notes.

So I went back to those first days of my new job: working in the ringing chamber; the clearing of the tower room; and, a few days later, the belfry. How had I made my notes? Had I used recording forms on a clipboard or did that method come later? No. It had been one of the spiral bound reporters' notebooks. A new one, I recalled.

I sat up and switched on the lamp. I'd been looking for typescript but had I actually typed the notes up? Well, if I hadn't, I still had the original record. All those notebooks were downstairs in the study. I never threw first copies away. Cursing myself for not thinking of this before, I ran down to the study and lifted the box of notebooks down from the shelf above the desk.

They were in date order so, logically, the one I needed would be second from the back. But the book I pulled out began with the transcriptions of the memorial brasses in the chancel, and the next with the ledger stones of the nave. I checked them all to no avail. The first, as I'd thought, contained details of everything in the tower except the belfry, which I knew came next. As far as I could tell no other records were missing and no pages had been torn out.

I put them away and went back to bed, puzzled. It looked as if I'd never done that recording at all, but I could remember writing awkwardly on the narrow walkway around the bell frames. I could remember reading the inscriptions back to Marina so that she could check them against the bells themselves. So what had happened to the book? Over and over it all went until my thoughts jumbled and I fell into a confused, half-waking dream of bells and books and Elwyn Pryce. And soon, this hypnagogic state became sleep, and sleep became morning.

* * *

The persistent shrilling of the telephone woke me: Adam, apologising for getting me out of bed. 'What's up? What time is it?' I yawned, wondering vaguely if I'd overslept.

'Half past six.'

'What! Adam...'

'It's all right,' he soothed. 'Nothing's wrong. Could you come in to work early, do you think? Something's turned up. Area G. I'll explain when you get here.'

I was at the rectory within twenty minutes but although I gave a passable imitation of life my brain, clamouring for the day's first caffeine fix, simply could not take in what Adam was telling me. John hovered behind me buttering toast, boiling eggs. Listening. 'Start again, Adam,' I begged. 'I'm not with you at all.'

He made an effort to control his impatience, and this time it got through. In view of the success we'd had with the dry ice, he'd been unable to resist trying it again. 'It was tricky without you to give me the warning but I thought I'd manage, and I went out before 11 to give me time to be in place. But when I got to the gate Pryce was already there, and he had someone with him. Don't know who. They were walking across the site towards the vault talking very quietly. There was nothing I could do except keep my head down and hope they didn't find my stuff. I'd left it covered but they'd only to lift the plastic and shine a torch and the game would be up.

'They paused a couple of times. Just listening, I think. Pryce lit a fag and they moved a bit closer and stopped a yard or two from the vault. The church clock struck the quarter. Still they just stood there. Oh... five minutes at least. I was getting cold and fed up and wondering what the hell they were doing when all of a sudden there's some swearing, then they both go hell for leather, falling over each other, round the church and out of the gate.'

He stopped. John, not speaking, put more coffee in front of me and a second piece of toast on my plate. His expression was unreadable.

'Go on,' I urged, wide awake now.

'Well, I damn near ran myself because there was fog pouring from the vault. I watched it rolling over the site and then it just... it sort of curled back on itself and disappeared.'

'What did you do?'

'Waited a bit then went and had a look. Nothing had been touched. Everything was exactly as I left it.'

I stared at him, my scalp tingling with instinctive reaction. John, still silent, spooned eggs into egg cups and sat down next to Adam. I transferred my gaze to him wishing he would say something. He didn't and Adam finished his story with an account of how he'd returned to the rectory, roused John, told him what he'd seen and brought him out to witness the untouched vault.

'So if it wasn't you and nothing was disturbed, who was it?' I asked, finding my voice.

'I don't know. I just don't know.'

'One of them...' I began lamely.

'Stephanie, listen. There was no-one else there. With all exits blocked except the west path and the Rector's Path anyone would have had to pass me. No-one did. No-one climbed the spoil heap – you couldn't without making a noise – and there was no-one hiding. Apart from the place we use by the church wall and the vault there is nowhere to hide.'

'John, what do you think?' I demanded, and was maddened when he too admitted that he didn't know.

'But you must at least have ideas! Both of you!'

Adam said nothing. John, after some nagging, conceded that several ideas had occurred to him but, not having witnessed the event, he was reluctant to voice an opinion. Which made me even madder.

'OK.' I stood up. 'Since you don't want to discuss it, I'll turn this early start to good account and do some work.'

Adam made a negating gesture. 'Sit down, Steph,' he said. 'It's not that we don't want to discuss it. We really don't know what to say. I was rather hoping you would.'

I sank back into my seat. 'Adam,' I said, very restrained, 'John, who at least witnessed the fact that the vault hadn't been tampered with, says that he doesn't feel competent to express an opinion. I, who saw absolutely nothing, am expected to pronounce on this. Yes?'

'Why not? You've never been particularly reticent about producing theories in the past.'

Which was true enough. 'All right,' I said cautiously, 'but I think you could say more than I, John.'

'And I could be wrong.'

'So what? At least we'd have a starting point.'

It was most unusual to see both of them so utterly at a loss. No, that wasn't right. Adam was, but not John. Notwithstanding his odd silence, John seemed almost serene.

I said, 'Right. If you're certain that apart from you, Pryce and the other party there was no-one else in the churchyard, and no-one else's dry ice in the vault, that leaves variants on one other possibility. It has to be paranormal. Yes?'

Adam's nod was reluctant; John's more confident.

'Very well. Now three options present themselves. The first is that Llantathan did it and that it was meant to scare you. Second, it could have been someone in the village rebelling, and it was intended for Pryce...'

I stopped, still trying to think it through.

'Go on, Stephanie,' John urged quietly.

'Well, the third possibility is that it was truly supernatural: an outside agency stepping in. And, judging by what you two haven't said, I'd guess that's your choice. Am I right?'

Adam sighed. 'As usual.'

I shrugged. 'It doesn't take great powers of deduction. The first two options won't wash, will they? If it had been intended for you, Adam, Pryce and the other one would have known and wouldn't have reacted as they did. Rebellion in the village? Unlikely. It would have to have been growing for a long time for someone to risk a confrontation with Pryce. The women might, but they wouldn't have the power.'

'So. Some independent supernatural agency,' John said. 'But good or evil, Stephanie?'

'Good. At least for us. It's either the devil, or what-have-you, turning on his own. Or it's God. And that's your department, John. Come on. I've said it since you wouldn't. Give us your ideas now.'

'I'm not inclined to think that this is the work of Satan,' he said. 'He may be called the Father of Lies, but he isn't stupid. Turning on his own here, when he's clearly onto a good thing... No.'

'So that leaves us with God.' I smiled suddenly. 'God with a sense of humour.'

John smiled too. 'Has that only just occurred to you, Stephanie? Yes, I think this was God intervening. He knew Pryce would be early and that you wouldn't be able to carry out your plan, Adam. So He did it for you.'

Nice of him, I thought. A pity he didn't stir himself before now. I didn't say it though: I knew how my bitterness upset John. Knew too how difficult all this was for him.

'So I saw a miracle,' Adam mused.

'Perhaps you did,' John agreed. 'But we must be careful. We don't know for sure, and if God did decide to intervene directly, we can't assume that He will do it again. Or that this is a sign of His approval of all our actions. Don't see it as God giving us carte blanche.'

'I don't see it as anything except that it was handy,' Adam stated. 'You, Steph?'

'Open mind. It depends on what else happens. If anything.'

John thought that was reasonable and told Adam to go on with his nocturnal tricks if he felt so inclined. They were obviously having useful effects.

After that there was time for more coffee and the washing up before work. John went to field an early phone call and Adam asked me whether I'd had any luck with the notes.

'No, and it's odder than I thought,' I told him.

'And you never missed the book?' he asked when I explained.

'No. I've always taken it for granted that I typed the notes up as I do with all my recordings. It's only eight inscriptions. If there was anything else I would have noticed long before now, but it suggests that I've lost a notebook with very little in it.'

'Lost?' he repeated. 'Or was it stolen?'

'Oh, I thought of that. But I never leave things around. I always keep everything in my bag... Oh!'

He looked at me, his eyes sharp. 'You've remembered?'

I grinned. 'I rather thing I have. I just hope, after all this, that that inscription ties everything together.'

VI

John spent the day in his study and I didn't see Adam again after breakfast. Hoping, now, that the matter of the bells would be wrapped up by the end of the week, I tackled my legitimate work with uncommon energy and went home at 4.30 feeling so good that I cooked a decent meal and ate it. And as I did so I retraced the incident which must have led to the loss of those notes.

It was so simple. Less than a week into my job I found that the strap of the big organiser bag I'd bought when I started the M.A. was almost at breaking point. I didn't need anything as big now, and I found a replacement in Chepstow that weekend. But I kept the old one with a vague idea of having the strap replaced one day. Clearly, I'd overlooked the notebook when I'd transferred my things. Wherever that bag was now, so must be the notes.

As soon as I'd finished my meal I went up to the bedroom and opened the wardrobe. Yes, there it was, squashed under a suitcase of clothes I no longer wore but might again. I dragged it out, excited and nervous, and unzipped the main compartment. Fluff, nameless crumbs and bus tickets but, through the lining I could feel treasure in a side pocket. I had it!

The belfry of St. Michael's, Llantathan, I read, housed a ring of eight bells arranged in pairs around a square and that in order they were named and inscribed as follows:

Treble. Recast at the Whitechapel Foundry in 1952. Sound bow inscription reads:

JUDITH

There is none that can resist thy voice

1952

My relief in finding the book was virtually wiped out by the realisation that this didn't help at all. Crestfallen, I decided to go down to the rectory.

Adam misjudged the look on my face. 'You didn't find it, then,' he said.

'Yes, but I'm none the wiser. The inscription's a quotation, but I don't know where from. It seems to suggest that the bell should be rung, but I still can't see the significance.'

'Leave it,' he advised. 'Something might click.'

He was sitting on the edge of his bed pulling on dark socks to complete a black ensemble of teeshirt, jeans and jersey. Going to do his thing in the churchyard later, no doubt. He looked just showered: damp-haired and shaved, but tired. As I watched him combing his hair in front of the mirror I thought that he seemed older.

There was nothing boyish about Adam, nothing to stir the mothering instinct. More than one member of his team had described him as a hard bastard and he looked it. Moody, difficult, awkward, yes, but that wasn't all he was. So many times I'd been the recipient of his thoughtfulness, his understanding. Now, watching him, I knew that I wanted to know more. Was he a man capable of love, of joy and pleasure and weakness. Was he, I wondered, anything like me?

He saw my studied reflection in the mirror and turned. 'What are you thinking about, Steph?' he asked.

'That you look older,' I said bluntly, if not with complete honesty.

'Yeah, well, I feel it.'

'No, I didn't mean it like that. You don't look older than you are. You're 33 this autumn aren't you? Oh, I don't know what it is. More mature... grown up...'

I was making a mess of this. He sat down again and pushed his feet into black canvas lace-up shoes. 'Before I started the job here do you know what I used to do, Stephanie? At weekends?'

I shook my head. I'd never speculated.

He tied the laces and looked up. 'I used to drink a lot; get stoned sometimes. I went to the cinema, to parties. I had girlfriends. Good times.' He stood up. 'Grown up... that's about it, Stephanie. God, you forget! I wouldn't mind having good times again.'

'Not long now, and you can,' I said.

He made a sound that was half laugh, half sneer. 'Is that what you'll do?'

'I don't know what I'll do when this is over. Carry on as usual, I suppose. For now... do you want any help?'

'If you like. Borrow John's sweater again. I think it's still in the kitchen where you left it.'

'As quiet as possible, Steph,' Adam whispered. 'We'll go round the back of the house and over the wall at the bottom of the garden. I haven't rigged up the line and I can't now, so as soon as you see Pryce you'll have to throw a small stone into the vault. Can you do that?'

'I think so,' I said, privately doubting it.

We scrambled over the wall into the churchyard and crossed to where I could see the corner of the tower and the vault. Then, abruptly, he pulled me back against the church wall in the angle of the buttress. In a moment I saw dark figures walking across Area G.

Elwyn Pryce's characteristic bulk was identifiable but I had no idea who the others were. It was too dark to make out anything much and they spoke too quietly for us to hear what they said.

They stopped within a yard of the vault. Its plastic covering, battened down by planks and bricks, stirred in the breeze. A match flared, and two cigarettes glowed red. I shivered. Adam put an arm round me, holding me close to his body for warmth. And comfort. I was very scared and I could feel his tension growing as the minutes passed.

The church clock struck 11. The little knot of figures seemed to draw closer together. Adam's arm tightened round me as the wind gusted suddenly and the plastic over the vault lifted at one corner, breaking from its restraints. I had time to think that now they would see Adam's dry ice paraphernalia, and then I couldn't think at all. From the vault's depths a great cloud rose, billowing then hitting the ground and curling up again in slow white waves that glowed with light.

I heard a cry of alarm, curses and a confusion of movement, and still the cloud boiled from the vault until the whole area of the excavation was engulfed. Then, as we stood there watching it, my fear gave way to fascination for, as it built and swirled, it changed into a thing of beauty.

'It wasn't fog, John,' I said later. 'Or mist or smoke or steam. It glowed and sparkled. Scintillated. Oh, I wish you could have seen it! Imagine billions of minute particles reflecting light and colour...'

'The scales from butterfly wings,' Adam said. He lit a cigarette and put it between my fingers. His face was drawn: etched with concern for me. And no wonder.

Out there in the churchyard I had experienced something beyond what we both saw and my reaction had terrified him. I was still weeping intermittently.

I will never be able to describe any of it adequately. No simile can convey more than a pale semblance of the cloud's radiance. Butterfly scales, yes. A rainbow broken to fragments. Sunshine dancing on waves. The clean, pure shining of a raindrop. The glitter of frost by moonlight. It was all that and more. That much we both saw. That was all we saw. Adam agreed that he too ceased to be afraid, but I felt more. Fascination became attraction and then compulsion until I broke from Adam's arms and began to walk towards that great shining cloud.

'I couldn't help it,' I said, crying again. 'It drew me. Everything about it was so...'

... wondrous. I could think of nothing but being in it, part of it, lost in it. I'd reached the edge of it when Adam dragged me back. I had just time to feel the particles on my face... my hands... and it was...

'... warm, John, and soft... Oh God! I was furious with Adam for stopping me.' I turned to him and held out my hand. 'I'm so sorry...'

He came to me and took the hand I offered – the hand I'd burned – and his eyes widened. 'Stephanie...'

And then I saw that the skin was perfect. Every trace of injury was gone.

'Stephanie...' His voice was broken as if he was going to cry. I put my arms round him and felt his body shaking.

'What is it?' John asked, hovering anxiously.

'Wait,' I told him, still holding Adam until the shaking subsided. 'It's all right.'

In a minute or two Adam pulled away and all but ran out of the room. John stared after him.

'Leave him,' I said. 'Look...' And I showed him my hand.

'The night we scared Pryce with the fire I burned this hand. I lied to you, John. I didn't cut it. I'm sorry, I thought you might veto more tricks if you knew. Although it was healing, I was going to have scars and Adam felt responsible. This hand came into contact with the cloud. Do you see?'

He looked from my hand to my face. 'Yes. Yes, I see, Stephanie,' he said quietly. 'I see very well indeed.'

He sat down heavily, still staring at me. 'What happened then?'

'Then it spread, thinned and started to disappear. In a moment it was gone. Adam was raging at me and I was crying. I felt so... disappointed. John, it couldn't have hurt me, could it?'

He reached out and took my hand, but gingerly, as if he was afraid to touch me. 'No, Stephanie, I don't believe it could have hurt you. Your hand is evidence of that. But... Oh, thank you, Adam.'

He was back, looking in control again, more or less, as he handed glasses of whisky.

'But what?'

'But perhaps we might never have seen you again.'

'You said it wouldn't have hurt me...'

'What if it took you with it when it disappeared? I'm probably being fanciful but...'

'Nice way to go Steph,' Adam said drily. 'Sorry I had to stop you, but the site report's not finished yet.'

We laughed and I was able to recover some sense of the ordinary. Well, ordinary for Llantathan, and I made some remark about the cloud's effect on Pryce and his friends. They didn't see it as a thing of beauty.

'Not from the noise they made,' Adam told John.

'I wonder what they did see,' I mused. 'Did it appear to them as something horrible or is it that they can't bear to be in the presence of that which is lovely and good? And it was good, John. I've no doubt of that. Whatever it was, wherever it came from, evil had no part of it.'

'I know,' he said gently. 'I can see that.'

Adam escorted me home again and reminded me about photos of Marina. 'Hang on a bit,' I said. 'I'll look now.'

But he shook his head. 'Bring some to work tomorrow. I can't do anything until then anyway.'

Which, translated, meant "I'm not going to be alone with you at this time of night when we're both shaken and not entirely sober". Not that I had the slightest ulterior motive then. The 8th loomed too large now to allow side issues any space at all. Or so I thought.

VII

Marina and I never got round to putting our pictures in albums so they were still in the original paper wallets. I shuffled through dozens taken over the last year, mostly on day trips and weekends away. Marina laughing at me from the bench under the pear tree in Gloucester. Marina eating ice cream in Bath, and leaning moodily on the Clifton suspension bridge. Marina scrambling out of the great ditch at Avebury. And always Marina in jeans or skirts and tops. Nothing ethereal. Nothing to suggest the ghost.

Then I remembered the folder of photos I'd found in my office desk. Where had they been taken? North Wales? Yes… that aimless drive through Snowdonia and, reaching the coast, the chance discovery of Tonfanau.

Tonfanau. How could I have forgotten that? Strange, fascinating, empty, haunted Tonfanau, where the sea met a wide beach below the deserted ruins of a military base. It was the weirdest place I'd ever seen. It should have been nightmarish: it was surreal enough; yet it was only beautiful and oddly poignant.

We were camping that weekend, our tent pitched on the sheep-nibbled grass by the Dysynni estuary. It was warm for late September and we swam and lazed for a day, made love on the beach under a moon just past full. There must have been pictures taken in a place like that. I put aside snaps of Llanberis, of the Snowdon railway, and Capel Curig and Dolgellau.

Yes. Here was our tent on the cropped turf and me on my knees frying bacon, and again in a green bikini sitting on a rock, my feet in the sea. Marina sunbathing. Marina standing on a cliff edge... Oh yes! Marina in the evening, the soft wind lifting her dark hair, blowing the hem of the white silk nightdress I'd made for her when she envied mine. The garment she was buried in. Oh God, how lovely she looked! How lovely she'd been.

I didn't cry. I wouldn't cry. I put the photograph aside, repacked the box and went to bed. And hoped, prayed, that come the 8th, Elwyn Pryce would be in hell.

'Perfect!' Adam exclaimed when I gave the picture to him next morning. 'Good quality, so it should blow up well on the projector. Background's nice and neutral too.'

He looked at it for a long time. I assumed he was thinking about technicalities until he said, 'This is how she was for you, isn't it? The woman you knew?'

I nodded.

'Funny... I never thought she was anything special. Not particularly attractive. Yet here she's beautiful.'

I picked up my bag and my coffee mug and walked to the door. 'I know she wasn't conventionally attractive. You might even say that she was plain. But for me that's how she was. Always.'

Adam spoke. His voice was controlled to lightness, flippancy, almost, but the underlying thread of bitterness was unmistakable. 'And always will be, now. It's a bugger isn't it, Steph?'

'Yes,' I choked, coffee splashing onto the steps as I fled to my room.

* * *

Adam came upstairs during the afternoon tea break to tell me that the diocesan architect had been out to look at the vault. 'It'll have to be completely excavated and the well investigated,' he told me. 'They think it's probably the cause of the damp. We'll do the digging, but the well is their problem. We'll finish everything in that area then get out of their way.'

'No more tricks, then?'

'Shouldn't think so.' He stood at the window for a couple of minutes, looking down on the site. Then: 'I'm going back to Caerwent on Saturday, Steph. They're working on the temple site now. Would you like to come with me?'

I looked up and nodded. 'It would be interesting. And if the weather's half decent I'll pack a picnic. We'll go and sit on top of the motte there. Yes?'

It wasn't going to be a very elaborate picnic: cooked chicken, tomatoes, bread rolls and strawberries with a pot of cream to dip them in; a bottle of Frascati and two glasses. The weather was better than half decent, and I was looking forward to the trip, curious to see how another organisation's excavation looked, and needing this day out. I'd fallen asleep thinking about the elusive quotation on the bell, and it was the first thing I thought of when I woke up. Whatever the wisdom of spending time with

Adam, a picnic at Caerwent was a more than welcome distraction.

The excavation was still in its early stages, so there wasn't a great deal to see yet. Adam chatted to the supervisor about what they hoped to achieve and about bringing the Llantathan team over during the second week in August. We go on as if life will just continue as normal after the 8th, I thought. When we might not even be here. Rationalisation again. Marina had been right: life would be impossible without it. Having a picnic was, I supposed, a part of that. If we really, truly, believed that we might die on the 8th, would we be sitting on a medieval motte in the sunshine, eating strawberries?

I put it to Adam when we were doing just that. He took another strawberry and dipped it in the cream. 'No, of course we don't really believe it,' he said. 'Part of me doesn't really believe any of this. Maybe it's like having cancer and being told that you have six months to live. All the evidence is there, but do you believe it? When every day you wake up and life goes on.'

'Yes. The vault; the shining cloud; the hex... all we know, all we've seen... At this moment all that has less reality, less importance than being here with you.'

He looked up from the strawberry punnet, his eyes dark shadowed, expressive, and I realised what I'd implied. But he said nothing. We finished the picnic, packed everything up and he held out his hand to steady me down the grass-slippery side of the motte. Neither of us spoke much on the way back to the car and when he dropped me off at Vine Villa I saw that same look and wondered where all this was going to end.

* * *

On Tuesday I worked late tidying up file notes which had been hanging fire while I dealt with my section of the report. I'd seen nothing of Adam all day, and precious little since the picnic. Probably as well, I thought, and knew I didn't mean it. At lunchtime Joyce, sitting with me on John's terrace, said that Adam was in one of the worst moods she'd ever seen.

'I suppose it's the vault,' I said, knowing that that was only part of it. The Clerk of Works was pushing to get his team in to investigate the well. Adam, his patience stretched, had explained that his own team could only work as fast as the archaeology allowed. Joyce, elaborately, said nothing.

At John's invitation I stayed for supper, and wished that I'd gone home. Adam was morose, John seemed distracted and I was, as usual, preoccupied with the bell mystery. I was beginning to think that we would have to take a chance on the ringing, and hope that we got it right. It was not a comfortable thought.

After supper Adam went upstairs muttering something about schedules. John and I did the washing up, then I set off for home. I'd just passed the war memorial when I heard footsteps and Adam's voice calling me to wait.

'It's getting dark, Stephanie,' he said. 'I'll walk up with you.'

I thanked him, and meant it. School Lane wasn't well lit and someone – Mal Bowen or Mervyn Pryce or one of the others – would be lurking somewhere near the house. Lurking, watching, was all they'd ever done but we were getting too close to the 8th to be sure that the status quo would be maintained. Howells had, apparently, put a stop to the hexing, but he might not be able to stop them arranging a convenient accident.

That evening we didn't see anyone hanging around which was, in a way, worse than the spying we'd grown used to. I would have been relieved if Adam had offered to stay for an hour or so, taciturn as he was, but as soon as he'd checked the house he said goodnight and went back to the rectory to try, he told me, to come up with a work schedule which would satisfy the architect.

I went through to the kitchen to make some tea and look at the day's post: the phone bill, a bank statement, and a big, bulky envelope. The feel of it suggested more local history bits and pieces, so I didn't bother to open it until I was ready for bed, and then all thoughts of sleep fled. I turned the contents over in disbelief, unable to imagine where this had come from. Newport, said the postmark. I looked again at the hand-written address. Where... *where* had I seen it before? That swanlike letter S at the start of my name... No covering letter. No clue. The postmark... that handwriting...

* * *

There was no chance to talk to anyone until after lunch. John and Adam were in Newport for a meeting with Alan Foster and the architect. Joyce was in and out. 'Bones!' she exclaimed as we passed briefly in the kitchen. 'Bits and pieces all along the side of the church. And there's a complete infant inhumation. Ceri's digging it now. Got to go!'

I worked with my door open, listening for voices in the hall, but it was almost one before John and Adam came back. I heard John, indistinct, in the kitchen, but not Adam. In a couple of minutes I saw him from the window, striding across the site to where Ceri was working, with Joyce nearby dealing with finds. I took my bag and went down to John's study.

When I apologised for interrupting he pushed aside a pile of church paperwork with evident relief. I said, 'Something's happened. No, it's good, I think, John, but it means that we're all going to have to make some more plans quickly. And I need your help. It's the bell again. And it might be another invitation to treat.'

He looked from my face to the package in my hands, bewildered. 'Sit down, Stephanie,' he said, 'and tell me about it.'

I pulled one of the chairs closer to his desk. Holding up the package I said, 'This came through the post yesterday. As far as I can tell from the contents, it's what Angela wanted me to have.'

Startled, John pulled out the contents and stared at the faded inscription on the brown paper: *My papers concerning Penelope's memorial. A.V.* 'Arthur Vine?' he said, and I nodded.

Inside there were two smaller brown envelopes. One, as Angela had said, held newspaper clippings and a list of births, marriages and deaths. The other contained, as well as receipts, correspondence and so on, Arthur Vine's rationale for the casting, hanging and ringing of the memorial bell. And a picture which looked as if it had been cut from a book. It showed two women, both holding a man down while one of them cut off his head. On the back was written: *Artemisia Gentileschi. Uffizi Gallery. Florence.*

He looked up at me in disbelief. 'Stephanie, who... how... Do you know?'

'I think so. Look.' I took a card from my bag and put it next to the outer envelope. 'See? Compare the 'S' and the old-fashioned 'r'...'

He stared. '"So sorry",' he read. 'Stephanie, isn't this the card you thought came from Mrs. Pritchard?'

'Yes. I'd say it's the same writing, wouldn't you?'

Still looking from the envelope to the card and back again, he nodded, slowly. 'You're right. We are going to have to discuss this with Adam and Joyce.'

'Today, John. After work. It's not just the implications. It's what's in here.' I picked up the picture. 'This must be a depiction of Hubert's bible story character, John, but who is it?'

'It's Judith,' he told me. 'Judith beheading Holofernes to save her people.'

* * *

As the team were leaving I packed up my papers and went to the window to pull the sash down. Adam, doing his usual check around the site, stood for a minute or so, staring towards the eastern end of the churchyard. Pryce, of course, leaning on the wall, staring back. Then I saw his head turn towards the rectory and up, fixing his gaze on my window. Adam, seeing, turned too. He lifted his hand in a half wave and walked towards the Rector's Path. I stayed where I was, arms folded, still looking down at Pryce until he reached up, pulled at his cap and walked away.

In the kitchen Adam, boots in hand, was just about to head upstairs for a shower. Joyce, he said, had gone back with the team to get the finds into the store, but John would bring her, and Gladstone, back later, collecting fish and chips for everyone on the way.

When Adam came down I went over what I'd told John. He compared the handwriting for himself agreeing, finally, that he thought I was right. Rose Pritchard. 'Though how she came to have this stuff I can't imagine,' I said.

'I think I can,' John told us. 'Evan Pritchard's been away this last week. What if he was the one who pushed Angela off the ladder and stole the package? His wife must have known something about it: perhaps where it came from; maybe a lot more than that. With Pritchard away she could get it into the post without him knowing.'

'Yes, but if all that's true, how does she explain that it's gone missing?

'We can't know, but she must have believed she was safe to do it,' Adam said. 'That, or it's a trick.'

'If it's a trick,' I replied, 'it's pretty stupid. It's given us what we need to know about the bell. We know now that Arthur's bell and Hubert's had the same name. I don't know the significance of that name, but I'm pretty sure that you do, John. So please tell us.'

He nodded, opened his big bible and began. 'Arthur's bell is, Stephanie says, called Judith. This picture...' he passed it to Adam, '...shows the Gentileschi painting of Judith beheading Holofernes. It's in the Uffizi Gallery in Florence. Hubert saw it during his Grand Tour and it inspired the naming of his bell. The story of Judith, by the way, isn't in the bible proper but in the Apocrypha. That's a collection of writings which weren't considered to be the word of God, but were thought to be edifying. Most bibles don't include them now, and I have to admit that I haven't looked at the Apocrypha in years.'

'So what about Judith,' I demanded. 'Why did she behead... what did you call him? Holofernes? Does it make sense?'

'Judge for yourselves,' he invited. 'It's a long story but I'll edit as I go.'

And so we heard about Judith, the good, beautiful and rich widow. When the land of Judah was threatened by Nebuchadnezzar and her town besieged, Judith put off her widow's weeds and, attended by her maid, set out to beguile the enemy general Holofernes. Convinced of her ultimate seduction and believing her to be trustworthy he allowed her access to his tent where she cut off his head while he lay in a drunken sleep. The siege was lifted and the land was saved. Judith was a heroine and she sang a song of triumph and praise. 'And the quotation on the bell,' John finished, 'is from chapter 16 of the Book of Judith, verse 14.'

'That has to be it,' Adam said. 'Does it all make sense to you now, Steph?'

My mind was racing. 'More, even, than Arthur Vine could have worked out. As far as I know, he didn't have a real Judith.'

'What do you mean?'

'Marina *Judith* Graham. Who, last year, laid her hands on the treble bell which bears the name of one of her own people. Do you see? Not only do we have the bell with all its history of prayer, with its three dedications to the service of God – thrice blessed – and its specific association with the defeat of evil; we also have its tie-in with Marina, who was also Judith, who was, however distantly, linked with the woman who killed Holofernes. I don't know if such things are possible but I'd suggest that when Marina touched the bell something of her went into it. She left her fingerprints on it. Traces of herself. At the very least she was in empathy with it and all it symbolises. And...' ...by now tears were running down my face... '...and the bell was recast in the year that Marina was born...'

We all stared at eachother, then John passed me his box of tissues, and Adam said, 'Well, if blessing the bell means something, then Marina's empathy should. But it's this business of faith and symbols again.'

'No comment,' John said firmly when we turned to him. 'I don't know and I refuse to go round in circles over it. All I'll say is that expressions of faith usually mean doing something positive. The whys and wherefores don't matter much. Grace comes from trusting God.'

'So we ring the bell,' Adam said. 'Let's do it now.'

'Hold on, Adam. We can't just do this any-old-how. As I understand it, when God told people to do something they did it his way. People had to go to particular places at set times and do specific things, like Joshua marching round and round the walls of Jericho. Isn't that right, John?'

'It is, and I think that Stephanie's correct because if you look at scriptural examples, the ones who did it God's way received special grace. If we go and ring the bell now, something will happen, I've no doubt. But it might not be all we want. 'I believe that we've been led step by step through this and all along we've held to the conviction that there is one day on which we can put a stop to the evil here. I see no reason for abandoning that conviction now.'

Adam said that he followed John's reasoning, but there were things he didn't understand. 'For instance, who told Howells that it would go with a Jew? And the bell... Marina... were they preordained? Where does the Cavendish bell come into this? Is the ringing comprehensive or do we still need to get hold of Howells? And who do we equate with this Holofernes character? Howells or Pryce?'

'Both and neither,' I said. 'It's Llantathan really. The bell will, in some way, destroy not only Pryce but all he stands for in Llantathan.'

'So Howells as well?'

'That's something I'm not sure of,' I admitted. 'I think we still have to hijack him if only because we can't afford to let him run around. We don't know when the sacrifice has to be made: sometime in the last two hours of the 8th is the closest we can get; but we do know that he has to be there. No Howells, no murder. Maybe that'll finish him. Maybe the bell will. Surely the two together will take care of the lot.'

'OK, but why can't we do it today? After all, Arthur Vine wasn't going to ring on the 8th.'

'No, and I think he would have come unstuck. He'd worked out a lot, but not everything. He didn't know that there was only one Howells, nor where the balance of power really lies. I think he took the victims' apparent death dates as actual dates, and never pinned down the significance of the 8th. He must have counted on the bell being effective as long as Howells was in Llantathan, and the anniversary of Pen's death fell within that period. No. We must stick to the 8th as John says.'

'Fair enough. But when on the 8th?'

'Leave that for a minute, Adam. Let's go back to your question about preordination. I haven't a clue but perhaps the ending with a Jew part was somehow built in when Josiah Abelson was killed. Isn't it the case in legend and myth that what you do to put a train of events in motion is, in a different guise, the way to stop it?'

'Touch of the Tolkiens there somewhere,' he muttered, but he was grinning. 'All a bit sword and sorcery.'

I laughed too. 'Seriously, Adam, I don't know and we're not going to know unless Howells tells us. I don't think it matters.'

'OK. So let's assume that we've got Howells in the church. We know we have to hang on to him until after midnight. When do we ring the bell?'

'Midnight,' I said. 'If only because it's a time of supernatural significance. It's a threshold, a point of transience. Let's not ignore things like that. The witching hour may be a cliché now but it's become that, presumably, because there's truth in it.'

'And the Cavendish bell? Do we do anything with that?'

Once things start falling into place they do so with ease and speed. All I'd ever read about the functions and lore of tenor bells assembled into the obvious reply. 'When it's over,' I said, 'one of us must ring the tailors. Nine strokes followed by another 228. One for every year this has been going on.'

'What does that do?' Adam asked.

'Traditionally it frees the soul from the body. The tenor always seems to signify endings.' I frowned. 'The big problem with these bells,' I went on, 'is that none of us knows a damn thing about how to ring them. Unless you do, John?'

John shook his head regretfully.

'You pull the rope,' Adam said.

'Ah, but it's how you pull it. Get it wrong and you can do a lot of damage. We'd better decide who's going to do this ringing and find someone to give some quick lessons.' I turned to John. 'Can you help there?'

He said, 'Yes, I think so. I'll talk to Faringdon. Leave it to me.'

'Thanks. Now, who's going to do it?'

'You are,' Adam decreed. 'If anyone should ring the treble it should be you.'

I started to protest but John added his voice to overrule me.

'It has to be you,' Adam insisted. 'Especially if we're not ignoring symbolic details. You have an affinity with the bell through Marina.'

'And if you think of it, aren't you a Judith too?' John's voice was quiet and very gentle. 'Aren't you, in a sense, a widow? Good, beautiful and rich?'

Adam broke the silence. 'Rich,' he drawled. 'That at any rate. Don't know about the other two...'

'Really, Adam!' John protested, sounding quite put out.

'Oh stop it, both of you!' I intervened. 'This is silly. Let's just agree that I'm the nearest thing we've got. All right. I'll ring that bell but one of you will have to ring the tenor. It's too big for a small person without experience.'

'Joyce isn't small,' Adam pointed out. 'She'll have to do it. The immediate aftermath could well be a shambles in which case John and I will have our hands full.'

'Right then, John, fix it up. Some lessons in basic bellringing for Joyce and me. And you, Adam, can break the news to her later. She'll love you for suggesting that she's big enough to pull 32 hundredweight.'

'She is,' he said defensively.

'Yes, but that's not how she wants to see herself or how she wants to be seen. She probably hates always being the one people lean on because she's big and practical. What she needs is a man who'll make her feel that she can lean on him sometimes.'

I stole a look at John. Adam said slyly, 'Ah well, that's John's mission in life.'

John started. 'What do you mean?'

'You are going to marry her when this lot's over, aren't you?'

'Am I?' But I thought he was unsurprised.

'She'll be very disappointed if you don't,' I told him. 'And so shall we. Adam's set on being best man and I want to be matron-of-honour in a frilly pink frock. So there.'

Never one to wilt under teasing, John grinned. 'Oh well, if you've got it all worked out I'll try to oblige.' Then, turning the tables neatly if, for once, not wisely, he said, 'And perhaps we'll do the same for you one day.'

I averted my face. Adam flushed and stood up. 'Will you explain all this to Joyce on the way back?' he asked. And John said he would. 'And,' he added, 'I'll do you a favour, Adam. I'll tell her about the bellringing.'

'Where is she going to sleep?' Adam demanded when he'd gone. 'Because I'm not having that bloody dog in my room. It's about time John sorted out another bedroom. He's got plenty.'

'So have I,' I said.

His smile was strange: almost a sneer. 'What do you mean by that, Stephanie?'

'It's practical,' I replied, hoping I sounded cooler than I felt. 'You're right about another bedroom here, but it can't be organised tonight so... Take it or leave it, Adam. Joyce and Gladstone in with you, or my spare room.'

* * *

Adam had little to say as we walked up to Vine Villa. I left him in the kitchen, moodily contemplating a mug of tea while I went to make up the bed in the spare room. When I came down again, I saw that the tea was untouched. 'Would you rather have whisky?' I offered.

He looked up and nodded, his expression bleak. I wondered why. Our plans had taken an amazing, near miraculous, leap forward and my determination had acquired a new dimension: confidence. I believed, as I had never believed before, that we were going to succeed. Surely Adam must feel at least something of that. Or was it simply worry because I had to meet Howells again? I put the bottle and two glasses on the table, found my cigarettes and sat down opposite him. Was there, I wondered, anything I could do... say... which might help? Anything which, unlike last time, wouldn't make things worse?

He opened the bottle and poured for both of us. I lit two cigarettes and passed one to him. We drank and smoked mostly in silence, but it wasn't an easy atmosphere and, when I finished my drink, I said that I was going to bed. I went round the house checking windows and doors and, at last, Adam stood up and followed me upstairs.

At the spare room door he paused and turned, his look entirely unfathomable. I crossed the landing to him and we stood there in a frozen tableau for what seemed an age, awkward in the silence. Then, 'Adam, love...' I began and got no further.

'Don't say what you don't mean, Stephanie.' He opened the spare room door.

'You don't know what I mean.' I didn't know myself either, but I did know that I should have left things alone and that was what I would do now. I went into my bedroom, closed the door, switched on the bedside lamp and sat on the edge of the bed, cursing myself.

Because of the circumstances we were in, the three of us – and, lately, Joyce – had become accustomed to a lot of mutual informality and blurring of privacy boundaries. Even so, I was unprepared for Adam to walk unheralded and unapologetic into my bedroom. 'No,' he said, his voice low and harsh, 'I don't know what you mean. So tell me.'

I knew that I couldn't. Instead, I tried to turn the tables. 'You accused me of treating you like a kid. What was it you said? Kiss it better? No, Adam. I don't want to treat you like a kid. I want to know what you want...'

Agitated, he took a step or two towards me, then away. At the window he lifted the curtain, dropped it and turned back. 'Does it matter what I want?' He looked, sounded, coldly furious.

'Yes, it does. Adam...'

There was a fierce tension in his movements as he crossed the room to where I still sat. His fingers closed on my arms and he pulled me to my feet and shook me. 'You want to know, Stephanie?' he demanded. 'Really?'

'Yes. Yes, I do'

'I want to marry you.'

* * *

It was after eight when I woke. I'd forgotten to set the alarm. Oh God... I sat up, pushed back my hair and felt sick as the fiasco of last night came back to me. Downstairs I phoned John.

'I'm going to be late in this morning. Would you tell Adam, please?'

'Adam's not here.' His voice sharpened with fear. 'I thought he was with you. He certainly didn't come back last night.'

That stopped my self-pity dead. 'I'll be there as soon as I can,' I promised. 'I need to talk to you anyway.'

'Stephanie...'

'As fast as I can, John.'

What now? Oh Lord, what had I done? Where could Adam be? I rushed through getting ready and ran down School Lane willing that Adam would be at the rectory when I arrived. But the absence of the Golf and John's face told the same story. Outside, the team, thrown by this unexpected crisis, was trying to sort itself out.

John produced coffee and toast, waiting for me to come up with explanations. I didn't speak until I was halfway through my coffee, and then I gave an account of the previous night's events after Adam and I reached Vine Villa.

'I was trying to be reassuring. All I said was "Adam, love". I didn't get a chance to say more. He was so angry.' Gratefully I took the cigarette John offered. 'I should have known better. I did something like this before and he was furious then. Last night I asked him what he wanted, and he said that he wanted to marry me.'

John was unsurprised. 'Go on,' he invited.

'I was amazed. I never imagined he was that serious. So I just stood there gawping at him and he told me that I needn't take it as a proposal. That he'd be damned if he was going to let me treat him as a security blanket or a Marina substitute.'

'A security blanket?'

'The things some toddlers carry around and take to bed instead of teddy bears. He's got it into his head that I only want him for comfort because I miss Marina.'

John's hand covered mine with an understanding squeeze. 'Poor Stephanie,' he murmured. 'Don't be too hard on yourself. It isn't surprising that you would turn to whatever comfort's to hand.'

Dear, kind John. Were there no limits to his tolerance? I shook my head. 'It's nothing to do with comfort,' I said. 'I can't explain and I don't understand. How, after Marina, can I feel like this? I loved her so much. I miss her... So how can I possibly want Adam?'

'I don't know,' he said. 'But I don't think you should feel bad about it. Stephanie, I've not been blind to the fact that Adam loves you. Or that your feelings for him are rather warmer than friendship. Yes, there was Marina and you will go on missing her, but Adam must be hoping that one day... Still, he might have shown a little more patience.'

'No, don't blame him. I don't. It's my fault, not his.'

The kitchen clock stood at 9.50 and still no sign of Adam. I, who on waking, hadn't wanted to go within a mile of him, now wanted only that he should walk through the door safe and well. John made fresh coffee and eventually I finished the tale.

We'd snapped and snarled at each other, hurting and hurt, until somehow it ended up a mess of accusations and insults. 'And I told him to get out,' I finished. 'He gave me such a look, and he went. I heard the front door slam and that's all I know. I cried a lot and in the end I fell asleep.'

'Poor Stephanie,' John repeated. 'And poor Adam.' He was concerned, but he sounded almost relieved too. 'I think he'll be back soon. I expect he was regretting his words as soon as he spoke. Let's leave it until lunchtime,' he advised. 'If he's not back by then, we'll see.'

That was wise. If Adam had gone in a fury and was cooling off somewhere he wouldn't thank us for raising dust. So I went upstairs to try to work, and John drove off to see Angela.

The morning dragged. I struggled with my report writing, stopping too often to make yet more coffee to achieve much. Joyce came up once, Gladstone at her heels, asking if I knew where Adam was. I said I didn't. She wasn't satisfied but she went away again leaving me to brood and fret.

Lunchtime arrived, but Adam did not, and neither did John. I wasn't prepared to take unilateral action, even if I'd known what action to take, so I went on pretending to work until the phone rang at half past two. Joyce was out on site so I ran down to the study.

'Stephanie?' Adam's voice, hesitant.

'Where are you? Wait...' I reached out and pushed the door to with my foot. OK Adam. Go on.'

'I'm in Bristol. I'll be back this evening.'

'Are you all right?'

'Yes. Stephanie, I'm sorry...'

'So am I. Oh Adam, this is crazy.'

I heard a sigh. 'I know. Will you tell Joyce that I've taken this as a day in lieu? Tell her... Oh, tell her anything. I'll see you later. Take care.'

I put the phone down and walked out into the hall as Joyce came in with a batch of finds. 'Adam just phoned,' I told her, and relayed his message.

She nodded, but the look she gave me was rather odd. 'What's he doing in Bristol? Did he say?'

'No.' Which was more or less the truth. 'Putting two and two together I'd say it was a woman.' Which was, again, more or less the truth. And Joyce gave me an even odder look. I went back upstairs.

I heard John come in soon after, and a buzz of conversation between him and Joyce. I knew I ought to go down and reassure John myself but I felt too edgy to talk to anyone. I'd tried to give Joyce the impression that everything was fine. Nothing to worry about. But things weren't fine. Not when Adam and I were caught, now, in a nasty emotional snarl-up and the showdown with Howells so close. Somehow, we had to put our own problems aside and concentrate on what lay ahead. If we went into this with anything less than single-mindedness we would fail.

* * *

Adam phoned me later, when he was back at the rectory. 'We have to talk,' he said. 'Could I come up this evening?'

'Yes. All right. We both said too much and not enough last night.'

I tidied up, loaded the washer, and sat down at the kitchen table with a gin and tonic. Adam was right: we had to talk. Do what we could to get us safely beyond the 8th. But it wasn't going to be easy because nothing we said could turn the clock back. However sorry we both were now, was it going to be possible to avoid a repetition of last night's acrimony? Remembering was dreadful and I mixed another gin, an action which had become uncomfortably close to automatic lately.

Not wise, I told myself, but what the hell? This was going to be a difficult evening. However sorry Adam was, I knew that he was going to want the answers I couldn't give him last night: answers I still didn't have because I didn't understand myself.

The first thing Adam wanted to know was whether I'd eaten. 'I had boiled eggs when I came in after work. I don't want anything else,' I said.

'Just gin.' He filled the kettle. 'I'll make some coffee, Stephanie.'

He put two mugs on the table. 'Now sit down and let's talk about you, about Marina, and about us. Look, I do realise that you and Marina regarded yourselves as life partners. John was right when he said that you were, in a way, a widow. Not for a minute do I want to detract from what you and she had. I know you loved eachother but something... I don't know... You and she had that row after York, but something was out of kilter before then. Stephanie, was it as good, as right as you say? Because I can't help thinking that if it was, we wouldn't be here now, talking about it.'

I took the empty coffee mugs to the sink and rinsed them. Brought whisky and glasses. Found a fresh pack of cigarettes. Anything to give me time to think. Finally I said,

'Adam, I can't deny that things with Marina weren't always right. Yes, things were, as you say, out of kilter. The nightmares... Llantathan... We did love eachother. I can't tell you how much, but...'

He nodded. 'But... It hasn't stopped you playing games with me.'

'I'm not playing games,' I said. 'And I don't want a comfort blanket or a substitute for Marina. If it's looked like that, I'm sorry, but games it isn't.'

'So tell me,' he urged. 'Tell me about the evening we talked about the bells. It was late and I was ready to leave. You said I could stay. Why? Why did you kiss me the night I brought you home after your dinner with Howells? What was I supposed to make of last night? What were you offering? Or, to put it another way, what did you want?'

I splashed more whisky into my glass. 'I didn't know what I wanted,' I said. 'Not at first. Only that I didn't want you to go. I was missing Marina, desperately missing her, but at the same time... Things had changed between us... I didn't want comfort, Adam. I wanted you.'

He pushed his chair back and came round to my side of the table. Bending, he put his hand under my chin, forcing my head up. It wasn't the first time I'd been kissed by Adam but there was a world of difference between mistletoe kisses last Christmas and what he did now. Now I was permitted a glimpse of what I might expect if he became my lover. A glimpse of an intense passion I'd barely begun to suspect. Still kissing me he pulled me to my feet, holding. And I? What did I do? I returned his kiss with a matching passion. And I scared myself silly.

He let me go. I sank back onto my chair and reached out for the cigarette packet. He refilled his glass. 'No, you don't want me just for comfort, do you?' he remarked, half to himself.

'I told you so.'

'I still want to know why, Stephanie.'

'I don't know! I don't know! I don't know how I can feel like this after...'

If I was confused before, it was worse now. I'd imagined that kissing Adam would be an enjoyable experience. I had never contemplated so wholehearted a response. Nor that I would feel as shaken by him as ever Marina had shaken me. It was different, yes, but it was no less powerful. When Marina made me feel so, I had called it love. Now Adam had done the same thing and from the corner I was backed into, I was forced to call it lust.

I stood up and went to pull the window blind down, and lock the back door. 'It's getting dark. Unless you prefer fluorescent light we'd better go into the sitting room.'

He followed me, bringing his glass and the bottle. I wondered, again, what the end of this would be. No. I knew what the end of this would be. Perhaps not tonight. Or next week, next month. But one day...

I reached to close the curtains, then turned, meaning to switch on the lamp. He was closer than I thought and I turned straight into his arms.

Waves of excitement and panic engulfed me. This wasn't safe. I thought, as I'd thought before, that I didn't know Adam at all. Still less did I know myself.

'Stephanie, what do you want?'

'I thought you knew.'

'Yes, I know. But I don't know what you want to do about it.'

He let go of me and I took a step back. 'If I told you to do whatever you want to do, what would that be?'

He looked at me. 'Whatever I *want* to do? I wonder if you'd enjoy that. Yes, perhaps you would. Is that what you want, Stephanie? To unload it all onto me? Because that way you don't have to take any responsibility for your actions?'

'No!' I was indignant. 'How can you say that? I was the one who invited you to stay that night.'

'I'm beginning to wonder if it would have been better if I had stayed,' he said. 'Maybe we wouldn't be in all this shit now.'

'And maybe things would be ten times worse. Adam, I don't know... I don't understand why, given the circumstances, I feel as I do, and all this is getting us nowhere. I think we have to put it aside until after the 8th. If we don't...'

'Is that what you want, Stephanie?' he asked, and when I said that it was, his look told me that he knew damn well that I was lying.

He refused coffee but I made some for myself and carried it back to the sitting room feeling tired and dispirited. I didn't seem to be able to take a step in any direction without chasms opening at my feet, but when Adam said that he was going, I could have wept.

I stood up to follow him to the hall but he stopped me, his hand closing on my wrist. Closing and holding. Hurting. He dropped his jacket on the floor and, swinging me round, pushed me down onto the sofa.

'Adam... what...'

'Shut up.'

I tried to sit up and was pushed back against the cushions, his mouth hard on mine. One hand tangled in my hair; the other dragged at my teeshirt, pulling it from the waistband of my skirt.

Slowly, agonisingly slowly, he caressed my body, exploring its curves as I had once seen him, in the archaeology store, run his fingers over the rounded form of a Roman jar. This sudden gentleness lulled me and when the pain – real pain – began, I was unprepared.

I must have been so naïve. It had never occurred to me that it was possible to use all the tricks and techniques of lovemaking to hurt. No previous experience had ever encompassed what Adam did that night. Kisses turned to bites and caresses to scratches. Gentle exploration became vicious probing. I cried. Oh yes. But I didn't fight. I couldn't, because every new hurt brought a new degree of pleasure I'd never imagined, and I didn't want it to stop. When he asked, his voice low, hard, if this was what I wanted, my sobbing, urgent response was an affirmation.

It did stop, though, as suddenly as it had begun. He stood up, retrieved his jacket and was gone. Perhaps he realised that there was only one end to this. Perhaps he'd never intended it to go so far. Or it might have been a performance to scare me into backing off. I don't know but, naïve as I was, even I could tell the difference between passion and playacting. Adam had wanted me every bit as much as I wanted him and how he found the will, at that point, to stop and go away I couldn't imagine. It was, though, the solution we needed. Having been left raging with humiliation I wasn't going to do anything which could be interpreted as game-playing.

By now anything other than detachment would have been impossible. Events were piling up like bills after Christmas and what control we had was in danger of slipping. I walked down School Lane next morning in a mood of resolution. It had been folly to allow what lay between Adam and me to take precedence. During the whole evening I hadn't given a thought to Matthew Howells. Llantathan had been forgotten and that was unwise.

* * *

It was a scratchy, uncomfortable day: busy yet irritatingly unproductive. I wanted to lose myself in writing, but couldn't do that until I'd done something else, and couldn't clear up the something else until I'd dealt with yet another something else. It didn't help, either, that Joyce seemed to be having one of those days too. I could hear her, down in the dining room, ranting at someone for forgetting to bring out the packing material she'd asked for, and could she please be allowed to get on with her own work instead of having to solve everyone else's problems because they were too wet to think for themselves. I was amused: Joyce in full flight was pretty spectacular; but then she came upstairs and started on me.

Ostensibly she was niggling about having to go and learn to ring bells: 'It can't be that hard, surely?' Her real reason, though, was Adam.

'He's in a foul mood again. I don't know what you've done or said, but we're all catching the fallout, and I for one am sick of it.'

If I said all I wanted to say, we would have outright warfare on our hands. Not a good idea at this stage, so I told her, as calmly as I could, to mind her own business.

Her follow-up attack, telling me that I ought to get out of Adam's life, was barely under way when John walked in. Though she had the grace to shut up, and I to assume a casual attitude, he wasn't fooled: he must have heard her halfway down the stairs, but he said nothing about it. Instead, he told us that he'd fixed up a basic ringing lesson for us with Nigel Faringdon.

'But he can't do it until the 4th.' He put a slip of paper on my table: details of time and place. Then, with a slightly conspiratorial smile at me he requested Joyce's company for coffee.

'Is it that time already?' she asked. I couldn't decide whether her amazement was feigned or not. 'Goodness! Yes. Thanks, John. See you later, Steph.'

I resumed my interrupted scribbling and tried to dismiss Joyce's accusations from my mind. The trouble was that I thought she was probably right.

* * *

It was an unusual weekend in that I didn't go anywhere near the rectory. Not even to church. Instead I caught up on odd jobs and, finally, I tackled the bags of Marina's clothes. Packing everything useful up and taking it all to the Salvation Army in Newport felt like a positive step and not as painful as I'd anticipated. Heartened, I turned my attention to the one room at Vine Villa which Marina and I had never got round to tackling: the breakfast room in the wing.

It had become nothing more than a passageway to the conservatory, and a place to store the boxes of books and specialist journals brought from Yorkshire. There were more books throughout the house: reference works and history texts crammed the study with lighter reading in just about every other room. I didn't need a breakfast room, but it would make sense to turn this wasted space into a library. So I measured for bookcases and made lists. It kept my mind away from worrying about Llantathan, about

Adam and about Howells who was, apparently, still away. He had to come back but would he come back soon enough for me to arrange to see him on the 8th? Everything, now, hung on that arrangement being made.

* * *

Perhaps it did us all good not to be in eachothers' pockets over the weekend. Certainly the atmosphere at the rectory on Monday morning was much better. Joyce had gone to see her parents in Cirencester and wouldn't be back until Tuesday. Adam, John told me, had spent much of Saturday in and out of the church, preparing for the 8th. 'And on Saturday afternoon he went to Faringdon's church to play with whatever it is he's doing with the projector.' On Sunday, I heard, he'd gone off to look at Goodrich Castle. Both days he'd come in during the evening and gone out again until late.

Upstairs it was warm already and I opened the window, top and bottom, standing for a few minutes to watch the team. They were still mainly concentrated in the area adjacent to the south wall of the church. The Clerk of Works had told Adam and Alan Foster that, come hell or high water, his team would be moving their equipment onto site on the 10th and starting work on the 13th. I wondered what Adam had said about that!

Soon after three, when the latest section of my manuscript had grown appreciably, there was a knock at my door. 'Come in,' I called, expecting John, or perhaps Adam, with tea.

But the tea bearer was Matthew Howells. 'I hope I'm not disturbing you,' he said. 'You look very busy.'

'Not if you've brought my tea,' I smiled. 'Do sit down. How are you?'

'I'm very well, and I'm glad to see that you look blooming.'

I simpered a bit and added a few trite comments on the weather and life in general for good measure, remarking that I would be pleased when I'd finished my latest piece of report writing.

'And when will that be? I was hoping to persuade you to have dinner with me again.'

I tried to look doubtful but interested. 'When did you have in mind?'

'Saturday. Could you, Stephanie?'

'I'm sorry Matthew. I have a deadline. More than one, in fact. At the present rate I'm not going to be free until... let's see...' I turned and looked at the calendar behind me. 'Next Wednesday... the 8th... By then I'll have this out of the way.' It was nonsense, but he wouldn't know that.

'Do you really have to work so hard?' he asked, and it seemed an honest question. 'You never seem to have any free time.'

'That's the way it goes. It'll be better in the winter. Matthew, I really am sorry, but I've other things too, which I can't put off. That is the first available evening.'

He gazed steadily at me. A smile lifted the corners of his mouth: a knowing smile. A smile of concession and admiration. And of complicity. The game was up but we went on playing. 'Then Wednesday it will have to be,' he said. 'Unfortunately I have another appointment that evening. I too work late sometimes.'

'Oh well, if you're going to be busy... the week after?'

Clever, his eyes said. 'That won't be possible, alas. I won't be here.'

Not kidding, I thought, putting a disappointed expression in place. 'I'd hoped you would stay longer. You said you might.'

'No. Business calls. Wednesday it is, but I'll have to be back at the Hall early, I'm afraid. No later than 10. So shall we make it drinks at seven? Where would you like to go?'

I named the place Joyce had suggested – Aphrodite's – and he agreed.

'I'll see you safely home afterwards, of course.'

'Thank you.'

Another long look, and I returned it steadily.

'You're a clever woman, Stephanie,' he said quietly. 'But don't overreach yourself.'

'I don't intend to. I have a reputation for thoroughness and I never commit myself until I'm sure.'

'Sometimes that's not enough.' He stood up, extending his hand. I offered mine and it was enclosed in both of his. There was sadness in his eyes and it stirred me to compassion. By any standards he was a monster. But so was Frankenstein's creation, and whose fault was that? I loathed his actions but it was beyond my capabilities to hate him now. 'Take care, Stephanie,' he said. 'You do understand, don't you?'

'Yes, I understand,' I replied.

He nodded. 'Until Wednesday. By the way, please don't waste any more evenings in the churchyard. Mr. Pryce is unlikely to return...' He sounded amused and I couldn't quite stifle a quick bubble of laughter. Was anything ever as crazy as this? As Matthew Howells closed the door I wondered if, maybe, I was, seriously, going mad.

* * *

That Howells knew what we were about caused me no shred of concern, though I declined to tell the others. Adam was rather too acute concerning my contact with Howells and far too inclined to want to intervene. Now, more than ever, I was determined that he must not. I would stay out of his way as far as possible and, if necessary, lie through my teeth.

Well, staying out of the way was easy enough. Adam really did have a deadline to meet. He was cutting his lunch breaks to the minimum and working later with any team members who were willing to stay on. On Tuesday and Wednesday I went in to college to type up my manuscript and although I did go in to the rectory on Thursday, I didn't stay for supper.

Friday I took as another lieu day and went off with John to Chepstow where we dodged showers to do some shopping and spend an hour in one of the second-hand bookshops. I bought some shoes and black stretch denim jeans: smart enough for Aphrodite's; practical for what was to follow. Lunch was pie and chips in a café overlooking the main street where John gave me an account of his first meeting with Matthew Howells. He admitted that the man was not what he'd expected.

'Quite charming, Stephanie,' he said. 'And apparently genuine. I think your assessment of him is correct. I'm glad. It makes me feel happier about what he did for me. Well, in a way it does. It doesn't make me happy to know that I must help bring about the death of the man who saved my life.'

'No... and I find it hard because I see him as a victim. But we have to remember Brian Bennett and Andrew Mason and all the others. Whatever he is or isn't, he killed them and he'll go on killing. John... if he wanted, really wanted, to stop it... if he repented, could he escape retribution?'

'If he turned to God, yes. God forgives all sinners if there is true repentance.'

'Yes, but could he escape whatever horrible curse he'd be under if he broke his contract with the devil?'

'He could. The instant he put himself in God's hands he would be safe. But not, of course, from Llantathan.'

'No. John, when we've got him in the church will you try to save him?'

'My dear, I can't save anyone. Only God can do that. But yes, I will try to persuade him to seek salvation.' He twiddled his fork, prodded the tines into the squashiness of a sachet of brown sauce. 'You do realise though that even with God's mercy and protection, he will still die. The natural order must reassert itself, and his death is long, long overdue.'

I sighed and pushed my plate away. 'Yes, I suppose... But if he escapes the curse... John, maybe I seem soft, silly about this. I've spent so long hating him, wanting him dead. But I can't hate him now. I know he's a murderer but however often I tell myself that, I can only pity him. I don't see pure evil when I look at him. All I see is a weak man gone wrong, and trapped. If he took pleasure in what he does then I would hate him, but I don't believe he does. Pryce and his crew... that's different... I'll shed no tears over them. But I wish that come Thursday morning it could be finished, broken, and Matthew Howells redeemed and alive. No, I know that can't happen. But I'd rather he died in God's hands than the devil's.'

'I'll do my best,' John promised, 'but I'd guess that if anyone can persuade him it's you, not me. He holds you in high regard.'

I shrugged. 'Maybe. And maybe he just wants to sleep with me...'

'Don't, Stephanie!' John's voice was sharp with command. 'Don't let your pity take you that far. Such a thing would be dangerous beyond words.'

'I know.' I smiled suddenly. 'I do know that sex can have mystical power but I didn't think you did.'

'I'm learning fast. No! Don't tease, Steph. Not that fast. But I do read...'

He was beginning to look uncomfortable. Time to change the subject or I wouldn't be able to resist a dig about Joyce. 'Anyway, John, what did Howells say about the vault? He did discuss it with you, didn't he? Adam said something yesterday afternoon.'

'Yes. Oh, he played along with the vandalism story. He dropped a few hints about Pryce being responsible and beyond that he didn't seem very interested. But of course I had to mention the empty coffin: that without any remains it couldn't be reburied.'

'Ah. So now he knows we opened it. What did he say? Did he offer any explanation for why it was empty?'

'Not a word. He said he understood perfectly and offered to have it removed if it was in the way. I told him that it wasn't, and that the archaeologists welcomed the opportunity to study such an interesting and well preserved example.'

'Oh Lord! What did he say?'

John grinned. 'He said it was fine by him.' Then the grin died and he said, 'Stephanie, he knows, doesn't he?'

I closed my eyes and sighed. 'Yes. Yes, he knows.'

'What are you going to do? About Wednesday?'

'Carry on as we agreed. What alternative is there? I'm meeting him for drinks. He's bringing me back by 10.'

'I wish I could be sure of that,' John said. 'I know you've got your safeguards but can you reasonably expect him not to harm you?'

'I don't know. I don't think he will but whatever he intends I've got to do it. There's no other way. John, *don't* let Adam know about this or he'll stop me going.'

'He'll make a fuss, certainly.'

'He'll let personal feelings get in the way,' I insisted. 'I've pushed him far enough as it is. John, if necessary, endanger your mortal soul and lie to him. Whatever it takes. Because I've got to meet Matthew Howells on Wednesday evening.'

I planned my weekend around avoidance of Adam: a supermarket run on Saturday morning; lunch with Angela, then bellringing in Newport in the afternoon. Amusing myself away from Llantathan in the evening would be difficult: the cinema, perhaps. And on Sunday I was going to Gloucester, staying overnight at the hostel. I'd booked Monday as a lieu day too so I needn't be back until very late. That still left Tuesday when Adam might try to stop me, but by then it would be too late to change our plans.

* * *

Angela had made a full recovery. No, she said, when I asked, she had no idea who had caused her accident. She'd seen and heard nothing untoward.

Over an excellent lunch she entertained me with recollections about her late employer. 'Yes, she was a strange lady,' she agreed. 'When I first came here I was very frightened of her. I thought she was a witch.' Angela laughed. She knew so much and we could never tell how she knew.'

'Was she?' I asked. 'A witch, I mean?'

Her consideration of my question was perfectly serious. 'No, I don't think so. But she did see things. She would often tell me to prepare for visitors when none were expected and sure enough someone would turn up. She knew that you and Marina were coming. That's why she had Vine Villa renovated.' She saw my surprise and smiled comfortably. 'But then, even I knew that someone would come.'

She rose to bring the coffee. Over her shoulder she said, 'Will you stay, afterwards?'

It seemed an odd question and I didn't know what to make of it. Bemused, I replied that it was hard to think about afterwards. 'It doesn't seem real.'

'It will be. I only wish Miss Vine could be here to see it.'

'Yes, so do I. I hope we can justify her faith in us. And her generosity.'

'You will.' There was a calm confidence in her voice. 'Miss Vine never made mistakes. She was a good lady and she knew what she was doing.'

Before I left I made an attempt to tie up yet another loose end. Something Marina had meant to do before she died. 'Angela,' I began, 'Could you tell me why, in view of all the so-called accidents, the incomers stay? They must be aware that every family coming into the parish loses a son. Some of them have been here for four or five years. Don't they see that all these tragedies are more than coincidence?'

'I've talked to a few of them.' She told me. 'In a roundabout way. My dear, I simply don't know what hold Matthew Howells has over them. Some of the wives are uncomfortable, yes, but once the leases are signed it isn't easy to get out. My guess is that money's involved. Or blackmail. Probably both.'

'Blackmail? You mean that these families know what really happens?'

'No, I'm not saying that. They may have suspicions but they don't know. And I think Matthew Howells ensures that they won't enquire too closely. Perhaps with money, perhaps because he knows unpleasant things about them.'

'Such as?'

'Well, I do know that Andrew Mason's father has a criminal record.'

'That's not uncommon.'

'No, unfortunately it isn't. But the nature of his crimes might have hampered his ability to make a new life anywhere.'

She wasn't going to tell me more but it didn't matter. I could guess and I could see that she was probably right. Knowledge of a murky past would be a powerful tool in the hands of... no, not Howells. Pryce. Angela knew a lot but she was a long way from the complete truth.

I didn't tell her. I didn't think she wanted to know. Very soon she would be gone from Llantathan to make a new life in London. I wished her happy and, in many ways, I envied her: she was a survivor. In more ways than one.

* * *

Joyce and I met outside Nigel Faringdon's suburban church at three in an uneasy truce, glad of the presence of John's friend and his voluble enthusiasm. 'So there's going to be ringing in Llantathan again,' he said with relish. 'About time too.'

Joyce and I exchanged looks. 'Well,' I said faintly, 'we hope so.'

'Good. Good. All the bells, this time?'

'Er... yes...'

'That's a relief. I wasn't here then but I can imagine what an unholy row they made when they rang on the middle six. Why they insisted on it I don't know when they had a fine ring of eight. But Llantathan people have always been pig-headed. I understand that people were most thankful when they stopped it after the war.'

As he led us up the stairs to the ringing chamber I thought hard. 'Of course,' I muttered to Joyce. 'How stupid of me not to realise.'

'Realise what?' she asked over her shoulder.

'Why they stopped ringing the bells altogether. When the ring was increased to eight the bells would have been retuned. Ringing on the original six would have sounded wrong. That's why they stopped.'

We stepped into a ringing chamber much like that at St. Michael's but warmer, full of the signs of constant use. 'So that's another mystery cleared up to your satisfaction.' There was an edge to her words: she was still annoyed with me.

I can't say that either of us showed any aptitude for bell ringing but the vicar was patient and at the end of our allotted time we knew enough to do what was necessary without danger to ourselves or the bells. Our strokes were uneven and they improved little so we were all relieved when Faringdon said he thought that would be enough for the time being.

'Just remember,' he said. 'Handstroke, backstroke. Keep it steady. Handstroke when you pull the sallie. Backstroke when you pull the tail rope. Don't forget.'

'Handstroke, backstroke,' Joyce repeated obediently.

We thanked him and cheered him with a donation to the bell fund then, out of sight of the church, Joyce began to giggle. 'Oh God, Steph! That poor man. He was in absolute agony! We were so bad!'

Her laughter was infectious and it carried us back into the town, to a chintzy teashop, our disagreement forgotten. I treated us to coffee and cakes and suggested a film later.

'Can't,' she said indistinctly, occupied with an oozing chocolate éclair. 'John's asked me to dinner at the rectory. Sorry.'

We parted amicably half an hour later and I walked round to Bridge Street to see what was showing at the

ABC. Deciding that I could not face "Supergirl", "Police Academy" or "Indiana Jones" however much I wanted to stay out of Adam's way, I drove home hoping he wouldn't see the car and that Joyce would tell him I'd gone to the pictures.

Perhaps she did: my evening was undisturbed until late. I packed my weekend case, washed my hair and went down again to watch television for a while. Of course that was when Adam turned up. I braced myself for the collision but it never came.

'I was at a loose end,' he explained. 'John and Joyce are all wrapped up with each other. Bugger all to do round here...'

Well, if that was all. I didn't mind his company so long as there was no danger in the Howells department, but Adam and I and late nights were a problem combination. After the last time I thought things wouldn't get out of hand, but I wasn't counting on it. With four days to go things were tense. This was not a safe situation, especially as Adam wasn't sober.

But he showed no signs of amorous intentions. Slumped in Marina's chair he watched a film, ate and drank what I provided for supper and spoke only to complain about John and Joyce.

'Nice for them,' I said. 'You should be pleased.'

'Nice for them but sickening for everybody else. I'm moving out once it's over.'

'Back to Newport?'

He shrugged. 'Unless you want a lodger. All right, all right! Sorry. Forget it.'

I didn't look at him.

'Not easy, Stephanie. Not... fucking... easy...'

'No.' I stood up and turned the television off. 'Adam, let's just agree to leave it alone. Next week...'

'We can agree to anything you like. Agreeing's the easy part.' He reached out and caught my hand. 'Will you marry me, Stephanie?'

I stood still, frozen by an overwhelming temptation to say yes. And he knew it. But sense – or idiocy – prevailed. 'Leave it, Adam. It's late. I'm tired. You're tired and drunk. We're both under a lot of stress...'

'I am serious.'

'I know you are. Listen, after Wednesday I promise you, we'll talk about it. Sort it out.'

'I don't see how, but I expect you're right. As bloody usual. OK...' He heaved himself from the chair and walked a mite unsteadily into the hall. Touching my cheek with the tip of one finger he said, 'Take care of yourself, love. See you... when?'

'Wednesday morning. I'm taking Monday off and I'm in college on Tuesday,' I reminded him.

'Oh Christ! I'd forgotten. You're going to Gloucester. Jesus... Wednesday...'

He stared at me, bewildered, as if Wednesday had finally become real. 'Stephanie, take an hour for lunch on Wednesday. I've got to see you alone before... before...'

'Yes. Yes, I will. Adam...' The fragile control was cracking. If he didn't go now, I would crumble completely.

He smiled faintly and shook his head. I opened the door and, as last time, he walked out into the night without a word or a backward glance.

* * *

I'm not sure now why I thought that a trip to Gloucester was a good idea. To put a sharper edge on my determination? Perhaps, but it savaged me emotionally and in ways I didn't expect.

It was predictable that, at the hostel, I should have been given that same attic room where, an age ago, I had written up my notes and yearned for Marina. Nothing had changed. Each piece of furniture was exactly as I remembered it. I closed the door, put my case down by the bed and walked to the window. It was closed: the weather was cool and showery; but even before I pushed the sash up, I could see the lawn and the branches of the pear tree moving against a grey sky. There was the bench strewn with a few immature windfalls. Oh God! *How* could this go on unchanged as if nothing had happened! How could this exist when she did not?

I turned away and unpacked my case. What was I going to do on a damp Sunday afternoon? Lunch somewhere: it was still early enough to catch a pub; then the cathedral.

So that's what I did, and found myself making comparisons with York. More than once I caught myself wishing that Adam was with me to talk archaeology in that easy companionship of last winter. Later, though, after dinner at the Fleece, I walked back to the hostel and the garden. The sky was clearing now but the grass, damp from the last shower, wet my feet and ankles as I trod a determined path to the tree.

If any trace of Marina existed still in this world it would surely be here where the compulsion of our love brought us together under this tree. It was colossal foolishness but it was in my mind as I sat there listening to the stirring leaves and the distant traffic on the London Road.

But the garden was empty of all human life but mine. There is nothing deader than dead. No matter what I did, where I went, I would never be able to break the truth of that. She, who had so often in life appeared to me as ethereal as a ghost was not, now, even that. In an instant, unknowing, she passed from life to death, ceasing so completely to exist that, for all the presence she left behind, she might never have lived.

But for Llantathan, but for Elwyn Pryce and, yes, but for Matthew Howells she would still be alive. Tonight, instead of restless sleep in a solitary bed, we would have lain in each other's arms, warm and safe in the great cocoon of our love, happy with ourselves and with the world. Above all happy in that singing, joyous love we had generated not because we would but because we were.

Even as I thought it, another image grew, a different scenario took shape. Even as I sat there remembering, raging at my loss, I wondered whether, if I'd said yes to Adam's proposal last night I might not be here now, but lying in his arms.

And still, always, the question: how could I want that when I'd loved Marina so much?

On Monday I was out of the hostel by 10. At the bank I cashed a very large cheque and then I went shopping. Clothes: I was looking ahead, determined to believe in life after Wednesday even if I couldn't imagine what it might be. Books. Records. Some nice porcelain for my mother and something I'd never had before: a silver cross on a fine chain.

After coffee and a bun I went back to the jeweller's and bought three more, for John, Adam and Joyce. Symbols again. And the last thing I did was to visit the best florist I could find. There I bought five vast bouquets for arrangements in the church and one small, neat posy of freesia to put on Marina's grave.

I was home earlier than I intended but I'd had enough. Gloucester had been as futile as it was disturbing. If I'd had any idea of using memory to evict Adam from my thoughts, the trip had been a failure and even the shopping on a grand scale had become tedious. Not bothering to unpack the carrier bags, I did nothing more than put the flowers in water in the back porch before I ran a bath and went to bed. I wanted as much sleep as possible now and tomorrow night. Anything could go wrong on Wednesday but if it did it must not be because I was tired.

And I did sleep those last two nights, easily, after a chapter or so of my book; without conscious thought of Matthew Howells, Llantathan and all that Wednesday would bring; nor of Adam and the tormenting bond between us. Not even of Marina. In the end my mind was in limbo, clear and uncluttered. I didn't even dream.

VIII

Wednesday morning dawned still and sunny. I turned off the alarm and lay for a minute or two watching motes of dust dancing in the thin shaft of light streaming between the curtains. It reminded me of the shining cloud.

Wednesday, 8th August, 1984.

The day we'd planned for, waited for, never quite believed in. Fully awake now, I analysed my state of mind and found excitement. I was keyed up but not afraid: the way I was on the day of an exam for which I was well prepared. It was good. I pushed back the bedclothes and swung my feet to the floor. My day was in motion.

A lovely day too: warm, but fresh after the rainy spell. The hedgerows on School Lane, parched and tired over weeks of drought, had taken on new life: green, damp and rich. Thick tangles of bramble promised a generous harvest in a couple of weeks: the heavy clusters of hard green berries were swelling and changing colour. Last year Marina and I had meant to make jam, wine, pies, but Llantathan intervened. In a hundred ways, large and small, Llantathan had screwed up my life. Today I would have my revenge.

Early for work I stopped off in the rectory kitchen as usual for coffee and found John looking very much as I felt, grilling bacon and tomatoes; frying eggs. He greeted me cheerfully and offered a second breakfast. I accepted a bacon sandwich and sat down.

Adam, opposite, lifted his gaze from the front page of the Guardian. 'OK, Steph?'

I nodded, smiling. He looked preoccupied but not fraught. It might have been any ordinary work day. And that's how it went on.

Joyce, busy with finds, didn't materialise until the morning break when she came up with my coffee, and stayed to drink hers. 'All right?' she asked.

'Yes. Are you?'

'A bit jittery now and then but nothing I can't handle.'

'It's going to be hectic later. Somehow we'll have to find time to get together, all of us before half past four. There won't be a chance after that. All clear on what we're doing in Newport?'

'No problem. How are you getting in?'

'With the site van. I've an appointment with my solicitor at 5.15. Then I'll get something to eat, and kill time until I meet Howells.'

'I'll be there.'

I asked her what arrangements she'd made about Gladstone. 'Miss Morton's minding him,' she told me. We refined a few details and she rose to go. 'John said that Matthew Howells knows that we know... knows that we're going to stop him.'

I nodded confirmation. 'It doesn't change anything, though. But for God's sake don't tell Adam.'

'No. John did warn me. But there'll be hell on when he finds out.' She fidgeted with her hair. 'Steph, I'm sorry about the other day. You were right: it's none of my business.'

'There was some truth in it,' I admitted ruefully. 'I'm sorry too, Joyce.'

'Couple of cats,' she grinned. 'Seriously, Steph, I don't want any bad feelings between us. Any of us.'

'I can't imagine bad feelings between you and John,' I said and her face lit with happiness.

'I must go,' she said. 'I've a million things to do. See you later.' She closed the door then opened it again and put her head round. 'Handstroke, backstroke,' she intoned, and dissolved into giggles.

I threw a ruler at her, laughing too. It hit the door as she slammed it and I listened to her laughter fading as she ran downstairs.

The rest of the morning passed, for me at least, industriously. By lunchtime I'd finished all the work I intended to do that day. I tidied my table, washed my hands and went out to meet Adam.

He was waiting by the church porch, smoking. 'Nice day,' he said. 'The weather report says it's here to stay till the weekend at least.'

By tacit agreement we made for the ramparts, following the path to the south-west corner. Neither of us said much until we sat on the grass, our backs against a low, mossy section of the medieval wall when Adam asked how I was feeling.

'Fine. More excited than anything. You?'

'On edge, but it's not bad. I'll be glad when it's over.'

'Hard to imagine, isn't it?' I said. 'It all being over.'

'Some things won't change.'

'I wonder what will change. Once the pressure's off and we can live without Llantathan on our backs.'

'Llantathan will always be on our backs. There'll be no happily-ever-after. It's changed us too much. Joyce and John... well... maybe. But you? Me? That's assuming we're still around tomorrow.'

'We will be.' I closed my eyes, turned my face to the sun. 'Better, perhaps, if I'm not.'

He swore. Grabbed my arms and pulled me round to face him. 'Don't say that, Stephanie! Don't even think it! For Christ's sake come out of that fucking shell and realise that you don't live in isolation. Do you seriously imagine that if you're not here tomorrow we're all going to say Oh dear, poor Steph, and carry on as usual? John loves you as a sister. Joyce is fond of you. And I... When you think about not being around tomorrow, remember how it feels to be the one left behind.'

He relaxed and let go of me. Neither of us spoke for several minutes. I watched the stream of traffic on the Newport road: small blocks of moving colour; flashes of sun on windscreens.

'Is everything ready for tonight?' I asked at last. 'Did you sort out the slide?'

'Yes. No problems. Stephanie, that's not why I wanted to see you – to talk about Llantathan.'

'No.'

'I wanted to tell you... wanted you to know that no matter what's happened between us already... what might happen, I love you. OK, so it's not what you want. If I could give you what you want, I would.'

'Adam, I...'

'No. I know. You don't have to tell me.' He lit another cigarette and stared out over the fields.

'On Saturday,' I began, speaking slowly, carefully, 'will you come to Vine Villa? Supper?'

It was a loaded question.

'Yes, I'll come.'

I put my hand on his arm, brown from the sun and the long days outside. 'I can't tell you what you want to hear,' I said. 'I can't promise that I ever will. And I won't insult you with anything less. All I can say is that there is no-one more important to me than you. It may be no consolation to you but if I don't marry you, I'm damn sure I'm not going to marry anyone else. And come tomorrow I want you to be there. Because I couldn't bear it if you weren't.'

Then I broke all the rules and kissed him. And for what remained of our lunch hour I lay in his arms on the grass. When we walked back, hand-in-hand, I knew that when Saturday came, I would capitulate. I would marry him.

In the afternoon I went back to Vine Villa to shower and change and to collect the flowers and the silver crosses. In the cool silence of the church I filled vases, lit candles and then sat in the Michael Chapel to write three small cards. Nothing elaborate. Names, the date and place and a simple message of love and goodwill. I frowned for a while over Adam's card wondering whether to add more but it seemed inappropriate to mix the personal with this. It didn't matter: the hour we'd spent together on the ramparts had said all that was necessary. All that could be said for now.

The church clock chimed quarters and halves and I felt the first edges of nervousness. It would grow as the hours passed unless I kept my mind occupied. What to do? There was nothing left to do now, nothing to check, nothing to discuss. Only John's benediction when he called us together in the afternoon tea break.

Until then I sat in the garden reading over the story of Judith and Holofernes and, now, parallels I hadn't noticed before presented themselves. There was Judith, bedecked and bedizened, going off with her maid to fascinate the enemy and win his trust. The text prettied it up but what Judith said, in effect, was "I'll make him want to screw me, then I'll top him". There's nothing new under the sun. It was, more or less, my ploy with Howells. So, then, I was Judith too, just as John had said. One aspect of a triple force which would destroy the enemy. The bell, Marina and I, made composite by some mysterious spiritual tie. I even had my handmaid, Joyce, to accompany me. It was so right. Far, far better than Arthur Vine could have envisaged.

I closed John's big bible and carried it back to the study. I was still nervous but something of that strange peace which had come with the shining cloud took up residence in my mind.

Joyce was sitting in John's battered armchair. She looked up at my entry and I knew she was having a fit of the shakes. Her hands were pressed between her knees, her face pale. I knelt beside her and held her. 'Handstroke, backstroke,' I murmured and was rewarded with a weak giggle. She sat up.

'I'm all right now. Just a minor freak.'

I nodded. 'Stage fright.'

'What time is it?'

'Nearly three. John and Adam'll be here in a few minutes.'

'God, I don't know if time's going fast or slow. I hate this waiting.'

The door opened. Adam. 'Hi,' he said. 'John's just coming. He's dressing for the party.'

'What...?' Joyce began, then saw for herself when he walked in, in full panoply. I remembered what he'd said about going as a representative of the Church with all its trappings, and I realised that his stole was red: the liturgical colour of Pentecost. Fire and blood. The Holy Spirit. It was sobering, but a comfort, and a strange experience to be ministered to so personally by my friend in his official capacity.

He began by making the sign of the cross on our foreheads with holy water. Then, at his request, we recited the General Confession, were absolved, and received Communion. I don't think any of us felt in a position to refuse whatever the state of our faith. He said a prayer of thanksgiving for the good in the world and beseeched God's help then and always, and pronounced a last collective blessing. Then individual blessings as, one by one, we hugged him, thanked him and wished him well. I distributed the crosses and cards and finally, as far as we could, we relaxed.

But it was awkward. There was nothing to talk about. We all knew our parts and speculation was useless. It wasn't long before we dispersed: John to pray in the church, Adam to finish some planning, Joyce to catalogue finds and I... I to put my posy on Marina's grave and to think about the three hours ahead of me in Howells' company. The Judith bit, bedecked and bedizened. But this Holofernes knew what this Judith meant to do.

IX

It was just before seven and Aphrodite's was quiet. Joyce, startling in a leopard print boiler suit, sat at a table by the window chatting to a girl wearing a painfully tight pink dress. She saw me but neither of us made any sign of recognition. Matthew Howells wasn't there.

Perched on a bar stool, I lit a cigarette and sipped a weak gin-and-tonic. Quiet background music, Cyndi Lauper, overlaid the conversation of the two girls. The minutes ticked by and Howells failed to appear. I heard Joyce laugh and, tense now, I longed to turn and say 'Handstroke, backstroke...' Twice the door opened to admit customers. Twice my heart rate accelerated then slowed with disappointment and a perverse relief. The small bar filled and the balance between music and conversation changed. A shriek of high-pitched laughter made me wince. When I tipped more tonic water into my glass, the neck of the bottle clattered on the rim.

Then he came.

Smiling, apologetic, easy. Smart, but not business-smart. Entirely appropriate for a provincial wine bar on a Wednesday evening. He sat beside me and went through the litany of social politenesses before he ordered a drink.

'Beautiful as always, Stephanie. I do like your shirt.'

Pure silk. *Bedecked and bedizened...*

'Thank you.'

Then the gloves were off. 'Why are you here tonight, Stephanie?'

'Because tomorrow you'll be gone.'

It was an ambiguous reply. He poured water into his Scotch from the glass jug set by the barman. Its weakness matched my gin.

'Why are you here, Matthew?'

'Because that's what you wanted. And because I wanted to see you again before I go.'

Very light sparring, this. Still almost a game.

'Because you know you won't see me again?'

'It's not likely, is it?'

'No.'

He looked at me earnestly. 'Stephanie, is there any way, anything I can do, to dissuade you from the course you're about to take? As you know, I'm an extremely wealthy man with considerable influence. I will gladly pay whatever it takes to settle you and your friends anywhere in the world, give you anything you want, if only you will let Llantathan alone.'

'We can't do that, Matthew,' I replied. 'I'm sorry. I really am so sorry for you, but it has to be.'

'Sympathy for the devil?' He seemed surprised. 'Oh my dear... You can't possibly succeed.'

I didn't answer.

'You can't, you know,' he persisted. 'You're not the first to try.'

'I don't suppose we are.'

'But do you know what will happen to you?'

'If we fail?'

'When you fail. Do you realise what Pryce will do to you? Especially to you?'

'Matthew, I am well aware that if – *if* – it goes wrong you, or Pryce, or someone else will kill us. I'm also aware of the possibility that somewhere between here and Llantathan you will try to murder me...'

'No!' he interrupted sharply. 'No. I gave my word that I would see you safely home. I give you my word now that I will never harm you or any of your friends. Pryce, however, is another matter. Yes, he'll kill you, eventually, but not before he's extracted payment for what you've done.'

'I can imagine,' I said drily, thinking of the ex-verger's grovelling terror in the night churchyard.

'I don't think you can. Don't underestimate Pryce, Stephanie. He might look like a shambling idiot...'

'Oh, I don't underestimate him. I've had a taste of the pain he's capable of inflicting, remember.'

'Your friend.'

'My lover,' I said with quiet savagery. 'Didn't you know that? Pryce did. She was more than all the world to me and he killed her. Oh yes, Matthew, I know what Pryce can do.'

He shook his head. 'Stephanie, please... Leave it alone. You do not understand this. You have no idea what you're getting into.'

'Matthew, I have spent the last year studying Llantathan and learning to understand it. No, I don't know everything, but I know enough.'

'Then, presumably, you know what will happen to me if your actions do succeed.'

'Not the specifics, no, but I know what must happen, and what will probably happen.'

'And you want that?'

'No. I don't want that to happen to you. I can't say the same of Elwyn Pryce. But if you break with Llantathan and accept the protection of the Church...'

'I don't believe that,' he said flatly.

'I do.'

'You wouldn't if you'd seen a tenth of the things I've witnessed. Stephanie, the Christian god is powerless compared with Lucifer. Do you think this never occurred to me before? Oh, it did. Often, at the beginning.'

'How did it begin?' I asked softly. 'Matthew, tell me about it.'

He smiled. 'What every historian wishes for... to talk to someone who was there.'

'Yes, of course. But not just that. So many times I've wondered how Llantathan came about. It took me a long time to understand, to believe what was going on. I don't know everything and there are things I never want to know. But I do want to know about you. You must realise how difficult it is for me. Damn it all, Matthew! Today is your birthday. You were born in 1717. You've lived for 267 years. I believe that, though it's nearly broken my reason to do it. Of course I want to know!'

I took a cigarette from the packet. He picked up my lighter and held it for me. 'Do you make comparisons,' I began. 'Do you think that people are healthier now? Happier? Is life better?'

'I don't think so. Human nature doesn't change except, perhaps, for the worse. The 20th century is no more civilised than the 18th. Less so, in many ways. People are greedier, more dissatisfied, less caring of each other. Casual cruelty is the norm...'

'What do you mean?'

He picked up his glass, drank, said, 'Who looks after the parents when they're old and frail? They go into a home. Isn't that cruel? It would have been regarded as shameful, when I was a boy. Now it's the accepted thing. Children...'

'Your generations exploited them in the mills and the mines,' I said quickly.

'And yours makes them unfit for society. It gives them possessions instead of values. It sits them in front of television sets instead of teaching them to be useful. Puts money in their pockets and robs them of morals...'

I thought he had a point. 'Would you go back, if you could?'

'Yes. Right back. To the days when I was poor. If I could. Stephanie, I never wanted any of this. Never.'

'Yet you did it. Why? Greed, Matthew? Ambition?'

He laughed. It was a hollow, mirthless sound. 'Yes, if you didn't know the facts you would reach that conclusion. I was never ambitious, Stephanie. Not beyond a natural wish to live in comfortable circumstances. Llantathan, when I bought it, was the fulfilment of my dreams. To build the estate up and live happily with my wife. Have sons and daughters... live to see my grandchildren...'

'What went wrong?'

'Weakness.' He tapped his glass. 'This, Stephanie. Drink, and the fact that my wife died. If she hadn't, I don't think I would be here now, talking to you.'

'Did they kill her?'

'No. She never recovered properly after the birth of our son. And then he died too. It's easier to be weak when...'

'Yes, I know. So what did you do?'

He glanced up at the big gilt sunburst clock over the back of the bar. 8.40. 'I hope this isn't some sort of Scheherazade ploy, Stephanie,' he said severely.

'No. A woman might talk herself out of time, but a man? Never!'

He laughed. 'How true! Will you have another drink? What is it?'

From the corner of my eye I saw Joyce walking towards the cloakroom. Howells, his back turned, ordering drinks, couldn't have noticed. I murmured an excuse and followed her. She grabbed me as I closed the door.

'Steph, how's it going?'

'No problem. Listen, if you don't want to hang around here you don't have to. He's not going to touch me. Any of us.'

'You believe that?' She didn't.

'Yes. He really doesn't want to. But he doesn't need to. So he thinks. It's Pryce who's the real danger, just as we thought. So go back to Llantathan if you want. Up to you.'

'Adam would string me up if I left you.'

'All right. Got to go.'

She nodded. 'I'll follow when you leave. White Datsun. Good luck.'

'You too.'

I settled myself once more and waited for Howells to resume his story. He didn't, immediately, saying instead, 'I hear the rector has a bad cold. He seemed well enough the other day.'

'John tends to get colds easily,' I replied. 'Which reminds me. Would you drop me at the rectory, please? I want to look in and see if he needs anything.'

'Isn't your Mr. Pembury around?'

'Probably not. Adam mentioned that he was going out for a drink somewhere.'

'Ah... Yes, I'll drop you at the rectory, my dear. But I won't come in for coffee if you don't mind.'

I had to laugh. 'No. But please go on with the story. They trapped you, didn't they? How? What were they doing? Witchcraft? Satanism?'

'Yes.' His face was hard now, and angry. 'At first, I thought they were keeping pagan traditions which were nothing more than an excuse for self-indulgence. A few silly, meaningless rituals as a forerunner to drinking oneself stupid and sleeping with the prettiest women in the village. That was nothing, Stephanie. No-one believed that those incantations had any power. But their leader then...'

'Another Pryce?'

'No. A man named George Bowen. But very much like Pryce. Vile. Inhuman. Bowen set those sessions up. He knew I didn't take them seriously but he knew that I liked to drink and I liked women. And, I suppose, that underneath I was wretched after I lost my family. But then something went wrong. Badly wrong. I woke up one morning next to a corpse. Bowen's daughter, with a dagger through her heart and a dozen witnesses to swear that I'd stabbed her in a drunken frenzy.'

'Did you?'

'I doubt it.'

'So then you were blackmailed into serious magic?'

'Yes. Very serious magic, Stephanie. Nothing I ever read in books came close to it.'

In a few moments he sketched the subsequent events which had tied him to Llantathan forever, and it was more or less as I'd surmised. The pact with the devil, the sacrifices, the promises of everlasting life, of riches and status. I wanted to know more, so much more, but now he kept glancing at the clock and more than once he checked the time against the thin gold watch on his wrist. He put up with a few more of my questions, admitting that he had made the two big donations for the church restoration. 'A dig at Pryce?' I asked and he nodded. Then: 'And I want you to know that I would have prevented Dr. Graham's death if I could. It was done before I knew.'

'Pryce has a lot to answer for,' I said. 'And the rest of them.'

'More than you know.'

I wondered if he could be persuaded to elaborate but now he stood and said, 'I'm sorry, Stephanie, but I must take you back to Llantathan.' He glanced at his watch again and I noticed that it said 8.30. That couldn't be right. I looked up at the clock. 'Why do you keep your watch an hour slow?' I asked.

'What?' He started. 'Oh, European time.'

He was in a hurry and I hoped that he wouldn't be in too much of a rush to get out of the car and walk with me to the front door of the rectory. But, as we left Newport, he eased up.

'Change your mind, Stephanie,' he begged again. 'Don't get involved in this.'

'I must,' I said. 'I can't let it go on. I can't let you kill anyone else. Can you understand that?'

'Yes, I understand. Can you understand that although I will not harm you, I will not be able to prevent Pryce from killing you?'

'Yes, I know. It makes no difference.'

He pulled off the road into a layby and my stomach gave a lurch. Dead in a ditch, I thought. Where was Joyce? I saw her Datsun pass us. She would find somewhere to wait until she saw us move off again. The Daimler's engine purred on. He turned and said, 'Give me your hand, Stephanie.'

I did, but warily.

'It's all right. I'm not going to hurt you. I can't help seeing this as a foolish waste of life, but neither can I help admiring you. All of you. You have values. And courage. You'll need it. Perhaps you will succeed. Who knows where you and I will be after midnight? You know that much, don't you?' He leaned forward and kissed me very gently. 'You are the only person who has ever felt sorry for me,' he said. 'Don't let midnight catch you out, Stephanie.' He kissed me again and let go of my hand.

Then we were back on the road. I noticed Joyce's car ahead of us, taking the left turn which would bring her into Llantathan by the alternative route. In another 10 minutes the big car was turning into the rectory drive. Oh God, I thought, this is it now. He switched off the engine, got out and opened the door for me. Walked with me to the kitchen door where the only light showed. Took the hand I offered. Kissed it.

'Goodnight, Stephanie,' he said. 'And goodbye.'

'Goodbye, Matthew,' I returned. And watched him walk back to the car. He lifted his hand in a brief salute, got in and, I suppose, turned on the ignition. Had Adam had time to do his stuff? He must have. The car pulled away a little, coughed, misfired and then there was a small, dull explosion.

Howells climbed out. I ran over to him.

'I wonder how you did that?' he asked, somewhere between anger and amusement.

'I didn't,' I snapped. 'How could I?'

'Someone did.'

'Don't be silly, Matthew. It's just gone wrong.'

'Daimlers don't just go wrong. I think...'

I never knew what he thought. A volley of screams – real screams of terror – split the night and I jumped, my scalp tingling. Well done, Joyce, I thought.

'What the...?'

'That's someone in trouble.' I grabbed his hand. 'Come on!'

I pulled him, half resisting, through the side gate and along the Rector's Path. Round to the front. We heard a loud, agonised moan coming from the church porch.

'Stephanie...' He hesitated, but he wasn't sure. Those screams were so good. His hesitation was enough. One more tug at his hand into the shadowy porch where Joyce slumped as one attacked, still moaning. Then one great push, catching him off-balance as he bent to look at the 'victim' and he fell, staggering, through the church door as it was opened. Hands seized him. Joyce scrambled inside and I skipped over the threshold. John, his vestments fluttering white, slammed the grille and snapped the padlock. He pushed the great oak door into its frame, turned the key, shot the bolts and dropped the three bars into place.

In the darkness I heard Howells' voice laden with wry, self-deprecating amusement. 'You'd think, after all this time, that I would have learned never to underestimate a woman.'

The tower room was a reasonably comfortable place to sit out a siege. It was defendable with fallback positions, and it had curtains. Like all the church windows its grilles had been wired and Adam had made bars for the door. We had food, water, a kettle to make drinks, candles in case of power cuts, bedding should we have a chance to sleep, and an Elsan in the ringing chamber. Howells looked round, noting everything. His glance rested on me, quizzical.

At Adam's invitation he sat down on a straight-backed chair close to the radiator, and offered no resistance when Adam produced handcuffs and fastened him by one wrist to the radiator's top pipe.

'There's no need, Adam,' I told him. 'He won't hurt us.'

'Maybe not, but it'll slow the other buggers down if they get this far.' That was true and I said no more. Howells frowned, but he didn't look seriously worried. John moved a chair and sat beside him, talking quietly.

'Tea or coffee, Sir Matthew?' Joyce called. 'Or we have orange juice and water.' He shook his head. 'Let me know if you do want a drink. Or something to eat.' The unreality of it all: the juxtaposition of normal, abnormal, paranormal made me wonder if this really was happening. It was so far from any scenario of my imagination.

Adam took a mug of coffee from Joyce and passed one to me. 'So far so good?' he said quietly. 'Any problems?'

'No. Everything seems to have happened just as it should. You certainly caused an interesting effect with the Daimler.'

'I didn't, you know.'

'What?' I stared at him. 'But it had to be you.'

'No. I didn't have time. I'd counted on him saying a longer goodnight.'

'He did that earlier. So what happened if it wasn't you?'

'I've no idea. I thought we'd had it.'

'Pre-empted again,' I murmured. 'Rather like the dry ice.'

'You think so?'

'What else?'

Joyce sat down with us, listening half to our conversation and half to John's low-voiced urgings.

'Did you find out anything more?' she asked.

'Not as much as I wanted. But he did explain how it started.'

Adam jumped. 'Do you mean to say that he knew? Knew before we got hold of him?'

'Yes. I'm sorry, Adam. He knew last week. I couldn't tell you. You'd have tried to stop me. I knew that I was safe, though, and it was worth it anyway, to be able to talk to him freely.'

'How much does he think we know?'

'Hard to say. That we have to hang on to him beyond midnight, but not the other means. He's certain that we've underestimated Pryce and he thinks we'll fail, though he admires us for trying. You know... he offered to pay whatever it took to get us away from Llantathan if only we would stop.'

'Well, he would.'

'Yes, but that was mostly because of what Pryce would do to us.'

'If he got the chance.'

The church clock chimed the hour. 11. I saw Howells look at his watch again and remembered my glimpse of it in the wine bar. It would be reading 10-o-clock now. European time? Surely not...

'They must have realised that something's happened,' Adam said. 'It won't be long now.'

'What's the weakest part of the defences?' I asked.

'The windows. They won't know about the grilles until one of them gets a belt. They'll soon work out how to disable the system, but it'll slow them down. Someone will have to fetch gear to...'

He stopped suddenly, listening. Yes. Voices. Howells heard them too, his expression indefinable. Perhaps he remembered that his rescue meant my death.

The voices died away and we heard the rattle of the porch grille. At the same time a heavy thudding began from the direction of the boiler room door. It soon stopped. It would. That door was triple barred too. It had to be: it gave access to the vestry.

For five minutes we heard nothing more. Howells' face was gloomy and he appeared to be taking little notice of John's urgings. I would have given much to know his thoughts then.

Another 20 minutes. Still no sound. And then the lights went out.

'What's going on?' Joyce's voice, annoyed.

'Power cut,' Adam told her. 'Don't worry. Plenty of candles.' I heard his clumsy rummaging then a match flared. 'Light some more, Steph,' he whispered. 'I've got to see what's going on.'

'Adam, no!' I protested. 'What if they're in?'

'They can't be. It'll take time for them to get one of the grilles down. 'I'll be quick. Anyway, I want to check whether I've still got power to the projector.'

Swiftly he unbarred the door while Joyce slid the bolts and turned the key. He opened it a little and listened, and then he was gone. We waited in silence, alert to every minute sound, trying to distinguish the natural from the human. Two minutes... three... five...

I glanced round the candlelit room. At Joyce, her hands between her knees again. At John, strangely majestic in his robes, his face sad yet serene. At Matthew Howells leaning against the radiator. His eyes were closed, his features taut with strain. As I looked at him, he opened his eyes and gazed directly at me. Very deliberately he moved his left arm forward, resting his hand on his knee. In the candlelight I caught the gleam of gold and glass at his wrist. European time? No... No! Greenwich Mean Time! His eyes and mine locked in the strangest complicity yet. His eyebrows lifted, questioning. I nodded.

Adam slipped back through the door and we secured it again.

All's quiet,' he said, 'but someone had a go at the grilles and shorted the whole caboodle. The projector supply's out too. It's a nuisance but it doesn't matter. We're nearly there.'

'We're not, Adam.' I glanced over my shoulder at Matthew Howells. His eyes were closed again. I summoned John with a gesture. 'Listen,' I said, and I told them about Howells' watch. 'And he said to me: "Don't let midnight catch you out". Don't you see? He... they... set this up over two centuries ago when time wasn't standardised, but now they're working to Greenwich Mean Time. We're working to British Summer Time.'

'God, we'd have looked so stupid!' Joyce said.

'Yes, though something would have happened. But now we've got an hour longer to sit out than we thought. Can we do it, Adam?'

'We should be able to. I'm assuming that they won't try these windows. Too narrow and we could disable them one by one. They'll go for one of the windows into the main body of the church. Then they'll have to get through this door. It can be done but it'll take time. We can retreat to the ringing chamber. It's a narrow stair. Doors top and bottom. Easy to defend. Time-consuming again, and we still have one last retreat. Yes, we should be able to hold out for an hour at the very least.'

He hunted in a box under the table and set up a camping kettle on a little stove.

'No joy with Howells, I suppose?' I asked John.

He shook his head. 'I cannot convince him that God does have the power to save him.'

'I know. I tried too. I think he must have seen some terrible things.'

'He has, poor soul. But there's time yet. Many a man has thrown himself on God's mercy when faced with certain death. Let's not give up hope.'

Adam made more coffee and distributed biscuits. And still, from outside, there was silence. We sat in the flickering candlelight not talking much. Tense, but not exceptionally so. Howells accepted a mug of coffee this time, but after a couple of sips he put it down and closed his eyes again.

Slowly, painfully, time slipped by. The clock chimed another half hour. Howells stirred. His eyes found mine again across the room. 'Stephanie,' he said quietly, 'A word...'

I went to sit next to him.

'Matthew...'

'Stephanie, I think I must concede.'

'It's too late now, isn't it?'

'I think so. You did this very well. But you do know that this isn't all?'

'Yes. I told you I was thorough. Matthew, for all that, it might have gone wrong. Why did you tell me about midnight?'

'Why not? I have no chance. You might as well have all the chances there are. It's possible, probable even, that you'll succeed. The little good I've been able to do now may atone for some of the evil.' He shifted his position and fixed me with an expression of mingled sadness and fear. 'I deserve what's coming to me. You don't deserve what they would do. I would hate to think of so good and lovely and great a lady falling into their hands. No-one but you ever pitied me...'

He seemed a child then: a terrified child. 'Matthew,' I said quietly, 'will you listen to me? It isn't too late to escape.'

'There is no escape,' he said dully. 'Spare me the preaching, Stephanie. I've had it all from the rector.'

'I won't preach,' I promised. 'All I want to say is that I believe you can escape the consequences. Whatever you've done, I don't want you to suffer. I really don't. Think about

it, please, Matthew. While there's still time. And...'   I
reached up behind me and unfastened my cross and chain.
'Take this, just in case.'

'What...?'

Before he could protest or refuse, I pushed the little
silver symbol into his hand and closed his fingers over
it. 'Let it be the best of all your birthdays. God bless you,
Matthew,' I said. And walked away.

Adam was jumpy. He lit a cigarette and began to pace
about, stopping every few seconds to listen. He looked at
his watch. Checked it against mine. Twenty minutes to go
and still he hadn't heard a sound beyond the door.

'I'm going to have another look round,' he said. 'It's too
bloody quiet.'

'Adam, don't be daft!' I said. 'Twenty minutes. That's
all. If we sit tight there's no way we can fail.'

'Unless they're up to something we haven't foreseen.'

'Like what?'

'Lord knows. Setting fire to the church... Stephanie, I've
got to see what's going on out there!'

'And what if they're outside the door waiting for that
very thing?'

In reply he took the big key from the lock, listened,
peered through. 'Nothing,' he said. 'See for yourself.'

It was true. Darkness and silence. Was it possible that
they'd abandoned Howells? With less than twenty minutes
now, perhaps they'd seen the futility of attempting to rescue
him in time and, unaware that this was not our sole gambit,
were waiting for us to come out. I chewed at my thumbnail,
listened again at the keyhole. The smallest sounds in an
empty church are amplified but I heard nothing. Even so,
I didn't like it. I shook my head. Adam swore, began to
argue, and it was then that all hell broke loose.

The only points of entry we'd always discounted, because they were narrow and easily defended, were the lancet windows in the south wall of the tower. Simultaneously all three came exploding inwards in an eruption of glass and lead glazing bars, and before we could act, they were in: three of the younger men followed by three more, and it was a shambles. One of them unbarred the door and when Adam tried to fend them off, to clear a path between me and the belfry steps, a swinging fist knocked him sideways and I was grabbed from behind. I heard Joyce screech and John's voice: 'In the name of God...'

'Get him! Quick!' A voice hissed. I thought it was Paul Williams. 'And take these bastards outside.'

Resistance was natural. I struggled and fought but with no effect at all. Joyce's screeching, punctuated by a stream of inventive abuse, was cut short by a yell of pain, and then I heard her sobbing. It might be hopeless now but I went on fighting. Anything to delay them. It seemed important. As I was half dragged, half carried through the porch, I hooked my right arm through the bars of the grille and hung on. As long as I could block them, they couldn't get Howells out. Let us have, at least, a partial victory.

I was dragged again but I held on, turning my arm to grasp the next bar with stretched fingers.

'Come on! Come on! What's the hold-up?'

'Bitch has gotten hold of the gate,' my captor replied, pulling again.

'Well break her fucking fingers!'

'I'll break your fucking neck!' I screamed. Then I screamed again in earnest as the man brought something hard and heavy down on my hand. Blood sang in my ears and the pain that shot through my arm as I was wrenched free almost put me out.

Hold on. Hold on. Somewhere, in some small corner of my mind, a voice spoke. Warm and calm, and familiar. *Hold on.* And I did.

They herded us together in front of the porch and now I saw, assembled on the path, Pryce, Bowen, Reece, Pritchard, Powell... The twelve. And on the grass to Pryce's left, his head lolling, held up by two of the younger men, a boy of about 16. Dear God! They were going to do it here! Here, in front of the church!

Oh no, the voice said. *Hold on. Forget the pain. Think!*

I took several deep breaths to calm myself and sort out what I was seeing, what the situation was. Adam had put the street light out, as he'd said and in the darkness it was hard to distinguish faces but I'd already recognised the senior twelve, directly in front of us. And the boy was held by... yes... Mal Bowen and Powell junior. John was to my left, stunned and holding a weeping Joyce. At my right hand Adam, on his feet and recovering fast. At least six of the juniors flanked us and there were two inside trying to free Howells. With the tools they had, it couldn't be much longer. I thought with detachment that I needn't have wasted my hand.

Minutes passed. Nothing happened. Nothing could until either Howells was free or midnight passed.

Time enough, the voice said. *Time enough yet.*

Richard Reece's son came out of the church, pushing past us. 'Howells won't come,' he called.

John's eyes met mine over Joyce's head and he smiled. I returned his smile and nodded. And, silently, I thanked God.

'Bring him out,' Pryce ordered. 'There's still time.'

Reece junior hesitated. He looked back at us and then at Pryce. He was frightened. 'It won't be any use Mr. Pryce,' he said, his voice wavering. 'He's gone over.'

'Bring him out!' roared Pryce.

Still he hesitated. Pryce took a step towards him and he shrank back to obey.

No.

If Matthew Howells had to die, he was going to die in peace.

I have no idea why I did what I did. Far less do I know why it worked. Why, or even if, I thought it would. All I know is that the voice in my mind spoke another word.

Tonfanau.

Marina, in floating white silk...

Looking towards her grave, to where Adam had rigged the gauze for the projection, I summoned her image. I don't know if the materialisation was the product of my mind or if the force of my will defied all physical laws and turned the projector on. I only know that in the darkness, under the shadow of an old rowan tree, a glow of light grew and her face and her form, lovely and ethereal, came into being.

Adam saw it, uttered something incoherent, and reached behind me to tug at John's sleeve. John looked and despite his shock he grasped the meaning of this. He began to pray. If he had ever stopped.

Still looking at the glowing image, I stepped forward and, pushing Reece's son aside, I pointed. 'Look, Pryce! Look at the one you murdered!'

Heads turned, following my outflung arm. Someone to my right gave a cry. Unease bordering on fear ran through them, shaking their unity.

'The Jew!'

'Tricks!' Pryce sneered. 'Nothing but tricks.'

He'd taken half a dozen steps towards the tree. Without doubt he had seen through this device and meant to rip down the gauze. But now he stopped, and a dozen or more voices were raised in cries of horror as the image, shining with a light that owed nothing to electricity, lifted its arm, turned, and moved towards their leader.

It was Marina. But a Marina transfigured, terrible in beauty and power. And in her hand I saw, and scarcely believed what I saw, the posy of flowers I'd placed on her grave. Like a queen she walked, the white gown floating and flowing around her, skimming the grass, light spilling from her body, every movement tracing rainbows in the dark. And she drove Pryce before her, crawling on his knees. Behind me came the second of the two men who had been sent to release Howells. He saw and groaned and fell back. All around me men were cowering, pinned by the vision, unable to run. Unable to move. And still Marina drove the grovelling Pryce along the path, and the brightness of her hurt my eyes.

'Go, Steph!' Adam said urgently. 'Go! The bell!'

I looked one last second on Marina's face. Then I turned and ran, half falling over the porch step.

Minutes.

Through the tower room where Matthew Howells, head bowed, sat as one graven in stone in the light of a solitary candle. No time to worry about him now.

I wrenched open the door at the foot of the stairs. Up, stumbling in the blackness to the ringing chamber. No light. My lighter in my pocket. I flicked it and saw, on the floor, curled like a velvet snake, the sallie belonging to Judith. Someone had taken no chances. I swore. Wasted a second on rage, and knew what I would have to do. Wasted another second as a mammoth fear ballooned inside me.

You can, the voice said. *You can.*

Shaking now, I mounted the ladder and, pain screaming in my hand, I pushed the trapdoor and scrambled onto the narrow platform beside the bells.

Go on!

Which one? The presence of the bells, nurtured in my imagination, pressed around me. Which one? Which was Judith?

I flicked my lighter again and the chamber danced with shadows. *Left,* said the voice, a whisper now, drowning in my rising hysteria. From the side loft below the belfry I heard a preliminary clicking. The mechanism of the clock.

Seconds.

I grabbed the bell frame to my left and held the lighter out over the sound bow of the bell. The tiny flame illuminated the gothic script.

JUDITH
There is none that can resist thy voice

I dropped the lighter, grasped the great wheel and set the bell in motion.

With one hand a redness of pain and all but useless, and without the force of the rope, I could not make her ring properly. Even so, I was unprepared for the excruciating clangour. Two strokes had me reeling but I kept on and when the bell's momentum took over it became easier. I couldn't see but I could feel the swinging arc as the moving mass of metal cut the air inches from my face. Again and again Judith spoke. Stroke after stroke resounding in the confines of the belfry, her voice escaping through the louvres to call out over Llantathan that the old order was gone. Stroke after stroke after stroke, and time meant nothing to me. Only the voice of the bell. The voice of Judith. The voice of God.

And then the Cavendish bell began to move, creaking on its mountings. I let go of Judith's wheel and collapsed to a huddle on the belfry floor, my head buried in my arms.

Elwyn Pryce was still sane as he was driven across the threshold of the church. As sane as he had even been. His terror, vast though it was, had not yet closed off his ability to rationalise, his capacity to hope.

The thing – the being – whose inexorable steps had cut him off from the safety of numbers and forced him along the path was a trick devised by that shit Pembury. Or the Hargreaves woman. Clever, but it wasn't real. The Christian god never permitted return. His Master, for his own purposes, counterfeited the dead, but this was no work of his. A trick, and it would fail. They had not the power to sustain it. Or one of his own would speak the word and release him from its thrall.

One of them... but they neither moved nor spoke... and his last sight of the tableau, before the blazing image herded him into the holy, the loathsome darkness of the church, showed him that the Hargreaves bitch and her friends were gone. The sphere of terror closed tight around him as the heavy oaken door swung silently shut.

Still the being that was and was not Marina Graham moved step by step in a white, shimmering radiance, light cascading about her. Pryce squirmed, dragging himself over the flags of the aisle in a desperate struggle to keep out of that spreading halation. With every second the brilliance increased in magnitude, dissolving the darkness as she trailed rainbow ribbons of incandescence from her fingertips.

Like an injured crab, the man scuttled, crawled, never lifting himself from his knees. He had no idea, now, which way he was going, and cared less. His one devouring aim was to keep a breadth of unlit space between himself and the being. Nor was he aware that his voice was raised in a long, ululating howl.

When his hands touched the carpet of the chancel steps he found himself caught between that aweful, advancing source of light, and another no less terrible. Behind him she came on still. Ahead, at the heart of the altar, a great aurora burned, building to fall in broad streamers spreading in a silent, searing tide across the sanctuary floor.

She stopped. Pryce huddled at the foot of the chancel steps, eyes closed against the impossible, intolerable brilliance. Yet still he saw, as if that light had burned away his eyelids... saw that she was raising her arms high and wide. Droplets of light fell in iridescent showers from the posy in her hand, and the movement of her arms filled the chancel with banners of dazzling, crystal colour, meeting, merging with the liquid diamond flood from the altar. At the instant of merging he heard, breaking the living silence, the voice of the bell.

Burrowing his head into his arms, still he howled and still he saw and heard. The bell, sweet and clear, speaking in defiance of the Master, was the voice of God. And with the note of the bell came another voice. Her voice. And for him, all three were one.

'Elwyn Pryce! Elwyn Pryce! Elwyn Pryce!'

Three times she called his name and three times the sound of that voice, ineffably sweet, infinitely stern, tore through his brain. For, behind his earthly name, he heard his secret name spoken: the name given by his Master.

'The Lord loves His people, Elwyn Pryce. His love and His goodness towards His creation are limitless and eternal but it is for no creature to usurp His power...'

She spoke, but her words meant nothing to him. She, this creature, this... angel of light... messenger of God...

had named him. How could the weak, the pathetic, the ineffectual god of the Christians have known what was between him and the Master alone?

The great streaming aurora pulsated around him, dancing to the voice of the bell. She spoke again and now, into the light, swarming as the heavenly host must have swarmed in the midnight skies of Bethlehem, came other beings. Rank upon rank, it seemed: an army, but an army of individuals whose identities poured out into the light and were, even so, a part of the light.

'Look!' she commanded. 'These are the souls God requires at your hands.'

His weakness crushed him but her power forced him to obey, to gaze at those inhabitants of the light, to know and to acknowledge them. Formless, faceless, yet they lived and were knowable.

'Are they known to you, Elwyn Pryce? Answer!'

'Yes... yes!' Though he whispered, barely croaked the reply, the effort of speaking gave him a transient courage. 'But I am not responsible. Howells killed them. Howells was killing them before I was born.'

She laughed. 'Matthew Howells was the instrument you used. As well brand the knife as the murderer. Do you imagine that God knows nothing of your part in this abomination? Did you and those who went before you think that because another worked your will, your hands were clean?'

The brief spark of defiance died. He whimpered.

'Has it not been said that the wages of sin is death, but the gift of God is eternal life? What will you choose: that which you have earned, or the Lord's mercy? He will listen. He understands the weaknesses of men but He is God and will be so recognised.' Her voice dropped, its crystal sweetness warm, sorrowful, pleading. 'Will you acknowledge the Lord? Will you accept His mercy and love? For He loves you. Even you. For the sake of that, will you deny the one you call your Master?'

It seemed as if all the eyes of heaven burned into him. Accept the love of the Christian god? Live in that terrible light? Cross the gulf and spend eternity in that holy company?

'No!' He raised himself upright on his knees. 'No! I am sworn to my Master and to him I will go. I have served him faithfully. He will not abandon me now.'

And he raised his voice in a wild, pleading cry.

Again she spoke. 'Elwyn Pryce, your choice is witnessed by your victims and your wages will be paid in full.'

Then he saw, in the light that was her right hand, another light burning, growing. That which had been a posy became a sword. A sword in size and form such as the grail knights might have wielded. Its hilt, grasped in her fingers, glowed ruby red. The blade, long, two-edged, shone now silver, now gold, and the air around it crackled with sapphire sparks.

She put her other hand to the hilt and, holding the sword upright, steady, struck straight and sure. The blade swept down in a fiery arc. Flames of rose and violet and gold leapt up. A mighty, crashing boom rolled round the church. Azure and amethyst flashed in jagged stabs of lightning. The stone under Pryce cracked asunder and every window blew out under the pressure of the whirlwind that ripped through the building.

The light swirled, closed in on itself in a sweeping spiral encompassing the shining beings and the envoy of God. Round and round it spun, shrinking to one intense beam, back into the heart of the altar leaving behind only the darkness and the chill of the night air blowing through the shattered windows, and the body of Elwyn Pryce.

Above, high in the tower Judith, her work done, stilled and was silent, and a second voice rang out. On the broken stone, close by Pryce's body, lay a small posy of freesia, fresh and fragrant, delicate and perfect.

AFTERWARDS

1984 – 1985

I have forgot much, Cynara! Gone with the wind,
Flung roses, roses riotously with the throng,
Dancing to put thy pale lost lilies out of mind...
...But when the feast is finished and the lamps expire,
Then falls thy shadow, Cynara! the night is thine;
And I am desolate and sick of an old passion...

Ernest Dowson

I

I became aware that the tenor was still. Gentle hands helped me from the floor and I opened my eyes to torchlight. Though the bells hung motionless, in my mind they rang on and on. John, his arm about me, spoke, but I heard nothing clearly. Half guiding, half supporting, he led me back to the steps and, with Adam's help from below, I made it down, blinking in the sudden real, electric, light.

Joyce put her arms round me carefully, mindful of my hand, as I began to shake, and then to laugh and to sob, and the sounds were strange to my tortured ears. Adam swept me up in his arms and I remember no more. My next brief awareness was of a bed – Adam's bed – the dim, distorted sounds of voices, and pain before the blackness came again.

I don't know how long that blackness lasted. It seemed only moments but when it lifted the grey, even light told me that it was dawn. Did I move or speak? Perhaps I did for Adam's voice said, 'Easy, Stephanie. Lie still. Everything's all right.'

I turned my head on the pillow. 'Did we...?'

'You did.'

'John? Joyce?'

'Yes, they're fine. Listen, you have some broken fingers but I've taped them. Don't worry about anything. Just rest.'

Fragments of memory came and went. 'Tell me... please...'

'Later, Steph, when you're feeling better.'

'No, now. Is it over? Finished?'

'Yes, it's over. Don't worry. Go back to sleep. You'll feel much better in the morning.'

I closed my eyes again and let all the half-formed questions fade away into peace.

Over.

Finished.

* * *

Adam was right: I did feel better when I next woke. They left me to sleep until late morning when Joyce came in with tea and toast on a tray. I looked up at her and said, 'Handstroke, backstroke,' and anxiety faded from her eyes. She fell into giggles.

'Oh God, Steph!' she exclaimed. 'You're something else! Can you sit up?'

I could, and did, dizzy at first.

She poured the tea and sat with me as I ate to make sure, she said, that I didn't scald myself. 'I've got the day off to look after you.'

'Day off?' I echoed. 'Oh Lord! Work! What's been happening?'

'Not a lot, actually,' she told me. 'Fortunately it started to rain soon after dawn so Adam phoned the college and told the team to stay put and start some post-ex there.'

'So Adam's taking the day off too.'

'What do you expect? There's been a lot to do. 'Stiffs in the churchyard, the church wrecked and half the village out of their minds.'

'Tell me!'

'Like I said, stiffs in the churchyard... OK! But I'll get John or Adam. I don't feel competent. Anyway, I've lunch to cook.'

Heading for the door with the tray, she stopped and turned. 'Oh, by the way, John's asked me to marry him.'

'And you will?'

'Offer I can't refuse,' she said. 'I always wanted to marry a millionaire with a big house.'

* * *

Over that day I had the story from John and from Adam. John's version had a theological slant, naturally, otherwise their accounts tallied. But it was Adam who was the first to elaborate on Joyce's vivid but inadequate summary.

Stiffs in the churchyard...

'To be accurate, Steph, in the church. Howells died where he sat in the tower room. And Pryce on the chancel steps.'

'It was Marina, wasn't it?'

He didn't reply.

'Did you see?'

'Yes, I did, Stephanie. Everyone there saw. Yes, it was Marina or something that looked like Marina. At least it was at first. How did you do it?'

'I don't know. Go on.'

'She changed. Still recognisable but... something else. I think John would be better at this than me. He doesn't mind using biblical similes and metaphors.'

'An avenging angel?' I suggested. 'How real was she?'

'Steph, no-one can look like that and be real. Not human real. I don't know. All I can tell you is that she was three-dimensional and when she walked into the church the hem of her frock trailed over the edge of the step.'

And then I heard how John, Adam and Joyce, unopposed, had followed me into the church, Joyce to take her place in the ringing chamber, John and Adam to witness Pryce's end. Adam struggled for words to describe the indescribable. He gave me, perhaps, the shadow of the reality but I, calling on my memory of the shining cloud, thought I could imagine a little of that celestial light. 'And so, in the end, she was Judith,' I mused. 'Judith with the sword. What happened? How did Pryce...?'

He knew what I meant: had she really beheaded him? The idea of a decapitated Pryce on the chancel steps, his blood flowing into consecrated ground, was sickening.

'No. What happened on her level I wouldn't like to say but his body was intact. Which is more than can be said for the church.'

I sighed. 'Poor John's got a real mess on his hands.'

'Poor John,' Adam told me, 'Is singing hymns of praise. No, it's not as much of a mess as you'd think. The Caldicot doctor reckoned that Pryce had a heart attack. There'll be a post-mortem, naturally, but since there wasn't a mark on him I can't see any problem there.'

'No, maybe not. But how is John going to explain the church windows?'

'Pretty much as we explained the vault.'

'But we didn't... Oh, I see! He's going to be mystified.'

'He does it very well,' Adam grinned. 'The archdeacon's been out already. I wouldn't mind betting that he has more idea of what's been happening than he's letting on. Anyway... The official line is that Pryce ran amok in the church, maybe with some sort of explosive, broke the windows, played merry hell up in the belfry and dropped dead with the effort of it all. I don't think anyone in Llantathan's going to contradict that.'

'No, but there was one other stiff in the church,' I reminded him.

'Oh yes, Matthew Howells. Now there's a thing. You'll recall that we had an empty coffin...'

'Adam, you didn't!'

'Didn't we, though! He's where he belongs, and no-one the wiser.'

'But someone will start asking questions about him, surely. A man like that doesn't just go missing. And what about his car on the rectory drive?'

'Not now it isn't. It's in the car park at the back of the Cross Guns.'

'You've had a busy night.'

'Not kidding. We've done all we could. As for the rest – someone, somewhere will cover up. He was confident. 'You'll see.'

'All right then. So what about the boy? I can't believe he won't talk.'

'John handled that. You'd better ask him but I doubt if he'll say much. All I can get out of him is that the family won't cause trouble.'

'Well, if John says so...'

Adam was right: Llantathan was in no state to contradict anything. It was as I'd guessed: with its raison d'être destroyed it could barely function and though John sang his rejoicing that the evil was vanquished, he wept over the devastation left behind. But the first days and weeks of his labours to aid and guide the village are his story. His, Joyce's and Adam's. I wasn't there.

* * *

On Thursday evening I went home. Home to a house which was no longer subject to spies. Where I could live, if I chose, in untroubled peace: a life free from the threat of Llantathan. And, if I wanted – and I thought I did – a life shared with Adam Pembury. His happy ending and perhaps mine too.

But was I still comfortable with that idea? If I hadn't seen Marina again... Not my Marina, no, but her beloved face, at least in the beginning. There's nothing deader than dead. It was still true. My Marina was dead. If she continued, it was in another form, as unreachable in that altered state as if she did not exist, and for me, she didn't. But that sight of her had disturbed whatever peace I might have achieved. Nevertheless, I had promised Saturday to Adam and I would not renege.

I didn't have to. Fate, or whatever, did it for me, with a side-swipe. On Friday morning the phone rang. I didn't recognise the voice of the woman who spoke such a confusion of words, but I knew the name. Mrs. Broughton. My mother's neighbour and crony at the senior citizens' club. My mother was in hospital, she told me. 'Very poorly.' Would I come at once?

Cancer, the doctor said. Inoperable. Terminal. 'Didn't you know?'

'No,' I told him. 'She didn't tell me. I knew she wasn't well, but she said it was something and nothing...'

How long? A few weeks at most. What did they recommend, I asked. The doctor and the sister hedged and, embarrassed, suggested that if I could afford it, I should have her transferred to a private nursing home or a hospice where she would receive the necessary pain control and personal care.

Who looks after the parents when they're old and frail...?

Could my mother be cared for at home? Yes, but it would be expensive. No matter. It was what she wanted. If the hospital could do no more for her, she would go home.

And so she returned to her beloved bungalow to lie diminished under the pink satin quilt amid the figured walnut and the silk flowers and the lace. There was no need for her to suffer and the cost which made it easy for her was immaterial.

And it was easy for her. Slow, at first. Dying by inches and fractions of inches. Given my mother's metaphorical backbone of steel, her whipcord resilience, I had imagined her going on and on. Fading away, eventually, at some incredibly advanced age, but falling victim to such a demeaning disease? No. My mother had never been a victim in all her life. Freed from pain and running true to character she recovered some of her vivacity and it carried her through the rest of August to her final decline.

I lived out a strange existence in her home. All her care was undertaken by nurses. I cooked and did the housework, following the routines I remembered from childhood. And she was, as she had always been, critical to the last.

'You should go home,' she said sometimes, when she was lucid. 'When all this is over. To Eldersfield, Stephanie, not that Godforsaken Welsh place. Go home, where you belong.' Mostly, by then, she wasn't lucid at all. She talked of my father, and his father, and someone else: a great-grandmother, I thought. 'We called you after them. I didn't want to...'

I knew that I owed my name to my father and grandfather who had both been Stephen, but I had often wondered where my second name, Margaret, had come from. I took my mother's hand. 'Why didn't you like my names, Mum?' I asked. 'What would you have called me?'

'I wanted to call you Shirley... Go home, Stephanie. You should go home...' Oh Lord! I thought, Shirley Temple... *The Good Ship Lollipop*... That explained why she always tried to make my hair curl...

In the quiet evenings I worked on the report and the History, wrote letters to John and Joyce and to Adam, and found Llantathan slipping away from me. John wrote of his ministry to the village and of the tragedy of the aftermath: of breakdowns and children taken into care; of Evan Pritchard's suicide and the car crash that claimed the lives of the whole Reece family. He wrote of the bleakness of the people: their aimlessness and lack of all motivation. But he wrote, too, of his personal happiness: his joy that no matter how long it took, with the evil gone, Llantathan would recover; and he wrote of Joyce. Plans for a spring wedding. Their insistence that I serve as matron-of-honour, with or without that frilly pink frock. Letters from Adam rarely mentioned Llantathan. He told me of progress at work, team and college gossip, books he'd read and of his flat in Newport. Not once did he refer to our indefinitely postponed rendezvous.

It was all unreal. Real was this bijou bungalow. Real the bitter wind and the salty rain, and the bleak Scarborough seafront where the booths and the arcades, shuttered for the winter against the elements, lined the promenade with paint-peeled, shabby façades. Real was my mother,

her thin arms bruised from the injections which eased her path to the grave. Real was the funeral and the lingering, subliminal smell of death in the house. Real the dealer who took away the walnut and the china and the embroidered supper cloths. Real was the box of papers and photographs and the few mementoes I kept. Real the estate agent and, eventually, the sale and the settling of her estate.

There was one other reality. When I left Llantathan, my mind a mad jumble of unprocessed impressions and worries, I took with me one ineradicable image: that of Marina, of her face in those last moments before I ran into the church. Llantathan receded in the face of my mother's impending death. John, Joyce and Adam became inhabitants of another world. But Marina... No... I'd taken her image with me to Scarborough, and it was still with me, no less clear, when I went home in the middle of November.

II

At first, I had trouble tying up past and present. When I left Llantathan in August the village was devastated. John had kept me informed of developments but I still expected it to be as I'd always known it. Christmas lights strung through the trees around the green and the crib in the churchyard were strange. Stranger still the sight of children playing outside. Odd to walk past the police house and know that its occupants were a Caldicot constable and his wife. Where was the Griffiths family now?

The Llantathan estate was, it seemed, in the hands of an administrator. No-one knew the ins and outs. What we did know was that The Cross Guns had a new landlord and served meals in the refurbished back bar. Elwyn Pryce's pig farm was vacant and at Richard Reece's surgery medical care was dispensed by a young and cheerful Dr. Ann Mortimer. Evan Pritchard's wife still ran the shop and post office and she at least looked as if she might adjust to a different life. When I went in to buy stamps for my Christmas cards, she smiled, and her eyes glistened wet. She knew, I think, that my thanks were for more than the stamps she passed across the counter.

There were new graves in the churchyard. Pryce had been cremated and his ashes scattered in Newport but the Reece family, Paul Williams – overdosed on tranquillisers – and his father Owain who, like Evan Pritchard, had blown his head off with a shotgun – they were there. And, of course, Matthew Howells.

I stood for a long time looking at the mound over his remains. He had, as far as I knew, died quietly, without the horrible mauling he had expected. They had found my cross still clutched in his fingers and buried it with him. His denial of Pryce's will suggested that, at the end, he had claimed God's mercy. I hoped so.

The following Monday I went back to work in my office at the college. Alan Foster welcomed me with open arms and a stack of paperwork. 'And don't forget the archive,' he said. 'Adam should be free to start on that by next week.'

'What is he doing now?'

'Finalising Llantathan. But the team's fieldwalking near Chepstow and there won't be any more digging until after Christmas.'

'Where will that be?'

'Back to Llantathan,' he grinned. 'More of the same, I'm afraid.'

'Not quite the same,' I murmured, but I don't think he heard me.

'Adam's in the unit office,' Foster went on. 'Why don't you go along and have a word with him?'

'I will,' I agreed, but I didn't. Not immediately. Truth to tell, I was scared. Before I left Llantathan I'd been close to agreeing to marry Adam. Now? I didn't know what I felt about him, and I was afraid to find out. Besides, there was that image of Marina, more vivid than memory, sharper than the clearest photograph. But... I'd promised him that Saturday. It was long postponed but I would, if he still wished it, keep my promise.

Just before lunch I steeled myself to knock on Adam's door. His barked 'Come in!' was repelling: he must be having trouble with his paperwork. With a hand that shook too much I pushed the door open and walked in. The not-quite-blond head with its wayward forelock lifted. Tossing his pen aside he stood up and came round the desk.

'Stephanie!' A smile broke through the surprise. 'Christ! It's good to see you!'

'Hello, Adam,' I said shyly, taking his outstretched hands. 'I'm back.'

'To stay, or just visiting? Is everything wound up in Scarborough? How are you?'

I laughed. 'I'm back to stay, and I'm fine.'

'How's your hand? Wiggle the fingers.'

I laughed again. 'Adam, that was ages ago! Look. No problem. You always were good at patching me up.'

He leaned against the desk, his hand groping automatically for the cigarette packet. 'No more of that, thank God.'

'No. It was weird to come back to Llantathan and see it looking so normal. I still expect Mal Bowen to be hiding in my rhododendrons.'

'They say Mal Bowen hides under his bed in the psychiatric ward,' he remarked. 'And he's not the only one. It was a shambles, Steph. And it's not much better now.'

'No, but at least there'll be no more killings. I still can't quite believe that we did it.'

'You did it,' he amended.

'We did it,' I repeated.

'We can argue about that later if you wish, Steph, but I'd rather forget it for now. What about lunch?'

I saw him most days in college, and he was friendly enough, but that was all. Probably, I thought, my prolonged absence had cooled his feelings and I wouldn't have been surprised to discover that there was another woman in his life. The promised Saturday was apparently no longer on the agenda but, just before Christmas, I discovered how things really stood.

A blazing fire warmed the greenery-decked, pine-scented sitting room at Vine Villa. Cards, including one signed *Rose* cluttered the mantelpiece and the side table was laden with festive goodies: chocolates, fruit, dates, nuts. I'd been wrapping presents on the hearth rug, a gin-and-tonic to hand, when the doorbell rang. Fear shot through me and died. It was a conditioned response. Nothing to be afraid of now. I stood up, shook out my skirts, and went to the door.

'Hello, Stephanie,' Adam said.

He followed me into the sitting room. 'Ready for Christmas?' he asked, his gaze taking in the decorative evidence of my preparations.

'As ready as I'll ever be.'

'Well, here's an early present,' he said, putting a bricklike box into my hands.

I raised my eyebrows. 'Can I open it?'

'Go ahead.'

I pulled off the red and green ribbon and opened the lid. And laughed. Sugar cubes. How odd that he'd remembered. 'Thank you,' I said. 'I shall treasure them.'

'You're supposed to eat them.'

'Oh, I will, don't worry. A drink, Adam? Glenmorangie?'

He nodded, still standing, while I poured it and got myself another gin. When I turned it was into the intensity of his gaze. And I knew that what had grown between us in those last weeks before the end had not cooled. Not for him, and not for me. My isolation in Scarborough hadn't changed a thing.

'I've come for the Saturday we never had,' he said quietly.

He took the glass and sat down. I curled up in a corner of the sofa. 'I wondered if you would,' I said. 'But you seem to have had other things to do. Having fun again, Adam?'

That laugh of his that was as much a sneer. 'You could call it that. I sat through all the Star Wars films the other week. I go to Dawn's parties again.' He swallowed the rest of his drink and lit a cigarette. Silently I passed him the bottle and fished my own cigarettes from my bag. He looked at me through the haze of smoke. 'And before you ask, there have been girls.'

'So? I've no claim on you.' Nor had I, but I didn't like this. I added defiantly, 'What you do is none of my business as long as you're happy.'

The sneer was undisguised this time. 'Happy? Call it that if you want. I wouldn't. There may have been a dozen women since you left, but I still love you. Nothing's changed, has it, Sweetheart?'

Sweetheart?

I couldn't look at him. 'No,' I replied softly. 'No, it hasn't.'

He splashed whisky into his glass. 'So. Here we are again, Stephanie. What are we going to do about it? The last time we talked...' He paused and I looked away, remembering. '...we had Llantathan to contend with. Now we don't. Shall we go back to that night? Start afresh?'

'What? So you can hurt me again?'

Another gin. At this rate I was going to be smashed. So bloody what?

'I did what you wanted.'

'You did what you wanted. Tell me anything else and you're a liar. Anyway, you didn't do what I wanted. Not entirely.'

His look was quizzical, amused. 'Not entirely? So... Back to that night, Stephanie? Start again? What shall we do?'

'What if I said anything you want?'

'I think I'd strangle you.'

'Would you?'

'No, but don't imagine It would end like the last time. It wouldn't.'

No, and I wouldn't want it to. Sense told me to walk away from this, but my body... Oh yes, nothing had changed, and the knowledge that last time had been the merest foretaste of what it would be was a goad, not a deterrent.

'When he was halfway through his fifth whisky I asked, 'How are you planning to get home tonight? You can't drive. Nor can I. And you won't get a taxi. Or are you staying with John?'

His eyes gleamed. 'What? Surely you're not going to miss such a wonderful opportunity, Steph? Aren't you going to ask me to stay?'

'What if I don't?'

'I don't think you're big enough to throw me out.'

I knew then that he'd planned all this before he arrived. Taken control. No options. *What are we going to do?* He knew what he was going to do. The question was when. I closed my eyes. How long could I wait? And another question. What sort of woman was I?

I was unsteady on my feet when I went out to the kitchen with vague ideas of supper. Dithering between the pantry and the fridge, not sure of what I was doing, I dropped cutlery on the floor, cursing.

'What are you playing at?' Adam, in the doorway.

'Supper,' I said. 'If I can...'

He crossed the floor. 'If it's for my benefit forget it. I don't want anything to eat.' He took the knives and forks from my fingers and put them on the table. One hand tangling in my hair forced my face up.

'Is this what you want, Stephanie? Is it?'

I looked up into his grey eyes. Fear, excitement, desire and some other emotion I wouldn't name rose to engulf me. I bit my lip. 'Yes. Yes. Adam... Please...'

He kissed me, and I knew for sure, then, how it was going to be.

III

When spring came Joyce and John were married. Not at St. Michael's, but at Nigel Faringdon's church in Newport. Just as we'd teased, Adam was best man and I was matron-of-honour, though not in pink frills. And as we all left the church, the bells Joyce and I had tortured that Saturday afternoon last August, rang out in what Nigel told us later was a quarter peal of Cambridge Surprise Major. The only surprise, Adam muttered, was that anyone would know it was different from every other bit of bellringing.

When spring came, Llantathan had begun to take on a subtly different look. The excavation team returned and, with John and Joyce at Allington, they took over the rectory completely for the duration. Now, on Friday lunchtimes, they went down to the Cross Guns for beer and sandwiches. Decent sandwiches. And, during the school holidays and at weekends, children played on the new swings in the beer garden.

When spring came, John began to think seriously about leaving the Church and, with the archive more or less set up, I started to make plans. When spring came, I knew I couldn't take any more.

Adam kept his Newport flat but every Friday evening he came to Vine Villa, staying until Monday morning. By day we had a lot of the fun he at least had wished for: out and about; at home, entertaining or doing nothing very much; working on the house or the garden. But the nights were something else.

He loved me – never for a moment did I doubt that – but he was incapable of expressing that love except through the infliction of pain. Oh, I'm not complaining. What he did was what I wanted. With the pain came the pleasure. If my body hurt, it also sang. There were times when we began to explore something different: tenderness; but it was unsustainable. Sooner or later the gentlest lovemaking turned to savagery. I wanted Adam. I wanted his love. What I didn't want was anything which resembled, in the slightest way, my relationship with Marina. And so I cheated myself and him. His violence was my way through the thicket of my guilt, and I would have nothing else.

But that wasn't why I left. What did it was the night when, swept into a spiral of desire, I forgot. I forgot Marina. The sheer happiness and fulfilment of that moment blotted her out so entirely that she might never have existed. I clung to Adam, sobbing with joy as I told him that I loved him. And he knew, and I knew, just what kind of love I meant.

It changed everything. The next day he asked me to marry him, something he'd not done for a long time. But by then I'd retreated behind a wall of guilt: telling Adam that I loved him was a negation of all Marina and I had been to eachother. I turned cold. He, hurt, became nasty. The pain of our lovemaking continued, but the pleasure was gone.

I began to dream about Llantathan, about the bells. But above all, about Marina. Dreams of red roses and gardens and her face. Dreams whose frightening reality lingered when I woke, to taint my days. And so I left. Not permanently the first time. A break, to see if some time and distance between us would help. It might have, if I'd done sensible things, but I spent much of that time in Gloucester, writing about Marina and the way it had been. And, I suppose, that's what did the final damage. In fixing my memories on paper, as I did, I turned Marina into an uncorrupted effigy, like a saint in a crystal casket: perfectly preserved forever.

When I came back and saw Adam again, there was no improvement. Leaving Llantathan became imperative. I had to allow him to find something better, cleaner and, after the last time we slept together I knew that I had to disappear. If I did not, one day he would surely kill me.

Not even to John did I confide my intentions and my destination. He, bless him, would never have broken my confidence willingly but sooner or later he might, inadvertently, have given me away. There had to be a break and that break had to be complete. One day Adam would, I hoped, acknowledge the sense of that. With the perspective of time and distance he would, eventually, see me for the damaged woman I really was. Then he would – must – forget me and be free.

I didn't realise, then, that Adam knew exactly what I was, and it made no difference. He wasn't going to forget. Ever.

ENVOI

Escape me?
Never – Beloved!
While I am I, and you are you,
So long as the world contains us both,
Me the loving and you the loth,
While the one eludes, must the other pursue.

Robert Browning

ACKNOWLEDGEMENTS

My thanks are due to the following for their generous assistance with information and advice:

Harkness Roses, Hertfordshire

Silver Cross UK Ltd., Yorkshire

Dr. Mark Lewis, Amgueddfa Lleng Rufeinig Cymru

Jonathan McDonald, pharmacist

Philip Ellis, bellringer

Malcolm Pryce, author

Jon at Oleander Press, Cambridge very kindly gave me permission to quote from Sue Lenier's poem 'Swansongs'.

The poem 'Why must you follow me when I come to the threshold of this holy place' is by Vita Sackville-West. It appeared in the Poetry Review in 1949 but as far as I am aware, it has never been published since. It was the subject of controversy due to its close similarity with 'St Augustine at 32' by Clifford Dyment, a poem which Sackville-West had been aware of prior to the publication of her own poem. I have been unable to discover any copyright information regarding this work.

Thanks also to my family and friends who supported and helped in many ways, particularly David, John, Matthew, Elisabeth, Catherine, Andrea, Ann, Julie, Marcus, Sally and Trevor, and everyone at the Coach and Horses, Caerwent.

Although its setting in Wales exists, Llantathan itself does not. The Hafren College, Papa Gino's and Aphrodite's in Newport are, likewise, figments of my imagination, as are the characters.

Christine Went,
Spring, 2022.
Yorkshire.